MARY MINTON

SPINNERS END

PAN BOOKS

First published 1989 by Century Hutchinson Ltd

First published in paperback 2003 by Pan Books
an imprint of Pan Macmillan Ltd
Pan Macmillan, 20 New Wharf Road, London N1 9RR
Basingstoke and Oxford
Associated companies throughout the world
www.panmacmillan.com

ISBN 0 330 42078 X

Copyright © Mary Minton 1989

The right of Mary Minton to be identified as the
author of this work has been asserted by her in accordance
with the Copyright, Designs and Patents Act 1988.

SPINNERS END

Mary Minton has been a teacher of creative writing at the Leicester Education Centre for nearly twenty years. Her interests include sailing and clothes designing, and she has always been an avid reader.

To my dear friend Jean Chapman,

whose knowledge of country lore delights me

*Only a warm heart will melt the ice-cold lens
of a camera.*

CHAPTER ONE

It was with reluctance that Edwin Chayter had agreed to having his eight year old daughter Francine living with him and, within half an hour of the furniture van arriving at the new house he was regretting his decision. She was here, there and everywhere, darting between the men carrying in the furniture, without any sign of the woman who was supposed to be in charge of her.

Francine, who had spent the first seven years of her life with an unhappy aunt in a gloomy house in a backwater, was in her element. She loved the big imposing house near the docks, loved the noise and was intrigued by the strange dialect of the men shouting to one another.

'Wochit, Charlie, or you'll 'ave those flippin' table legs orf . . .'

''Arry lad, don't yer know yer bloody right arm from yer left? Git yer clodhoppers up them stairs . . .'

Francine was also intrigued by the man she had been told was her father, a big, bearded man with wild-looking dark hair and a fierce expression. *He* roared at everyone in sight.

She had been in some of the downstairs rooms but was unable to see anything from the windows because the panes had been whitewashed over. What she wanted to see was the docks, the river, the ships. Ships were such exciting things that carried people to wonderful places all over the world. Not that her Aunt Amelia thought them exciting. She said they took people away from you and they never came back.

Francine waited until the men had gone outside for some more furniture then she ran nimbly upstairs to the first floor and began peeping into the rooms. In the first three there was furniture but here the panes were also whitewashed. Then she glanced into the next room and immediately saw it was different. This one had a projecting glass roof. She stood staring at it thinking how strange, why a glass roof? Who could look out of that? She went further into the room, noticed a stool then drew in a quick breath as she saw a camera. She had been told that her father was a photographer, had seen some of the photographs he had taken and had had his camera described to her, but she had never seen one.

With a feeling of awe she walked slowly towards it. It was so beautiful, with its lovely polished wood, its gleaming brass fittings and the scarlet leather bellows. She drew up the stool, climbed on to it and was running her fingers gently over the soft leather when her father shouted, 'Don't you dare touch that!'

She was snatched from the stool, none too gently, set on the floor, had her hand slapped and a finger poked at her chest. 'I told you to sit on the chair in the hall, didn't I? Warned you what would happen if you so much as moved and you disobeyed me, didn't you?'

She said, 'Yes, Papa,' as she had been taught to address him, 'but I liked touching the camera.'

The finger was now wagged under her nose and his expression was more fierce, if possible, than ever.

'You do *not* touch it. Is that understood? And if you as much as set foot in this studio again, without my permission, I shall thrash you soundly. Do you understand?'

She nodded and looked up at him steadily from large, widely-spaced grey eyes, which disconcerted Edwin Chayter, who found it unbelievable that this elfin child should look at him so fearlessly, when he could have underlings trembling in his presence.

Grabbing her by the hand he ran her out of the room, then at the top of the stairs he seized her round the waist, carried her down the stairs into the hall, where he all but dropped her and yelled, 'Where is the dratted woman who's supposed to be looking after my daughter?'

A green baize door at the end of the hall was flung open and a little scullery maid, her mob cap awry, came hurrying out. She stopped on seeing Edwin and bobbed a curtsy. When she kept on bobbing he roared at her to stand still and demanded to know where Miss Tindle was.

The girl, looking terrified, said in a whisper, 'She's gone, sir.'

'What do you mean – *gone*? And speak up, girl!'

'She's left, sir, she had words with Cook. And – and Cook says she's leaving, too.'

'Oh, she does, does she? Well, we'll see about that!' He pushed Francine towards her. 'Look after this child and don't let her out of your sight!'

The girl promised, started to bob again then remembering took Francine by the hand and lifted her on to a leather-covered chair. 'You'd best sit here, Miss, and please don't move or you'll get me the sack.'

Francine gazed at the ginger-haired girl with interest then she smiled. 'My name is Francine, what is yours?'

'Evie.' She rubbed her hand down her coarse sacking apron and looked around, her eyes full of worry. 'There's been nothing but trouble since I came 'ere. Cook 'as been raising the roof and the master, well, you could 'ave 'eard 'im at Billingsgate.' Evie's hand suddenly flew to her mouth. 'Oh, I'm sorry, Miss, I forgot he was your dad.'

'That's all right,' Francine said happily. 'Aunt Amelia told me he was very bad-tempered. Today is the first time I've seen him.'

'The first time?' Evie eyed her in astonishment. 'Cor love a duck. Fancy never 'aving seen your dad. Why 'aven't you?'

Edwin came out of the kitchen then, the green baize door swinging after him, and ordered Evie to take charge of his daughter. She was to keep her in the kitchen and not let her out of her sight. Evie promised, took Francine by the hand and led her away. A moment later Francine was standing in front of a small, plump woman with a red face and tight lips who, she was told, was Mrs Dodge the cook.

The woman began a tirade: the kitchen was her domain and if the master thought she was going to put up with kids running all over the place he was greatly mistaken. And he needn't think either that she was going to be bossed around by nursemaids. If anyone else came in here throwing their weight around she would chuck up the job. There were plenty more waiting for her – cooks with her skills were in great demand.

Evie glanced at Francine, raised her eyes towards the ceiling as though to say, not again, then stood to attention. At last when Cook seemed to be running out of breath she ordered Francine to go and sit on the stool in the corner and warned if she moved from it she would go back to her father.

Francine hitched herself on to the stool and looked around her with interest. Coming to the kitchen was, to her, just one more lovely adventure. What she liked was the gleaming black-leaded grate with a huge fire burning. Aunt Amelia never really had a proper fire. There were gleaming copper pans too on the shelves.

A door at the far end of the kitchen opened and an older girl came in. She removed her coat and a small black shawl which covered her head and hung them on a hook on the back of the door, talking as she did so to Mrs Dodge.

'I've brought the meat and told the butcher what you want for tomorrow. The boy will deliver at six in the morning and collect your order for the rest of the week. And now, I think we'll have a cup of tea, it's sharpish outside.'

The cook bridled. 'Don't you start giving me orders, Reilly, or you'll be out on your backside. I've had enough to put up with for one day!'

'And don't you think that *I* am having a lot to put up with too?' The girl had a soft, lilting voice. She took a piece of braid from her pocket and tied back her long dark hair. 'I have been trained as a cook and what am I doing here? The work of three.'

'Well, I am cook here and what I say goes. One word to the master and you'll be out.'

'I don't think so, Ma'am, him wanting to get me into his bed an' all. Not that I would, mind, not for all the tea in China.' She had still spoken softly but Cook shouted at her.

'Shut your mouth! We have company.'

The girl turned and seeing Francine she said, 'Oh, the poor wee mite, she's arrived then.'

She was going towards Francine when Cook snapped: 'Reilly, you leave her alone, d'ye hear? It's the master's orders. That aunt of hers has spoiled her rotten, let her have all her own way. She's wild, a rebel, needs checking.'

Francine stared at Mrs Dodge, astonished to hear herself so described. Her aunt had never let her have her own way, she was always telling her not to do this or do that, always scolding her and telling her she must learn to be a lady.

The girl said, her head up, 'My name is O'Reilly, Ma'am, and I'd be pleased if you'd use it. Either that or my God-given name of Kathleen. I might add that I was brought up to make a stranger feel welcome and as this mite is motherless, I wanted to say hello to her.'

'And I say you'll leave her alone. Also, as I am in charge of this kitchen I'll call you what I like.'

Kathleen walked across the kitchen and took her coat from the back of the door. 'In that case . . .'

'What do you think you're doing?' The cook's voice held uncertainty.

'Leaving, that's what. I only came here to fill in. I worked as cook in a good house, I have excellent refer-

11

ences. Either you use my proper surname or my Christian name-' Kathleen put on her coat.

'Look . . . O'Reilly, it's been a bad morning . . .'

There was now a placating note in Cook's voice.

Kathleen took off her coat and after hanging it up, went over to Francine and held out her hands with a smile. 'Welcome, Miss, I hope you'll be happy with us.'

Francine, a great warmth spreading through her, returned the smile and thanked her.

After that she watched the lovely Kathleen moving about the kitchen. She was tall and walked with what her aunt would call an elegance, like two of the ladies who came to visit her. Kathleen had long dark lashes in contrast to her very blue eyes.

Francine also liked the way Kathleen had stood up to the bossy Mrs Dodge. She seemed quite unafraid of her. Not like poor Evie, who was terrified of getting into trouble. While all the talk had gone on she had stood at the sink scraping carrots then peeling potatoes, never once looking round.

It was difficult for Francine to sit still while all the activity was going on in the house, but she tried to be patient, not wanting to cause any more upsets.

What did puzzle her was Kathleen saying that her father had been trying to get her into bed. As she understood it, only wives slept with men. Her mother was dead, so she had been told by her aunt, and although Francine had asked to know about her mother Amelia had refused to discuss her.

'She was my much loved sister,' she said, 'and I cannot bear to talk about her.'

And, as according to her aunt all the photographs of her mother had been torn up after her death, she had no way of knowing what she looked like. She hoped she had been pretty like Kathleen.

It seemed to Francine that she sat for hours on the stool, watching Mrs Dodge making bread, rolling out an apple pie, Evie fetching and carrying for her. Kathleen was in and out of the kitchen, reporting on the progress of the removal men, taking a dustpan and brush upstairs once a carpet had been laid, then disappearing with polish and dusters.

When she reported that the beds were now in the bedrooms and said she would make them up, she asked if Francine could come with her. Cook gave a definite no, she was to stay in the kitchen, it was the master's orders. Kathleen then took the woman aside and after some whispered talk Mrs Dodge agreed, although seeming reluctant. Kathleen held out her hand to Francine and smiled. 'Come along, you can help me to make up the beds.'

Francine slid off the stool, unable to believe her luck. Mrs Dodge called after them, 'And don't you be all day about it, O'Reilly, d'ye hear?'

One of two men who were about to carry a carpet into one of the downstairs rooms began to tease Kathleen, wanting to know when she would walk out with him. The other man laughed and said, 'Never, she turned me down and I'm better lookin' than you.'

Kathleen, hands on hips, pretended to be weighing them up and her vivid blue eyes held laughter. 'Well now, I've five fellers lined up wanting to walk out with me, so if two of them drop out I'll let you in.'

The men groaned then, chuckling, went on their way. Kathleen said, 'You have to have a bit of fun or you may as well be dead.'

As they went up the as yet uncarpeted stairs, Francine asked her what she had said to Mrs Dodge, to let the woman agree to her helping Kathleen.

'I told her, didn't I, that you'd get corns on your bottom if you sat on that stool any longer.'

Francine laughed at this and Kathleen stopped and gave her a hug. 'Oh, you've got a wonderful infectious laugh. My family would love you. I'll take you to meet them on my next half-day off.'

13

Meet a *family?* Francine felt so joyous at all the things that were happening to her she felt sure it must all turn out to be a dream.

They went along a passage on the first floor with Kathleen explaining that Francine's bedroom was at the end. She added, 'Actually, it's one of a small suite of three. One big room was made into two, a sitting room and a bedroom for your nanny and your bedroom leads off. It used to be a dressing room, so it's small, but comfortable. No doubt your father will find someone else to look after you.'

Francine eyed her in dismay. 'I don't want anyone to look after me. I want to be with you and Evie.'

'Oh, now, hold on, Miss Francine. You're the master's daughter. He wants you to be educated. You have to be, otherwise you'll grow up a dunce.'

Francine declared she didn't care and was so upset that Kathleen put an arm around her and led her into the sitting room. A fire which had been lit, had burned low. Kathleen took the tongs and put coal from a brass coal bucket on to the embers. Then she patted the rug. 'Come and kneel here and we'll have a talk.'

Big tears hung on Francine's lashes and Kathleen wiped them gently away. 'You've been so good, I don't want to see you crying.'

Francine, whose bubble of happiness had burst, shook her head. 'I never cry usually, but I can't help it, I so much want to be with you and Evie. I've never had people to be kind to me, like you and Evie . . .'

'Glory be to God,' Kathleen said under her breath, 'what have they done to you, child?' Francine looked up at her, the big grey eyes full of pleading.

'Couldn't *you* be my nanny? You could ask my father.'

'Well now, there's a big problem, Miss Francine. I wasn't all that clever meself at school. I learned the three Rs, and I know on the map where England and Ireland are, but that's about all.'

14

Francine gave a wan little smile. 'You're just saying that. I'm sure you know a lot more.'

'Let's say a wee bit more. Cheer up, your nanny might be a lovely woman. You know, Miss Francine, I was told you were a happy child and that you lived with a very quiet aunt. So if you could be happy with a woman who didn't have much to say -'

There was the sound of running footsteps and Evie burst into the room. 'Cook's getting mad! She wants to know what you're doing, says you must be talking to the furniture men.'

Kathleen got up. 'Holy Mary, does she expect me to make the beds and dust and polish in two minutes. What does she think I am?' She turned to Francine. 'Come along, I'll sneak up sometime and make the beds. If I don't go down now she'll take it out on you. We'll have another talk later.'

It was bedtime before they had their chat. Kathleen had been allotted the task of taking Francine up to bed. Cook had been in a temper all day, complaining about the men having to have cups of tea and something to eat. She called them time wasters in spite of them never having stopped since they arrived. Edwin had gone out and so Francine had not seen him again since that morning.

When Francine was washed and ready for bed Kathleen asked if she had a doll or a teddy to take to bed with her. Francine said no, she had never had either, her aunt didn't believe in children having dolls or animals.

Kathleen stared at her. 'I can't believe it. Why ever not?'

'She says that children get fond of them and if something happens to them, like getting hurt or lost, the child breaks his or her heart.'

Kathleen shook her head. 'It's beyond me, but I can tell you this, Miss Francine, you'll have a doll to take to bed with you tomorrow night, and that's a promise. I must go now or I'll have Cook after me, don't forget to say your prayers. I'll leave this bit of candle burning but don't touch

15

it, mind. I'll come up later and put it out when you're asleep.'

Kathleen dropped a kiss on her brow and smoothed back the chestnut-coloured hair that curled at the ends. 'Bless you, Miss Francine, sweet dreams.'

Francine whispered her nightly prayer. 'God bless Aunt Amelia, and Papa, make Mamma happy in heaven and make me a good girl.' Usually she ended on an amen, but this evening she went on, 'And God bless Kathleen and Evie and please, *please* God, let me stay in Papa's house.' After a pause she added, 'If you *can*, would you make Papa love me. Amen.'

Francine unclasped her hands, opened her eyes and looked around the room, at the flickering shadows on the walls. Her aunt had always left her in darkness, and although she had never really been afraid in the dark she liked the feeling of having movement in the room. The shadows were dancing like she was, dancing in her mind. What a wonderful day it had been, in spite of having to sit still for so long at times on the stool. When Cook went out of the kitchen Evie would come hurrying up to have a few whispered words with her, to ask her if she was all right. Once, she had brought in one of the new kittens for Francine to hold for a moment. She was unable to leave it, she said, because its mother would fret. She wasn't well. She had a bit of a fever.

Francine hoped the cat would soon get well then perhaps she would be allowed to stroke it and play with the kittens. Aunt Amelia would not have an animal in the house – she said they got lost or they died then you were full of grief. Francine had often wondered why her aunt was always weepy. She cried a lot. Said fate had been hard on her. She never laughed or even smiled. And yet she had not been unkind to the girl. It was she who had educated her. Sometimes she would tell her niece interesting stories about countries she had visited. She seemed very clever, she could speak French like a native and had been teaching

16

Francine herself to speak it. In fact, one day, she had been telling her how well she was doing when she had stopped in mid-sentence, paused then said, 'Francine, I'm sorry, but I can't have you here to live with me any more. I've decided to go into a convent. I need to find peace of mind.'

Francine knew about convents and nuns but did not understand what she meant by peace of mind. She had been about to ask when Amelia went on, 'You are going to live with your father, but I must tell you that he doesn't really want you. He's a busy man and will be moving into a new house at Spinners End.'

The only thing that had registered with Francine then, was the fact that she would be seeing her father. It was something she had dreamed about. And when it did sink in to her that he didn't really want her to live with him she didn't really blame him. He was a very busy man and was unused to children. It would take time for them to get to know one another. Her eyelids began to droop. It might take a long, long time but surely they would eventually become close. Her very own papa . . . Francine slept.

It was Evie who woke her the next morning. She had brought a can of hot water for her to wash in. She poured some into the basin then said, 'Can you manage to wash yourself, Miss? Cook's poorly and Kathleen's having to see to the master's breakfast.' Evie wore her habitual worried frown. 'Your Dad wants to see you.'

Francine, who had lain cocooned in the feather bed, shot up, tossed back the bedclothes and asked, a panic in her voice, why he wanted to see her. As she slid off the high bed on to the floor Evie tried to restrain her.

'It's all right, Miss, you needn't 'urry, 'e doesn't want to see you until after breakfast. And I think, but I'm not sure, that it's good news.'

'What sort of good news?' she wanted to know, but Evie shook her head, she was unable to say any more. Kathleen would explain, and after telling Francine to get washed before the water got cold, she picked up the can and scuttled out.

Francine gave a little shiver as she left the warmth of the bedside rug and trotted across the floor to the washstand. There was no carpet in this room, but although the boards were uncovered they were beautifully polished and were warmer to walk on than in her bedroom in her aunt's house. Why did her father want to see her, after ignoring her most of the day before? What good news could it be? Perhaps he was going to take her out with him!

Francine plunged the flannel into the water. She wrung it, soaped it, washed her face and then her neck. How wonderful it would be. But then Evie had said she *thought* it was good news. Her father might have decided to send her to school. At one time she would have welcomed it, but if she was sent away she might never get to know her father properly. And anyway, she wanted to stay here with Kathleen and Evie.

Francine suddenly decided that worrying about it would not change anything, but all the same she seemed to be all fingers and thumbs and took a long time getting dressed. She tidied away her nightdress and slippers and took stock of the room for the first time. It had been difficult to see much the night before by candlelight. The room was smaller than the one she had been used to, but it was cosy. The quilted coverlet had a pattern of rosebuds and the bedside rug picked out the rose colour. The curtains were olive green velvet. There was a large wardrobe in mahogany, a chair, a chest of drawers and a small dressing table with a swing mirror.

As she brushed her hair she studied herself in the mirror. Her eyes looked enormous in her pinched-looking face and she wished, as she had wished so often, that she was prettier. She would have liked to have had lovely blue eyes and dark hair like Kathleen, instead of which it was brown – chestnut-coloured her Aunt Amelia called it. Her father was dark-haired and had eyes almost black. Was she like

18

her mother? Her aunt once said that her mother had been very pretty but had never described her. Francine stood quite still as she heard a man shouting somewhere along the passage. It sounded like her father's voice. Oh, dear, he was in a bad temper again. It was not, she felt, a morning for good news.

She tied her hair back with a piece of blue ribbon and after straightening the lace collar on her dark blue velvet dress she prepared to leave.

All the doors along the passage were closed so Francine had no idea which was her father's room. She hurried along, not wanting to meet him in a temper and ran down the stairs to the kitchen.

Kathleen greeted her with a smile. 'So there you are then! Did you have a good sleep? Evie said she had a job to wake you.'

'Yes, I did, thank you. Evie says that my father wants to see me.'

'That's right. But not until after breakfast, and he won't be down for another quarter of an hour or twenty minutes. You've time to have your breakfast, you can have it in here. There's some porridge and I'll do you a lightly boiled egg. Go and get a warm by the fire.'

'Kathleen – why does my father want to see me?'

'It's all right, Miss Francine, don't look so worried. I put a plan to him about you last night and I think it might work . . .' Kathleen busied herself as she talked, putting a tablecloth and cutlery on a big tray. 'Mrs Dodge said she couldn't do with having you in the kitchen all day and when your father talked about going to the domestic agency to get someone to look after you, I ventured to put a proposition to him.'

While Kathleen swung the grill plate over the fire and laid some rashers of bacon on it, Francine swallowed hard as she waited to know her fate.

'There now, that's got the breakfast started. I told him that my Auntie Bridget used to be a teacher until she was married. My uncle died recently, leaving her not very well off. I said I was sure she would be willing to give you lessons and take you for walks.'

'Oh!' Francine looked up at her, eyes shining, feeling sure that anyone Kathleen recommended must be a lovely person. She only hoped that her father would think so, too.

To her joy he accepted Bridget Brogan. But his expression was no less stern as he eyed her.

'But remember this, child, if you disobey her in any way, or don't work hard at your lessons you shall be sent to school.'

Francine pressed her palms tightly together. 'I like learning things, Papa, I really do and I promise I shall do everything, *everything*, that Mrs Brogan tells me.'

'Very well. There's one thing more. You do not go roaming all over the house. You either stay in the kitchen or in the rooms allotted to you.'

'Yes, Papa.' Some of the light died in Francine's eyes and Edwin Chayter wished she did not make him feel so guilty. He spoke sharply, 'Off you go and remember what I told you.'

'Yes, Papa.' She walked sedately out of the room, but once outside, when she saw Kathleen, she ran to her and flung her arms around her skirt.

'It's all right. Your Aunt Bridget will be looking after me. Oh, thanks, Kathleen. Thanks a lot. I feel so happy. The happiest I've ever been in my life.'

Kathleen felt a restriction in her throat. The poor wee thing, what sort of life had she been living when a woman coming to teach her could be a highlight in her life? Kathleen vowed then she would do everything she could to make Francine's life brighter.

CHAPTER TWO

When Francine caught her first glimpse of Bridget Brogan the following day and saw a plain woman, dressed in black, her small mouth giving her a prim look, she felt disappointed. But then Bridget greeted her with a warm smile, and Francine knew it was going to be all right.

Bridget said, in a quiet voice, 'I'm pleased to meet you, Miss Francine. I feel sure we shall get on well together.'

'I know we shall,' Francine said.

Kathleen said she would show her aunt the rooms and they went upstairs. Bridget nodded her approval, and especially of the good fire burning. Children could not be expected to learn if they were shivering.

It had been arranged she would come at nine o'clock every morning, give Francine lessons until twelve, have lunch, then take the child for a walk in the afternoon. She would leave at four o'clock. After that Kathleen would take over.

The first day was a delight to Francine. Not only was Bridget a good teacher who made each lesson interesting, but she would answer any questions she cared to ask; not like her Aunt Amelia who would tell her to stop asking so many questions, it made her head ache.

If the morning lessons were a pleasure for Francine, the afternoons were a revelation. She was used to walking along a quiet avenue with her aunt, then out on to country roads. Bridget took her along thoroughfares teaming with people and traffic.

Men with carts shouted to those pushing barrows to get out of the way, and those with vans yelled to everyone to get out of the way. They cut through a narrow alleyway where women were exchanging gossip in loud voices from open windows on either side.

They came out into a street market where everything from jellied eels to pots and pans seemed to be sold. Here, if anything, the noise was louder, with stallholders shouting their wares. Francine, wide-eyed, had a constant smile on her lips. She would have liked to linger to look at the stalls but Bridget urged her on.

'Another time. I wanted you to get acquainted with Spinners End today.'

Francine looked up at her. 'Why is it called Spinners End?'

'Probably because people living here many years ago spun cloth. It was easy to load on to ships crossing the ocean. Tomorrow I shall take you to the docks.'

The docks, tomorrow? What other wonderful thing could happen?

That evening Francine received her first doll and she thought that nothing, no matter what it was, could be more wonderful than that. Kathleen gave it to her when she was ready for bed.

'I made it quickly,' she said, 'because I wanted you to have it to cuddle tonight, but you shall have a better one later.'

She had made it from pieces from the rag-bag. She had used cochineal for the mouth and tinted cheeks, and had marked in the eyes and nose with the black lead used for the kitchen range. She was about to apologise for the roughness of the doll when Francine murmured, 'It's beautiful! I love it, I shall love it till the day I die.'

Kathleen felt a lump come into her throat. 'Oh, don't, you make me want to cry. I shall take you home with me next Wednesday when I have my half-day and then you'll have a nice surprise. I won't tell you what it is.'

She tucked Francine up in bed, dropped a kiss on her brow and left the small curled-up figure, her cheek pressed close to that of the doll.

22

When Kathleen went back to the kitchen she exclaimed, 'I feel I could kill that aunt of Francine's *and* her da'. That child has never had a doll in her life. She told me about it yesterday but it wasn't until she was all but weeping over the rag doll I made last night that I realised what she had missed. That father of hers should be horse-whipped! He could afford the very best for her.'

Evie agreed. 'We were poor but us kids always 'ad a peg doll or a wooden spoon one. Me mam would tie a bit of cloth round the 'ead for a shawl and a bit round the middle for a skirt.'

Kathleen gave a firm nod. 'Exactly. It's a disgrace that people with money should deny a child -'

'That'll do, O'Reilly,' snapped Cook. 'There's plenty of kids never had a doll and are half-starved into the bargain. Now get on whipping up that cream, and you, Taylor, get those vegetables done, the master's bringing two friends home for dinner.'

When Mrs Dodge went into the larder Evie whispered to Kathleen, 'Well, anyway, you got the old bag to use your proper name!' Then after a pause she added, 'Are you really a cook?'

Kathleen grinned. 'Sort of. At me last place when Cook was ill I took over and cooked for the family for six weeks. The mistress was a lovely woman and when they were all going out to India she put on me reference that I was an excellent cook.'

Evie eyed her in astonishment. 'Then why did you take the job 'ere of housemaid?'

'Because I like moving around. If you're cooking you're stuck in the kitchen all the time. I like meeting people when I answer the door, and all that.'

During the past two days, with all the moving in, Kathleen had worn a print dress and a big white apron. And had done so in the mornings at the old house, the master never having clients to be photographed until the afternoon. But with the meal almost ready and the table laid in the dining room she went to change.

She liked wearing her black dress, her frilly apron with the big bows at the back and her little white cap. This evening she put up her hair and knew she would draw glances of approval from any male who might arrive. But not from the master. She had lied when she said he wanted to get her into his bed, wishing to seem important to Cook when she was hinting at getting her the sack.

Kathleen sighed. Heaven knew how many Hail Mary's she would have to say when she went to Confession.

And it was not that she wanted to get into Edwin Chayter's bed. Apart from the fact that he was about the most bad-tempered man she had ever met, her brothers *and* her grandmother would kill her, so they would, if they ever heard of such goings on.

But this was not to say that the master was celibate. When guests came for dinner there was usually one attractive female left whom he was supposed to be seeing home. But did he see her home? He did not. He took her to his bed. Oh, he was always very careful about it and Kathleen knew that if she had not been late to go to bed herself she might never have known. It was the subdued laughter of a woman she could hear coming from his bedroom that gave the game away. Although Kathleen had never seen the 'bed guest' leave she knew, even without hearing the laughter, when the master had been entertaining by the fact that he never on these occasions had early morning tea brought to his room. He would give instructions that he would be sleeping late.

She did suspect, however, that tea was made in the bedroom. Once when a cupboard had been left open she saw a spirit kettle on a shelf, but before she could note whether there were also cups and saucers, the master was back and the cupboard locked.

Kathleen had come to the conclusion that although

24

Edwin Chayter was a bad-tempered man he had enough respect for his staff not to flaunt his women to them.

It was half past eight when he arrived with two men. Kathleen took their hats and coats, her gaze modestly lowered. The taller of the guests gave her hand a squeeze and she heard him say to her master as they moved away, 'A nice piece, Edwin. Mind if I poach on your preserves?'

'Not on my preserves, Godfrey,' came a surprisingly light-hearted reply. 'But you would be poaching on the preserves of the swineherd who is walking her out.'

The three men laughed and Kathleen was fuming. How dare he assume she was not worthy of anyone better than a swineherd to walk her out.

Later, when she carried a tureen of soup into the dining room she had to restrain herself from pouring it over her master's head. But none of the three men even glanced in her direction; all were in earnest conversation about the new techniques in photography. They were still on the same subject when they settled to their port and cigars.

Kathleen was over her earlier temper but she brooded about Edwin Chayter's remark until Mrs Dodge demanded to know what was wrong with her.

When told, Cook dismissed it with a wave of the hand. Didn't she know that all men were animals where women were concerned? Her husband had been no different from the rest.

It was the first time she had mentioned her husband and Kathleen, curious, asked if he was still alive.

'He's not. He died six years ago and it was the best thing he ever did as far as I was concerned. I'll say no more than that, except to advise any girl I know to stay single.'

Oh no, Kathleen thought, being a spinster was not for her. She wanted her own man, her own little home and children. Then she sighed and made up her mind not to tell any more little white lies, like saying the master had tried to get her into his bed, or God would punish her and she might die a spinster.

The following morning Francine asked Bridget's permission to have the doll with her while she was having her lessons. Bridget agreed, but asked her to sit the doll in a chair as she wanted Francine to do some writing.

When the doll was seated Francine said, 'Her name is Gabrielle. I think that was my mother's name.'

'I see. You have a French name too, was your mother French?'

Francine turned, looking thoughtful. 'I don't know, ma'am. I think my grandmama may have been. Aunt Amelia taught me French. I don't know an awful lot, of course, not yet.'

Bridget beamed at her. 'Then I shall teach you some more. I learned it when I was at the convent. Mother Superior was French and we had long conversations. Perhaps one day your Papa will take you to Paris.'

Francine was not very sure about this, but she might be able to go on her own some day. Aunt Amelia had been and she said it was a very beautiful city. The strange thing was, when she talked about Paris she always looked so sad.

'Well, now . . .' Bridget opened a book. 'To begin with today we shall talk about the Kings and Queens of England.'

Francine did not like history very much but she listened carefully because her aunt had told her it was important to know about it, so she could hold a sensible conversation when she was launched into society.

Francine decided that 'being launched into society' must be very interesting indeed.

When Bridget took her to the docks that afternoon Francine thought that one pair of eyes was not enough to take in everything. Although there had been a lot of activity the day before, here it was on a much vaster scale. There was a constant movement on the Thames, of small

26

rowing craft, tugs, coal barges and sailing ships. And the noise everywhere was deafening: hooting from the tugs and huge cranes creaking as they loaded and unloaded goods from ships at the dockside.

There was a babbling of strange tongues, which reminded Francine of the Tower of Babel in the Bible. Bridget pointed out some men with strange hats and pigtails, who she said were Chinamen. Other men wearing what looked like white nightdresses were Arabs. A group of drunken sailors sang songs. Bridget steered her away from these.

Francine's gaze went to men swarming agilely up the rigging of ships, while men below were bustling around on deck. The tangy smell of fruit and the heavier aroma of spices mingled with that of tar, oil, paint, new timber. . .

Although she was loving every minute of it she became a little confused after a while and Bridget, perhaps aware of it, put an arm across her shoulders and led her to where there were warehouses, ships' chandlers, shops that sold pies and soup, a cobblers . . .

Bridget said she thought that was all for now. Tomorrow morning they would talk about commerce and sea voyages.

Francine thought she had seen more in two days than she had seen in the whole of the seven years she had lived with her aunt.

That evening Francine was so tired after her adventures she fell asleep without saying her prayers.

Bridget did not start the French lessons until the following day and was surprised at how much her little pupil knew. She tested her memory when they went for their afternoon walk, in a much quieter area this time, and was further surprised at how much Francine had absorbed from the morning lesson.

'You have a very retentive memory, child,' she approved. 'It will be most valuable to you in the future. You may marry a wealthy man who will want to travel.

When we are a little further on with French, I may start you on Italian, or German. We shall see.'

Although Francine was pleased at the praise she was longing for Wednesday to come around, so she could go to meet Kathleen's family. She had learned from Evie that the O'Reillys were a large family, but that was all. The little kitchen maid seemed to be in constant fear that Cook would find her talking and get her the sack for idling her time away.

When the Wednesday came at last and Bridget was getting Francine ready for her outing she said, 'Now mind your manners and speak only when you're spoken to. You'll like the O'Reillys, they're warm-hearted people.'

Francine learned some more about the family from Kathleen during their ride on the horse-drawn tram. Kathleen told her that her parents had died when she was young and that her grandparents had brought them all up.

'Himself drinks a lot,' she said, 'he could empty the river Liffey if he had a mind, but he's a kindly man for all that. When Herself scolds him you could hear her from here to Dublin but she has a big heart and she'll love you, I know it.'

Francine asked how many brothers and sisters Kathleen had and was told four brothers and three sisters. One of the boys was married.

When they got off the tram they walked along a street where a few tall, narrow houses seemed to be wedged between what looked like derelict warehouses. All the houses had a short flight of stone steps leading up to them. Most of the houses looked shabby, with peeling paint, but the steps were clean and the brass knobs on the front doors gleamed. Kathleen stopped about halfway along the street and said, 'Well, here we are! This is where we live and where most of the family work.'

As they climbed the steps, Francine, the doll clutched to her, could hear sounds coming from the house, but was unable to make out what they were. When Kathleen opened the front door and went in the sounds which became louder seemed to be coming from upstairs.

Kathleen called, 'Are you there, Gran?' and a small, wiry woman, with bright bird-like eyes, came out of the room on the left to greet them.

'So there you are then! And this is Miss Francine. How are you, child? You look cold. It is cold. If it rains, it'll be snow as sure as sure. Keep your coat on while you go upstairs and meet the family then you can come down and have a cup of cocoa and a bite of gingerbread.'

The old lady then said in an aside to Kathleen, 'You didn't tell her, did you, about the surprise?'

Kathleen shook her head and girl and woman exchanged smiles.

'Good. Come along then, follow me.' They climbed the uncarpeted stairs with Francine wondering what the surprise could be.

The sounds were louder when they reached the first landing and it seemed there were a lot of people talking. When they went into a room all sounds ceased. Mrs O'Reilly said, 'This is the wee girl I told you about. Her name is Francine. Make her welcome now.'

There were smiles and greetings from all sides. Kathleen went around the people saying, 'This is me brother Michael and this is Declan and here's Milo . . .' Then there were the girls, but Francine didn't hear the names of any of them. She had caught sight of a frame full of dolls and she gazed at them, her eyes round with awe and wonder.

Kathleen laughed. 'They're wooden Betties, we make them to sell.' She picked one up. 'See, her arms and legs move. The boys make the dolls and the girls paint the hair and faces and make the clothes. But we have a *very special doll* for you.'

She went to a door near to her and opened it. 'Grandad, will you bring it in.'

A man, as sprightly as his wife, with twinkling blue eyes

and silvery hair and beard, came in, a broad smile on his face.

'And there you are, me little beauty. A queen of a doll.'

Francine could only stand and stare, tongue-tied, as she looked at the beautiful doll with a china face, big brown eyes and lovely fair curly hair. It was dressed in a dark green velvet coat with matching bonnet, the bonnet lined with rose-coloured sateen.

Big tears welled up and ran slowly down her cheeks and there was a chorus of 'Ah–' from all those in the room.

Kathleen took the doll from her grandfather and held it out to Francine saying softly, 'It's yours to keep.' She made to take the rag doll from her but Francine clutched it to her, and it needed a great deal of persuasion to get her to lay Gabrielle down while she took the new doll to hold. Then Kathleen said, 'And now, we shall go downstairs and you shall have some of Gran's gingerbread, then later I'll bring you back and you can see the dolls being made, the wooden Betties, that is.'

Francine took small bites of gingerbread and had sips of cocoa, but her gaze never left the armchair where Mrs O'Reilly had coaxed her into seating the dolls side by side.

It wasn't until Francine had finished the gingerbread and the cocoa and thanked Mrs O'Reilly that she began to take stock of the room. It was long with a fireplace at either end, as though two rooms had been made into one. In each grate a log fire burned cheerily. A table ran almost the whole length of the room. It was white scrubbed wood, like the one in the kitchen at home, but this one had hollowed out circles all round the edges which were lined with what appeared to be tin. Strange, what were the circles for?

Kathleen said, 'Well, Miss Francine, are we going to the workroom to see how dolls are made? Leave your own two here, they will be perfectly safe. Gran will look after them.'

30

Gran confirmed this, she would guard them with her life.

And so Francine was initiated into the world of doll-making, and also into a family who seemed to accept her as one of their own. She saw Kathleen's brothers fashioning the dolls, shaping them with chisels from uniform pieces of wood. She identified each man and girl by his or her allotted task. Michael and Declan shaped the head and body; Milo made the arms and legs, then all three men took turns at smoothing the wood on a small whirring machine. Graine joined on arms and legs with elastic threaded through holes in the body; Therese and Cecilia painted on the hair and faces while Mary made the clothes. Mary was married to Milo.

Francine learned that the largest proportion of dolls were sold without clothes but those that were clothed wore either a simple cotton dress in one piece with a drawstring at the neck, or a skirt and top of red or green cloth.

While they worked one or the other was always talking to Francine, wanting to know what she had seen when she went to the market and to the docks. She described scenes to them but her gaze never left what they were working on. Cecilia asked her if she would like to make dolls and Francine nodded.

Michael teased her, saying then she would have to live here because they started work at six in the morning and didn't finish until perhaps nine or ten o'clock at night.

Francine said, her expression solemn, that she would not mind the work, but she could not leave her papa. She glanced up then and saw Kathleen and her sisters exchange glances but was not sure why.

She would have liked to know how her china-faced doll was made but she had not seen Kathleen's grandfather since he brought her the doll and of course she dare not ask.

After a while she became aware of an appetising smell

coming from downstairs and Michael said, 'I think it's time to eat.' They all agreed and minutes after this Mrs O'Reilly looked in and said, 'It's ready and don't be lingering.'

Work stopped immediately and they all began to troop out.

Francine then learned what the hollowed-out surfaces on the table were for. A huge pan of stew was passed around and everyone helped themselves to a portion.

Kathleen smiled at Francine. 'We've no time to wash up plates.'

Francine was not really hungry but she took some stew to be polite. And ended up eating it all. It was delicious.

Then bread was passed around, the gravy was mopped up and after that Therese brought in a big dish of rice pudding.

There was a lot of talk and laughter. One or another of the men told a tale, something that had happened long ago. Did they mind the time that Farmer Finnigan's pig got loose and the whole village was after catching it. Not for Farmer Finnigan, but for themselves. What a feast someone had, they never did find out who found it.

There was a great burst of laughter at this.

Before the meal was finished a boy of about twelve or thirteen came in. Kathleen said it was her brother Rory, who worked as boot boy in a big house.

His grandmother said, 'And is this supposed to be your half-day off? 'Tis five o'clock.'

Michael shook his head. 'It's a shame it is, but what can he do? Nothing. He either puts up with it or leaves.'

A slow smile spread over Rory's face. 'I don't mind, a guest gave me half a sovereign.'

'Half a sovereign?' came a chorus of voices.

He held up the coin. 'I worked for it, didn't I. He had me running messages for him all over the place and if Mr Tench had found out I would have been for it.'

His grandmother held out her hand for the money. 'I'll save it for you.'

Rory began to plead. 'Gran, I'd like to buy a bike with some of it. I can get a secondhand one for three bob.'

'Hand it over, boy.' The old lady still had her hand held out. A look of defiance came over Rory's face and there was a sudden stillness in the room.

'No Gran, not unless you promise to give me the money for the bike.'

'Who is boss in the house?' the old lady demanded. '*I* say what you can and cannot have.'

Rory's head went up. 'If I hand this over you'll make a dishonest man of me because I'll never tell you if I ever get any more tips.'

'Right. Then you'll be the first dishonest one in this family. Mary, get him some stew.' Mrs O'Reilly sat down and the room was so quiet that when Mary pushed back her stool to go to the kitchen the sound was startling. Francine found that her hands were tightly clenched.

After a moment the golden coin was on the table and Rory was pushing it across to his grandmother. She took it and put it in a pocket of her dress then said, 'When I do the accounts up at the weekend you shall have your money for your bike, Rory. Now shall we get on with the meal.'

Colour had come to Rory's face and Francine felt sorry for him.

She and Kathleen left shortly after this, with all of them giving Francine a warm invitation to come again.

The two dolls had been put into a linen bag and Francine had agreed that Kathleen should carry it for her. As they walked along the street to get the tram she said, a little hesitantly, 'Kathleen, why was your grandmother so unkind to Rory, then saying he could have the bicycle. I felt sorry for him.'

'You had no need to. There are rules and Rory knows them. Gran is the boss, she handles all the money, no matter what any of us earns. She pays the accounts, the rent, buys the food and gives us money for our clothes. Gran might have a sharp tongue but she's not mean. Rory would know he would get his bike eventually.'

'Then why didn't he just give her the money straight away?'

'Because he's a rebel. He's a lovely lad, but he has big ideas. He wants to conquer the world.'

'Is that a bad thing?'

Kathleen glanced quickly at her small charge. It was something an older person might say. Had she ever had a proper childhood? Was she only starting now, having dolls to play with? The expressions flitting across the child's face in the workroom had made Kathleen feel like weeping. She said, 'What are you going to call this new doll?'

Francine was silent for a while then she looked up. 'I think I shall call her Lavinia. Aunt Amelia had a friend with that name and she was very elegant.'

'Well now, that's an elegant name, isn't it?'

They didn't talk very much on the way home. Francine felt sleepy after all the excitement of the visit but when they arrived home she was wide awake and anxious to have her dolls to look at again. To her surprise there was a third doll in the bag. A wooden Bettie who was wearing a scarlet felt skirt, a black jacket and a woolley hat with a pompon on top.

Francine, eyes shining, held it out. 'Is this for -?'

Kathleen nodded, smiling. 'Yes, it's yours. The family wanted you to have it so you now have three dolls to play with. But that's for tomorrow. It's past your bedtime.'

When Kathleen had tucked her up and gone, leaving the stump of candle casting flickering shadows on the walls, Francine eased herself up in bed and looked at the china-faced doll and the wooden Bettie in the chair in the corner. She had Gabrielle with her in bed.

Three dolls! She could hardly believe it. What a wonderful afternoon it had been.

34

CHAPTER THREE

During the next few days Francine did not even catch a glimpse of her father and when she asked Kathleen about him she was told he was away, but would be returning late Sunday evening.

Francine had obeyed her father and not been anywhere near the studio, but the fact that he was away put the mischief into her. She would just take a peep in. She could manage it after her morning lesson when Bridget sent her upstairs to wash her hands.

At twelve o'clock, Francine, with her heart beating a little faster, looked cautiously along the passage, then carefully turned the knob of the door. Once inside she closed the door and stood gazing around her, surprised at the change in the studio.

On the wall facing her was a country scene of trees and a river, with swans on the water. In front of it was a rustic wooden seat. To the right were three tall-backed chairs, the seats upholstered in dark green velvet. There were two stools, also covered in green velvet. Rugs on the polished oak floor gave the room a cosy look.

She was disappointed at first to see no sign of the camera, but on opening a door on the right she found it stored away. The room was full of equipment; there was a sink with a tap, box files and many different kinds of bottles holding liquid. Above the sink was a thin rope with clips attached to it. She knew that photographs had to be developed, her aunt had explained this to her, but she had no idea of the process.

Francine would have liked to linger, but knowing that she would soon be missed, she left. Perhaps there might be another opportunity when her father was away to look again.

By the time she had washed and dried her hands she had decided that although she would like to make dolls, what she really wanted to do was to photograph things, and people.

When she confided this to Bridget that afternoon when they went for their walk, Bridget held up her hands in horror.

'That is man's work, child. Put that idea out of your mind at once. Your father would never countenance such a thing.'

Francine thought of Rory who was a rebel and decided that she would be a rebel, too. When she grew up she would be a photographer.

At bedtime she told Kathleen what she had decided and Kathleen eyed her with some curiosity. 'You're a strange child, Miss Francine. Most girls of your age want to play at being grown up, having a home and a husband and children of their own. And here you are wanting to be a photographer. I suppose it's in your blood, inherited from your father.' Kathleen smiled. 'But there, these are early days. When you grow up you'll probably fall in love with a nice young man and you won't even give photography a thought.'

'Oh, I will, Kathleen, I know it.' There was something so positive in the tone Kathleen sighed and said no more.

When her father had not arrived by the time Francine went to bed on Sunday evening she made up her mind to stay awake, just to know he was home. But sleep overcame her.

The next morning when Evie brought up her hot water Francine asked about him and was told he was home. 'I 'aven't seen 'im, though,' Evie said, 'but I did 'ear him coughin' when I passed 'is room.'

Coughing? Was he ill? Although Francine had no intention of calling to see if he was all right, she found herself, when she was dressed, knocking gently on her father's bedroom door. There was no reply and turning the knob, she looked in.

To her astonishment there was a woman beside him in the bed. Both were fast asleep. Francine, full of excitement, closed the door again quietly. Perhaps her father had married again and she had a stepmother. She ran down the stairs and all but fell into Kathleen's arms.

When she gabbled out her story Kathleen looked alarmed.

'Oh, Miss Francine, you didn't go into his room?'

'I only peeped in, they were asleep. The lady had lovely golden hair. Is she my stepmother? Please say yes.'

'No, she – oh, God.' For once Kathleen was lost for words. How do you explain to a child about a man taking a woman to his bed, other than his wife? She hated to disillusion her but it had to be done.

'No, she's not your stepmother, Miss Francine. I'll try and explain later who she is, but you are *not* to tell Evie, or Cook, about her. Do you understand?'

Francine said yes, the light going out of her eyes. Kathleen then told her that breakfast was ready, and a moment later watched the small bereft-looking little figure go walking away.

Blasted men. Why hadn't the fool locked the door? But then he wouldn't expect anyone to go in. He had left a note on the hall table to say that he did not want morning tea.

Kathleen hoped that Francine would not pursue the question of the woman in her father's bed, but no sooner had she gone upstairs to do some dusting than Francine was tugging at her skirt, wanting to know about the lady with the golden hair. She turned to her.

'Look, Miss Francine, there are some things best left alone until you are old enough to understand, so just leave it, will you?'

Francine knew tones of voices and accepted it would be

37

no use asking any further questions, but she was puzzled. Who *could* the lady be?

Bridget arrived and the bedroom incident was temporarily forgotten as Francine told her excitedly about the two new dolls and all about visiting Kathleen's home. It took Bridget some time to get her settled down to her lessons.

That afternoon they were coming downstairs ready to go for their afternoon walk when the doorbell rang. Kathleen came hurrying out of the kitchen to answer it. She said, 'It's visitors for the master, come to have their photographs taken.' Bridget drew Francine aside while Kathleen let them in.

There was a smartly-dressed man and a woman with two children. Kathleen said, 'The master is expecting you, sir.' She led the way upstairs.

Francine whispered to Bridget, 'Do you think I might go and watch them having their photographs taken?' to which Bridget once more showed horror.

'Certainly not, child. Having one's photograph taken is a private thing, very private indeed.'

Francine had never had a photograph taken but could think of no reason why it should be private. But perhaps this was something else she might find out in time.

That evening at bedtime she was going upstairs with Kathleen when they met her father on the landing. He stopped.

'Good evening.' He addressed himself to Kathleen. 'I trust my daughter is settling down and behaving herself.'

'She is that, sir, she is very well-behaved and Mrs Brogan has nothing but good to say about her, an intelligent child, she says.'

'Excellent.' He stepped aside to let them pass then went down the stairs. Francine stood watching him and at the forlorn look on her face Kathleen felt like shouting after Edwin Chayter, 'Why don't you talk to your child, love her, wish her a fond goodnight?'

Francine looked up at her. 'I don't think my father likes me, not even a little bit.'

'Of course he does! It's just that men don't show their feelings like women. They have so many things on their mind. Your father would no doubt be worrying about the photographs he had taken, if his clients would be satisfied with them. It's very important that they should because it's his livelihood. Without his work there would be no money.'

Francine said, her expression solemn, 'I believe you, Kathleen.'

Kathleen grimaced. That was her trouble, she always talked too much when she was trying to convince someone of something. The Father had told her so when she went to Confession. Oh, Lord, what a mixed-up world it was. All it needed for this child to be made happy was for her father to give her an affectionate word.

She put an arm around Francine's shoulders as they walked along the passage. She would try to make up a special story tonight to suit the occasion.

But she ended up repeating the story of Cinderella and hoped that Francine would dream of a prince coming to court her.

But it was not of a fairy godmother or a prince that Francine dreamed that evening: it was of Rory and he was taking a photograph of her. When she awoke the following morning she hoped that Kathleen would take her to her home again this coming Wednesday. Kathleen did and the first person Francine saw when they went into the house was Rory. He had his bicycle, which was in pieces in the passage. He looked up from sandpapering one of the wheels.

'Hello, Kathleen, hello, Miss Francine. I got the bike.'

'So I see.' Kathleen patted his black hair, which curled a little. 'You're a lucky lad. Where's Gran? Upstairs?'

'Yes, and she's in a foul temper. Grandad broke one of her favourite ornaments last night. She told him to get out and he did. Now she's worrying herself sick because he hasn't come back.'

'Oh, dear. I'll go up and have a word with her. Miss Francine, you stay here for a moment.'

As Kathleen went upstairs a door opened on the landing and Mrs O'Reilly came out. 'Oh, so there you are, and no doubt you'll have heard about all the trouble.'

Kathleen, who had reached the landing, tried to soothe her. 'Grandad will be all right, he can take care of himself.'

'Take care of himself? It was cold enough to freeze a corpse last night and if he fell down and couldn't get up and was there all night, it would be the death of him. And who is it who would have to be sitting up nursing him? Me, that's who.'

Kathleen took her grandmother by the arm and led her to another room on the landing. They went in, then there was silence.

Rory looked up at Francine and grinned. 'You're seeing a bit of life, kid, aren't you? Real life, not the make-believe world that you live in.'

Francine was puzzled. 'What do you mean by make-believe?'

'Like fairy stories, where Aladdin rubs a lamp and has everything he wants and where a prince rescues a princess and they live happily ever after. They're all rich in your world.'

Francine hesitated a moment before replying. 'It's not really like that. My father has servants but he doesn't seem very happy. And I don't think he likes me very much.'

Rory sat back on his heels and studied her with interest. 'Why is that, do you know?'

Francine shook her head. 'No, and I can't ask him. You are lucky, you can talk to your grandmother and she listens.'

Rory was silent. He lifted one wheel, laid it against the wall and began sandpapering the other. When he continued to be silent Francine wished she had not said

40

so much. It was the most she had talked to someone she hardly knew. Perhaps he thought her unkind for saying what she had done about her father. She went on, 'Papa is a very clever man. He's a photographer.'

'I know. I want to be an engineer, I think. I might even go to sea.'

Kathleen who had come out of the room and was on her way downstairs called, 'Don't take any notice of our Rory, he's going to be something different every time I see him.'

Rory took this in good humour. He winked at Francine and told her that his sister was exaggerating as usual. Kathleen then took Francine into the kitchen to make her a cup of cocoa.

She had a slice of fruit cake this time and as she munched it she listened to Rory whistling as he worked.

Kathleen, who had been listening too said softly, 'He's a lovely whistler, is our Rory. One time, when your father might be away I'll persuade Cook to let me stay overnight. I'll have you with me so you can hear the singing. Me brothers and me sisters have lovely voices, they blend in beautifully together, it can bring tears to your eyes.' There was a dreaming in Kathleen's eyes then and Francine found herself wishing that her father would go away again soon.

The visit that day was not such a happy one for Francine as the previous one had been. All the family were quiet because Kathleen's grandfather had still not come home. Mrs O'Reilly was sure that something dreadful had happened to him.

'He could be lying at the bottom of the river,' she wailed, 'and if he was he would never be the same again.' Mrs Logan's husband had never been right since he had fallen into the river, always coughing and wheezing. And if he wasn't in the river, where else would he be? If he had gone to friends they would have let her know.

The boys kept telling her he would be all right. Had he

41

not stayed away once for three days and where had he been? Sleeping it off in a pub. And another time when he had gone to a Wake he did not show up for nearly a week!

But none of this consoled Mrs O'Reilly.

When Kathleen's grandfather had not come home by the time they had to leave, she had the promise that someone would be in touch to let her know what had happened to him.

The next morning when Francine came down for breakfast Kathleen was saying to Cook, 'I was hardly out of me bed this morning and dressed when I heard a hammering on the back door. It was me brother Milo. He told me that Himself had come home at midnight, stone cold sober. He had fallen asleep in a pew at the back of the church and the Father had found him.'

Cook said, 'He wouldn't have got away with that with me, I can tell you!'

To which Kathleen replied: 'And he didn't get away with it from Herself. Milo said you could have heard her across the river, but when Himself began to cough she was fussing him like a child. He was to go to bed and she would bring him a hot poteen.'

'Your grandmother's daft,' declared Cook. 'Completely daft. I would have been hitting him over the head with a rolling pin.'

'I think I might have wanted to had he been my husband,' Kathleen said. Then after a pause she added softly, 'But you see, in spite of all her shouting, she loves him.'

Cook sniffed. 'Love? Bah! A load of rubbish.'

Evie came in from the back carrying a bucket of coal and Cook began scolding her. She'd taken long enough to get it, had she gone all the way to a coal barge for it?

Kathleen told Francine later that her grandfather was all right, he had come home. Francine's knowledge of married couples was limited. Those she had met when her aunt had taken her out to tea seemed to be quiet and well-

42

mannered. So why should Kathleen's grandparents have all this trouble?

She thought then about her father. On her visits to these married couples both parents would kiss their children goodnight when brought down by their nannies before going to bed. They really did seem to love their children. So why did her father not love her? Did he think her unattractive? Perhaps if she had been pretty, like her doll Lavinia?

But then Gabrielle was not pretty, nor was Bettie, and she loved them both, almost as much as she loved Kathleen.

Two days later Kathleen was told by Cook that she must change her half-day off from now on to a Saturday, as the master needed her during the week. He was getting more and more bookings from clients wanting their photograph taken and she could attend to the ladies, who might want to tidy themselves before the sittings.

Kathleen said she liked having her afternoon off in the middle of the week, but supposed there was nothing she could do about it. Cook told her she ought to be thankful she had such a good job. The master was getting a number of bookings from a wealthy clientèle after the successful exhibition of his work.

To Kathleen's query of 'Exhibition?' Cook gave a knowing nod. 'Saw it in *The Times*. Evie brought the paper down to make firelighters and I just happened to spot it.' She took a piece of paper from the mantelpiece and held it out. 'Getting known, he is. I'll be asking for a rise soon.'

Kathleen took the paper and read: '*The illustrious members of the Photographic Society met for the presentations of the annual awards. There were two sections, landscapes and portraits. Mr Edwin Chayter was a very worthy winner of the first section for his delicate handling of the four seasons of the countryside* . . . Kathleen stopped and looked up. 'My goodness, isn't that

43

wonderful? An award winner. Miss Francine will be very proud of her papa.'

Francine, when told, showed no outer excitement but was quietly pleased, hoping that this success would put her father in a better mood.

But as far as the staff and Francine were concerned, there was no change in his attitude. He still ignored his small daughter and roared instructions to anyone in sight.

Bridget showed a great interest in Edwin's success and whether by accident or design she and Francine were invariably on their way out for their walk when people arrived to have their photograph taken. The clientèle varied. One day it would be a stern, distinguished-looking man who Bridget was delighted to recognise. 'A member of Parliament,' she confided to Cook and Kathleen.

Another day a father and son came, and the next day it was a young couple with their two families and a nanny holding a baby in christening clothes.

Francine began to look forward to her bedtime because Kathleen described everything that went on in the studio.

'The people have to sit absolutely still through the count of six while your father is actually taking the photograph. If they move a fraction the plate will be ruined.'

When Francine declared that she would never be able to sit still Kathleen explained there was a rest at the back of a chair to hold one's head still. 'It can't be seen. Oh, but I must tell you, Miss Francine, about a very, *very* attractive family who arrived today after you and Bridget had gone for your walk. Their name was de Auberleigh.'

'A lovely name,' murmured Francine.

'Yes, it is. There was mother and father, three sons and three daughters. All the boys were fine fellows, but the eldest, was about the handsomest boy I've ever seen. *He* did not need a rest at his back. Oh, he was tall, straight-backed, had a military bearing. His hair was dark and thick and his eyes were *very* dark.'

'What is his name?'

'A strange one. Mr de Auberleigh introduced him to your father as his eldest son, Tyson.'

'Tyson? It is strange. Kathleen, do you think I could have a look at the photograph of the family, when Papa is not there?'

'I wouldn't dare let you, Miss Francine. You know how he is about the studio. I would get the sack at once if I let you do it. And if you went in on your own and he caught you I bet you'd be packed off to school right away.'

The threat of school was enough to take Francine's mind off any thought of sneaking into the studio.

Edwin Chayter became so busy he not only had to employ a man to come in daily to help him, but started taking appointments on a Saturday afternoon, which meant that Kathleen could not have her half-day off then, either.

Cook told her she would see the time was made up to her but it was a month later when Kathleen was told she could have the whole of the next weekend off, as the master was going away. Cook told her to take Francine with her.

Francine could hardly contain her excitement. Nearly two whole days with Kathleen's family! Evie had the weekend off too, but she was not so happy about it. If she went home, it would be all work and looking after the kids. She thought she would go to her gran's instead. She liked her gran, who gave her a good meal and fussed her a bit.

Kathleen was up extra early to get all the chores done, but it was nearly eleven o'clock before they set out to get the tram. The November morning was raw and foggy. Sounds were muffled, which seemed somehow to emphasise the mournful tone of the foghorns on the river.

Kathleen gave a shiver and said it was all so ghostly, the foghorns and dim shapes appearing out of the mist. Francine thought it all very thrilling.

The journey took longer than usual because traffic was

45

slowed and when they did get off the tram Francine wanted to run to the O'Reilly home and knew she was hoping to see Rory.

Rory was not there but the rest of the family were, including Kathleen's grandfather, and they all gave her a warm welcome and told her how they had missed her and Kathleen.

'A terrible miss,' Mrs O'Reilly said. 'It's not right to deny a girl her half-days off, and was it being made up to her? It was not, the master was doing her out of half a day!'

Kathleen smiled. 'We're here, Gran, and that's the important thing. Now, tell us all your news.'

It was mostly about neighbours, two of them dying and Mrs Donovan's youngest daughter giving birth to triplets and her man not having worked for seven months, God help her. Then there was Father Dougan being sent to Rome and wasn't that an honour? And their cousin Ann had made up her mind to become a nun. The family all wept with joy at this. A lovely girl, an angel if ever there was one.

After Francine had had the usual cup of cocoa and piece of cake Mr O'Reilly came in to take her upstairs to look at his own little workroom. His wife called to him to mind his tongue and he gave her a broad grin and a bow and told her he 'would an' all'.

Upstairs, he opened a door she had not noticed before and he ushered her in saying, 'The holy of holies – only the good people are allowed in here.' He then apologised for the time they had met before, when he had given her the doll but had not seen her again before she left. He had been indisposed that day, his heart, you know.

Francine was only half-listening. She was staring at rows of tiny carved animals, dozens of them, of every description: horses, cows, sheep, cats, dogs . . . and none of them any more than three inches high. She looked up at him, her eyes full of wonder. 'Do you make them, Mr O'Reilly?'

'I do, Mavourneen, every one of them, by hand. A master craftsman, me work is in demand. Pity me heart keeps playing me up. I have to have me rest, you see.'

Francine pointed to a dog and asked what kind it was. He picked it up, a dog with a slender body and long fur, so delicately carved one felt if the dog moved the fur would swing.

'Now that is an Irish wolfhound, known in some circles as a Borzoi. There's not many of them about. Only the wealthy people here will have one, or a couple, as pets.'

'But they're so small! What do you carve them with?'

'A wee knife.' He picked one up and held it out. 'It's just practise, Mavourneen, like every other job if you want to make it perfect.' He took a piece of wood from a side table. 'This is how you go. You have to see an animal in the piece of wood, if you know what I mean. I see a kitten in this.'

He began to chip away at the wood and before long there was the shape of a kitten sitting on its haunches. And within another quarter of an hour the kitten had an endearing expression as it yawned.

Francine laughed. 'Oh, she's lovely. Do you give them names?'

'No, I leave that to the people who buy them. You can give this one a name if you like. The person who buys her eventually won't know.' He beamed at her, 'That's just a secret between us.'

Francine felt suddenly shy. 'I called the lovely doll you gave me Lavinia, but I think the kitten should have an Irish name because, well, because you're all such . . . such lovely people.'

'Now isn't that nice of you to say so. Well let me think, you could call her Shula.'

Mr O'Reilly laid the carved animal down, saying he would have to finish it later. He must rest now, his heart was playing him up. He took Francine into the next room where his family were making the dolls. And there she spent the next hour, watching and learning.

They had the big meal at one o'clock on a Saturday because the family wanted a little time off. There was a rabbit stew with apple tart to follow and Francine was allowed at the end of the meal, after much pleading, to take a soapy rag over the tin 'plates' and polish them with a dry one, ready for the next meal.

But it was the evening that Francine felt she would always remember. The men went out for what appeared to be called 'a jar or two' and when they came back they were merry and full of laughter.

Normally Francine would have been in bed and fast asleep at nine o'clock but Kathleen had kept her up to hear the singing.

The table was pushed to the back of the room and the stools arranged around the two fires.

Milo played an instrument called a concertina and the men and the girls began to sing.

This song was about a place called Galway Bay and Francine thought it was the most beautiful singing she had ever heard, the singers harmonising, telling a story that was lovely and yet sad at the same time.

The next one was called *Danny Boy* and no sooner had they started singing than a clear, younger voice joined in and Francine saw that it was Rory. He sang a verse on his own.

> '*Oh, Danny Boy, the pipes, the pipes are calling,*
> *From glen to glen and down the mountainside,*
> *The summer's gone and all the roses falling,*
> *And it's you must go and I must bide . . .*'

Francine was lost in the scene, the haunting melody, and she felt little shivers go up and down her spine.

The summer's gone and all the roses falling and you must go and I must bide . . .

48

Then they sang a lively song called *Phil the Fluter* and they all got up to dance and Declan picked Francine up and swung her around and she thought she would die with happiness. She found herself thinking that if only her father loved her, she could tell him all about this wonderful experience.

On the Sunday morning they all went to church and in the afternoon the girls and young men told stories of Ireland, about the Little People and other fascinating legends.

On the Sunday evening they left later than Kathleen intended and when they arrived home she said urgently, 'Nip upstairs, Miss Francine, and get undressed and I'll bring up your cocoa.'

Francine was in her nightie when she recalled one of the stories about a mother who longed to see her son who had gone far across the sea. One day, she had stood in his room and whispered how much she wanted to see him – and the boy came home.

And she thought that if perhaps she stood in her father's studio and whispered how much she loved him he might love her in return.

She went quickly before she could change her mind and was standing just inside the door in a pool of moonlight, when she heard a roar of anger from her father.

'How many times have I told you not to come in here? Well, you'll have to be taught a lesson.' He began slapping her on her arms, then, putting her over his knee he picked up her nightdress and thrashed her soundly.

Kathleen, hearing the punishing slaps as she came up the stairs, put down the cocoa and ran to the studio and when she saw what was happening she shouted, 'Mr Chayter, *sir*, stop! Stop it at once!' And without even realising it was her boss she was shouting at she snatched Francine from him and hurried out and along the passage.

Then, feeling the small body shaking with soundless sobs she put her cheek to that of the child and whispered,

'Oh, Macushla, don't, don't. He didn't mean it, he's a tormented soul.'

In the bedroom she wrapped a blanket round Francine and sitting in the chair rocked her to and fro. The sobs were now small hiccupping ones but no less heartbreaking for that. And when she gently wiped the tears from the young cheeks and saw the desolation in her eyes Kathleen felt that she herself was crying inside.

How could he have done this? Did he not realise his own strength and the awful pain he could inflict on such tender young flesh?

In the studio Edwin Chayter sat, head bowed, hands to his face. God help him for the way he had behaved to a child who had always looked at him with eyes full of love. Yet although he knew she was not responsible for what had happened in the past he could not overcome his hatred towards her. She would have to leave the house, go to school, before he ever lost control of his temper again.

CHAPTER FOUR

Kathleen slept with Francine that night, holding her close and soothing her when she whimpered in her sleep. The next morning when she got up she drew the covers over her gently. Let the child sleep, there would be hurt once she awoke.

Evie took the jug of water up for Francine to wash and when she came back to the kitchen she said, 'The poor thing, she looks like a little white ghost, she does. That father of 'ers oughter be thumped.'

'That's enough from you,' Cook snapped. 'It's none of your business.'

But when Francine came down she said quietly, 'Sit down, Miss Francine, Evie will bring your porridge.' The next minute she was saying in an aside to Kathleen, 'But she only has herself to blame, you know. She was warned not to go into the studio.'

Francine had whispered tearfully why she had gone before she fell asleep but Kathleen did not bother to tell Cook, feeling sure she would never understand.

Francine hardly touched the porridge, nor the lightly-boiled egg, but nothing was said to her.

Bridget always arrived well before nine o'clock but this morning when she arrived Edwin Chayter called to her from the landing that she was to come to his study. Francine, who had heard the order, looked fearfully at Kathleen.

'Do you think Papa will send me to school?'

Kathleen prevaricated. He might, but then he might not. He had been angry the previous night, but he might have got over it by now. She was not to worry. He might have wanted to see Bridget for a number of reasons.

51

But when Bridget came to the kitchen she confirmed that Francine was to go to a school. 'But it's to a private day school, Miss Francine. It's to prepare you for boarding school, but that won't be for several months.'

'There now,' Kathleen said smiling. 'That's not too bad, just going to school through the day. You'll get to know girls your own age. I'm sure you'll enjoy it.'

Bridget then said, 'There will be other changes. You are to live with me, Miss Francine. I shall take you to school in the morning and collect you in the afternoon.'

Then she added to Kathleen with what, for Bridget, was a mischievous smile, 'I thought we could share her. I can have her with me one weekend and the next she can go to the family. I am, after all, just a stone's throw away.'

Kathleen was laughing. 'Why, that's wonderful. Do you hear that, Miss Francine?'

Francine said yes, it would be very nice. She liked Bridget and she loved Kathleen, but she was being turned out by her father. Would he ever want to see her again?

Kathleen knelt down and took the small, cold hands in hers. 'Your papa is not abandoning you, my love. He's thinking only of you. He has a lot of chemicals in his studio and he feels you just can't stay out of it. They're chemicals that could cause you harm if any were upset, so I'm sure he feels that until you are a little older you would be better away from the temptation of going into the studio.'

Francine said yes, she understood, but it did not take away the hurt of not being able to live with her father. And Kathleen, looking at the little woebegone figure longed to hold her to her and chase away her unhappiness.

Bridget took over then, speaking gently. 'Well now, my dear, you don't have to go to school until next Monday, so I shall still give you lessons in the mornings and we shall explore other places in the afternoon. I know you would like that.'

Francine had thought she would not be allowed to go

to the O'Reillys on the Saturday afternoon, but apparently it had all been arranged.

They all made a fuss of her and Mrs O'Reilly said she had especially made her a gingerbread man, but to her consternation Francine refused to touch him, saying with pleading, that she just couldn't bite off his hand, or his head, could she?

The old lady said it was just cake, but she understood the way she felt, and brought her a buttered scone.

Mr O'Reilly told her he had a lot of 'poorly' dolls and if she liked she could come to his dolls' hospital and help to make them better.

His wife was frantically shaking her head at him but he took no notice. Miss Francine, he was sure, would make an excellent little nurse. And he was right. She was full of compassion when she saw dolls minus a leg and arm, a foot, or whose face or head had been broken.

'The poor things,' she grieved. 'Can you make them right again?'

'Of course, Mavourneen, I'm a doll doctor.'

She looked at him with admiration. 'You can do anything, Mr O'Reilly, can't you?'

'With your help I can. Now then, where do we start?'

Francine was fascinated as she watched him make a foot with wire. He then wrapped it all around with bandage. Then he made a paste, put it on, and told her when it was dry that the foot would be as good as the other one.

He glued pieces of a face together, explaining how careful one had to be that not too much glue was put on the joining pieces or the doll would look disfigured. When the doll's face was properly finished it was impossible to see where the joins had been made.

She saw an arm being put on, a leg and a kid body being repaired and was completely fascinated. Next time she came, he said, he would show her how dolls' wigs were made.

53

When she went to see the rest of the family working with the wooden Betties she told them all in a breathless way what she had just witnessed and the girls asked her if she would like to try her hand at painting a face. She nodded quickly and drew in a breath, overwhelmed at actually taking a part in the making of the dolls.

She was given a wooden head, some small pots of paint and a brush, and worked, painstakingly, her tongue between her teeth.

When she had finished and there was complete silence for a moment she felt dreadful. Then Milo was saying, 'This child has genius. The doll has expression, who does this face remind you of?'

Old Mr O'Reilly who had come in, said, 'She's the dead spit of Jinny at the Hare and Pheasant, same saucy smile. They'd all recognise her.'

The men agreed. Declan said, 'Miss Francine, when you leave school there'll be a job waiting for you here.'

Francine was pleased, but knew it was photography she really wanted to do.

They were in the middle of having dinner when Rory came in. He gave them all a cheerful greeting and took his place at the table. Kathleen said, 'One of these days our Rory, your boss will get to know that you keep popping in at home and you'll get the sack.'

He grinned. 'Who's to tell him? I had a message to go for one of the guests.'

Francine felt so happy after her visit to the O'Reillys, but when on the Sunday evening Kathleen said her father wanted to see her all her unhappiness returned. She was trembling. 'Why? Have I done something to upset him?'

'No, Miss Francine, no. I think he probably wants to say goodbye to you.'

Kathleen let Francine go into the study alone. Edwin Chayter looked somewhere beyond her head and told her he would not be here on Monday morning. He wanted her to know that he had had a letter from her Aunt Amelia who was settling down very well. He added that she wished, as he did, that she would pay attention to her lessons and behave herself.

Francine said, 'Yes, Papa,' then he waved a hand dismissing her and she turned away, trying not to cry.

Kathleen took her hand. 'Everything all right?' Francine nodded and repeated what her father had said and Kathleen felt furious. That wretched man to treat his child in such a way. Evie was right when she had said he ought to be thumped. And at that moment Kathleen thought she would have welcomed the chance to be the one to do it.

The school uniform was a navy dress with a white sailor collar and Francine was also to wear a navy coat and hat, the hat having a wide, turned-up brim. Kathleen wished that Francine could have worn a warmer colour, for her face was drained of colour, paper white. But when Bridget arrived for her she managed a brief smile.

Edwin Chayter had arranged for a cab to collect them. Bridget had been given money so they could travel by cab back and forth from school. When it arrived, quick goodbyes were said, with Kathleen promising she would see her the following weekend. Cook came to wave her goodbye. Evie was wiping her eyes.

Then they were clip-clopping away, with Francine staring straight ahead. The straw in the cab stank and Bridget said they would travel by horse tram after this unless the weather was very bad.

The school turned out to be a large private house, one of four opposite a small park. It looked well cared for. A maid opened the door to them and asked if they would take a seat in the hall, she would inform Mrs Treadwell they were here.

The next moment they were ushered into a room on the left and Francine was welcomed by the headmistress, a rather austere-looking woman, but with a surprisingly pleasant manner. She said, 'We are pleased to have you with us, Francine. Mrs Brogan tells me you are well-behaved and a dedicated pupil, that is all we ask. But of course if you should misbehave you will be punished. Is that understood?'

'Yes, Ma'am.'

'Good. Miss Stead teaches the younger children and she will take charge of you. It's quiet at the moment but within the next ten minutes the other pupils will be arriving.' She picked up a small bell from her desk and rang it and within seconds there was a knock on the door and a tall, thin, younger woman entered.

She smiled at the headmistress but when Francine was introduced she stared at her in a shocked way. The next moment, she had recovered herself and smiled in acknowledgement. If Francine would come this way she would show her the cloakroom.

Bridget told Francine she would call for her at four o'clock then Francine, heart beating fast, followed Miss Stead.

In the cloakroom the woman's manner changed. She had told Francine to take off her hat and coat and hang them up, but when she made to hang them on the nearest peg she said, 'Not that one! Are you stupid? Can't you read? Don't you see it has someone else's name above it?'

For some reason Francine felt suddenly calm, and she walked along the stand slowly looking for a peg where she would find her own name. When she found it she hung up the hat and coat, and smoothed her hand over the coat.

'Are you trying to be awkward?' demanded Miss Stead, 'because if you are you shall suffer for it!'

Francine suddenly thought of old Mr O'Reilly's saying to her, 'You'll make friends, but you'll also make enemies. Ignore the enemies, they are not important in your life, but if they persist in being nasty treat them in a quiet way.'

So Francine met the angry stare calmly. 'No, Miss Stead, it's just that I'm new and I have to find my way around.'

The woman was about to reply when there was the sound of running footsteps and the chatter of young people. Four girls burst into the cloakroom, laughing, then stopped abruptly as they saw their teacher.

Miss Stead upbraided them for their boisterous behaviour, told a fair-haired girl called Sophie Denton to take charge of the new girl then commanded the other three to follow her.

When they had gone Sophie grinned and said, 'You've soon fallen foul of "Ready Steady Go". What have you done or said?'

Francine told her about the incident of the clothes peg and Sophie looked surprised. 'Is that all? She really does have it in for you, doesn't she? Never mind, *we* shall look after you.'

Francine thought she had obviously made an enemy in Miss Stead, but then she was also sure she had made a friend in Sophie.

And she had. At the end of the first day Sophie told Francine she felt as though she had known her always, and Francine smiled and said she felt the same way, too.

When Bridget came for her that afternoon Francine had so much to tell her she was sure she would never get it all told before bedtime. She spoke about Miss Stead and how she seemed to hate her and about Sophie and how lucky shewas that she could sit beside her; the other girl had left two days before. And then there was Mademoiselle Jolie, the French teacher, who was delighted that she could speak such good French. Francine had to stop to draw breath several times during the relating of every little incident.

She said that some of the girls were not very nice to her but Sophie had told her they were jealous because Mademoiselle Jolie had praised her for her accent and knowledge of French.

Francine's final offering about her first day at school,

before Bridget told her gently she must calm down, was to say that Sophie's father was a surgeon.

'Indeed,' said Bridget smiling, then added, 'so we can safely say you enjoyed your first day at school.'

'Oh, yes,' Francine breathed. 'I cannot wait for tomorrow.'

Francine set out joyously the next morning for school, but no sooner had Bridget left her and she encountered Miss Stead than the woman shouted to her to go and wash her face, she was filthy.

Francine put her hand to her cheek and told her she had washed earlier but she was pushed towards the cloakroom and told if she did not do as she was told she would be punished.

Sophie, who had more or less arrived at that moment watched Miss Stead striding away then turned to Francine. 'What's the matter with *her*? There's nothing wrong with your face.' Francine, who felt herself trembling, hung up her hat and coat in silence then she poured some water into a bowl. Sophie came over to her.

'Take no notice of her, Francine. She must be ill. She's never been *good*-tempered but she's never been as bad as this.'

Francine managed a smile. 'I'll be a *good* girl and do as I'm told.'

Sophie laughed. 'That's right. We'll beat her yet.'

But it was not easy to beat Miss Stead who very definitely had it in for Francine. Once she accused her of not paying attention to her lessons. This was when Francine was copying down notes from the blackboard and was absorbed in the work.

'Stand up, girl!' she commanded. Francine stood up. 'If you do not pay attention you shall be brought out and caned.'

Francine opened her mouth to say she had been paying attention when Sophie tugged at her dress and shook her head.

'Let that be a warning to you. Now, get on with your work.'

Francine sat down and the two girls exchanged puzzled glances.

At midday the pupils were served soup in the dining room and those who wanted it could bring a snack from home. Everyone could talk then but it had to be in low voices and there was to be no laughter. The younger pupils sat at one table, the older ones, whose classrooms were upstairs, at another. Two who acted as monitors saw that the younger ones behaved themselves.

It was not only Sophie who commiserated with Francine over Miss Stead's treatment of her. One girl who sat behind her in the classroom said, 'You were working away, I was the one who should have been picked on. I felt lazy and I also had a pain in my stomach.'

Another girl suggested that Francine should complain to Miss Treadwell, but Francine, alarmed, said no, she would probably only get into more trouble. She liked coming to school. To which Sophie said that she liked to have her as a friend.

At this a girl sitting opposite sneered and said, it was a good job Francine wasn't teacher's pet in Miss Stead's class as she was in the French class. After all, she was a nobody, just a photographer's daughter and that was being a *nobody*.

Sophie leaned across the table. 'Let me tell you something, Claribelle Boulder. Francine's father won one of the highest awards in the country for his work. And, what is more, she is the granddaughter of Lady Telberry Coherte, and she is not a *nobody*.'

The girl looked at her plate and said no more.

Afterwards Francine said to Sophie, 'But I'm not the granddaughter of the woman you mentioned.'

Sophie grinned. 'That's true, but she wasn't to know, was she? Mama says you have to be somebody to get on in this world. Although,' she added, 'I think it must be exciting to be the daughter of a photographer.'

Francine had not realised until then just how much she must have told Sophie about herself.

There was no more trouble from Miss Stead for the rest of that day but on the following one she accused Francine of throwing paper pellets at a girl in the front row to attract her attention.

This time Francine denied throwing anything and Sophie stood up and confirmed this. At this Miss Stead was so angry she was visibly trembling. She ordered them both to come out.

Sophie received two sharp cuts of the cane, one on either hand. Francine had six, which had the class gasping. This was unheard-of, even for Miss Stead. She ordered the two friends back to their seats and warned if there was any more disobedience from either of them they would know about it.

At the break many of the girls, including the one who had sneered at Francine, complained about the treatment. Two of the girls said they had seen the pellets on the floor when they came in that morning; Miss Stead must have put them there out of some sort of spite. There was so much discussion they were ordered by one of the monitors to be quiet.

Sophie whispered to Francine, 'But what's happened to the woman? She must be mad.' Francine shook her head. Her hands were so swollen she could hardly hold the spoon to eat her soup. And during the afternoon when they all had to do some writing she found it was impossible to grip the pen. Immediately Miss Stead pounced on her. She came up and demanded to know why she was not writing. When Francine explained she told her to hold out her hand.

The cane was brought from her side and two vicious cuts were given to Francine, causing her to cry out with agony.

Sophie jumped up and told her to stop. At this Miss Stead seized Francine by the hair, drew her to her feet and dragged her outside into the hall.

There she started slapping first her arms then her face.

Sophie came running out and tried to drag her away but Miss Stead began pummelling on Francine's back with both fists. Sophie then began yelling for help.

Miss Treadwell, the first to appear, said in a stern voice, '*Miss Stead*! Desist at once! Do you hear me?'

Miss Stead's arms fell to her sides but her eyes were wild and her hair had fallen into disarray.

By then all the children had come out of the classroom and two of the teachers from upstairs, followed by some of the older girls, came running down the stairs. Miss Treadwell told one of the teachers to take over the younger class and the other to accompany Miss Stead into her study, she would follow in a moment. The headmistress then turned to Francine and asked if she was all right. Francine nodded. She then said she would send someone for Mrs Brogan to take her home. In the meantime one of the monitors would look after her.

Sophie asked quietly if she could go too and after a moment's hesitation she was given permission, but told not to talk to Francine. They went into an ante-room.

Francine was not aware she was crying until the girl pulled out a handkerchief and wiped the tears gently away. She said, 'I really think you must have a hot drink, Francine. I'll leave you for a moment. Will you be all right?'

'Yes,' she whispered, 'Sophie is here.'

When the girl had gone Sophie put an arm around her and for a moment they cried together. Then Sophie was wiping Francine's eyes and then her own.

There was only one thing Francine wanted to know — why Miss Stead should hate her so. When the girl came back with a cup of sweetened tea she asked her, but even she had no idea of the reason.

CHAPTER FIVE

It seemed to Francine she had been waiting hours before Mrs Treadwell came back to the ante-room. Then she saw that Bridget was following. Bridget came over, a look of compassion in her eyes, and squeezed her shoulder.

'Mrs Brogan will take you home, Francine,' Mrs Treadwell said. 'She will explain about Miss Stead. I will see you again next Monday.' To Sophie she added quietly, 'Go back to your lessons, Sophie, I shall be with you in a few moments.'

Sophie and Francine exchanged glances but were unable to say anything. Bridget was holding out Francine's hat and coat.

A cab had been ordered to take them home and when they were seated Bridget took Francine's hands in hers and turned them palms upwards. 'Poor wee mite,' she said softly. 'We'll talk about it when we get home.'

The skin on Francine's right fingers was broken and Bridget gently rubbed soothing ointment on her hands and bandaged both. Then she told her quietly about Miss Stead.

'She's had a tragic life, the poor creature. She was in service when she was younger. She had a baby, a little girl, but was unable to keep it. She was forced to have it adopted, which was a great grief to her. Then her father died and her mother became bedridden.'

Francine looked at her, puzzled. 'What happened to the baby's father?'

'Oh—' Bridget gave a little cough behind her hand then, leaning forward she picked up the poker, stirred the logs on the fire which sent sparks shooting up the chimney. 'He had to go away. Miss Stead hasn't seen him since.'

'Does she ever see her baby?'

'Normally she wouldn't have done. When you give a child away for adoption you relinquish all rights to it. That means the child regards the people who have adopted her as her real parents.'

'But that is awful!' Francine exclaimed.

'It's the law. As it happened in this case Miss Stead found out who had adopted her little girl, I don't know how, but from then on she kept going to the house to catch a glimpse of her. The people were wealthy and the child was always in the care of a nanny.'

Bridget was silent for a moment staring into the fire, then she went on, 'For a whole year Miss Stead kept following them when they went for a walk, or she would stand at the railings and watch the child playing in the garden of the house. Until then she had kept in the background but, one time, the child was alone for a few minutes and when the ball she was throwing came near to the railings and she came to collect it Miss Stead plucked up courage and spoke to her. 'Hello,' she said quietly, 'how are you?'

The little girl tossed her hair back and said in an arrogant way, "People like you have to go to the servants' entrance," then she turned and walked away.'

Francine, who knew the meaning of rejection, the other way around said, a catch in her voice, 'Poor Miss Stead.'

Bridget nodded slowly, 'Poor Miss Stead indeed. She had known she was shabbily dressed, but she had been unable to work because of her mother being bedridden. All she had hoped for was just a kind word from her child. It's so sad.'

Francine was silent for a moment then she looked up. 'But why was Miss Stead so unkind to *me*?'

'Because unfortunately, my dear, you resembled her daughter, with the same oval-shaped face, chestnut hair and big grey eyes. She was hurting all the time at the way the girl had behaved towards her. The hurt became bigger until it turned to a hatred for her child, and she took her hatred out on you. It was a terrible thing to do but who are we to judge the actions of another?'

'Will Miss Stead lose her job?'

'I'm afraid so. When her mother died Mrs Treadwell offered her the position of teacher at the school. She said that Miss Stead was self-taught but most knowledgeable. She hinted to me today, however, that she *would* try and find her work elsewhere.'

Francine knew a relief. Although she felt sorry for Miss Stead over the loss of her little girl, the pain of the caning was still too raw in her mind – and fingers – to want to be taught by her ever again.

As Francine was free from going to school until the following Monday Bridget gave her lessons each morning. In the afternoons they went to the market, to the docks and on walks in a little out-of-the-way park. Although Francine loved her visits to the docks she thought she enjoyed the market best of all because of the jocular cries of the stallholders to persuade people to buy their particular wares.

'Come along, lidees! Ow's about a dollop o' tripe, give yer old man a treat, it'll put thunder in his belly!'

'And what'll it put in me?' yelled a big woman. There was a roar of laughter and the stallholder joined in.

'Yer too sharp for yer own good, Maggie, yer'll cut yerself!'

Bridget, who had been looking at some material on a stall on the opposite side, came over and hurried Francine away. Francine was laughing. 'The tripe man has a funny face, hasn't he?' Then she added, 'Some tripe had a lovely pattern, like a bee's honeycomb.'

'And that is what it is called,' Bridget replied, her lips twitching. 'The other two kinds are known as Reed and Thick Rib.'

'Oh,' said Francine, looking towards the next stall.

At this one a woman with a voice as raucous as any man

64

was shouting, 'Fresh gingerbread, ginger parkins, apple turnovers, Sally Lunns, Maids of Honour . . .'

Bridget stopped and had a little chat with the woman, asking after her family while she went on serving her customers. Before they left Bridget said she would have two Maids of Honour for their tea and handed over a penny. The woman, with a smile, popped in a broken teacake.

'She's a good soul,' Bridget said as they walked away. 'A hard worker. Her husband died leaving her with eight young children to bring up. Sometimes she's up all night baking. Her house is spotless, I don't know how she gets any sleep.'

There was a man selling cough mixture that was guaranteed to cure any cough in Christendom! Bridget declared the mixture to be no more than liquorice water.

There were a number of stalls that sold jellied eels which were served in small dishes, with a tiny two-pronged fork. Francine had no desire to taste eels. But she did like herrings, which were thirteen a penny. Cook at Spinners End used to bake them in vinegar.

She lingered at the fruit stalls, liking the sharp smell of lemons which mingled with the tangy one of oranges, which according to the stallholder had arrived that *very* day from Seville!

A man at a secondhand clothes stall was holding up a bright pink dress in satin, which was soiled, and shouting, 'Come on, me old loves, put that on and your old man'll 'ave you up them apples and pears in the wink of an eye.'

Francine was beginning to learn the Cockney dialect and knew that apples and pears meant stairs. She wanted to linger, especially as the women were laughing and shouting remarks back, but again she was hurried along by Bridget.

Bridget usually bought her fish at the docks, it was cheaper she said, but as there was a sleety rain starting she bought a piece of skate at a fish stall. Francine thought skate a funny sort of fish with so many tiny bones, but she liked the taste of it.

The sleet was icy, stinging their cheeks, and they got the tram home. Bridget toasted the teacake for tea and they had the Maids of Honour afterwards and Francine thought it was lovely to eat round the fire on such a cold and miserable day.

She said she was looking forward to seeing Kathleen and the family on the Saturday and Bridget said it would have to be Sunday this weekend when they called because the family would be busy, very busy. It was the Christmas trade, you see. They had to make such a lot of dolls they were working all the hours that God sent, sometimes not even stopping to have a meal.

When Francine asked why, she was told they had to 'make hay while the sun shone', which did not make any sense to Francine, seeing there was no hay involved, only dolls.

Bridget patiently explained that the biggest trade was at the Yuletide when Father Christmas needed a lot of dolls to put into the stockings of children all over the world.

Francine was very puzzled about Father Christmas. Aunt Amelia had told her there was no such person, he was just a myth, but Francine knew there *was* a Father Christmas because other children talked about him when her aunt took her visiting. They had shown her toys brought by him. He came over the rooftops in a sleigh, drawn by a reindeer. She said, 'Bridget, do you think I will be going home to spend Christmas with my father?'

'I'm not sure about that, Miss Francine. I think Kathleen mentioned he might be going away. But she did say if this was so you could spend Christmas with her family. I am invited on Christmas Day for my dinner.'

Although Francine thought it would be very nice to spend Christmas with the O'Reillys, she would have liked

66

to have been with her father on that day, as other children were.

On the Sunday when they went to Kathleen's family she was not there, nor did Francine see Rory. The family as usual made a fuss of her but she did not spend a great deal of time with any of them, they were too busy. There was a great deal of running up and downstairs carrying boxes and a man with a cart and horse taking the boxes away.

With Bridget feeling they were a bit in the way she told Francine they would leave early. When they did leave, Francine found that Milo had packed her a few pots of paint and a brush and some dolls' heads, to paint when she was at home. Francine was delighted and could hardly wait to get started.

She was painstaking and had completed six before bedtime. Bridget laughed when she saw them and named various people each doll reminded her of. 'You have a gift, my dear. I can see you starting a business when you're older.'

'No, Bridget, I love dolls, but I want to be a photographer. I will be one, I know it.'

'Right! But now it's time for bed, you have to go to school in the morning. I had a note from Mrs Treadwell, saying you'll have a new teacher. She's young, rather stern-looking, but you will not be caned again, and that is a promise.'

It was not until then that Francine realised she had been dreading going back to school. Now she found herself looking forward to seeing Sophie again. They would have so much to talk about.

Both girls were there early the following morning and Sophie's smile was wide. 'Oh, I'm so glad you came back, Francine, I would have *died* if you hadn't. I missed you awfully. Tell me what happened, *all* of it, *we* don't know a thing.'

Bridget had made Francine promise not to repeat Miss

Stead's story and although it was hard for her not to tell Sophie she did keep her promise.

Miss Watson, the new teacher, was younger than Miss Stead. She was plain, rather drab, but she did make the lessons more interesting.

At midday Sophie and Francine exchanged news. Sophie said her mother was upset that she had been caned and had been to see Mrs Treadwell to say her daughter would be withdrawn from the school if such a thing ever happened again.

'Mama is very soft-hearted. Papa says she spoils me. He is strict. I think he was disappointed because I was a girl. All men want a son, don't they?'

A son? It suddenly dawned on Francine why her father had no time for her and she wondered how it had not occurred to her before. *She* was an only child and her mother was dead. He would never have a son unless he married again. Poor Papa. She wished then she could grow up quickly and give him a son-in-law. That at least would be better than no son at all.

When Sophie questioned her about her family she was able to explain why she was living with Bridget. She also told her about the O'Reilly family and Sophie declared she was the luckiest girl alive to know such interesting people.

'I never meet Papa's friends,' she said, 'and Mama and her friends talk about nothing else but balls, soirées and who is wearing what and which man has proposed to which girl. So dreary.'

Francine realised as Sophie went on talking about her family that she belonged to a very different world from her own, one peopled by those with wealth and position. Although Sophie was her own age she seemed to know a lot about grown up things. Sophie and her parents went abroad to France every summer, sharing a large furnished house with an aunt and uncle and their family.

Sophie then went on, 'We are also spending Christmas

with the same uncle and aunt. I love Aunt Leonora, she is Mama's sister and they get on splendidly, but the rest of the family are a bit stuffy. But I do like Christmas and all the presents.'

Francine looked up. 'Sophie, does Father Christmas come down the chimney with your presents?'

She eyed Francine with surprise. 'Why yes, of course. Mama always writes to him to tell him where we will be staying. I love that part of Christmas, it's so exciting getting up to see what is in your stocking. Last year I hung up a pillow case too, to take all the toys.'

A pillow case? Francine felt awed. She had never even hung up a stocking. Aunt Amelia always gave her some presents on Christmas morning but it was usually clothing, underwear mostly, perhaps a white pinafore and some-times a dress.

It was Kathleen who told her that as her father would be away for Christmas she would definitely be coming to stay with the O'Reillys. In the next breath she added with a smile, 'But you will be going home two days beforehand to wish your papa a happy Christmas. He's leaving to photograph people at a holiday resort in the French Alps.'

Francine was suddenly filled with a quiet joy. Her father wanted to see her. Her eyes bright with tears, she thanked Kathleen and said how pleased she would be to spend Christmas with her family.

Kathleen gave her a hug. 'And *they* are looking forward to having you, Miss Francine. It's a long time since we had someone in the house young enough to hang up a stocking.'

A *real* Christmas. Francine's eyes were now round with wonder as she asked if she would actually *see* Father Christmas come in his sleigh. Kathleen said she thought it was doubtful. He was here and gone like a flash of light-ning, he had so many houses to visit. 'But when you wake in the morning,' she said, 'all your presents will be there for you.'

The days before Francine was to see her father were the longest she could ever remember. Then at last she was setting out with Bridget for Spinners End.

She felt shivery with excitement. She had never been near the market in the evening and everywhere looked so beautiful. There had been a fall of snow and in the moonlight it was turned to silver on the roofs of the market stalls and the naptha flares wavering in the wind cast a warm glow over everything. Even the gas-lit shops around the market held an attraction with their hanging bunches of holly and mistletoe.

Outside the butchers shop was a row of turkeys hanging up and below them one of rabbits. An assistant was reaching up with a pole to get a turkey down for a customer.

Then there was the lovely red glow of charcoal stoves where one could buy a roast potato or some chestnuts. Francine had never seen these before and laughed at a group of young people who were dancing about and yelling as they tried to peel the skin from their hot potatoes.

The market was busier than she had ever seen it and one of the stallholders was shouting, 'Watch out for the pickpockets!'

At this Bridget took Francine's hand and led her out of the crowd to the pavement where there was at least a little more room to move.

'And now we must hurry,' she said. 'We don't want to keep your father waiting, but I thought you would like to see the market at night.'

As they neared the house Francine's heart began to beat a little faster. Would her father perhaps take her on his lap and talk to her, as she had seen other fathers do with their children when Aunt Amelia had taken her visiting?

Kathleen opened the front door and whispered to Bridget that as the master had just this minute come in they could nip into the kitchen and see Cook and Evie.

Cook actually greeted Francine with a smile. Well, and wasn't it nice to see her again. Evie's little pinched face wore a smile too. "Ello, Miss Francine, 'ow you bin? I ain't 'alf missed you.'

The two girls talked, at least Francine did most of the talking, telling Evie about school while the other three women chatted about Christmas. Then a bell on the wooden board rang.

'That is your papa, Miss Francine.' Bridget fussed about straightening Francine's hat, tugging down her coat. 'There, off we go.' Kathleen called after them, 'The best of luck.' And Cook told Bridget they were to come back afterwards to the kitchen and have a cup of tea.

Edwin Chayter was standing with his back to the fire. He still had a fierce look but his voice was quiet as he bade them 'Good evening.'

Although he asked them to sit down he remained standing. Then he said to Francine, 'I trust you are doing well at school.'

Bridget answered for her. 'Yes, indeed, sir. Francine is doing extremely well. Her teachers are well pleased with her.'

'Good. So, child, you do know that you will be staying with Mrs Brogan over Christmas, for I shall be away. I have given Mrs Brogan some money to buy you a dress, a party dress, which she seems to think you need.'

'Thank you, Papa. It's very kind of you.'

Bridget had helped Francine to make a little book of pen wipers from oblongs of felt. Francine had embroidered the cover with a camera. With Bridget's permission to get down from her chair she went over to her father and held out the tissue-wrapped package.

He undid the wrapping. 'Pen wipers, most useful. Thank you.'

Francine waited a few seconds in case he wanted to say more. He did, but only to wish both of them a happy

71

Christmas. Then he said they must excuse him, he had work to do. He strode to the door and opened it.

The next moment they were outside with Francine wondering if he had smiled at her. She thought he had, a small smile, and felt pleased. It was a step forward.

Edwin Chayter went back to the fire and stood, his hands clasped behind him. God, who would have believed it could be an ordeal to wish a child a happy Christmas. If only she had not looked at him in that wistful, appealing way. He studied the camera on the front of the book of pen wipers. Whose idea was that? It was neatly done, and done in detail. How many times had she sneaked into his studio to study his camera? He went over to his desk, dropped the pen wipers into a drawer and slammed it. If she thought she was going to get round him with such a gift she was mistaken!

When Bridget and Francine went back to the kitchen Cook, Kathleen and Evie all stopped what they were doing and waited. Cook said, 'Well?'

Francine raised her head and said proudly, 'Papa has given some money to Bridget to buy me a *party* dress. And, he smiled at me.'

'He did?' Kathleen beamed at her. 'Now isn't that lovely. Oh, he'll soon be having you at home again. He's going to employ an assistant after Christmas so he'll have more time to spare for you.'

By the time Francine was back in Bridget's house the brief smile she thought her father had given her had developed into quite a broad one. She was right: it was just a question of time, of getting to know her properly.

Although Francine had ben excited at going to see her father it was nothing to what she felt on Christmas Eve, knowing that when she hung up her stocking before she went to bed, it would be filled sometime during the night by Father Christmas.

Although all the orders of dolls had been sent out the family were still working, and would be working even on

Christmas Day. There would be shops needing more after Christmas. They were a cheap line, especially the undressed wooden Betties, which sold all the year round. They needed to, said Mrs O'Reilly grimly, the profit was minimal for worker and seller alike.

The living room was strung with coloured paper chains, some of which Francine had helped to make. As well as the paper chains there were pieces of holly, full of bright red berries, pushed in at the side of pictures on the walls and in some ornaments.

Then came the moment for Francine to hang up her stocking. Kathleen pinned it with a clothes peg to a piece of string stretched across one of the fireplaces, saying that Francine would find it filled when she came downstairs the next morning. But she was warned that if she tried to stay awake to see Father Christmas she would find her stocking empty.

Francine closed her eyes tightly when Kathleen tucked her up in bed and although she was sure she would never be able to sleep, it seemed only minutes before Kathleen was telling her that Father Christmas had been.

Francine was quickly out of bed and slipping her arms into the dressing gown Kathleen held out. Her stomach was quivering with excitement as well as the chill of the bedroom.

But a warm room greeted her and she ran to the fireplace where her stocking was hanging. She gulped as she saw two tiny dolls' heads peeping out of the top of it. Kathleen unpegged the stocking and held it out.

One was a clothes-peg doll and the other a wooden spoon doll. She now had a family of five dolls! Francine looked up at Kathleen, her eyes shining, then feeling more things in the stocking she brought them out one by one. An orange and an apple, some nuts and a tiny story book. 'Oh!' she exclaimed, and again, 'Oh!' as she brought out six newly-minted pennies.

'He left *all* of these for *me*?'

'And look behind you,' Kathleen said softly.

Francine turned and then she was staring from a draped dolls' cradle to a wooden pram. 'They're both yours,' Kathleen told her and Francine walked slowly towards them, disbelief on her face.

The next moment, hearing what sounded like controlled laughter she glanced towards the living room door and saw faces peeping round. Then the family were there, all except Rory, laughing, but some of them with tears in their eyes. Francine ran to them and began gabbling about all there had been in her stocking then she said to old Mr O'Reilly, a catch in her voice, 'And he left me a dolls cradle *and* a pram as well!'

He picked her up and held her to him. 'I know, Mavourneen, we wrote to Father Christmas and asked him to bring them for you.'

'You did?'

She put her arms around his neck and two wet cheeks met.

Then Mrs O'Reilly was saying, 'Well come on now, all of you, this won't get us any breakfast.'

The family dispersed. Later, when Francine was sitting rocking the cradle with all her dolls in it, she heard Mrs O'Reilly saying to Kathleen, 'Her first real Christmas, and wasn't it a lovely sight to watch to be sure. Some of you will have to be marrying soon, like Milo, and give us grandchildren.'

'Cecilia will be obliging once she's married,' laughed Kathleen. 'She says she wants six at least.'

'And may the Lord grant them,' replied Mrs O'Reilly piously.

The house was filled with the lovely smell of turkey roasting and sage and onion stuffing, when Bridget arrived. She was carrying a parcel which she told Francine was her father's Christmas present to her.

The next moment Francine was staring at a white muslin dress with a frilled hem, and a wide pale blue silk sash.

When Bridget held it up in front of Francine there were 'Ooohs' and 'Aahs' and Francine found herself unable to speak.

The old man patted her on the head and said gently, 'It's too much to take in, isn't it, wee Mavourneen?' She nodded then smoothed a hand over the skirt. Her own father's present. She could hardly believe it. Bridget said they would wrap up the dress for now, she could have another look at it later. Bridget then went to talk to the womenfolk and Francine spent the time before dinner between giving her dolls a rock in the cradle and pushing them around the living room in the pram.

She would have had them near her at the table when the meal was ready but Mrs O'Reilly declared there was a time for eating and a time for play.

The turkey was carried in with everyone declaring it was 'done to a turn'. Mr O'Reilly had just begun to carve it when Rory came breezing in.

'Happy Christmas everybody. Hello, Francine. How did you like your cradle and your pram? Grandad and the boys spent hours making them.'

There was a split second's silence then everyone seemed to be talking at once, with Mrs O'Reilly's voice overriding all.

'To *send* to Father Christmas, of course, child. He hasn't time to make everything, now has he?'

Francine shook her head, solemn-eyed. Then as she looked from the old man to each of the boys a slow smile spread over her face.

'They're lovely. Thank you all.'

Rory, looking a bit sheepish, had taken his place at the table, then they were all chattering as the girls served the meal.

There was Christmas pudding to follow and when Francine felt something hard in her mouth she discovered a tiny silver slipper, which meant, they said, she would not die a spinster.

In the evening when all the work was done the family sat round the fire and there was a popping sound as chestnuts were roasted and a cracking of nuts when Milo, who had big strong hands, crushed them in his palms.

Afterwards they all sang carols and then the men sang Irish ballads, and when Francine was in bed, her rag doll Gabrielle clutched to her, she thought no matter how many more Christmasses she would know in her life, this one would forever remain in her memory.

CHAPTER SIX

During the months that followed Francine and Sophie became such close friends that every incident, every experience in their separate lives was shared. Francine loved to hear about all the birthday parties that Sophie was invited to and about the games played, and Sophie drooled over the time Francine was invited by a nephew of Bridget's on to his ship and they had coffee in the galley. And every time she talked about the O'Reillys a look of longing would come into Sophie's eyes.

The O'Reillys were now Francine's 'family', and when she tentatively asked the old couple's permission to call them Grandad and Gran, they were delighted. But, warned the old lady, if she did then she must be prepared to be scolded by them if necessary.

Francine nodded happily at this. Then she *would* be part of a proper family.

She had not seen her father since Christmas, but it no longer worried her. When she started growing up she would show him she could be as useful to him with his photography as any son. How this was to be achieved she had no idea, but she had the faith of Mrs O'Reilly that God answered as many prayers as He possibly could and every Sunday morning when she went to church with Bridget she lit a candle and prayed fervently that her father would accept her back home again some day.

There did come a day when it seemed a part at least of her prayer was to be answered. This was when Kathleen told her that Rory was going to work for her father.

'Rory is?' Francine looked at her wide-eyed. 'In the studio?'

Kathleen nodded, laughing. 'When I knew the master

was wanting an odd-job boy I spoke for Rory and after your father had met him he agreed to take him on.'

'Oh, Kathleen, he, he—' Francine was so excited she could hardly get the words out, 'he can learn all about photography and teach me.'

'Now hold on, he's going as an odd-job boy. He'll be sweeping up, emptying the waste bin, running errands, carrying your father's equipment when he does outdoor work.'

'But he'll be *there*,' Francine persisted, 'and he's sure to learn something.' Kathleen agreed but told her she was not to hold out too much hope. But Francine hugged herself, knowing that it was God's way of eventually bringing her close to her father.

When she related this to Sophie the following day she did not get an immediate response and it was then she realised that Sophie had been quiet from arriving at school. When Francine asked if something was wrong Sophie told her that they would not be going abroad for the summer this year. Her mother was not very well. The doctor thought it would be unwise for her to travel.

'I'm sure Mama will get better soon,' Sophie went on, 'but what makes me so cross is the way my cousin Tyson looked at me when he knew. I'm sure he was glad that *I* was not going.'

Francine had looked up at the name Tyson. She had heard it only once before and when she asked Sophie her cousin's surname and was told de Auberleigh, her heart began a slow beating. She told Sophie that her father had photographed her cousin and his family.

Sophie was intrigued. 'Well, how strange. Have you met them?'

Francine said no, but Kathleen had seen them the day they arrived at the studio and mentioned that she thought them a handsome family.

'I agree,' Sophie said, 'But Tyson, especially, always

looks so – so–' she sought for the word and came up with, 'he always looks as if he knows *everything*.'

Francine ventured to say she thought he sounded interesting, to which Sophie retorted that she would not think so if she met him.

Francine hoped she would, in spite of Sophie's remarks.

Because Sophie would not be away for the summer the two girls tried to make plans for spending some time together and came up with the idea that if Sophie could get her mother to invite Bridget and Francine to tea, then Bridget might invite her back to tea and she could see the market, the docks and perhaps meet the O'Reilly family. Francine thought this a wonderful plan, and hoped it would work.

But before this could take place Sophie arrived at school one morning full of indignation. The doctor had brought her mother a baby boy through the night and no one had told her.

'I think Mama and Papa are very mean for not having mentioned they were going to order one.'

Francine said she thought it would be lovely to have a baby brother then asked where her parents had ordered it from.

Sophie shrugged. 'I don't know, there must be *some* place you can go to.' Then her expression suddenly softened. 'He's a funny little thing, with his face all screwed up, and he can certainly yell but, well I suppose I shall get to love him when he gets older.'

Sophie talked about babies, wondering why they were only brought to a house where a mother was ill in bed. Francine, who had not been involved with any newly-born babies, could offer no answer, but said she would ask Kathleen, she would know, having brothers and sisters.

When Francine asked about babies Kathleen said gently, 'God sends them and He chooses whether it will be a girl or a boy. And the reason a mother has to be in bed when the baby arrives is to keep it cosy and warm, they're such tiny creatures, so delicate. They can't be taken out of doors for several weeks.'

'Why is that?'

'Because they come from a warm and cosy place.'

'Where?'

Kathleen smiled and wagged a finger at her. 'Now that is a secret, one you'll get to know when you are married.'

'Oh,' said Francine. 'I shall tell Sophie tomorrow.'

Sophie accepted the explanation but was anxious to impart the news to Francine that she would be invited to see the baby. Then she added with some regret that it would not be until after he was christened. He was to be called Roderick, Jonathan, Alfred, Charles, after their two grandfathers and great-grandfathers.

Francine said she thought she had only one name, but then she didn't have any grandmothers or great-grandmothers.

'Of course you have,' Sophie said. 'Everybody has grandparents and great-grandparents. I have four names – Sophie, Eleanor, Mary and Elizabeth.'

Francine once more took her problem to Kathleen and was told her grandparents and great-grandparents would probably be dead, so Francine was left envying Sophie who had four names, which made her seem very important.

It was two months later before Bridget was invited to bring Francine to tea. It was for a Saturday afternoon, which meant that Francine would miss going to the O'Reillys, but Kathleen said she must go. It was good to experience a different way of life.

Francine wore her best pale blue coat and matching pill box hat and a fur necklet and muff, which Bridget had made her from an old fur coat. Kathleen declared her to look very smart.

They took a cab and arrived at a three-sided cul-de-sac of elegant three-storeyed houses, with a circle of shrubbery in the forecourt.

An elderly maid answered the door and then Sophie

came running. 'Mama is waiting!' she exclaimed. 'Oh, I'm so glad you could come. Roderick is sleeping at the moment but nurse will bring him to the drawing room when he awakes.'

They were taken to the drawing room where a tall, fair-haired woman in a silver grey dress greeted them.

'Mrs Brogan, Francine, I'm so pleased to meet you. Do please sit down.'

It was all very formal, reminding Francine of the houses she had visited with her Aunt Amelia, but whereas her aunt's friends had ignored her Sophie's mother addressed herself to her, saying how pleased she was that Sophie had found such a nice friend.

To Francine, Mrs Denton was like an angel with her fairness, her sweet expression and her gentle voice. And what Francine especially liked was the way Mrs Denton talked easily to Bridget, not only about the weather, but about her work. 'Francine praises you to Sophie, says you are a wonderful teacher. Mrs Brogan, do you know that I wanted to be a teacher, longed to be one, but my parents would not allow it. In their opinion a girl had to be nurtured, like a hot-house flower. I may look frail but I'm really quite strong.'

The maid came in to say that the baby was awake, should nurse bring him down?

'Oh, yes,' Mrs Denton said, her face alight with pleasure. 'He's a darling child, hardly ever cries.'

Sophie glanced at Francine and raised her eyes ceiling-wards as though to say, Not again! But then her mother said softly, 'How lucky I am to have a lovely daughter *and* a son,' and Sophie lowered her gaze.

The nurse was elderly and although she hardly looked at the baby as she put him into his mother's arms, Francine found herself thinking, she loves him too.

The baby was in a beautifully embroidered gown and an embroidered cap to match. He was dark with very blue eyes. 'Just like his dear papa,' Mrs Denton murmured.

Francine was invited to come and see him, but was warned by Bridget she was not to touch him.

Francine was entranced with the baby. He yawned like an old man then put his fist to his mouth and Francine laughed.

'He's beautiful.' She longed to take hold of his hand and had to restrain herself. The baby's hands were constantly moving. One time he fixed his gaze on a vase and became cross-eyed then his mother laughed and waved a hand in front of his eyes.

The next moment she handed the baby back to his nurse. They must not let him get excited, and tea would be coming in very soon.

Francine was sorry to see the baby go.

They had wafer-thin sandwiches and cakes that were fairylike. Mrs Denton and Bridget discussed various subjects, checked some dates in history, while Sophie and Francine talked in low voices about Sophie wanting to see the market and the docks. Francine said that Bridget was going to ask if Sophie could pay them a visit.

To the delight of both girls permission was granted and it was arranged that Sophie would spend the whole of the following Saturday with Bridget and Francine.

Sophie said on the Monday morning, 'I knew I would get permission, Mama was greatly taken with Bridget and with you. She thought you a lovely, well-mannered girl and Bridget a very knowledgeable woman. Oh, I can't wait for Saturday to come!'

On the Saturday there was snow on the ground but this only added to the pleasure of both girls. Sophie was brought in a carriage just after nine o'clock and from then on they packed the day. From the start Sophie was enchanted with Francine's small bedroom and her dolls; the room because it was cosy and the dolls because Francine actually *knew* the people who had made them.

They went to the market, and to the docks, where Sophie was constantly exclaiming with delight and when they went to visit the O'Reillys in the afternoon she could hardly speak for excitement.

The family treated her as they did Francine and this intrigued Sophie the most. Fancy being able to talk to grown ups as she and Francine talked to one another. She said she thought Francine to be the luckiest girl she had ever known, and Francine wished that although she would not want to exchange lives, how wonderful it would be to have parents who loved you *and* to have a baby brother.

They had one more visit each but when the school eventually closed for the summer holidays the exchange of visits increased and it was during an afternoon at Sophie's house that Francine finally met Tyson de Auberleigh in the flesh. She was awed by him, thinking him the most handsome and elegant young man she had ever seen.

He acknowledged his introduction to her with a brief nod of his head and then ignored her, but she was glad about this because then she could feast her gaze on him.

He was tall and very straight-backed. His thick hair was dark, and his eyes were dark too, and piercing. He used his hands as he talked to Mrs Denton, and even they seemed elegant to Francine. Slender hands, long-fingered.

He did not stay long but when he had gone Francine knew he was the type of man she would want to marry and thought she must be in love.

She had to tell Sophie, even though she felt sure she would laugh at her, but to her surprise Sophie said in a dreamy way, 'Well, I could never love Tyson, but I think I could love Rory.'

And it was then that Francine knew her first pangs of jealousy. Rory was someone who was very special to her and although they had never been together long enough for her to learn anything from him about photography she was quite sure that she would one day. Sure, in fact, that he would play a big part in her life when she grew up. But had no idea how she knew this.

And so the two girls went on dreaming in their childish

way until the end of August when Bridget broke the news to Francine that she was to be sent to boarding school in Exeter in September.

Francine stared at her shocked. 'Boarding school? Oh, Bridget, I can't go, I *won't* go. There's Sophie, she's my only friend.'

'I know, but it's your father's wish.' Bridget was distressed. 'I've tried to talk to him but he won't listen, his mind is made up.'

Francine's mouth took on a stubborn line. 'I won't go. If Papa tries to make me I shall run away.' And nothing Bridget said would make her give in.

When Sophie knew what was planned she was aghast. 'You can't go! Not without me. Mama was saying to Aunt Lavinia the other day that she loved you like a daughter. I shall tell her to speak to Papa. If *you* go to boarding school then I shall go too.'

A week later they were told that Sophie would also be going to the same boarding school. The girls were so jubilant at this news it was not until much later Francine realised what she would be losing. She would not be seeing her dear O'Reilly family, or Bridget.

Kathleen consoled her. She would be home for the Christmas break, then Easter and before she knew where she was it would be the long summer break again.

Three days before Francine was due to leave for Exeter she was summoned to Spinners End to say goodbye to her father. This occasion was little different from the last, except that his instructions were longer. After telling her she was to do everything she was told he said, 'I am giving you the best education I can afford, to prepare you for the time when you will be launched into the world. You will write to Mrs Brogan once every month and she will keep me informed of your progress.'

Francine, without seeking permission to speak to her father, said, 'May I write to you too, Papa?'

'It will not be necessary.' He spoke sharply. 'That is all.'

In no way this time could Francine say her father had smiled at her. His expression was glowering. She slid off the chair and Bridget took her by the hand.

Outside Bridget said, 'Men get embarrassed at showing their feelings and so appear to be much more stern than they intend.'

'What did Papa mean by saying I would be launched into the world?'

'Well, one day a husband will have to be found for you, so you will go to balls and soirées, meet men socially.'

Francine thought this would be quite unnecessary as she had already decided she would marry someone like Tyson de Auberleigh.

When she went with Kathleen the following day to say goodbye to the family she had, for the first time, a talk with Rory about photography. His brothers kept teasing him, saying he was showing off and Francine got cross because she wanted to know as much as possible.

Rory told her about the plates and how they were developed, some in the light and some in the darkroom. And he told her how when you looked through the lens at people having their photographs taken they were upside down and she looked up at him in surprise, thinking this very strange.

'But how would the photographer know what they looked like if they were upside down? They could be fidgeting.'

'Photographers know by experience,' he said airily.

Rory talked about the ingredients used for developing and Francine thought him very clever. He told her about the importance of light and shade and how her father was making a big name for himself with his landscape photographs.

'When you go to Exeter,' he said, 'observe clouds, the movement of them, watch the sun chasing shadows across the hills, the land.'

Francine felt her stomach contract with excitement.

'You must always be observing, Miss Francine, it's the only way to become a photographer. Observe people too, their expressions.'

'Now, stop that, clever clogs,' scolded his grandmother. 'If you fill the poor child's head with all that nonsense she'll have no room for her lessons.'

'Oh, I will, I will,' Francine exclaimed. 'I want to know *everything*. I want to be a photographer.'

'Of course you can't.' Rory was scathing. '*You* are being trained to be a lady! Boarding school and all that. *I* am going to be a journalist photographer. Your father says I have the making of one.' This was said with pride and it hurt Francine that her father would say such things to Rory when he couldn't even be nice to her.

Her head went up. Well, she would show him *and* Rory what she could do. Just wait until she grew up.

Bridget was to take Sophie and Francine to Exeter and as Francine had never been on a steam train before it seemed like one big adventure, dulling the emotion of saying goodbye to everyone.

But after being at Oakleigh Manor for a month the 'adventure' faded. It was not that any teacher was as cruel as Miss Stead but discipline was rigid and both Sophie and Francine admitted that if it had not been for having each other they would have wanted to run away.

The main joy Francine had was observing the countryside. Rory had told her to study trees, leaves, watch their movement, watch rivers, streams. Sophie's joy when going for their daily walk with the rest of the young pupils was to catch the eye of a farm boy and give him a smile. Sometimes, but not often they would meet a crocodile of boys from another boarding school in the area and they would be told sharply by the teacher in charge to look straight ahead. The girls didn't, of course, they cast surreptitious glances and giggled behind their hands, including Francine.

As the girls settled in there were other pleasures, banned

pleasures, when in the dormitory a girl would share the contents of a parcel she had from home. Sophie and Francine did not fare too badly in this respect, as Sophie was sent a cake and sweetmeats from home every other week and Francine would receive from time to time a fruit cake from Bridget, some gingerbread from Mrs O'Reilly and a parcel of small cakes from Kathleen, which Cook had made.

These little secret midnight feasts made up for all the strict discipline exercised by the teachers. Sophie was the fun-maker and Francine her willing assistant, and in time they came to regard being at school as a normal way of life.

Francine's French teacher spoke of her as a natural, and this and botany were her favourite subjects. Sophie was a steady all-rounder, but the dance lessons were her favourite.

Bridget wrote every two weeks but Kathleen once a week, even if it was just a few lines. Once Rory penned a few lines and Francine treasured these, especially as they told her more about photography.

When one of the other girls had a birthday Sophie asked Francine when her birthday was. Francine told her not until the twenty-fifth of August the following year, and Sophie looked at her puzzled. 'You didn't tell me you had had your birthday.'

Francine shook her head. 'No, I didn't tell anyone. Papa is always so busy I don't suppose he would remember.'

Sophie thought this quite dreadful. Francine should have had a party, gifts; she *must* have one next year, *she* would remember, and her mama would give her a party if no else did. Francine hastened to tell her that Bridget would, or Mrs O'Reilly, it was just that they had not known about her birthday.

The time at school did not fly for Francine as Kathleen had predicted, but the vacations at home did. Christmas seemed just like a dream when she was back at school again. She had stayed with Bridget, spent a lot of time with the O'Reillys, seen her father just once. Rory she saw only at short intervals. He was wrapped up in photography and could talk of nothing else, which delighted Francine but drove the rest of the family to distraction.

His grandmother said, 'Photography and cameras! That's all we ever hear from him these days. Says he's saving up to buy a camera so's he can take all our photographs.'

'And wouldn't that be a lovely thing now,' Rory said. 'Then your great-grandchildren could see what you and Grandad looked like when you were alive.'

'So you'll have us buried in our graves before we've even thought of dying!' she exclaimed.

He put his arm around her waist. 'I'm teasing you, Gran. I want a picture of you now so I can keep it under me pillow at night, and I couldn't be closer to you both than that, now could I?'

She gave him a push, 'Oh, go on with you now, you can't get around me with all that soft talk.' But the smile she gave him was indulgent.

It was incidents like this that sustained Francine when she was back at school, the love that existed in the family, also the love they showed to her. She had had gifts from all of them at Christmas; some clothes for her dolls from the girls, a dolls' house made by the boys and some tiny, beautifully carved pieces of furniture made by old Mr O'Reilly. Mrs O'Reilly had crocheted her a fine lace collar for her velvet dress and Kathleen had made and embroidered two lace-edged handkerchiefs. In the corner of one was a clown so she would always have laughter in her life and in the corner of the other one was a fairy godmother, complete with a wand, to grant her all her wishes.

Bridget thought these lovely sentiments and dabbed at her eyes before presenting Francine with a warm knitted scarf and hat and gloves to match.

Edwin had given Bridget some money to buy Francine some serviceable clothes for school, but Bridget had recklessly spent some of the money on a gold bracelet with a small charm on it in the form of a pixie, so that Francine could show the girls at school.

It was this gesture particularly that brought home to Francine the thought and love that had gone into all her gifts, and she thought then how lucky she was to know such people, to be a part of their lives. And vowed she would never complain about the discipline at school again.

But of course she did complain as did all the other pupils, about the food, the icy dormitories, the chapped hands and chilblains, the ill-treatment from the older girls, who acted as monitors, the sly nips on arms, where bruises didn't show. They shed tears at night when they were homesick and commiserated with other girls when they were tearful.

And friendships were forged, some for life, as Francine was sure her friendship with Sophie would be.

Each time she was home she was told how much she had grown. Once Bridget said quietly, 'And in stature of mind, too. You've gained knowledge, Francine, not only academically but of human nature. I find you making excuses for their failings.'

Francine protested at this. 'I make no excuse whatsoever for the way my father has treated me over the years.'

'Be patient, Francine, I think he is changing in his thinking towards you, he—'

'So how long do I have to wait? Another year, two years, a lifetime before he acknowledges me as his daughter? On his deathbed?'

Bridget quickly crossed herself. 'Don't say such a thing, it's tempting providence. Things will change, I know it, just as I know that my name is Bridget Brogan.'

But there was no change in Francine's life until she was sixteen when she was invited by Sophie's family to spend a summer holiday with them in Monte Carlo.

Francine, who could hardly contain her excitement, had one fear, that her father would not allow her to go. But possibly because they would be staying in the de Auberleigh villa he gave his consent.

CHAPTER SEVEN

Sophie was as excited as Francine about the forthcoming holiday to Monte Carlo because she had not been abroad for some years. It had something to do with her father's finances. There had been summer holidays spent in small country houses of relatives in England where space was limited, so Francine had not been invited.

But it was different with the de Auberleigh villa in Monte Carlo, there was plenty of room. 'They have hundreds of bedrooms,' declared Sophie, the great exaggerater.

The girls talked about clothes. Edwin Chayter had been generous in this respect, giving Bridget carte blanche in providing the necessary wardrobe for Francine, as befitting the station of the de Auberleighs. Bridget had a friend who was a dressmaker and with Kathleen also involved they studied the latest fashion magazines.

There were to be simple cottons for daytime but as Sophie and Francine were to join the families for dinner there had to be something more dressy for evenings. Pure silk, shantung, voile, and zephyr were chosen and Francine had a feeling of entering a fairy-tale world.

Even before some of the dresses were completed the three women were remarking on the change they made to Francine. She was quite a young lady . . . a very lovely one . . . she would send few young men's hearts beating faster . . .

Although all this was spoken in an undertone, Francine caught the gist of their remarks and was excited about it. Perhaps Tyson de Auberleigh would notice her this time.

Two days later Bridget was asked to accompany the family to Monte Carlo in the role of nurse-companion to the girls. Both were delighted, Sophie remarking it was much better to be supervised by Bridget whom they liked than a dragon of a woman they hated.

When the O'Reilly family knew about Bridget going too they were all agog and when Bridget described travelling on the boat train from Victoria and explained that they would eat and sleep on the French train Mrs O'Reilly said, 'Well now, and isn't that something to be telling our friends and neighbours.'

If anything, Rory was more excited than the rest of the family. He had heard clients of Edwin Chayter's talking about Monte Carlo and knew all about the casinos where a man could win a fortune on the spin of a wheel. When his grandfather also showed a great interest in this his wife told him tartly there were also men who could lose a family fortune on the spin of the wheel and added that it had been known for a man to put a bullet through his brain when this happened. Rory grinned and said he thought that Monte Carlo seemed a very interesting place indeed. This brought the wrath of his grandmother on his head, who warned him if she ever heard of him gambling as much as a penny she would take a stick to his back.

Then of course he teased her and giving her a hug rocked her to and fro. 'Now Gran, you know perfectly well you wouldn't do such a thing. I'm your favourite boy, remember.'

She gave him a push. 'Now get away with your sugary talk, you'll find out what I'd do if ever you have a bet on anything.'

Rory just laughed and gave her a smacking kiss.

Francine liked these times when he was teasing his grandmother but she would get mad at him now he no longer gave her information about photography. When she asked him why, she always got the same answer, it was not a job for young ladies. This time he told her it was not the job for the daughter of a wealthy man, and she ought to concentrate on learning behaviour suitable for her position in life. He was a little scathing and she flared up.

'I think you enjoy annoying me and you've got big-headed since you went to work for my father. I don't know why. My father is a working man like anyone else. The only difference is he's taking photographs of people, instead of road sweeping or being a carpenter or a tram driver.'

His grandfather was nodding his head in agreement but Rory was annoyed. 'That's a stupid thing to say! How can you compare a road sweeper with a man like your father who is an expert at his job? You had better not let him hear you say what you've just said to me. A road sweeper indeed!'

'I never get the chance to say anything, do I?' she retorted. 'I'm a nobody to him, of no importance.' There was a catch in her voice and Mrs O'Reilly scolded Rory.

'Now look what you've done with your tongue that runs away with you, made Francine cry.'

Francine swallowed hard. 'No, Rory hasn't made me cry, Gran O'Reilly. Nobody could make me cry, not for anything like that anyway. I just get mad at him because he won't accept that someday I shall be a photographer, and a good one. Rory is jealous, of course. He can't bear to think that a girl could do something better than himself.'

'Better? Than me? How big-headed can *you* get?'

The old lady snapped, 'Stop it, both of you, you're behaving like spoilt children. You, Rory, are a young man and Francine is on the verge of womanhood. Act your ages the pair of you.'

There was a silence and Francine found herself seeing Rory with a new awareness. On every school vacation she came home to the O'Reillys and growing up with them had made her unaware of changes. Now she realised that Rory was a young man and a very attractive one. And judging by his expression he was seeing her, not as a child, but as a girl on the verge of womanhood.

He smiled suddenly. 'We'll never see eye to eye about women wanting to do a man's job, Francine, but I suppose that won't stop you dreaming about it. I have to go now, I was just given the afternoon off. Enjoy yourself and think of me when you're swimming in the lovely warm water of the Mediterranean.'

'Swimming!' Mrs O'Reilly flung up her hands in horror. 'She could drown.' She turned to Francine. 'Don't you dare come back here drowned and have us all weeping and wailing. We want you back as you are now.'

Francine smiled. 'I promise I won't come back drowned. I love you all too much for that. And anyway, I can't swim.'

'But I bet there'll be plenty of men willing to teach you.' Rory picked up his cap. 'I'll have to go or I'll have your dad bawling his head off at me. Don't forget to send me a picture postcard. Of a casino, of course.' He grinned as his grandmother raised a fist at him and, after touching Francine lightly on the cheek, he was away. The old lady shook her head. 'That one'll break a few girls' hearts before he's much older.' Her expression was indulgent, as it so often was when speaking of Rory. 'But there, none of the men in our family have rushed into marriage.' She glanced at Francine. 'They know when the right one comes along.'

Francine, who could still feel the touch of Rory's fingers, put her hand to her cheek. If only he would accept her need to take up photography when she was older they could make a good team.

Two days before she was due to leave for the holiday she was summoned to say goodbye to her father. Kathleen opened the door to Bridget and Francine and whispered, 'Rory is out on an errand. He sends his love, in case he's not back before you leave. Your father is waiting and I'm

94

sorry to say he's not in a good mood. Cook says to come to the kitchen before you go.'

Francine had long since given up expecting her father to treat her as a daughter, and was surprised when she went into his study with Bridget to be greeted in a quiet manner. He invited them to be seated then looking at Francine said, 'You are growing up.'

She was wearing the outfit she was to travel in, an oatmeal coloured dustcoat, a matching dress trimmed with royal blue braid and a cream straw hat. Francine felt pleased that her father had at last seemed to be more aware of her, but then he said, 'See you behave in a grown up manner when you are abroad,' spoiling her small pleasure.

'Of course, Papa. I shall write to you.'

He told her it would not be necessary, Mrs Brogan would keep him informed, but for once Francine answered back.

'I should like to write to you, Papa. It's the least I can do after all you have had to spend on sending me abroad and fitting me out with clothes. I do appreciate it.'

'Very well.' He began to sort through some papers and Bridget gave her a nudge and they both got to their feet. Francine said goodbye and he raised a hand acknowledging it.

'See you behave yourself.'

Francine had to clench her hands to stop herself from asking him to say something else for a change. Bridget hustled her out then reprimanded her gently, 'Your father sets boundaries, Miss Francine, you should know that by now. Today you overstepped them. You were lucky that he did not deny you your holiday.'

Francine stopped and stared at her. 'Papa said himself that I am growing up. How much longer am I to be treated as a small child?'

'You are growing up, but are not yet *grown up* and in that there is a vast difference. I would advise you to remember it in future, Miss Francine, especially when you are in the company of Sophie's family and the de Auberleighs. You are a minor in their eyes and you must not speak to them unless you are spoken to. They will have no time for rebels in their midst.'

It was Bridget's quiet manner that subdued Francine. She said she would remember her manners. She did, however, wish she could grow up quickly and be a successful photographer so that she was not treated as a nobody. But then, she reflected, she was not a nobody with the O'Reillys, she was *family*.

When Bridget and Francine went into the kitchen Cook and Kathleen, who had been talking, looked up expectantly. Francine answered their unspoken question. 'Papa turned out to be in quite a good mood. He gave me permission to write to him.'

'He did?' Kathleen flung up her hands. 'Wonders will never cease. He's been like a raging bull in a china shop all morning.' Cook, looking grim, confirmed this, then she yelled for Evie.

'Taylor! What d'ye think you're doing in that dratted pantry. Get out here and put the kettle on.'

Evie came running and seeing Francine beamed at her. ''Ello, Miss Francine, 'ow you bin?'

'Kettle,' Cook snapped. Evie pushed it from the hob on to the fire then brought out cups and saucers, and Francine watching her thought how little Evie had changed over the years, same pinched face and scrawny body. The biggest change Francine saw was in Mrs Dodge. When she first met Cook her hair was dark, now it was heavily streaked with grey and her body was hunched with rheumatism. Her voice, however, was still sharp. She said to Francine, 'So you're off to foreign parts. Good luck to you, I say. I couldn't tackle a two mile train journey these days. It's me rheumatics, play me up something cruel. I will say this, Miss Francine, you do your father proud. A proper lady you look.'

Cook kept Evie doing jobs all the time they were there and when they left Francine said to Bridget she felt sorry for Evie, having to work day in and day out for a woman like Mrs Dodge. Bridget told her that the woman had been kind to Evie in many ways.

'In what ways? Evie looks half-starved, she never stops working and -'

'Evie is not starved, she gets decent food, but she has suffered a lot of trouble in her home life. When her father died and her mother married again her stepfather ordered Evie to come home to look after the family. When she did go home he molested her, did unspeakable things. She was bruised from head to foot. It was Mrs Dodge Evie ran to and it was Cook who told the police. The stepfather was sent to prison and is still there.'

When Francine asked Bridget what she meant by unspeakable things she was told she might learn when she was older. It was not something normally discussed, even among adults.

Francine thought then what a strange world they lived in. Here she was bound for a luxury villa in Monte Carlo while Evie was at the beck and call of Mrs Dodge and had a home where a stepfather had done unspeakable things to her.

Francine had already said goodbye to the O'Reillys but Kathleen told her before she left Spinners End that she would call and see her the following evening for an hour at Bridget's house.

Kathleen arrived at seven o'clock. She was wearing a cinnamon-coloured dress trimmed with pale blue and her darker brown big brimmed hat was circled with pale blue velvet ribbon. Francine thought she looked very elegant. Kathleen talked as she unpinned and removed her hat.

'And I suppose you are both packed and ready for your adventure?'

Francine gave a breathless laugh. 'Bridget has just

locked the two trunks and now I really believe the holiday is not just a dream.'

Bridget said, 'A man will collect the luggage later and a cab will take us to Victoria station in the morning to catch the boat train. I've met Mrs Forbes, little Roderick Denton's nanny and I think we shall get on quite well together.'

Before Kathleen left she had a few minutes alone with Francine. She said softly, 'A whole new world will be opening up for you Francine, enjoy it and learn from it.' Kathleen seemed a little choked then and after giving her a quick hug, took her leave.

The whole new world opened up for Francine the moment she arrived at Victoria station and saw the gleaming brown boat train with its gold lettering and air of luxury. A porter escorted them to their carriage and an attendant took over and showed them to their allotted seats.

The de Auberleigh family were already in Monte Carlo and Sophie's father was to follow a day or two later.

Francine likened the carriage to a drawing room. The floor was carpeted and the plush seats had lace-edged linen squares on the backs of them to protect the upholstery from the pomaded hair of the men. Although Bridget and Francine had arrived in good time there was a constant activity on the platform, with families, couples arriving, some passengers with masses of luggage. All the people were well-dressed and most of the men had an air of authority as they hailed porters.

Then Francine suddenly sat up as she spotted Sophie coming towards their carriage. Sophie, seeing Francine, began to run, but must have been checked because she slowed to a walk and threw out her hands with a frustrated gesture.

Then Mrs Denton came into view with an older man cupping her elbow. Behind them was Roderick with his nanny, Mrs Forbes. Roderick, a shy, gentle boy, in sailor suit and hat, looked agitated. His hair, which had been so dark when he was born was now golden and hung in ringlets. Mr Denton, according to Sophie, had little time for his son because he was of such a nervous disposition.

Mrs Denton was in a delicate pale blue dress and coat which seemed to emphasise her fragility, but when they were on the train she gave an order to the attendant in a firm voice. She greeted Bridget then explained that she, with friends, would be in an adjoining compartment and with a sweet smile left, which had Sophie saying with a sigh, 'Thank goodness for that. Mama has been on at me since getting up.' She gave Francine a broad grin. 'Now we can talk.'

At last they were all seated. The two women were on one side of the carriage, with Roderick pressed close to Mrs Forbes' side, and Francine and Sophie sat opposite, talking in low voices about every small thing that had happened since they last met. They broke off only at departure time, when both girls showed excitement and Roderick an interest in all the people on the platform calling last-minute instructions and waving to friends and relatives as carriage doors were slammed. There was a great hissing of steam from the engine, the shrill sound of the guard's whistle, then the train began to move.

'We're away, Roderick.' Mrs Forbes took hold of his hand. He smiled then and for a while seemed fascinated by the clouds of steam blotting out everything. Then they were out of the dimness of the station and into grey morning where heavy clouds seemed to be sitting on the roofs of grimy buildings and equally grim houses. Francine thought how lucky she was to be going to blue skies and living in luxury for a number of weeks.

There was much to delight and enchant Francine during the long journey to Monte Carlo – the novelty of having meals and sleeping on train and boat. She had never tasted such food, nor experienced such deferential treatment from waiters. Both she and Sophie were allowed to stay up for dinner and they not only enjoyed dressing up for these occasions but Francine was impressed with the napery, the crystal, the silver.

Francine spent quite a lot of the time telling Roderick stories. Some she knew from her younger days and some she made up, but all she told him had to have a gentle theme. He had nightmares if anyone spoke of goblins or witches.

She kept a day-to-day diary and reading it over was surprised at how many times she had referred to the poverty they had seen on the way in farmland, town and village. *'A harsh contrast,'* she had written, *'to the big houses of the landowners and to the wealth of the travellers.'* She had a sudden feeling that Rory would have been pleased with these contrasts. She was observing.

CHAPTER EIGHT

On the last stage of the journey the train was delayed by some object having to be removed from the railway track. It was midnight when they arrived at Monte Carlo and Francine, who expected to find everything in darkness, was surprised to find lights in buildings and houses.

Mrs Denton, who seemed to be the least tired of the party said, smiling, 'Monte Carlo never sleeps.'

There was more activity than there had been in London. At Victoria station passengers had arrived at intervals. Here everyone disembarked together. Among people waiting to greet passengers were men displaying cards with the names of hotels written on them.

A tall man with a soldierly bearing came hurrying up and greeted Mrs Denton with outstretched arms. 'My dear Helena, I thought you must all be lost in a mountain pass.' He kissed her on both cheeks.

'Frederick, how tiresome for you to have had to wait so long. Let me introduce you to Francine.' Francine learned then that the tall, beautifully groomed man was Mr de Auberleigh, Tyson's father.

Poor Roderick was almost falling asleep on his feet and their host hailed a manservant to carry the boy to a carriage.

There were two carriages. The girls, Roderick, Bridget and Mrs Forbes travelled in the second one. Francine, who had felt sleepy during the last stage of the journey, was now wide awake and taking in the scene, the sounds, the clip-clop of horses' hooves as carriages drew away, voices, some weary, some full of laughter. There was the sound of hissing steam from the station, the clank-clank of engines shunting. The raucous voices of vendors offering fruit for

101

sale. 'At midnight!' Francine exclaimed, and was reminded by Sophie that they were now in *Monte Carlo*. The night was balmy and later when they were travelling along a winding road the mingled fragrance of pines and flowers drifted through open windows.

On the slopes were beautiful villas where lights cast a warm glow over trees and shrubs. Then as they rounded the next bend Francine had her first glimpse of the sea. She felt awed. A high riding moon silvered the water, which was still as a pond.

They had been climbing for quite a while when the carriages turned left and travelled along a short drive before drawing up outside a white painted villa. It was the largest Francine had seen. Not only was it long, but it went back a long way. There were balconies at each of the wide windows on the first floor, with pot plants trailing greenery through the fretwork. Coloured lampshades in various rooms on the ground floor cast a kaleidoscope of rose pink, green, gold and blue on the forecourt.

Francine had no time to take in more. Manservants and maidservants came hurrying out and the guests were shown into a spacious room, with a beautiful mosaic floor.

The rest of the de Auberleigh family came in and then Francine had eyes only for Tyson de Auberleigh who, with the others, greeted his aunt and her friends. Francine had dreamed of meeting him again, but was unprepared for the strange emotions he aroused, a shivery, excited feeling unlike anything she had ever experienced.

Francine was introduced to Mrs de Auberleigh and her three sons and daughter, but as with the father, their acknowledgements were brief, and Francine was sure that Tyson did not recognise her from the last time they had met at Sophie's home.

Tonight, he was looking even more attractive than before. He was wearing a white evening suit with a black bow tie, the white emphasising his suntanned skin.

Francine felt suddenly jaded and was glad when Bridget

and Mrs Forbes asked to be excused to see their charges into bed.

Even the exuberant Sophie seemed deflated as a maid escorted them to their bedroom.

Francine and Sophie were to share a room at the end of the first floor corridor. Bridget said briskly, 'Now no lingering, get washed and undressed and into bed. I shall look in on you in a few minutes.'

Usually when Sophie stayed overnight at Bridget's house the two girls at bedtime would be chatting away, talking over everything that had happened during the day, but now the girls were silent as they undressed in an automatic way.

Then Sophie said in a woebegone voice, 'Why is it that I find myself wishing I was back at home?'

Francine, who had always regarded Sophie as being more worldly-wise than herself, adopted the role of consoler.

'It's been a long journey, the delay tired us. I think we'll feel better in the morning after a good night's sleep.'

'You sound just like my old nanny.'

Francine said she felt like an old nanny then both girls were giggling. But they were in bed and on the verge of sleep when Bridget looked in. She bade them goodnight and closed the door quietly behind her.

When Francine awoke the next morning she found it difficult to place where she could be. The room was flooded with sunlight. Then, remembering, she flung back the bedclothes and sliding to the floor she ran to the window. There she stood entranced. To the right was the harbour, full of beautiful white-painted yachts. Down the slope that led to the beach bougainvilia spilled over arbours, walls and arches. Sky and sea were an unbelievable blue and golden coins danced and sparkled on the water. She ran to shake Sophie awake. Sophie groaned and said she had seen the sea before but the maid brought their hot water and so she too got out of bed.

The only ones in the dining room when the girls went down were Bridget, Roderick and his nanny. Bridget said that the ladies and the menfolk were having breakfast in bed and that the de Auberleigh sisters and brothers had gone swimming with a party of friends.

Bridget said that after breakfast they would go to the beach, but warned the girls to put on their bathing shoes because the beach was all pebbles and shingle. But as it turned out there was quite a big patch of sand at the foot of the steps leading from the house to the beach, which was a treat for Roderick who wanted to make sandpies and sandcastles.

Sophie, who had been praying that she and Francine would not be expected to help Roderick with his sandcastle building, was delighted when a nanny from a nearby villa asked if her charge, a boy named Christopher, could play with Roderick.

Mrs Forbes said yes, of course. Bridget did not look too happy at having a third party in the nanny, but before long the three women had seated themselves in deck chairs and were chatting away like old friends. Sophie grinned at Francine and suggested in a low voice that they go exploring. To the delight of both girls Bridget gave her consent but told them they were not to go out of sight and must not speak to any strange men. They gave promises, both of them demure.

But once on their own they were laughing. What joy to get away! Sophie looked about her, saying they must look for two attractive young men, but out of the line of vision of Bridget. At the moment Francine, who was enjoying the sun and the lovely clear air, was not a bit bothered about meeting attractive young men, but at the same time she knew deep down that she was hoping to meet up with Tyson.

Then people started to come on to the beach and she was intrigued at the different types. The women, all elegantly dressed, carried parasols. The men too were well-dressed but looked less formal in flannel suits or white blazers with stripes of navy, green, red or blue.

Soon afterwards whole families arrived and arranged themselves in circles in their deck chairs.

Then Sophie, excited, noticed a young man they had met casually during the train journey. She said they would go and make themselves known but Francine told her to go if she wished, she would wait. Sophie hurried off, calling over her shoulder to say she would not be long.

Two minutes after this Francine caught sight of Tyson de Auberleigh and her limbs went weak. He was wearing a white towelling robe and droplets of water glistened on his dark hair. He was talking to a dark-haired girl who was looking at him in a provocative way. Francine then saw the de Auberleigh party approaching. Tyson's two brothers and his three sisters were dressed for walking. If they had been swimming they showed no sign of it.

Francine, not wanting to be noticed, hurried to the water's edge where she stood looking out to sea, hidden by a bathing hut. Perhaps because of seeing the family together, she had a sudden feeling of homesickness, as Sophie had done the evening before.

And yet she had day-dreamed of coming to Monte Carlo, of being with Tyson, and decided she was being foolish. She should be grateful for this wonderful oppor-tunity. She *must*, it was foolish to feel sorry for herself.

She looked towards the horizon and realised what clarity there was in the air. What wonderful pictures could be taken. She walked on slowly, observing children paddling. One small girl, being held under the armpits by her nanny, was kicking her legs and laughing joyously. Francine was smiling at the child's antics when a voice behind her said, 'It is Francine, isn't it?' The next moment Tyson de Auberleigh was peeping under the brim of her straw hat. The colour rushed to her face.

'Yes, it is,' she said. He was still wearing his white robe.

'Not swimming? No, of course you're not, what a stupid thing to say.'

'What are you doing on your own, Francine?'

'Just observing. I was watching the children, thinking what lovely pictures they would make, that is, if I had a camera. My father is a photographer, but of course you know, he photographed your family.' She stopped suddenly, overcome with embarrassment. What a fool he must think her, gabbling on.

But he said, 'I think you must have been very deep in thought and I startled you. I'm sorry.'

His words and manner were so unexpected Francine felt touched by them, she had thought him arrogant and he was treating her gently.

'Shall we walk on, then you can study some more of humanity.' There was a teasing in his voice, but he followed this up by asking how she found conditions for photographing and was immediately serious. 'I should imagine the light must be perfect, although I haven't studied the subject.'

'Oh, yes, everything is startlingly clear. Look at the people in that small boat out there. One can see each feature of the two men and the woman and child. If I was specialising I think it would be children, they are so natural and have so many changes of expression. They have such a lovely innocence.'

'And when they are older?' The teasing was back in his voice.

Francine said, 'A child soon loses that innocence and sons soon learn to twist parents and others around their little finger, mothers especially. Adults wear various masks putting on the kind of face they want the other person to see.'

Tyson turned his head quickly. 'You certainly are observant for someone so young. Who taught you this, your father?'

'No,' she said quietly. 'I think it must have been life.'

He stopped and faced her. 'Francine, you are too grown up for your age, you sound as if you had already found the worst in everyone. How old are you, eighteen?'

She was pleased and flattered, but said, 'Not quite.' Then she smiled. 'Don't despair of me, I haven't lived life to the full and become jaded.' She had read this in a book. 'I'm just beginning to live. It's my first holiday abroad. I'm enjoying myself.' This was true now.

A group of young people hailed him and he said, 'Francine, I must leave you, we are going swimming from a friend's yacht. I shall see you at dinner this evening. Go on enjoying yourself but don't go talking to any strange young men.'

She smiled. 'I won't unless they speak to me.'

He wagged a finger at her. 'You behave yourself, Francine.'

She watched as he went sprinting towards the group, a lithe figure with a joyousness in him. Or was it an echo of the joyousness in herself? It was a dream come true. Tyson had not only noticed her and remembered her name but had talked to her as an equal. She had turned and was walking slowly back in the direction where Sophie had left her when Sophie came running up.

'I wondered where you were, Francine.'

'I met Tyson, we talked.'

'Talked, you and Tyson!' Sophie eyed her in some astonishment. 'I can hardly believe it. In all the years of meeting him I don't think we've exchanged more than a few words. We've never chatted, nor have I done so with any of my other cousins. I think they've always regarded me as a junior and therefore beneath their notice.'

'Tyson took me to be eighteen,' Francine said dreamily.

'He did? Well, don't let him know otherwise.'

Sophie went on to talk about Stephen, the boy they had met on the train. 'He had to meet his parents but he said he would look for me tomorrow and perhaps bring a friend. Come along, we must get back to Bridget, we don't want to get into her bad books the first day.'

But the three women were so deep in conversation that they didn't even notice Sophie and Francine until a picnic basket was brought down from the house, then Bridget asked if they had met any of the family on the beach and when Francine told her only Tyson, Bridget said there would be guests for dinner that evening so the girls must decide what to wear.

It took both girls some time to make a choice. Eventually Sophie decided on a lemon silk and Francine on a delicate green voile. On the front, which hung straight from neck to hem, was a scattering of tiny embroidered daisies. From the waist at the back were bunched pleats with a large bow also bearing daisies.

Usually Francine wore her hair tied back with a ribbon but for this occasion Bridget dressed it, sweeping it up on top and letting the curled ends fall over a green velvet band. Tendrils of hair touched her cheeks. When Francine saw her reflection in the long mirror she was astonished at the change. Sophie stared at her.

'Francine, you look lovely. If cousin Tyson was interested in you on the beach this morning in your blue cotton dress then I'm sure he'll fall head over heels in love with you this evening.'

When Mrs Denton saw them in their finery she said, 'My goodness, we have two beautiful young ladies on our hands. It seems only yesterday they were children.'

Sophie suggested they take a peep into the dining room and Francine was entranced by it. The walls were of stone and in a number of alcoves small fountains played, a musical sound in the stillness of the evening. A beautifully polished walnut table reached nearly the length of the room and down the middle were small bowls of roses with settings of silver, and crystal goblets.

Sophie, after counting the number of settings, declared there would be six guests. And she was right. There were three young men and a middle-aged couple and their daughter.

The girl, an elegantly dressed fair-haired beauty, made Francine feel she had faded into insignificance, especially as Tyson's face was alight with pleasure as he greeted her.

'Octavia, I'm delighted you were able to come.'

She laid her hand on his arm in a possessive way, her smile all-embracing. 'You knew I would if it were at all possible.'

When they assembled to take their places at the table Tyson noticed Francine and gave her a brief smile, but it was in an abstract way, as though trying to place where they had met.

When they were all seated for the meal Sophie and Francine were sat at either side of Mrs Denton near the top of the table where Mr and Mrs de Auberleigh presided. On the opposite side, to the left of his mother, sat Tyson and the girl Octavia. The girl's dress was off the shoulders and her skin was as creamy as the satin of her dress. Francine wished she could have been seated at the other end of the table.

To her surprise when the first course had been served Mr de Auberleigh, who had seemed to Francine to be an aloof, austere man, chatted to Mrs Denton and included the girls in his conversation.

He asked Francine if she had enjoyed her first day in Monte Carlo, adding, 'I know of course you must have felt very tired after the journey but what was your impression?'

'I thought everything quite wonderful, sir, especially the sea, it's such an amazing blue. It's the first time I've been to a seaside resort, although of course I have seen photographs of them.'

His eyebrows went up. 'Do you mean to say you have never been to a resort in England, Brighton or–?'

'No, sir. I lived with my aunt for several years and she did not enjoy very good health.'

109

'I see.' Francine noticed then that Mrs de Auberleigh was regarding her with some curiosity. She had seemed to Francine to be somewhat aloof, too. Now she smiled and the smile softened the rather severe planes of her face and, for the first time Francine saw a resemblance between Mrs de Auberleigh and her sister Mrs Denton.

'Papa,' Tyson broke in. 'Octavia's parents are making up a party to go to the Dolomites this winter for skiing. I've been invited, would you mind if I go?'

His father's mouth tightened. 'I think this should be discussed at a later date, my boy.'

Tyson leaned forward, his expression eager. 'Octavia says that some of the peaks assume fantastic forms. If we—'

Perhaps he noticed that his mother was shaking her head at him for he said, 'Yes, of course, this is really not the time to suggest such a project. Sorry.' He glanced at Octavia who raised her beautiful shoulders as though to say, 'Well, if you think I am not worth fighting for . . .'

After that Tyson's manner seemed a little stiff.

Not so Sophie's manner. She was in her element trying to attract the attention of the young man who was paired off with Tyson's eldest sister. When Sophie persisted in trying to break into the conversation her mother whispered something to her. Then Sophie attacked the food on her plate in a furious way. Mrs Denton looked distressed and spoke again to her daughter who, this time, mumbled an apology.

Francine looked around the table and noticed many different expressions, which in some cases must have been forced because eyes did not match the brightness of the manner; she saw a tiredness behind Mr de Auberleigh's kindly interest in herself. She recalled saying to Tyson that morning about adults putting on masks to hide their real feelings.

When Octavia's father, Mr Manning, let his mask slip for a moment he looked utterly bored. His wife kept laughing over-heartily then at times would look annoyed. Had her maid tightened the laces of her corsets too much? One of the three young men would look sullen on occasions and Francine wondered if he would have preferred to be seated beside another of the de Auberleigh girls.

Francine thought it strange that in this exotic setting there should be all this underlying boredom, annoyance and ill-feeling.

If Tyson had glanced in Francine's direction she was not aware of it and was glad when the meal was over. It was dusk and candles had been lit, softening the expressions of all those at the table. The women automatically got up to withdraw, leaving the men to their port and cigars. Sophie, who was about to follow the women to the drawing room, was forestalled by her mother who said that Bridget was waiting to see the girls up to their room. Sophie protested. 'But Mama, this is a special evening! Surely for once Francine and I are not to be banished like children.'

'It's late. Off you go. Goodnight dear. Goodnight, Francine.'

Even Sophie had enough sense to know it was an order and must be obeyed. But she grumbled all the way to their room. 'One minute Mama says we are young ladies and the next treats us as infants.'

Francine went to the window. The sky was a canopy of indigo velvet, with stars so near you felt you could reach out and take one, and the sea was again touched with silver. It was all so beautiful yet she felt strangely unhappy. Everything was so different, such luxury she had never before experienced. The food alone was out of this world, so why was there this unrest? Did she want this way of life? Yes, yes, she did, as long as Tyson de Auberleigh could be a part of it. But he was not and probably never would be. She must reconcile herself to this. Tomorrow she would write to her father and to Kathleen, so she could read the letter to her family and to Cook and Evie.

Sophie said suddenly, 'I can't stand Octavia Manning, and neither can my aunt, I can tell. Uncle approves, though, because the family is wealthy. I'm sure he would like the joining of the two families, and to create an empire.'

'But your uncle didn't approve of Tyson going with the family to the Dolomites.'

'Oh, he would approve all right but he wouldn't want to give Octavia the impression that she could take over the reins.'

Francine, with a newly-found philosophy, accepted that Tyson was not for her and set out to enjoy the simple pleasures of the beach, the sea and the sun.

The following day Sophie's father arrived. Francine had met him once or twice but had felt uncomfortable with him because of his aloof manner. Today, however, he exuded goodwill to all, even kissing Francine and greeting her in French.

The girls learned later that they were all to go to a party on the Mannings' yacht that evening.

Sophie said with some excitement, 'Perhaps the engagement of Tyson and Octavia is going to be announced. If so, there will be champagne.'

Francine felt a sudden pang, realising then she was still vulnerable as far as Tyson was concerned. She had been able to cope while he was out of sight, but how would she feel seeing him again this evening . . . with Octavia?

CHAPTER NINE

Francine decided to wear the simple white muslin dress Bridget had made her, for the Mannings' party. This had Sophie gazing at her in surprise.

'Why that one, Francine? You have others much more – grown up.'

Francine remained adamant about wearing the white muslin and as it turned out, the dress drew compliments from Mr and Mrs de Auberleigh and from Tyson.

Taking her by the shoulders Tyson held her at arms' length. 'Francine, you look lovely.' He turned to the others. 'Doesn't she?'

There were quick nods of assent then his father said, 'We must go, my boy, the carriages are here.'

Tyson took time to take Francine's matching muslin cape from her and drape it around her shoulders. The hot colour, which had just receded from Francine's cheeks after the compliment, flared up again and she was glad when Mrs Denton took charge of her.

When they arrived at the harbour it was full of activity – visitors alighting from carriages, a movement of people on the yachts and everywhere was colour, in the dresses and in the pennants moving gently in the breeze. The muted sound of music mingled with that of voices and laughter.

At the de Auberleigh dinner party the night before, there had been a sombre air, but here was a gaiety Francine had never seen before.

As they approached the Mannings' yacht several couples on deck came hurrying to the rails and began to wave. Then Octavia was there, outstanding in emerald green chiffon. She waved and Francine saw Tyson, who had stepped out of the carriage in front, smile and raise a hand in greeting to her before turning to help out the ladies.

Two young men who were standing apart from the others on deck drew Sophie's attention. With a mischievous smile she said as she nudged Francine, 'Now then, I find people like that rather interesting. How about you?'

Francine, entering into the spirit of the evening, gave her an equally mischievous smile. 'Could be . . . We shall have to find out, won't we?'

The girls joined the others to board the yacht, where they were greeted by their host and hostess. Within seconds of stepping on deck more guests arrived and without really being aware how it had happened Francine and Sophie found themselves paired off with the two young men at the rail, who had been introduced as Peter Kingsley and Glyn Jordan. Sophie made a proprietory claim on Glyn, who was tall, golden-haired and most attractive. Peter was smaller, and dark with a rather shy manner.

Waiters were moving among the guests with trays of drinks and Glyn asked the girls if they would care for champagne. Sophie promptly accepted but then Mrs Denton was there seeing that her daughter and Francine were given fruit drinks. When she left them Sophie said under her breath, 'Spoilsport,' which had Glyn laughing. Perhaps they could sneak some champagne to the girls later.

Peter shook his head. It might not be wise, if the girls were not used to it. It was heady stuff.

'Heady, yes,' said Glyn, 'but if you haven't tasted champagne you've never lived.' To which Peter replied quietly that if you had a hangover then you could wish youself dead.

A tall, elderly man who had approached remarked, 'Paradise in the evening perhaps, but Hades in the morning.' He turned to the girls. 'Take no notice of my nephew, young ladies, he has no right to lead you astray.'

Glyn just laughed. 'Uncle, let me introduce you to our two charming guests.' He gave Sophie and Francine's names and introduced his uncle as Lord Holcombe.

Francine, not having met anyone titled, was impressed. A lord? Wait until she told Kathleen!

Glyn drew out some chairs at a nearby table and invited his uncle to join them. He accepted.

Since first being introduced to Francine, Lord Holcombe had looked at her once or twice in a puzzled way. Then he said, 'Miss Chayter, your father and I are acquaintances, but I did not know he had a daughter. Your face is so very familiar. Have we met before?'

'No, sir, I would have remembered.'

'Strange,' he mused, 'you do remind me of someone. I wish I knew who it was. Perhaps I will remember later. You are on holiday in Monte Carlo?'

Francine explained she was a guest of the de Auberleighs.

Holcombe sat rubbing his chin. 'That does not ring a bell. I wish I knew who you reminded me of.' He gave a small wry smile. 'At my age an incident like this could keep me awake all night. Ridiculous, isn't it?'

Glyn teased him. 'Oh, come, uncle, you never go to bed anyway until daybreak. The casinos would miss you if you decided to spend *one* night in bed.'

His uncle laughed. 'How true.'

'The casino?' Francine exclaimed. 'It must be very exciting if you win. Is it really true that one can win a fortune in an evening?'

'It is, but alas fortunes are also lost.'

Glyn laughed. 'My uncle should know, he's won and lost several fortunes. He once lost the ancestral home and won it back three days later.'

Francine was shocked. 'Your ancestral home? Oh, sir, how could you bear to lose it?'

115

'Only a born gambler could, my dear. As he loses it he convinces himself he will regain it very soon.'

Sophie said grimly, 'But when some men lose their all they put a bullet through their brain. At least, that is what I was told.'

Lord Holcombe teased her, saying she was a very blood-thirsty young lady.

Waiters came round with trays of tidbits, delicacies to Francine. There was an informality about the evening that delighted her. Many people stopped at their table to have a word, people who knew Glyn and Peter but who included Sophie and Francine in the conversation. Then Tyson's three sisters, who had more or less ignored the girls, stopped by for a chat. Sophie said after they had gone it was simply because they had been in the company of Lord Holcombe, but Francine didn't agree. She had been aware of a shyness in them. The sisters left to join the three men who had paired up with them at their parents' house.

Francine caught glimpses of Tyson now and again, but he never came near, Octavia, no doubt, being too much of an attraction.

At dusk the whole scene changed. The lights from the yachts cast moving reflections in the water and above where the night sky was quickly moving in, more and more stars were appearing. Francine stood with Sophie and her mother at the rail in silence for a while then Sophie said that they had promised to return to Glyn Jordan and Peter Kingsley. She was reprimanded by her mother. Young ladies did not go seeking out young gentlemen. She had allowed them a freedom earlier because of the informality of the party, but they must now accompany her. As it turned out they found themselves part of a lively group.

Ships and various voyages became a talking point with the older people and although Sophie grumbled at always having to be saddled with adults Francine quite enjoyed hearing about India, Greece, Rome and Egypt. She was

116

especially interested in Egypt and when she mentioned this Glyn suggested she talk to Peter about it. He had been there several times, for his father was an archaeologist. Peter proved a mine of information about the treasures found in tombs and about the old temples. He spoke of the massive columns, the wonderful stone carvings. He described a journey up the Nile, the people they had encountered, the different tongues spoken.

'It must be very impressive to see the pyramids,' Francine mused.

Peter pulled on his lower lip. 'Impressive from a distance, yes, but most people find them disappointing on closer inspection. They're quite rough to climb. My father does have some photographs, I shall put some in my pocket and if we meet again, which I'm sure we will, I can show you the various attractions.'

Francine said a little dreamily, 'I would love to travel and take photographs of all the interesting places. I want to be a photographer.'

'You do?' Peter eyed her in faint astonishment. 'It's not exactly an occupation for a young lady.'

'Why not? Why should it be the prerogative of men to work? More and more women are going into commerce and into industry.'

'Maybe, but is it right? Women are fragile creatures who need protecting. Their place is in the home, to take charge of it and be there with their husbands, with their children.'

'But why should they stay at home before they marry and sit doing embroidery or some such task and be bored?'

Peter asked if she was bored in Monte Carlo and she said no, because this life was something new to her, it was her first holiday abroad, but she added she would not take kindly to such a life for always. When she was back home she would be returning to school to finish her education, and when that was completed she hoped her father would allow her to take up photography. Francine added the

117

information that her father was a professional photographer.

Peter and Francine had moved away from the group, but Glyn, who had obviously been listening to the conversation, asked if he might take part in the discussion. Then Sophie followed him and when the four of them began talking about the problem the rest of the group joined in. Things were becoming quite heated when Lord Holcombe stepped in and wanted to know what was going on.

Peter explained briefly, saying that all the girls apart from one wanted freedom to do what they wished with their lives but all the men were against it.

Of course they were against it, said the old man. They had been spoiled by their mothers and had had it instilled in them by their fathers that they were the superior sex. It was time young ladies had a say in their lives. When there was an immediate outcry from the men at this, Holcombe held up his hand. 'Please allow me to finish. I do make a reservation. I think if a young lady wishes to follow an occupation before marriage she should be allowed to do so. But once she is married then she must give her whole attention to her husband, her children and to her home.'

The girls agreed to this but the men were still against any young lady following an occupation outside her home.

Francine said, 'May I say something, please? If a woman is trained to do a job and happens to be left a widow, then wouldn't she be at an advantage if she could earn money to keep her home going and be able to feed and clothe her children?'

There were some protests at this. The husbands would provide for such an event.

Francine said, 'But what if the man has not provided for such a contingency? As the law stands, a husband can make a brother the sole beneficiary, with instructions for him to take care of his family. But that brother can opt out of his obligations. And this has been known to happen, not only in this society but in other walks of life.'

Francine received applause for this and the colour suddenly rushed to her cheeks as she felt she had been talking too much. But when she mentioned this it was not only from Lord Holcombe she got support but from Peter and three more men. Miss Chayter was talking common-sense, they said.

Some of the girls and their escorts started arguing among themselves and Holcombe, who had been studying Francine as he had done earlier in the evening, suddenly exclaimed, 'Now I know who you remind me of, Miss Chayter. It's a friend of mine, Madame Dupont. It was the photography I think, that set my mind going. Gabrielle was once married to a photographer. You are so like her – you have her fine bone structure, a fragile beauty. She is a very lovely woman.' He drew her away from the others.

Francine felt suddenly icy cold. Gabrielle? Was it possible that this Madame Dupont -?

'Miss Chayter, are you all right?' The old man's voice held concern.

'Yes, I – ' Francine pressed her palms together. 'It was just that I think my mother's name was Gabrielle. It seemed such a coincidence that Madame Dupont should have been married to a photographer. But then I was told that my mother had died when I was young.'

'Coincidences do happen,' he spoke gently. 'I'm so sorry to have distressed you, Miss Chayter. Gabrielle has never mentioned a child and I'm sure she would have done, for we've been friends since she came to Paris, and that must be, oh -' he spread his hands, 'fourteen, fifteen years ago.' He looked around him. 'I'm sorry but you must excuse me.' He gave a brief smile. 'It's casino time, where if Lady Luck is on my side I shall win a fortune. It's been a pleasure meeting you, Miss Chayter, I'm sure we shall meet again.' He spoke to Peter who was standing near and when Peter came over Holcombe left.

Francine wished that she was leaving then, or at least could spend some time on her own to think about this Madame Dupont. But Peter was teasing her, telling her what a furore she had caused airing her views on women taking up employment.

'But many of them thought you made sense, Miss Chayter. I left Mrs Frobisher telling them about her niece who was made homeless because of her husband's gambling. He was so heavily in debt that the house had to be sold to prevent his going to prison.' Peter drew her back into the group.

There were still those for and those against, and in the middle of the discussion Tyson arrived, without Octavia, to tell Sophie and Francine that Bridget was waiting for them in a carriage on the quayside. Sophie was furious at being treated like a child whose bedtime had arrived; Francine was pleased to be leaving so she could be alone to think over the evening and what had evolved.

Tyson was there long enough to hear Francine being praised as a young lady with a great deal of sense and when they left with him accompanying them to the carriage he remarked, 'So, it's been quite a profitable evening for you both. Each of you have admirers. But you, cousin Sophie, should be aware of Glyn Jordan. He has a penchant for young ladies.' He turned to Francine, smiling. 'But you, Francine, have fared better with Peter Kingsley, who is a much more dependable person.'

Francine, annoyed that Tyson should stay away all evening then make superior remarks when he did show up said, 'A man can be a gentleman in company and a blackguard when alone with a young lady.'

Tyson laughed at this. 'My goodness, you sound as if you had suffered from the attention of a number of blackguards.'

Sophie snapped, 'Well, there is one thing, cousin, *you* were not at hand to prevent such a thing happening!'

Tyson was immediately serious. 'If either of you have suffered any indignities I want to know about it and action will be taken.'

Sophie sighed. 'You can sleep dreamlessly, we are both still virgins.'

'Stop it, Sophie, stop trying to be a show-off, it does not become any young lady.' Tyson looked angry.

They had to stop to say goodbye to their host and hostess and thank them for a wonderful evening. Then Mrs Denton was there, apologising to the girls for sending them home before the party was over. It was her husband's wish.

Tyson led the way down the gangplank, the straight set of his shoulders somehow showing disapproval and when they stepped on to the quayside he turned to Sophie.

'I suggest you guard your tongue, Sophie, it could get you into trouble.' Then after a pause he added softly, 'Believe me, it is sensible.'

Sophie laughed. 'Do you know something, Tyson de Auberleigh? For the first time in my life I find myself liking you.'

His eyebrows went up. 'You mean you have never . . .?'

He looked so astonished Francine found her lips twitching. Sophie patted him on the arm and grinned. 'But from now on I'll make it up to you.'

To this he replied smiling, 'Now I know you are bound for trouble.'

Tyson took them to the carriage and Bridget greeted them and asked if they had enjoyed the evening.

They both said yes indeed. The carriage moved away and they leaned forward to wave to Tyson. Sophie kept on waving but Francine found herself taking in the scene, the stars with their shimmering brilliance vying with the moving reflections of lights from portholes and decks on

121

the water; and she suddenly felt tears spring to her eyes, without really knowing why.

CHAPTER TEN

Sophie talked non-stop about the events of the evening while they were undressing and continued when they were in bed.

During their train journey to the Principality, Bridget had told them the history of Monte Carlo, but although she had mentioned that members of royalty of many countries had visited Monte Carlo over the years and gambled heavily, it was Sophie who passed on overheard conversations of the adults to Francine about the mistresses of various men.

It was gossip Sophie had overheard on the yacht that evening. There were women who were unhappy either because their husbands were tight on the purse-strings or spent too much time with their mistresses. Then in the next breath she added, 'But then of course, there are the women who cuckold their husbands.'

Cuckolding was a new word to Francine and when she asked what it meant Sophie said, 'It's the opposite to men taking women to their beds, of course.'

'But why do they?' Francine asked.

'Because they fancy them, I suppose, like we take a fancy to different young men.'

'But we don't go to bed with them.'

'Because we're not married to them. Glyn's father apparently has a mistress, a beauty by all accounts, but she leads him a merry dance. He's a banker and should be more circumspect. Glyn likes the ladies too. I think he's fun to be with but I would never marry him,' Sophie laughed. 'Not that I'm likely to get the chance. He'll be married, I'm sure, before I even have the chance to finish school. You made quite a hit this evening with a lot of

123

people, Francine. You seemed to get on very well with Peter, do you like him?'

Francine said yes and because she knew she was not going to get an opportunity of thinking over what Lord Holcombe had told her she pleaded tiredness and told Sophie they would talk again in the morning.

But Sophie was too wide awake to settle for sleep.

'Tell me, Francine, what were you and Lord Holcombe discussing so earnestly? I had a feeling he had taken to you.'

Francine hesitated. Although Sophie enjoyed gossip she could keep a secret if asked. She had proved this during all the years of friendship and it would be so good to talk over the problem with Sophie. Francine drew herself up in the bed.

'Sophie, I'm going to tell you something but it must not go any further.'

'It won't, I promise.' Sophie exuded excitement.

After Francine had explained about the conversation between Lord Holcombe and herself, Sophie had it all settled.

'But of *course* Madame Dupont is your mother. In the first place, you have this strong resemblance to her. Secondly, there is the name Gabrielle.' Sophie began ticking the items off on her fingers. 'Thirdly, she was married to a photographer. Photographers do *not* hang from trees! Then there is the time sequence. Lord Holcombe said he first met her fourteen or fifteen years ago, and you were told your mother had died when you were very young. Francine, this woman just *has* to be your mother. I would accept *one* coincidence, but there are so many signposts here leading to a relationship with her.'

Francine felt a shivery excitement run through her. Her very own mother . . . She daydreamed for a moment then reality crept in. She looked at Sophie, a fear in her eyes.

'But why did my mother leave? Had *she* been having

124

an affair? My father has no time for me. Oh, Sophie, supposing I'm . . . illegitimate?'

Sophie eyed her in a speculative way for a moment then shook her head.

'No, I'm sure you're not. If your father had had an inkling that you were not his own daughter he would not have brought you to live with him when you were younger, or fed and clothed you and paid for your education.'

This made sense to Francine and relief flooded over her, but she still found it difficult to understand why her mother had made no attempt to get in touch with her over the years. She could have done so while she had been living with her aunt Amelia. But then Amelia was deeply religious, and even though her sister might not have had an actual affair, but might just have fallen in love with some other man, she would still have considered it a sin.

Sophie commented, 'Do you know, Francine, I don't think this is the last you'll hear of your mother. Lord Holcombe will probably think about it at some quiet moment and decide to pursue it.'

'It would be wonderful to find out if Madame Dupont is my mother,' Francine said, a wistful note in her voice. 'Papa and Aunt Amelia are the only close relatives I have. Papa doesn't want me and even Aunt Amelia doesn't bother to write.'

'But you have us,' Sophie said earnestly. 'Mama loves you as a daughter and to me you're a sister.'

'I know Sophie, and I do appreciate it. It seemed fated that we had to meet at school.'

And there were also the O'Reillys who were family too, Francine thought. She should be grateful. But it didn't stop her wanting to know more about the woman who could be her mother.

They were settling for sleep when Sophie said she wondered what the next day would bring. Glyn had mentioned they would probably see them on the beach. At that moment Francine was not sure she wanted to see

Peter; it was more important to have time on her own to sort things out in her mind.

The following morning Bridget insisted that the girls sat quietly for a while on the beach, as they had had a late night. There was plenty to observe, for there were many more people than before on the beach.

This was true. People were arriving in quite large family parties. Deck chairs had already been set up and servants were in attendance to see everyone settled.

One party had servants setting up small tables, laying out champagne bottles in ice buckets. Although all the women were wearing large-brimmed hats, they held parasols too.

When they were all seated an elderly autocratic-looking woman lit a cheroot and observed other groups in the vicinity through lorgnettes. Bridget said smiling that she doubted whether anyone could put *that* lady in her place!

When Bridget agreed to the girls going for a walk and Sophie suggested looking for Glyn and Peter, Francine said she needed solitude. Sophie glanced at her, said she understood and asked how long Francine needed. It was agreed they would try and meet in twenty minutes.

Francine was looking about her for a quieter part of the beach when she saw Tyson. Her heart gave a little lurch. He was walking towards the water's edge deep in thought. He stopped and gazed out to sea and Francine saw an air of desolation about him. She walked slowly towards him. When she spoke his name he turned to her, startled. 'Francine, hello, I was miles away.'

'Where were you?' she asked lightly. 'On an ocean-going liner?'

'Not quite. Perhaps on a yacht, one belonging to Octavia's parents – they left this morning for a few days' cruise along the coast.'

'And you weren't invited?'

A wry smile touched his lips. 'Unhappily, Octavia and I quarrelled last night.'

'Well, you know the saying, absence makes the heart grow fonder!'

'It's a fallacy. She's a desirable young lady and there are other men aboard. She could be engaged when she returns.'

'If so, then you will not be the loser, will you?'

Tyson eyed her with a steady gaze. 'Quite the sage, aren't you?'

'Well, surely it makes sense.' Francine now spoke seriously. 'If a girl switches her affection from one man to the other in a matter of days then she couldn't really be in love with the first man, could she?'

Tyson was looking at her in a slightly amused way when Sophie came up.

'Hello, I was looking for Francine then saw you together having such an earnest conversation.'

'Francine is a very interesting young lady. In a few words she has freed me from the bondage of love.'

Francine said in alarm, 'Oh, no, you – I –'

He patted her arm. 'Say no more, dear Francine. Believe me, you have done me a service this morning. There was I in the depths of despair because I had quarrelled with my love and now I find she no longer fits that role.'

His expression was serious but Francine had seen a mischievous glint in his eyes before he asked, 'Shall we take a stroll towards the water's edge?' He held out a curved arm to Sophie and the other to Francine. Sophie hesitated and looked around her and Francine guessed she was thinking of Glyn and Peter, but she accepted the invitation.

'Why not? After all Tyson, you are quite a personable young man to be seen with.'

He inclined his head. 'Thank you, cousin, for those kind words. And now shall we view the revellers who are enjoying the sun and their wine?'

Several groups were drinking wine, with servants hovering. The colourful dresses and parasols of the women

127

and striped blazers of some of the men, and the bright chatter and bursts of laughter made for an air of conviviality. Francine found herself enjoying the morning.

Tyson had been discussing various people on the beach when after a pause he said, 'Who are you looking for, Sophie?'

'No one in particular,' she replied, her tone casual. Then she added, 'At least, Mr Kingsley and Mr Jordan did say they would see us on the beach this morning.'

'Then you had no right to agree. You are two unchaperoned young ladies.'

'I thought we were *well* chaperoned at the moment,' she retorted. 'And if we had met them we would simply have exchanged pleasantries and walked on.'

'Good. It seemed to me you were exchanging a great many pleasantries with the young men last night and I did warn you about Jordan.'

Sophie stopped and withdrew her arm. 'And since when did you become my keeper? My mother was never far away from us. If you had been so concerned you would have noticed. But you were too wrapped up in that – that she-wolf Octavia.'

Tyson threw back his head and laughed. 'Oh, she would be surprised to hear herself called such a name. And for your information, cousin dear, I was well aware of what was going on all the time last evening. I know that quite a few men showed an interest in both you and Francine.'

'Very true, but then if you were such a dedicated watchdog then you must also have noticed that we were with a small party of people most of the time and my mother must have approved or she would have taken Francine and I away.'

'Of course. I was simply trying to point out that you ought not to make assignations with young men on the beach, or anywhere else for that matter.'

Sophie threw up her hands. 'Now it's an assignation!

128

You do realise of course that you are including Francine in these supposedly underhand dealings?'

Tyson turned swiftly to Francine, who had drawn slightly apart from them.

'Francine, forgive me, I had no intention of doing any such thing. Sophie has totally misinterpreted my meaning. I only want to protect you from men like Glyn Jordan.'

Sophie glared at him. 'Francine is not besotted with Peter Kingsley, nor am I with Glyn Jordan, not like you are besotted with Octavia Manning. We have more sense than to get involved with anyone. Satisfied? Now if you will allow us to walk along the beach to where our chaperone is awaiting we will take our leave.'

But before Sophie could storm away they were being hailed by Lord Holcombe, waving a silver-topped cane. He was wearing a cream suit and his panama hat was set at a jaunty angle. He raised it as he reached them. 'Good morning. I spotted you all and thought it would be good to have some young company for a change. I've been plagued by that doddering and boring old wretch Fellsworthy. Couldn't get away from him, he kept hanging on to my arm.' He gave them a beaming smile. 'And how are you all this exquisite morning?'

'Splendid,' enthused Tyson.

'Bad-tempered,' declared Sophie. 'My cousin is trying to play the heavy father and telling Francine and I what we should and should not do.'

'And that is not such a bad thing, my dear, if the advice is sound. What do you say. Miss Chayter?'

Francine, whose heart had given a lurch when he hailed them, smiled. 'I think Mr de Auberleigh was being overly worried that we might be molested by young men because we were unchaperoned for a while.'

'And he was right. There are some rather wild young men about who would very quickly take advantage of two charming young ladies on their own. On the other hand –' he was now addressing Tyson, 'I found these same

129

young ladies most sensible last night, both in their speech and behaviour.'

Sophie laughed. 'Bravo, sir, thank you.'

Tyson smiled and gave the old man a slight bow. 'I concede to your experience, my lord. I think perhaps I was over zealous in my duty.'

'That is a very generous admission, my boy. Now then, I will tell you what I particularly want to mention. I've been asked by friends to invite some guests to a Bal Masqué next week, and I wondered if you and the young ladies would be interested. Your families too, will of course be invited.'

Tyson was all smiles. 'It sounds delightful, sir, and I'm sure I can accept on behalf of myself and the girls, and the families.'

'Oh, yes,' breathed Sophie and Francine in unison.

'Splendid.' Lord Holcombe gave a slight bow. 'Now that this is settled, I shall take my leave of you and indulge in my morning pastime for an hour. And trust I don't lose my all on the spin of the wheel.'

'Don't you dare, sir,' Tyson teased, 'or you will plunge our spirits to zero.'

'And we can't have that, my boy, can we?' He raised his hat, bade them au revoir and left, walking with buoyant steps.

'A Bal Masqué,' Sophie said, eyes shining. 'How wonderful.'

All animosity between Sophie and Tyson was forgotten as they discussed the invitation and what roles they should assume for the fancy dress ball. Sophie told Tyson he should go as the devil because he had a devil's peak in his hair but Tyson said there would be plenty of devils there without adding another.

He walked along the beach with them and although Francine noticed Glyn and Peter talking to a group of people, Sophie had obviously not seen them so Francine made no mention of it.

Some people hailed Tyson and when he asked to be excused for a moment Sophie took Francine's arm. 'Come along and we'll tell Bridget about the invitation.'

But Bridget had news for them. The family, including the girls, had an invitation from Lord Holcombe to dine at his hotel that evening.

After lunch when the girls were alone Sophie said to Francine, 'You were responsible for the invitation from Lord Holcombe. He's taken with you, he never took his eyes from you last night and this morning when we met. I wouldn't be surprised if he asked for your hand in marriage.'

Francine was indignant. What nonsense, Lord Holcombe was old enough to be her grandfather. Sophie seemed to see this as no obstacle.

'Think of all the advantages – travelling, having your own way. No more school. You could perhaps take up photography at last. A young girl can always twist an older man around her finger.'

'Sophie, stop this nonsense at once or I won't go tonight.'

'All right, all right, I won't say any more. What dress are you going to wear?'

'The green, I feel happy in it, like I do the white muslin.'

Sophie approved the green frock and said that Francine looked lovely and very grown up in it.

Before they left they learned that Lord Holcombe had a suite of rooms in the Hotel de Paris, which was next to the casino. Francine had been impressed by the buildings at a distance but seeing them at close quarters gave her a breathless feeling. It was all so beautiful, the gardens, the flowers, the tree-lined walks, the casino with its gleaming copper roof and the Moorish embellishments, the twin towers and lovely facade of the hotel.

And then there were the elegantly dressed, bejewelled women stepping out of carriages and the equally elegant men in evening dress.

131

They were met by Lord Holcombe who took them to a small salon for drinks. Mrs Denton allowed the girls to have a small glass of wine, which had Sophie muttering that the quantity was not likely to go to their heads!

There were two other guests, friends of Lord Holcombe, a Mrs Freech-Taylor and her daughter Honor. The girl, who was tall and fair and seemed aloof turned out to be most pleasant and chatted freely to Francine and Sophie. The pair were here for only a few days then were going on to Nice.

Then somehow Honor and Tyson were holding an animated conversation. Francine thought Tyson looked more handsome than ever with his skin lightly tanned and she had to force herself to stop gazing at him. It did occur to her that men were fickle. Only that morning, Tyson had been miserable over Octavia and now, judging by his attitude towards Honor it seemed to be a case of off with the old and on with the new.

Before they went in to dinner Lord Holcombe spoke quietly to Francine, saying he had something important to say to her. Francine panicked. Had Sophie been right and he was going to propose to her? His next words had her heart pounding.

'I telephoned Madame Dupont in Paris this afternoon. She is your mother, my dear, and is anxious to meet you. We must talk about it some other time. I felt sure the news would add to your enjoyment of the evening.' He was beaming at her.

Add to her enjoyment? Francine felt that her whole body had turned to jelly. How was she going to sit down to dinner when she was aching to know more details about this mother she had thought to be dead.

A manservant came to announce that dinner was ready and it took Francine all her strength to smile at Lord Holcombe and thank him for his kindness.

Then they were all on their feet and moving towards the dining room.

CHAPTER ELEVEN

Afterwards, Francine wondered how she had sat through a seven-course meal without having been aware of what she had eaten.

The ladies did not as was usual leave the men to their port and cigars; it was the wish of Lord Holcombe that they all withdrew to the drawing room for a talk then, later, he would take Francine and Sophie and her parents to have a quick look into the gaming room.

Sophie was responsible for this by asking if it were possible. She had received strong, disapproving looks from her father and a gentle scolding from her mother, but Sophie had simply smiled blandly at Lord Holcombe and thanked him.

They discovered that a tunnel led from the hotel to the gaming rooms and to Sophie at least, it gave an added spice to the adventure. While the visitors waited outside the room Lord Holcombe spoke to someone inside. The next moment they were ushered in, but asked to keep in the background.

All Francine had wanted to do was to get back to the villa where she could share the news of her mother with Sophie, but once inside the casino she found herself caught up in the atmosphere. Although a gaming salon was a far cry from a church Francine had the same feeling of awe, of timelessness and of history as she had in church.

In the chill of the stone edifice of God's house, with candles flickering she would think of the countless thousands of people who must have come to pray over the centuries, people of the soil whose lives and that of their families depended on a good harvest, on them and their cattle having good health in order to exist.

Here in this bright, warmly-lit room people came to pray to the god of gold for a winning streak, people who already had wealth, the famous and the infamous; kings, queens, princes of various lands. There was drama in the sombre-looking walls, people taking their own lives.

People spoke in low voices and the only other sounds were the voices of the croupiers calling to the players to place their bets. Then there was the clicking of the ball as the wheel spun.

The gamblers were mostly men, with only a sprinkling of women playing. One elderly woman, whose face was scored with lines, had a bright, feverish look in her eyes. Her fingers were loaded with rings studded with gems, mostly diamonds, whose facets sparkled under the many lights. She wore a plumed headdress and sat so still she could have been asleep. She had lost twice then she won and her bony fingers were like claws as she drew the chips towards her. She won twice more and although Lord Holcombe said her winnings were high she was as poker-faced as most of the men.

Mrs Denton broke up the visit to the casino by saying that Sophie and Francine must leave, Bridget would be waiting in the carriage for them. When Sophie begged for them to stay a little longer her father said sternly, 'You will leave at once, Sophie and Francine.'

Francine had been hoping that Lord Holcombe might say something about seeing her the following day but when she thanked him for the evening he simply smiled and told her it had been a pleasure having her company.

The girls said goodnight to the others and a servant conducted them to the carriage, with Sophie grumbling at having to leave.

She was still grumbling when they were in the carriage and Bridget told her quietly she should be grateful that Lord Holcombe had included both girls in the invitation. When after a few minutes Francine had made no comments about the evening Bridget wanted to know what was wrong. Francine made the excuse that it had all been so exciting she felt tired, but this did not fool Sophie. The minute they were alone in their room she said, 'I've never known you feel tired through excitement so what happened earlier? I noticed Lord Holcombe having a cosy chat with you. What was that about?'

Francine, who was sitting at the dressing table pulling pins from her hair turned slowly to face her.

'He told me that Madame Dupont *is* my mother and wants to meet me.'

Sophie's whole face lit up. 'I told you she would be, didn't I? Oh, Francine, this is wonderful news. Is she here in Monte Carlo?'

'No, in Paris. How am I going to get to see her, Sophie? I must.' Francine gave a despairing sigh. 'I feel so frustrated. If only Lord Holcombe had told me more. She's *Madame* Dupont so has obviously married again. Is her husband alive, does she have other children?'

Sophie said eagerly, 'My aunt and uncle and family always have a week in Paris on the way home. I don't know if we are to go with them but I can ask Mama. I do think if my uncle knew the reason you wanted to go he would invite us all, if we are not already invited. Men are not supposed to take any interest in such things, but I'm sure they must be intrigued by such a situation as well as the women. And you must admit this *certainly* is intriguing.'

Francine pulled out the rest of the pins holding up her curls and shook out her hair. Then she looked at Sophie, her expression worried.

'My mother must have done something awful for Papa to turn her out of the house and not allow her to take me with her.'

Sophie pulled up a chair and straddled it. 'But was your mother turned out, Francine? She might have run away with some man she had fallen in love with and didn't want the encumbrance of taking you with her.'

When Francine, who could not believe any mother would willingly abandon her child, protested at this, Sophie pointed out gently it was something she might have to face.

'No.' Francine spoke firmly. 'That I refuse to believe. I'm sure it was my father's way of punishing her. He didn't want me but he was determined that she must suffer. And the fact that she wants to see me makes me realise how much she must have suffered over the years. Just imagine your own mother having been parted from Roderick when he was a baby. It would have broken her heart.'

'But my mother is a gentle, loving person, Francine; at the moment your mama is an unknown quantity.'

Francine turned a beseeching gaze on her. 'I have to believe that she didn't just abandon me.'

'Yes, of course. I'll speak to Mama in the morning and find out if we are likely to go to Paris. If not, then you must let Lord Holcombe know and I'm sure that he will arrange something.'

Francine became alarmed. 'No, Sophie, no. If your family will be going straight home after the holiday then I must go with them. Can you imagine my father's reaction if he learned I had stayed behind to visit my mother in Paris? Heavens, it doesn't bear thinking about. Even if I had the opportunity of going to Paris with your parents and the de Auberleighs, how would I dare admit to Papa that I had visited her?'

Sophie said, 'Let's take each hurdle as it comes.'

The next morning Francine learned that the family *were* planning to stay in Paris for a week, on their way home, and that Lord Holcombe would be with them. Francine was quietly excited, Sophie madly so.

Later that day they discussed the fancy dress costumes for the Bal Masqué. Bridget said she would make them if they chose simple styles and, after much deliberation Sophie said she would like to go as a Shepherdess and suggested Francine go as a witch, pointing out that no one would guess their identity. She was no simple shepherdess! And who would ever think of Francine as a witch?

As the costumes took shape the girls' excitement grew. But for Francine the main reason for going to the ball was the anticipation of perhaps having an opportunity to question Lord Holcombe further about her mother.

Bridget proved to be a wizard at making certain items. She constructed a cone of cardboard for the witch's pointed hat, covered it with black sateen and skilfully attached a covered brim. She produced some old wire, shaped it into a shepherd's crook and wound narrow strips of cotton around it, for Sophie. To make Francine look old she combed out some grey yarn to create a wig. A broomstick was borrowed from the gardener, and an ankle-length cloak completed Francine's costume to perfection.

Sophie's outfit consisted of a full hessian skirt, white apron, a laced-up bodice with full sleeves and a mobcap to go over a wig of black yarn, which fell in two plaits over her shoulders.

Both girls shrieked in delight when they had a dress rehearsal the night before the ball and saw their reflections in the mirror. They donned their masks and Sophie asked who could possibly recognise them. She wore a black half-mask with sheep's eyes painted on it (her own work) while Francine's was a full one of a witch's face, which had been bought. It was a really evil face, and when Francine raised the broomstick and cried in a croaking voice, 'I lay my curse on you,' Sophie, Mrs Forbes and Bridget all dissolved into laughter, although Roderick looked tearful.

As Bridget wiped her eyes she said to Francine, 'You do realise, of course, that this costume is going to repel all the young men?'

'On the contrary,' Sophie exclaimed, 'it will draw them – they will all want to know who she is. Everyone is curious about the person they fail to recognise at once. It's a test of their skill. Nothing gives them greater pleasure than to announce, "*I* know who you are", and then give the name. They are children, they have to be shown to be clever among their friends.'

Bridget was still smiling. 'You seem to be an expert on men, young lady.'

'I am. So is Francine. She observes their expressions, sees them through the lens of a camera, as it were. I read their minds.'

There was silence for a moment then Bridget said, 'Well now! After all that clever observation shall we pack the costumes ready for tomorrow evening?'

The older people had decided to go in evening dress but Tyson's three sisters came down wearing medieval costumes and sporting decorated silver half-masks. His two brothers appeared as cowled monks.

Mr de Auberleigh gave his approval to the costumes, with a special mention of Francine's. 'Excellent, my dear, excellent. It should be a good evening. Are we all ready? Tyson has gone ahead with friends. I have no idea who he is representing. It could be an executioner or a court jester.' He sounded annoyed that Tyson was not travelling with them.

As they prepared to leave Bridget and Mrs Forbes came to wish them well and Francine noticed some of the servants peeping over the landing rail.

The gaiety started almost as soon as the carriages had reached the road. Other carriages carrying revellers converged and laughing greetings were exchanged by the men, with promises to have drinks together when they arrived.

It was not until they were on their way that the girls learned that the ball was to take place in a château. It was quite a long drive but with everyone in such a good humour it was not important.

When Francine caught her first sight of the château she drew in a quick breath at its beauty. It was ablaze with lights but what caught her imagination were the many turrets and the crenellated battlements against the sky of indigo velvet, where stars were diamonds and the Milky Way a path of seed pearls leading to paradise. A truly fairy castle.

Francine smiled to herself, thinking it was no place for a witch to be.

As they drove through parkland along a tree-lined drive the sounds of revelry came to their ears, and when they reached the forecourt it was like being caught up in a world of make-believe. Men in animal costumes played Ring of Roses with Bo Peep; two clowns rubbed shoulders with a circus trainer and a bear. A parson and a cardinal were talking to Romeo and Juliet.

Then a man came to usher everyone indoors and Francine and Sophie and their party joined other revellers who were moving up a magnificent marble staircase where they were to be greeted by their host and hostess. Above all the chatter and laughter could be heard the muted strains of an orchestra, playing a plaintive air.

On the staircase were pirates, matadors, gondoliers, jugglers, a number of Madame Pompadours, serving wenches, Can-Can girls, queens, flower sellers . . . but so far Francine had not seen another witch.

The person Francine was hoping to identify her was Lord Holcombe. There were so many questions she wanted to ask him, but the ballroom was crowded and seeing so many people milling around it seemed an impossibility to single out one person. Mrs Denton kept saying she knew this person and that but when Francine asked casually if she could see Tyson, Mrs Denton laughed. 'Now that is something to tease your mind, Francine dear.' In the next breath she said to Sophie, 'Oh, there is your father's friend Mr Frobisher in the role of executioner and he, dear man, would weep if someone killed a fly. Astonishing, isn't it?'

Francine wondered what character Lord Holcombe would choose to represent. He was a gambler, had fun in him. A clown? A juggler? And what about Tyson? He, she felt sure, would choose someone adventurous, a high-wayman or pirate. There were a number of these characters.

Two men, one dressed as a court jester and the other as a magician, approached Mrs Denton and asked permission to dance with the young ladies. When it was given and the girls accepted, the magician held out his hand to Francine and said in a throaty voice, 'Will you do me the honour, Mamselle Witch?'

Francine got up and replied in squeaky tones, 'Thank you, M'sieu,' and added, 'I think we are well matched, but when we dance will you make allowances for my great age?'

'Of course, but being a magician I can make you any age you wish to be, sixteen, seventeen, eighteen.'

'Eighteen I think, M'sieu, for I cannot remember being that age.'

'Then I shall be twenty, no twenty-two, and we shall dance on clouds.' He led her on to the floor and when Francine looked back she saw that Sophie was already placed with her court jester. And it was then that Francine had a little sneaky feeling that their partners could be Glyn and Peter. They were the right heights and it was the sort of thing she felt Glyn would do, switching partners.

It was a waltz and the magician said, 'You are an exquisite dancer, Mamselle Witch.'

'But as the partner of a magician, how could I be otherwise?'

'Ah, but if I wished I could make you trip. I am a wicked man.'

Being masked, Francine became bold. 'I adore wicked men, they are so much more interesting, exciting.'

'Wonderful, wonderful! I will not allow you to escape me at midnight.'

Midnight, the unmasking . . . Francine suddenly experi-enced some qualms. If her partner happened to be a

140

stranger, or even if he were Glyn, she had laid herself open for liberties to be taken with her bold statement that she adored wicked men.

But the next moment she dismissed this thought. No person could take anyone seriously at a Bal Masqué.

When the dance was over and her partner brought her back to her seat he demanded to sign her card for at least three more dances, or he would turn her back into being two hundred years old again. Francine laughingly accepted.

When the two men had bowed themselves away Sophie said, 'I had a suspicion that I was dancing with Peter and that you were with Glyn.'

As Sophie did not seem put out by this Francine told her that she had thought the same thing, then added, 'Glyn will ask you for some dances later, I'm sure.'

To this Sophie laughed. 'And I shall surprise him and refuse. By the way, I recognised Tyson – he's a French Lieutenant wearing a dark beard but he forgot to wear a wig to match. He does have a very military bearing. He will be loving himself! I don't care who I dance with, I just want my card filled.'

Francine was not surprised that Sophie was approached for dances but was astonished that she herself should have so many partners when her mask was so revolting.

She danced with all sorts of characters, but because they all tried to keep their identity secret by disguising their voices she was not certain she had danced with any man she knew. One time she was sure that the king she was waltzing with was Lord Holcombe, but then a girl passing called, laughingly, 'Don't forget, Henri, that you promised the next waltz to me.' He called that he would not forget and Francine felt thwarted.

Although Francine enjoyed the fun she found herself longing for midnight to come, not only to be able to ask Lord Holcombe about her mother but to be able to discard her mask which was becoming more and more uncomfortable.

She was dancing with her magician again when he said. 'The witching hour is approaching; then we shall know the truth.'

Francine's heart began to race. He had dropped his throaty tones and spoken softly and she knew then he was not Glyn. Her face burned at the way she had talked so glibly of adoring wicked men.

A clock began to chime the hours of midnight and as people tore off their masks there were shouts and laughter. 'It's you! . . . Oh, you fooled *me* . . . I never guessed . . . I knew, of course it was you . . .'

Tyson, after removing his own mask and magician's hat, took off Francine's mask and wig and dropped them on the floor. Then, drawing her to him he kissed her gently on the lips, murmuring, 'I think I've fallen in love with you, dear Francine.'

Francine was unable to answer for the restriction in her throat.

The next moment three men came up and one slapped Tyson on the back. 'Honor said it was you, but I didn't believe her. Come along, we're all over there.'

Tyson tried to protest as they dragged him away, but then someone took Francine by the hand and was saying urgently, 'Come with me, my dear, we might not have another chance of a talk.'

It was Lord Holcombe in the robes of a sultan. He took her into an anteroom and there told her about her mother.

CHAPTER TWELVE

Three days after the Bal Masqué everything still had an air of unreality to Francine. Even the story of her mother seemed unreal too, although she desperately wanted to believe it.

'Gabrielle is tall and very beautiful,' Lord Holcombe had said 'She's fair in colouring, Francine, and has a great warmth. Men adore her but she is most circumspect. She told me that after her marriage she had a mild flirtation, nothing more, but your father accused her of having an affair and turned her out of the house and eventually disowned her. She assures me that you *are* his child and I believe her.'

'Papa will never accept me as his daughter,' Francine said bitterly. 'I'm sure of it. I think he hates me.'

'Your mother took you to your Aunt Amelia until she could make a home for you, but when she had and came back for you your aunt refused to hand you over.'

Francine was indignant. 'Why? What right had she to keep me from my mother?'

'Because she believed that your mother *had* been having an affair and that she was unfit to bring you up. And your mother could not apply to the courts because of involving the man she had flirted with. He not only held a position in high places, but he was married with children.'

Francine was silent and Lord Holcombe touched her hand gently. 'But quite soon now you shall be reunited and what a wonderful occasion that will be. I'm so sorry, my dear, that I've been so long in telling you about your mother. I intended to earlier, but no sooner had we arrived than an old friend of mine took ill and I've been with him until now.' He smiled. 'All my dressing up for nothing. I

143

didn't recognise you in *your* costume, and I'm quite sure no one else would.'

Francine, going over that conversation now thought, oh, yes, Tyson had, but after his declaration that had so moved her she had not seen him since. Sophie told her he was spending a lot of time with Octavia and her family.

Francine had been hurt at first, but had come to accept that he belonged to this unreal world. He had told her he had fallen out with Octavia, then had come to the Bal Masqué with Honor and after making the declaration of love at the unmasking he had not even bothered to seek her out in the hours that followed. The ball had not ended until five o'clock in the morning.

Francine did not tell Sophie about Tyson, but she did recount the story of her mother. Sophie was not impressed: if Gabrielle had been so anxious to have her daughter with her, she would have done something about it before now. When Francine pointed out the difficulties of involving the other man she said – rubbish, that was years ago, it was just an excuse.

Francine thought about this for a while then she said, 'My father always acts as though he detests me, yet he pays for my clothes, my education and this holiday.'

'Perhaps he loves you deep down, but can't show it. Some men are so arrogant they can't show their true feelings.'

Francine found this heart-warming and had hope that her father might truly acknowledge her as his own beloved daughter some day. And although she was longing to go to Paris and meet her mother, and hankered to see Tyson again despite the way he had treated her, she made up her mind to enjoy herself in Monte Carlo, for she might never get the chance to come again.

That same night in bed Sophie declared she was bored being by the sea all the time, she wanted a change. Glyn had met someone else at the ball and had hardly taken any notice of her. He had not asked her for a dance, not even after the unmasking and she said that Peter had not even been at the Bal Masqué. He and his parents were moving on to Nice.

The next morning when Sophie told Bridget that she and Francine wanted to do some walking, Bridget said she would come with them.

During the next two days they visited the harbour, where Sophie drooled over the handsome officers in charge of the yachts, went to the Royal Palace where she fell in love with one of the guards, and explored the small shops in the narrow streets.

One evening they were invited, with Mrs Denton, by Lord Holcombe to go by motor car to the top of La Turbie, where they witnessed the most glorious sunset; the sunsets being a local tourist attraction. The air was cool and seemed to intensify the scents from the orange trees, roses and pine trees.

'How wonderful,' Francine murmured. 'I'll never forget this.'

'And there are more pleasures to come,' Lord Holcombe said softly. 'Paris, your mother. I hope I might have the pleasure of showing you Paris, Francine, for it's a city close to my heart.'

Tyson sprang to Francine's mind. Would he be in Paris with them? At the moment he was on the Mannings' yacht on a trip along the Mediterranean coast. She had a longing to see him.

But Tyson did not return until a couple of days before they were all due to leave for Paris. He glowed with health, his skin was deeply tanned and he looked happier than Francine had ever seen him. He greeted both girls with a kiss on the cheek and asked how they were but before they had a chance to reply he was talking about Octavia and what a wonderful person she was.

Sophie said scathingly afterwards, 'Octavia, Octavia, we'll be hearing about her for weeks ahead. Pray heaven she won't be coming to Paris with us.'

Francine was annoyed with herself for feeling so upset over Tyson's devotion to Octavia, but then she had a letter from Kathleen which restored her good spirits.

Kathleen wrote a newsy letter, telling her about each member of the family. Himself had not been drinking for over a week, then he made up for it by going to three Wakes and not being sober for several days. Herself had ended up throwing a bucket of water over him then was mad that she had mattress and bedding to dry off!

Rory had had a shilling a week rise in his wages from Edwin Chayter and had had a tussle with Herself to let him keep half of it as he wanted to save up for a camera. Rory won.

'Your Da, for some reason, Francine, has been in a better temper this last week. Cook says she thinks he must have fallen in love, but we haven't seen him with anyone. He actually smiled at me yesterday, I got such a shock I nearly fell down the stairs. Sorry, that's not a nice thing to say about your Da, but his smiles are as rare as buttercups in December.

'More nice news. Evie is walking out with a lad called Jackie Pennystone. Cook says he must only be "tenpence to the shilling" to be walking out with Evie, but I like him and Evie is over the moon about it. She actually looked quite pretty the other evening when she was going to meet him. If that's what love does I'd better start falling in love! I've been looking quite haggard lately. Old age creeping on!'

Francine smiled at this. Kathleen had a rare beauty with her jet black hair, lovely blue eyes and red lips. Wherever she went she drew the attention of men. But why did she not get married? She must be twenty-four or twenty-five. Women were considered to be settled into spinsterhood at that age. Oh, no, Kathleen would never end her days a spinster, she was too warm, too loving. Perhaps she had simply not met a man yet she wanted to marry.

146

After Sophie had read the letter she remarked sagely, 'Kathleen's probably in love with your father.'

Francine looked at her wide-eyed. 'In love with Papa? Oh, no, she couldn't be. He's so cold and harsh. I don't think he has any love in him to give.'

Sophie grinned. 'I could fall in love with him.'

'Fall in love – with Papa? Sophie, you couldn't! He's – he can be brutal.'

'He's masterful,' she said. 'Women like masterful men.'

'But you've always said you wouldn't be dominated by *any* man.'

'That was before I had grown up.' Sophie's eyes were full of mischief.

Francine dismissed it. 'You haven't grown up, you're behaving more like an infant. What you are saying is utterly ridiculous. Life would be terrible living with someone like Papa.'

'It could be bliss, I think he could be a very passionate man. He must be to have turned your mother out of the house. *He* had to be the master, she was *his* woman. She was a fool to flirt with anyone else. Perhaps children never see their parents as being attractive, but I can assure you, Francine, that your father is a very attractive man. And if he wants a young bride I shall apply.'

Francine got up, saying she refused to discuss such a thing any further but when Sophie said, teasing her, that she might be her stepmother one day Francine began to see the funny side of it and within seconds both girls were laughing.

Later, when Francine went over their conversation in her mind she knew she would never see her father in the role of a loving, attractive husband. The hurt of his brutality toward her would always remain.

As the time drew near for them all to leave for Paris Francine began to worry. Supposing her mother wanted her to come and live with her, would her father allow it? Would she want to live with her mother? The O'Reillys had become her family, how could she bear to leave them? Then there was Sophie, and yes, Tyson. Although she hated to admit it she felt she couldn't bear Tyson to go out of her life, even though he had shown no particular interest in her since the night of the ball. Was this what was meant by being obsessed with someone? On the other hand, she would not want Rory to go out of her life either. But perhaps the love she felt for him was more the love of a sister for a brother. He, like Tyson, had never shown in any way that he would be bereft if she was to go out of his life.

The day before they were due to leave for Paris, Francine was told there had been a change of plan. She was to travel on ahead with Mrs Denton and Lord Holcombe would accompany them. The rest of the party would follow in a few days' time. Some urgent business had cropped up which involved Mr Denton and Mr de Auberleigh.

After much reflection and on the advice of Lord Holcombe, Francine had decided to confide in Sophie's mother about Gabrielle, and now both families were aware of the delicate situation.

Francine was about to ask if Sophie could travel with them when Mrs Denton forestalled her by saying, 'Lord Holcombe thinks that perhaps it has all turned out for the best. It will give you a chance to have a restful journey to prepare you for meeting your mother. Sophie, bless her, can be quite excitable. That is why my sister has stayed behind, to keep an eye on her.' Mrs Denton smiled.

Sophie was indignant about being left in Monte Carlo. 'I know why, of course. It's simply a ruse for his lordship to have you more or less on your own so you can get to know him. I would lay a bet that he'll have proposed to you before we arrive.'

Francine, who had vaguely been aware of some manoeuvring about the travelling arrangements was uneasy but she said firmly, 'Well, if that is so he'll be wasting his time. I am not prepared to marry anyone and no one can make me.'

'Good. That is what I wanted to hear. Oh, Francine, I so wish I was coming with you.'

Francine consoled her. They would meet again in a few days' time and she would have a store of things to tell her.

Mrs Denton and Francine left at six o'clock the following morning. Sophie, her aunt Leonora and surprisingly, Mr de Auberleigh, got up to see them off. Mrs Denton made the excuse that her husband was sleeping heavily and she had not the heart to rouse him, adding that he would be upset when he knew they had gone.

To this Sophie whispered to Francine, '*Not* Papa.'

Then they were getting in the carriage. Lord Holcombe was to meet them at the station.

Francine found the lengthy journey to Paris not only pleasantly restful but vastly interesting, as Lord Holcombe had a deep knowledge of the city's history.

'Do you know it is built on chalk?' he began, and when Francine and Mrs Denton exclaimed, 'Chalk?' he laughed and assured them that Paris was not likely to collapse while they were there. There were deeper deposits of sand, limestone, clay and plaster.

He told them that at one time the people used to draw their water from an artesian well and that now the statue of Louis Pasteur stands on the site. He described how a primitive company of tribes were formed and how the men knew how to polish stone, how to weave cloth and till the soil, and spoke of the Celtic invasion of 500 BC and then went through the subsequent eras and the building of Paris. Francine was fascinated.

'Paris is a city of contrasts,' he mused, his expression gentle. 'She has beautiful buildings and wide boulevards, but she also has her little alleyways, her rabbit warrens and hovels. Despite the grandeur, you will always be able to find the herbalists, the little milliners and dressmakers and never will the tiny cafés be done away with. I will show you the beauty, Francine, but I will also show you the poverty.'

Once when Lord Holcombe had gone to speak to friends on the train Francine said, 'What a wonderful man he is. What knowledge he has, how interesting he makes history. I wish he had been my teacher.'

'I'm very fond of him,' Mrs Denton said. 'I know he gambles heavily, but many people have learned from his tolerance, his philosophy. He's so pleased that he's been responsible for arranging this meeting with your mother. His own mother died when he was a baby and like you, Francine, an aunt brought him up in his early years, a cold woman with no love to give. But of course in your case, your aunt did care for you. His father spent most of his time abroad.'

'Did Lord Holcombe marry?'

'Yes, but tragedy dogged him. Four years after they were married his wife gave birth to a son. The baby was stillborn and his wife died the following day.'

'Oh, Mrs Denton, how absolutely awful. Did he never think of marrying again?'

'There have been women in his life, but he's never seriously contemplated re-marrying. This is what he told me. Sometimes I wish I could have been his daughter and given him love.'

After this, Francine felt a great affinity with Lord Holcombe and wished that she, too, was in a position to show him affection. She was glad she knew about his life, glad she had been able to travel with just these two people, or she would never have learned about the private tragedies, or known the gentle relationship that had seemed to grow between Mrs Denton and Lord Holcombe during the journey.

As the train approached Paris Francine became aware of some of the poverty that Lord Holcombe had mentioned. She saw rows of houses that were just hovels.

But once they arrived at the Gare du Nord she was caught up in the cosmopolitan atmosphere; all was bustle and noise and there were many tongues being spoken. They were to stay at an hotel which Lord Holcombe made his home whenever he was in Paris. It was about a ten-minute drive, he said. It was nearly midnight but it could have been midday judging by the number of people abroad and the traffic.

Francine had found a magic in Monte Carlo the night they had arrived, in the lighted villas and the stars so large and twinkling. Here, people thronged the pavements, some walking decorously, others in high spirits. A group of young men in evening dress – 'slightly inebriated' said Lord Holcombe – teased passers-by who all seemed to take it in good part. Elegantly dressed men and women stepped out of chauffeur-driven motor cars and went into restaurants.

Their hotel was in a quiet thoroughfare and had a sombre air. The walls were panelled in dark oak; carpets, curtains and bedcovers were in muted tones, and yet Francine had a feeling of homeliness. Lord Holcombe had suggested ordering a meal but Mrs Denton said she was ready to retire, and although Francine would have liked to have stayed up she thought it wise to say that she was tired, too. They arranged to breakfast together at ten o'clock.

A middle-aged maid, a motherly woman, came to attend to Francine. She ran a bath for her, brought warm towels and afterwards offered to brush her hair. Francine accepted and enjoyed the luxury. The woman, whose name was Thérèse, asked her about London, for she had a daughter who had married and gone to live there, but she had never been herself.

Her daughter, it turned out, lived in the dockland area. Francine was delighted to describe the area to her; the East Enders were wonderful, warm-hearted people, with so much humour. Thérèse beamed at her but there were tears in her eyes as she told her how much she missed her daughter. Still, it made her happy to know she lived among such people.

Because of this conversation, Francine went to bed with thoughts of her dear O'Reilly family. And possibly because they were last in her thoughts before she drifted into sleep she dreamed about Rory. He was scolding her for having taken a photograph of her mother that made her look ugly. 'She's a beautiful woman,' he shouted at her. 'Why did you make her look like a witch? Tyson de Auberleigh has tainted your mind with evil.' Rory lifted her on to a high shelf and told her she must sit there until she could think beautiful thoughts. But no sooner was he about to move away when he turned and lifted her down. Then he kissed her and told her he had loved her from the first day they had met.

Francine awoke to find it still dark, her heart racing. What an odd dream. Why should the word evil come into it? She knew her mother was beautiful and why should Rory say that Tyson had tainted her mind? Had she perhaps tried to make him jealous when she wrote glowingly of Tyson to Kathleen? One could do things unconsciously, she had learned that at school. She had been disappointed that Tyson had not bothered to get up to say goodbye to them when they left Monte Carlo. But why should she be disappointed? She meant nothing to him, he had proved that. Octavia was obviously the kind of girl he wanted. Would she be coming to Paris with the de Auberleighs? Francine tossed restlessly. She must forget Tyson. Once they were home again, it was unlikely she would be coming into contact with him. Her mind ranged over every member of the O'Reilly family, over the night of the Bal Masqué before she fell asleep again.

She awoke to find daylight and a fire blazing in the grate. She had not heard a sound. Sun touched the rooftops opposite, dispelling the unhappy part of her dream.

It was the day she was to meet her mother! She flung back the bedclothes.

But at breakfast Lord Holcombe told her she would not be seeing her mother until the following day. A message had been left at the desk early that morning. He offered no explanation and Francine refrained from asking. She was deeply hurt that she had waited so long to meet her mother and now their meeting had to be postponed. What else could be more important? She felt suddenly bitter. Probably a simple thing like a fitting with her dressmaker.

After breakfast Mrs Denton said gently, 'I know how you feel, Francine. I could see your disappointment when you learned that you would not be seeing your mother today. Unfortunately she is governed by her work, and an extra rehearsal had been arranged.'

Francine looked at her bewildered. 'Rehearsal?'

'Your mother is an actress, Francine. She didn't want us to tell you, but I feel you have a right to know.'

An actress . . . Francine found it difficult to take in. Had she always been in the acting profession, was that why her father had turned her out?

In answer to Francine's question, Mrs Denton said she thought it was probably something Gabrielle had taken up to make a living, after arriving in Paris.

Lord Holcombe said with a forced brightness, 'The day will soon pass, Francine, we shall go sightseeing. There is so much to show you.'

Francine made an effort to respond. It was not Lord Holcombe's fault and by the time they were ready to leave she was beginning to be intrigued about her mother's profession. She made up her mind to enjoy the day if only for Lord Holcombe and Mrs Denton's sake.

Lord Holcombe's knowledge of Paris took the edge off Francine's disappointment. They drove and they walked and as the earlier days of the city began to unfold Francine found it impossible not to be caught up in the atmosphere.

She learned that the Sorbonne had been founded by a

Robert de Sorbonne in the middle of the thirteenth century, and that its art students were the most turbulent of all the pupils. They regularly visited cabarets and places of ill-repute and many of them had to pledge their coats in order to pay their debts.

She also learned that sons of peasants were accepted at the Sorbonne but that they lived in hovels and took their lessons sitting on straw in the streets or in the college. They lived on practically nothing and had only one set of garments to their name, but knew at the end of it there could be honours.

Later Lord Holcombe talked about the many crafts in the city; the weavers all lived together in the Rue de la Tissanderie; the tanners by the waterside and the masons in the Rue de la Mortellerie. He told them about the tailors, how they must cut out their work in their own shop and in view of the public. Material was provided by the customer who must know that no piece of it had been kept by the tailor.

They walked by the Seine and while Lord Holcombe stopped to watch the men fishing on its banks Mrs Denton and Francine explored the many little stalls that sold art prints and postcards, pottery and delicate hand-made shawls. Francine was wondering whether Kathleen would like a small vase with the Eiffel Tower painted on it or one showing the Sacré Coeur, and had one in each hand when a voice behind her said: 'It depends on who the present is for.'

Francine tensed and her heart began a slow pounding. There was only one person with that deep-timbred voice. She turned slowly to find a smiling Tyson.

'Surprised?'

She said yes, but no sound came. She tried again. 'Yes, very. I thought the family were not travelling until a few days' time.'

'They aren't, but I felt I wanted to be in Paris, so I caught the next train after yours. I had no idea where to look for you all today and actually, it is sheer coincidence that we've met like this. How is that for Fate?'

Mrs Denton came up then and her look of astonishment had Tyson laughing. 'Hello, Aunt Helena. Thought I would join your party.'

By this time Lord Holcombe had joined them, and there was so much talking and laughter and explanations that Francine had time to pull herself together. She was quietly pleased when Lord Holcombe said, 'And now we are four! Where shall we go next?'

Francine was content to go anywhere, anywhere Fate would take them. She would be with Tyson. The sun seemed suddenly to be shining a great deal brighter.

CHAPTER THIRTEEN

The rest of the day was pure joy to Francine. They had a light meal then went exploring again. Sometimes the four of them would walk together, but when they had to split up on crowded pavements Lord Holcombe would walk with Mrs Denton and Tyson with Francine.

Tyson mentioned her mother, and sympathised with her. He was gentle and talked softly, saying how much parents meant to a child, although perhaps they did not realise it. When he voiced the wish that Francine and her mother would have a warm relationship together, Francine said she hoped so too, but deep down she doubted it. Just as photography was the most important thing in her father's life, she felt intuitively that acting came first with her mother.

Francine asked Tyson what had made him make up his mind to come to Paris before the rest of his family and he smiled down at her. 'You were the attraction, Francine. I knew I would miss you.'

'Miss me?' Her tone was derisive. 'Oh, Tyson, what a story you tell. After the night of the ball you've practically ignored me. Your attention centres on Octavia.'

'Do you know why I stayed away? Mama advised it. You were young, vulnerable, she said. It was not fair to you for me to pay you attention. Then, oddly enough, when I told her I had made up my mind to come to Paris she encouraged me. You know how she detests Octavia . . . Anyway, she gave me the name of the hotel where you'd all be staying. I must have just missed you all this morning. But she also told me I was to treat you as a sister.' He gave a shout of laughter, looked around him then said soberly, 'A sister? I'm head over heels in love with you.'

Francine felt a tremor go through her. 'Don't,' she said quietly. 'Don't say such a thing, it's wrong when you can't possibly mean it.'

He stopped, turned her to face him and looked deeply into her eyes. 'I was never more serious about anything in my whole life. I laughed, yes, because it seemed ludicrous to me to think of you as a sister when my emotions are in such a turmoil.'

Francine looked away from him then seeing Mrs Denton glancing over her shoulder she said, 'We must walk on, your aunt is looking for us.'

They walked on and because of what he had told her and because of his closeness she felt herself trembling. She stared straight ahead. 'I can't accept that you're in love with me, Tyson. Only a short while ago you were in love with Octavia.'

'No, not in love, I was besotted with her. Every man, every woman, is besotted with someone in their lifetime. I soon realised that I was just another conquest to her. I told her this, and after I had done so I felt better. I knew that when you had come into my thoughts so much, yes, even when I was with Octavia, that it had to be love for you. I knew a tenderness towards you that I had never experienced with anyone else. You must believe me, Francine.'

She looked at him then and was aware of his emotion. She wanted to tell him that she was already half in love with him, but instead said, 'Your mother was right when she told you I was too young. I like you, Tyson, I like you very much, but I don't want any involvement, not with anyone.'

'Then I have hope that someday you will grow to love me, and what more romantic place could a couple be together than in Paris? I'll make you love me.' He was smiling again, confident he could win her over, and she could not feel annoyed with him because he had charm and was so *very* attractive.

A few minutes later the four of them were together again. Lord Holcombe had mapped out an itinerary, his aim being, he said, to show them the places that many tourists never saw, and for them to see some of the main attractions from a different angle. The actual visits to these places could be undertaken when the rest of the family arrived.

He took them to narrow alleyways, so narrow that neighbours could have shaken hands across them from the windows of the three-storeyed houses. They went to the Rue des Ménétriers, which was the home of the jugglers in the fourteenth century, who had to pay a toll at the Petit Pont by singing a song and exhibiting a performing monkey. The jugglers, Lord Holcombe told them, were skilled also at singing, dancing, reciting, they could play a harp or a bugle, jump through a hoop, bandy jests and show off performing animals.

The jugglers built their own hospital cum church, St Julien des Ménétriers in the Rue St Martin, the beginnings of which were through two of the jugglers meeting a paralysed woman in a go-cart, from which she never moved, living on the alms of the charitable. The paralytic woman was the first patient in the hospital.

Lord Holcombe then took them to the home of a friend of his, where they saw peacocks, which the friend said had been bred there for the past two hundred years. Francine, who had seen only pictures of peacocks, was awed by their beauty, the iridescence of the feathers when their tails were spread in a fan.

From the attic of the house they had a panoramic view. Francine gasped at the cupolas of the Sacré Coeur bathed in a golden glow that seemed to float above the mist on the river Seine; saw a clutter of terracotta chimneys on the old houses of Paris, the irregular rows creating strange patterns. The pots were all different sizes and to Francine they had character, the smaller ones seeming meek, the taller ones arrogant and the tipsy-looking ones held a jauntiness.

Later, they dined in an hotel where they enjoyed canapés de langouste, côtelettes de Chevreuil aux raisins, and savarins Montmorency àla crême, and where from the window, they had a fine view of Notre Dame.

When Mrs Denton asked if it was possible for them to visit Montmartre that evening Lord Holcombe said yes, of course, then proceeded to describe Montmartre in the days of the revolution, as just a hill with a gun on top. 'It was a refuse dump,' he said, 'and stinking.'

Mrs Denton laughed. 'Sir, you are destroying all of my illusions. I was told it was most interesting, that artists sold their paintings there, that it was a romantic place.'

'And so it is.' Lord Holcombe smiled. 'We shall go this evening and we shall all be romantic. I shall pretend that I am young again, and that you, dear lady, are free to be romantic.'

Mrs Denton teased him. It was a dangerous proposition, one that she thought they must dispense with.

'Why?' Tyson asked. 'What is wrong with pretending? We shall be *two* romantic couples out for an evening's stroll. That is, if Francine is agreeable.'

Francine answered lightly that it sounded intriguing and Lord Holcombe said, 'Then it is settled.' There was a look of mischief in his eyes. Warm colour touched Mrs Denton's cheeks, but the glance she gave him held affection.

Francine found herself looking forward to the evening.

And she was not disappointed. From arriving at Montmartre she was caught up in a romantic atmosphere. Young couples were strolling about, their arms around one another's waists, there were girls, their heads resting against a young man's shoulder, something that one did not see in the normal way. There were mixed groups, talking volubly, gesticulating as they tried to put over some point of art. There was laughter, teasing.

Although there were no moon or stars visible, gas lamps cast a warm glow over the cobblestones. Some artists stood beside their displays of paintings, others were working by lamplight. Flames wavered in the slight wind that had arisen and there was a strong smell of tar that reminded Francine of the time she had whooping cough as a child and Aunt Amelia had held her over a workman's tar wagon to give her ease. Aunt Amelia . . . how remote she seemed.

There was a balloon man, a pedlar hawking cheap jewellery, a pieman and a man selling hot potatoes roasted on the glowing coals of a brazier. Tyson said the smells were making him feel ravenous again and suggested they go into one of the many cafés for a nightcap.

The one they chose was crowded, but they were lucky that two couples were vacating a table as they went in. Although there were some people who looked like tourists the rest, judging by their conversation, were art students. Some of them were shabbily dressed; there were those who talked with their hands, were excited, some had pinched faces and looked as if they had not eaten for days, but there were others who joked.

The café was old, the floorboards bare and posters on the walls faded almost into anonymity; but to Francine it was alive with people who had frequented the café in another age. How many artists had become successful, how many had slipped into obscurity? There was a wealth of subjects for any photographer.

After the refreshment they strolled around, looking at the work of the artists. There were landscapes, portraits, studies of dancers, views of Paris and also some paintings that puzzled Francine. To her, they seemed as though the artist had put blobs of various coloured paint on the canvases, or streaks. Then Lord Holcombe brought their attention to a painting a short distance away. 'How clever!

With a few brush strokes the artist has portrayed a starved and shivering mongrel.'

Francine looked at the painting but could find no resemblance to a dog; to her, it was just a black background with brown and dirty grey streaks on it.

Mrs Denton said softly, 'The poor creature, I feel I want to take it home and give it a good meal.'

Tyson remarked that when he had first seen impressionist painting during a previous visit to Paris he felt that he was being duped, but now he was full of admiration for the artists.

Francine looked from one to the other and seeing rapt expressions on their faces felt bewildered. Why was she not able to see a dog?

Lord Holcombe bought the painting for Mrs Denton and asked Francine if she would choose one, not necessarily from this display if she preferred something else. Out of politeness Francine tried to refuse but when Lord Holcombe insisted she looked for something not too large and saw a small, simple country scene. A young man who was standing at the door of a cottage with a lamb in his arms was looking towards mountains which were bathed in mist. The young man reminded her of Rory.

Francine thanked Lord Holcombe and told him that the painting would bring back very happy memories for her. While the artist was trying to find a wrapping for Mrs Denton's painting she was holding it away from her and Francine, glancing at it, was surprised to suddenly have a glimpse of the dog they had been talking about.

'I can't believe that I could see an animal in the painting,' she exclaimed. 'Who are these Impressionists?'

Lord Holcombe explained. 'First there was reality in painting, then with the birth of photography came true reproduction. Artists needed to push aside the barriers of the classical tradition, so they experimented with light and painted broad, general impressions of reality. Is that clear, Francine?'

161

'I – think so.'

The canvases were wrapped and Tyson offered to carry them. As they strolled around they talked art and Francine found the talk most rewarding. Before they left Tyson bought Mrs Denton and Francine a balloon each and told them if they made a wish when they released them the wizard would grant them their wish. Francine was pleased that Tyson had this whimsy in him.

The balloons drifted off into the night and caught up by a current of air were soon whisked away. Under the gas lamp Mrs Denton wore a dreamy expression and Francine wondered what she had wished. Her own wish was that her mother would tell her she had been heart-broken at having to leave her, and give a valid reason for having done so.

They were all exhausted by their sightseeing and were content to return to their hotel. Francine went to bed experiencing the excitement of anticipation, knowing she would at last be meeting her mother the following morning.

Lord Holcombe had told her that her mother lived in the sixteenth arrondissement, saying it was the most elegant part of Paris. He described it as resembling a quiet country town, with a long main street, containing small shops and churches, with avenues branching off where there were villas set among trees, and houses in walled gardens. A peaceful place. Her mother's house, he said, was three-storeyed, painted white with delicate wrought-iron balconies.

The wall surrounding her mother's house was high and a gardener opened heavy gates the next day to let the carriage through. Francine was impressed with the setting, for although the garden was not large it was well-kept and boasted marble statues and urns at various strategic points.

A manservant ushered them into a hall with tiger skins scattered over a golden expanse of parquet flooring. Oil paintings adorned the walls and a marble staircase rose from the well of the hall and branched out on either side of the landing.

Another manservant came, took their hats and coats and the first one said, 'Madame is expecting you, your Lordship. This way.' They followed him up the wide stairs with exquisite wrought-iron balustrades then went into a nearby room.

Francine had a brief impression of luxurious furnishings before a woman rose from a chaise longue and came forward, a delicate green chiffon morning gown floating around her. She held out her arms.

'Ma petite – c'est si longtemps . . .' Her mother's voice broke. Then Francine was in her arms and they were both weeping. After a moment she was being held away and her mother was cupping her face between her palms, 'So exquisite.' Her voice was soft. 'How I have longed for this moment, but it was impossible to have you with me, circumstances, your papa, so angry . . .' She asked to be excused for a moment and turned to greet Lord Holcombe and to be introduced to Mrs Denton.

While the adults made small talk Francine studied her mother. Her fair hair had a silver sheen to it; her eyes were more violet than blue, her features clearly defined and her skin had the texture of magnolia blossom. Francine thought she had never seen a more beautiful woman ever. It was not only her features, her colouring, but she had an aura, impossible to describe. It must be something she had acquired in the theatrical world.

Gabrielle clapped her hands. 'Now we must all have a talk. I want to know everything that has happened, but every little thing.' She turned to Francine. 'You have been staying in Monte Carlo, did you enjoy it?' Before Francine could answer she rushed on, speaking partly in French and partly in English. 'Lord Holcombe tells me you have many admirers, so many claiming dances at the Bal Masqué – tell me about all these admirers.'

They were interrupted by a maid entering with a card on a silver salver. Gabrielle looked at it then tore it in pieces. She spoke so quickly in French Francine could only catch a smattering but made out that a gentleman had called and she was to tell him it was not convenient. There was more that was spoken in an undertone she was unable to translate. Her mother was angry, spots of colour burned on her cheeks. When the maid had gone she flung out her hands.

'These people! I tell them I shall not be available until the evening and what do they do? Arrive on my doorstep, and expect to be entertained. Ah, entertained.' She rang a bell and two servants came in with light refreshments. She turned once more to Francine.

'When I saw you last you were – ' she cradled her arms and made a rocking movement and tears were in her eyes again. 'And now, you are . . . a beautiful young demoiselle.' She wiped her eyes with a wisp of a handkerchief. 'You must call me Gabrielle.'

Francine felt taken aback. 'Not Mama?'

'My image, ma petite. My public. Lord Holcombe tells me you know about my work, so you will understand why I must remain, to my public, young and beautiful. In the new play I must act the part of a girl who is eighteen. You do understand?'

Francine said yes, of course, but felt she was being denied the right to acknowledge either parent. She had never been in a public place where she could address her father as Papa. And now she was to call her mother Gabrielle as though she were an elder sister. How would she be introduced, as a niece, a protégée?

Gabrielle asked to speak to Lord Holcombe and Mrs Denton on their own, then she wanted to be alone with Francine for a while. They went into an anteroom and Francine had time to look about her.

The thick carpeting was cream, the armchairs, sofas, covered in jewelled-coloured velvets – ruby, emerald, turquoise and amber. There were small tables in white and gilt, chairs with spindly legs, beautiful glass ornaments, a small crystal chandelier, curtains in cream caught back with thick loops in gold, their pelmets trimmed with gold braid. A painting of her mother hung in an alcove; it had been done when she was younger and there was an innocence then in her expression. She wore a low-cut dress in dark green silk that shimmered.

Her mother came back to the room alone. She was smiling. 'And now, ma petite, for our talk.' She drew up a chair and took Francine's hands in hers. 'I had to know from Lord Holcombe and Mrs Denton the position at home. He, of course, knows little of your home life but Mrs Denton tells me you are happy with Bridget. She feels very affectionate towards you and regards you as a second daughter. I am pleased, yet jealous too, ma petite. Your father is responsible for this position. He would not believe that I was never unfaithful to him. It was not in my nature. I could have a hundred men at my feet, but I would never allow myself to be intimate with any one of them.'

Her mother sounded sincere but at the same time Francine felt she must keep reminding herself that her mother was an actress. She said, 'Your name Dupont – did you marry again?'

Gabrielle shook her head. 'Ah no, I did not, Francine. I merely invented a husband to stop suitors pestering me. I still love your father and would go back to him if he would have me, even after all these years, and our divorce but alas – ' She spread her hands and there was a sadness in her eyes.

Francine reached out a hand, 'Oh, Mama – sorry Gabrielle, I forgot.'

Tears welled again in Gabrielle's eyes. 'Ma chère, I am sorry too. I would like nothing better than to be known as your mama, but it is impossible. Tell me about your Aunt Amelia. Poor girl, she was once disappointed in love . . . and has never recovered. She wrote to tell me she was going to be a nun! It was the only letter I have ever had from her and yet we are sisters. It is so hard to believe.'

Francine talked briefly about her life with her aunt and enlarged on the fact that Amelia had been a mother to her. She spoke about her father, how he had educated her and saw that she wanted for nothing. She did not even hint at the hurt of his rejection.

Gabrielle got up and said she must bring back Lord Holcombe and Mrs Denton. It was Lord Holcombe who said they must leave and let Gabrielle rest. They would be dining with her that evening.

When they drove away Mrs Denton said, 'Your mother is a beautiful woman, Francine.'

Francine agreed, but was not sure how she felt towards her mother at this stage. Then Lord Holcombe told her that Tyson had also been invited to dinner. He smiled. 'I think your mother perhaps sees him as a possible suitor for you.' Francine made no reply. She was wondering how she would explain to Tyson that she was not allowed to address Gabrielle as Mama.

When he was told he declared he was appalled. How could any woman treat her daughter in such a way. He was sure he would want to tell her so. Lord Holcombe replied, 'I think that would be most unwise, Tyson and, in fact, when you meet Gabrielle I don't think you will want to.'

And he was proved right. Tyson, who had been so determined to dislike Gabrielle, seemed to fall for her within a moment of their meeting. He was full of compliments and she was vivacious in return, flirting outrageously with him, but with great finesse, making an apology about it. How could one help flirting with such a charming, handsome young man.

Over dinner the talk was of the theatre, with only Mrs Denton bringing Francine into the conversation. Never having been to a theatre Francine was lost in the names of the various famous actresses, apart that is, from Sarah Bernhardt.

Lord Holcombe told how he had become completely captivated by La Bernhardt in her role as Zanetto the Minstrel Boy in *La Passante*. 'Such an astonishing voice,' he declared. 'Sheer magic.'

Gabrielle nodded. 'Ah yes, *un artiste dramatique*.' In a lower voice she said, 'If I had had a voice like that I would have been in heaven.'

'Heaven forbid!' Tyson teased. 'Then I would not have met you.' Gabrielle and Lord Holcombe laughed; Mrs Denton looked solemn and Francine sat wooden. She had come to spend the evening with her mother and all they could talk about was the theatre and actors and actresses. As for Tyson, she wanted nothing more to do with him. He was all talk, telling her how much he loved her then completely ignoring her since meeting her mother. And Lord Holcombe was almost as bad, fawning over Gabrielle.

Mrs Denton had tried to change the subject several times but without avail. Once when she glanced at Francine in despair Francine forcing a smile said, 'Gabrielle lives such an interesting life, doesn't she? I'm sure there are so many stories about the theatre and its people that it could take weeks to go through them all.'

Conversation suddenly ceased and the gaze of Lord Holcombe and Tyson turned on her. But Gabrielle, seemingly taking the remark as a compliment gushed, 'Oh, chérie, I'm so pleased you enjoy hearing about the life. I, of course, am steeped in it.' Then she added, a sudden sadness in her voice, 'My one regret is that actresses, unless famous, are not accepted by the aristocracy.' She gave an expressive shrug. 'And why? I do not have lovers and am not a kept woman.'

Mrs Denton coughed and tried discreetly to make Gabrielle aware of Francine's presence. Gabrielle's hand went to her mouth. 'I forget we have a child in our midst.

But of course in France these things are more widely discussed. There is none of the Victorian attitude here. Did I tell you about Rachael Felix, who was the daughter of an itinerant pedlar and who became the honour of the theatre, and was on the best of terms with the future Napoleon the Third. She – '

They were interrupted by a maid who brought a message for Mrs Denton. The hotel had telephoned. She was to call her sister Mrs de Auberleigh in Monte Carlo at once. It was most urgent.

Gabrielle at once led Mrs Denton to the telephone. Tyson followed.

When they returned Mrs Denton was pale but calm. Her dear father had died. The family were returning to England at once to make all the funeral arrangements. Her sister wanted her to join them in England in a couple of days, by which time the arrangements would have been made. Right now, Mrs Denton just wanted to return to the hotel. Gabrielle offered commiserations and then took Francine aside. 'I'm so sorry your visit had to end in this way, chérie. There is something I must say to you. The theatre is my life but do not get the impression that I have no time for you. I love you, Francine, in spite of the way I have behaved, but I dare not let myself love you the way I want to. I cannot have any intrusion to detract from my acting. It's like a disease. Only one who is in the acting profession could understand. Try not to hate me, ma petite. Come again and see me, and perhaps in time we can get to know one another.'

They embraced and Francine whispered, 'May I call you Mama, just this once?' At this Gabrielle burst into tears and Francine knew that this time her mother was not acting.

When she had her tears under control she murmured, 'Say it once more, chérie.'

'Mama, I love you, may I write to you?'

'But of course!' She cupped Francine's cheeks between

her palms and her lips were trembling. 'There is nothing I would like better than to hear from you. God bless you, child.' They kissed then parted.

CHAPTER FOURTEEN

The journeys to Monte Carlo and Paris had been full of excitement for Francine, full of new impressions, but the journey home two days later was just something to be endured. Mrs Denton was unhappy and Tyson spent most of his time with acquaintances, either talking politics or playing cards. Mrs Denton was full of regrets that she had not visited her father more often. 'We were very close when I was younger,' she said, 'but as Papa became older he became more and more tetchy and I could do nothing to please him. He and my husband did not see eye to eye and so our visits became less and less.'

Francine tried to console her, saying that at least she did have happy memories to look back on and Mrs Denton nodded, yes, she supposed so, then she lapsed into silence.

It was late when they arrived at Victoria. The de Auberleighs' carriage was there waiting and also one with Bridget and Sophie beside it. Sophie practically knocked Francine over as she greeted her then Bridget caught Sophie by the arm and shook her head at her. Sophie, dressed in black, made an effort to control her excitement.

After greeting Francine affectionately, Bridget told her that Sophie had permission from her father to stay with them during the next few days. Mrs Denton said a tearful goodbye to the girls, and told Francine she would come and see them when all the trouble was over. Tyson said he hoped to see her again soon, then Bridget, Sophie and Francine were in the carriage and on their way to the East End.

Once out of sight of the others Sophie exclaimed, 'I would have died if I had had to stay in that awful atmosphere! Why do people have to be so miserable when

170

someone dies? If Heaven is such a wonderful place as we are led to believe then relatives should be glad that Grandpapa is going there.'

Bridget silenced her. It was sacrilege to talk in that way with her grandfather lying dead; she must control herself. Sophie sighed then placing her palms together she laid them against her cheek, indicating to Francine they would have a talk in bed.

Although Francine had been longing to get back to London everywhere seemed somehow alien to her, especially Bridget's house which gave her a closed-in feeling after the spaciousness of the villa and the hotel in Paris. And although she had always enjoyed a bedtime talk with Sophie she now felt reluctant to answer the numerous questions she flung at her once they were alone. Had Lord Holcombe proposed to her in Paris? . . . How had she got on with her mother? . . . What did she think when Tyson turned up in Paris? Had they gone to any theatres? . . . What places of interest had they seen?

Francine told her firmly that no, Lord Holcombe had not proposed, had not even hinted that he liked her a lot. Her mother had been delighted to see her and told her she must come again soon, they would now correspond with one another. No, she said, they had not been to any theatres, there had been no time. She would tell her more the following day, she really was quite tired after the journey.

But this in no way dimmed Sophie's demands to know more. Did Francine not realise how she had felt when she had been left behind when they went off to Paris? 'You would have felt the same, Francine, so please, please tell me.'

And so Francine related all that had happened, as briefly as she could. No doubt in time she would tell Sophie things in more detail, but she found she couldn't bear to dwell too much on the visit to her mother. Perhaps because she felt it should be something just between the two of them.

Then Sophie began to talk about her family and how her grandfather's death could affect them. Her grandmother was dead and as there were no sons living her aunt and her mother should be sole beneficiaries. Her grandfather was a wealthy man, so it would be wonderful if some money could come to her mother. Her father had been struggling for years to make ends meet.

'I just began to realise the value of being rich when we went to Monte Carlo,' she said. 'Papa would have liked to have had a little gamble, but was unable to afford it. He was dependent on my uncle for the holiday. It must be awful to be beholden to others for treats like that. If I marry it must be to someone rich and I shall insist on having an allowance to myself.' Then she laughed. 'I shall probably be punished for saying such a thing and find I'm married to a pauper.'

There was a tap at the bedroom door, with Bridget telling them to settle for sleep, it was late.

'There's always tomorrow,' Sophie whispered. 'We shall talk our heads off, I have lots to tell *you*.'

The next morning, after a cosy breakfast and an exchange of news, Bridget told Francine she should go and see her father, to let him know she was safely home. She suggested it might be wise if Francine made no mention of having met her mother.

Francine's head went up quickly. 'Of course I shall tell him, Bridget! I'm still upset that he allowed me to think she was dead. It was a dreadful thing to do.'

'Then tread warily, my girl. Your father probably thought it was for the best – your mother *had* deserted you.'

'No, Bridget, she didn't. Papa turned her out, wrongfully accusing her of having an affair with someone. She was innocent.'

'Maybe she was, that is her side of the story, but there

is another side and you must not condemn until you know the truth. So, as I said, just tread warily.'

Kathleen opened the door when they arrived at Spinners End, and gave a squeal of delight on seeing Francine. 'You're back! Oh, the family will be over the moon, what a miss you've been. Let me look at you. My, don't you look well. Come into the kitchen and have a cup of tea before you see your Da. Hello, Sophie, you look well, too. I'm dying to hear about your holiday, we all are. Evie's going to get married, oh, yes, we have our news too. Isn't it marvellous? She's so excited she keeps dropping things and Cook gets mad.' Kathleen flung open the door to the kitchen and shouted, 'We have visitors, guess who it is.'

There were cries of pleasure from Evie and even Cook managed a broad smile. 'My, aren't we honoured. The travellers. Come and sit you all down. Evie, what are you gawping at, pull up some chairs.'

It was Sophie who did most of the talking, while Francine watched Evie. The little kitchen maid had changed so much in the last few weeks. There was a look of animation about her, of happiness. As Kathleen had said, she looked pretty at times. That was what love did for you, Francine thought.

After so much had been told about the holiday with Evie oohing and aahing, Cook began to talk about her rheumatics and how she would not be able to manage her job much longer. She had had to shuffle along with a stick the week before. What she needed was to end her days in a little country cottage.

Kathleen jollied her along. That was a long way off, they couldn't do without her. What would the master say if she told him she wanted to retire?

'Oh, *him*,' Cook said in disparaging tones, then she apologised to Francine. 'Sorry, Miss Francine, but he's forever on the grumble.'

Kathleen nodded. 'It's true, he has this wonderful chance of going abroad to photograph this expedition and you would think he's being dragged there by the hair of his head instead of it being an honour. He's been chosen to go out of ten of the best photographers.'

Evie said, 'Perhaps your Da'll feel better when he knows you're back safe and sound, Miss Francine.'

Francine refrained from saying she very much doubted it. She asked Kathleen about Rory and was told he was delivering some photographs to a house in Hampstead, but would be seeing her perhaps that evening at home. Francine said she hoped so, and was amused by Sophie's envious glance. Bridget and Sophie left shortly afterwards.

Kathleen then went up to tell Edwin Chayter that his daughter had arrived, leaving Francine with small tremors running through her body. Within minutes Kathleen was back to tell her to go up. She squeezed Francine's shoulder and whispered, 'Good luck.'

When Francine went into her father's study, after his brusque 'Enter' to her knock, it seemed to her that time had stood still while she had been away. She had last seen her father sitting in the same position, his expression as forbidding as always. He motioned her to a chair and finished some writing he had been busy with. Then he laid down his pen.

'So you are back. I trust that all went well for you.'

'Yes, thank you, Papa, it was most enjoyable especially because -' Francine took a quick breath, 'because I met my mother.'

A white, pinched look came about her father's nostrils, then anger flared in his eyes. '*You did what*? Who was responsible for this underhand piece of work?'

Francine felt surprisingly calm. 'There was nothing underhand about it, Papa. It happened by sheer chance, one of the coincidences that occur in life.' She explained how it had come about then went on, 'Naturally, having been led to believe that my mother was dead I was anxious to meet her.'

'And no doubt she told a pack of lies.'

'What is truth and what are lies? Although you turned me out of your house you have paid for my schooling, my upkeep and for my holiday abroad. For that, I'm very grateful.'

'And I suppose you now want to live with your mother?' His eyes still held anger.

'No, I have no wish to live with my mother. She has her own life to lead, as you do. Fortunately, I've had affection from the O'Reilly family, Bridget and Mrs Denton.'

'I turned you out of my house for your own good.' His jaw was out-thrust. 'I regarded you as an intruder and did not feel responsible for my attitude, or my actions towards you. And I refuse to discuss this any further.' He picked up his pen.

Francine made no move. 'There are certain things I need to discuss with you, Papa. I have no wish to return to school next week.'

'Ah.' His eyes had now taken on a steely look. 'So you *do* intend to be with your mother. Why did you lie to me?'

'I don't lie, I have no need to. I want to learn about photography and that is not a subject I can take at school.'

He glared at her. 'Well, you certainly will not learn it from me. You will go back to Oakleigh Manor and that is an order. Now please leave, I have work to do.' He waved a hand dismissing her.

'I am not going back to school, Papa. I've been taught deportment, I have high marks in most subjects, I speak French fluently and am fairly proficient in German and Latin. There must be a photographer somewhere who would welcome a pupil.'

Edwin Chayter stood up and thundered, 'You are insolent, girl! If you raise any further objections about returning to school I shall find a husband for you, someone strong enough to control you.'

Francine felt a momentary fear, knowing her father was

175

capable of carrying out such a treat. But she held her head high. 'If you insist on such a drastic course then I shall run away.'

'And where would you go?' A sneer touched his lips. 'You are sixteen, vulnerable to every type of charlatan. You would have to earn money. Where? In a brothel?'

Francine, angry now, got to her feet. 'You have a depraved mind. I feel sorry for you. No father should ever speak to his daughter so.'

He raised his hand to strike her, then let it fall to his side. 'You see the way you affect me?' he shouted. 'Go and live with your mother, I'll even pay your fare. But before you go it's best that you know something about her. Gabrielle is a stranger to the truth and lives only for the admiration of men. Did she beg you to go and live with her? No, of course she did not. She doesn't want you, never did.'

Francine was stung to retort, 'You were married to her. These are not the kind of remarks a man makes, even about his ex-wife – a *gentleman*, that is.'

All the anger seemed suddenly to drain from him. 'But then I don't consider myself a gentleman, not any more. Gabrielle stripped me of what dignity I had, humiliated me in front of her lovers. Oh, yes, there were others.'

Francine felt tears rising. 'I don't believe you. You're only saying it out of jealousy because she had a mild flirtation with another man.'

'Is that what she told you? Ha!'

'I believe Mama. You're taking your revenge out on me for your jealousy by hating me. You've always hated me!'

He stared at her for a moment then shook his head. 'Revenge has nothing to do with it. You say I hate you – I don't know . . . But I *do* know that I don't want you living with me!'

Francine looked at him with pleading. 'Papa, couldn't you try to let me live here? I need you. I have no contact with close family. It's so important. When I see families together I feel like a – like a lost soul. I have a great love for photography, doesn't that convince you that we belong together?'

'No, it does not! I can see your mother's face in you, and it drives me mad with torment. I don't want you here. And another thing -' his voice had risen, 'I will not let you learn photography. You will go back to school in Exeter and if you attempt to disobey me you shall be married – and not to a young man. And if you carry out your threat to run away it will be a waste of time. I shall have you brought back. So take heed. Now get out, while I still have my temper under control.'

She was at the door when he called, 'And remember this. You might have met men of determination in your life, but you will not meet a more determined man than I.'

Francine left, and once outside the tears welled up and rolled slowly down her cheeks. She walked along the landing and stopped startled when Kathleen said gently, 'What's happened? Come on, love, we'll go into my room.'

They sat on the bed and when Francine had finished relating all that her father had said, Kathleen laid an arm across her shoulders.

'The poor tormented soul. He's living in a hell all the time, a hell of his own making. It must be terrible bearing a grudge all these years. He needs your pity, Francine.'

'Don't I need pity too?' Francine asked, her voice breaking. Two big tears hung on her lashes and Kathleen pulled a handkerchief from her pocket and wiped them away.

'Your papa needs it more. He must never know any happiness at all. You'll have to make up your mind about going back to school.'

'No.' Francine drew away from Kathleen. 'That I will not do! I shall run away. I'll think of somewhere to go. And no one will change my mind about that. I have the same determination as my father to have my own way too, at least about certain things. It's a matter of principle. Why should I be married off to an older man just because I don't need any more schooling?'

Kathleen sighed. 'I think we must talk again when you're over this awful meeting with your father. You'll probably feel better when we go home this evening. Everyone is so looking forward to seeing you.'

But although Francine felt joyous at being back with her O'Reilly family, she had lost none of her determination to run her life the way she wanted.

There were shouts of pleasure when she arrived with Kathleen.

'Well, and there she is . . .' Mrs O'Reilly held her at arm's length. 'My, haven't you filled out and look at the colour of your skin! I'm not going to tell you how bonny you look or you'll get big-headed.'

The family in turn all gave her a hug and paid her a compliment, all that is, except Rory. He touched her on the cheek and said, 'Well, and what was it like living among the toffs?'

'No different from living among the workers,' Francine replied pleasantly. 'There are the good and the bad, the kind ones and the mean ones.'

Old Mrs O'Reilly chuckled. 'That's telling him, Mavourneen. Young Rory likes to get in a dig at the ones with money.'

Rory simply grinned. 'Perhaps I should have said, how did you get on living among so much luxury and eating all that fancy French food.'

'I liked it for a time,' Francine said smiling, 'but what I'm looking forward to very much is some of the delicious O'Reilly Irish stew.' They all applauded and Mrs O'Reilly beamed at her.

'You'll go far, Francine, girl, with all that strategy at your fingertips. You'll have to give our Rory some lessons.'

Rory, a little put out, but trying to hide it, declared that he believed in plain speaking and was met with laughter from the others. 'Plain speaking, *you*?' teased Declan. 'You go every crooked which way to get what you want.'

His grandmother raised her hand. 'There *is* stew for supper, especially made for your homecoming, Francine, and no one told me it was a favourite with you, so how's that for foretelling your needs? Graine, push the pan from the hob on to the coals, it'll soon heat up. And then we'll hear all of Francine's news.'

The first question old Mr O'Reilly asked was about the Casino, and when he knew that Francine had been inside it he clucked his tongue – why had he not thought to give her a few bob to have a go on the wheel?

Milo said, 'A few shillings wouldn't have been any good, Grandad. People there bet in pounds.'

'Hundreds of pounds,' Francine said. 'In some cases thousands, and men have been known to lose their ancestral homes.'

'Thousands of pounds you say,' mused the old man. 'There's a thing now! And losing an ancestral home? And me lovely wife, bless her, gets her dander up if I as much as bet a tanner on the horses.'

'Sixpence would go a long way towards making a dinner,' Mrs O'Reilly retorted. 'But it isn't just sixpence you squander, is it? It's all the money you spend on swilling beer down your throat.'

Her husband was indignant. 'Swilling beer, do you call it? Twopence or threepence is all I spend, woman, and a man must have something to live for.'

The arguing might have gone on had not Declan said, 'Now, now, you two, this is no way to be going on when we're just welcoming Francine back.'

'No, it isn't,' said Mrs O'Reilly. 'I'm sorry for the both of us, it's just that he makes me that mad with all the talk of money as if it grew on trees. But there, I've had my say.'

'Money doesn't always bring happiness,' Francine said

quietly. 'Some wealthy people seem very discontented at times.'

'So it wasn't all milk and honey holidaying abroad,' Rory taunted.

Francine looked directly at him, her gaze holding his. 'It was an experience, Rory, one I wouldn't have missed. I think you would have enjoyed it. There was a clarity in the air I've never known here. The sea was an unbelievable blue and the stars at night were so large and seemed so close you felt as though you could have reached up and taken a handful.'

There was a moment's silence then Rory said softly, 'I think I would like to go there someday,' and the smile he gave her was tender.

With a brightness that Francine had lost since the interview with her father, she talked about the people, describing the elderly woman on the beach who was smoking a cheroot and eying everyone through a pair of lorgnettes. Francine gave an imitation and they all laughed. She told them about the party on the yacht and about the stateroom being as big as a drawing room and Mrs O'Reilly said, 'Well! Would you believe it.' Then Kathleen wanted to know about the real live Lord she had met and Francine described him as being so kind and how he had shown them all the out-of-the-way places in Paris; and about the sons of peasants being at the Sorbonne in the thirteenth century and living on practically nothing and sleeping on straw in the streets, and how two jugglers were responsible for the building of a hospital and a church.

They all listened spellbound and whenever Francine paused they would beg for more. When she felt she had covered most things she concluded, 'As I said, it was an experience I would not have wanted to miss, but it's lovely to be back among you again.'

The old man said, 'And it's glad we are to have you

back, Mavourneen, and it's good to know that living among the lords and ladies hasn't changed you one whit.'

Rory came up to her afterwards and lightly tapped the tip of her nose. 'D'ye know something? I envied you that holiday and I've made up me mind, *my* mind,' he corrected himself, 'to save up and go to Paris someday.' He grinned. 'And I might even take you with me if you behave yourself.'

'Now isn't that something to look forward to,' she teased him, speaking in the Irish brogue. 'Sure and the thought will keep me going for many a year.'

'Not so much of the many a year. I'm doing well at the photography. Your Da still shouts at me, but grudgingly admits I have the making of a genius.'

Kathleen, who had come up, laughed. 'A genius, is it? Well, you'd best be hurrying up so we can all feel the benefit of it before we're dead and in our graves.'

Francine felt a shiver go through her. 'Oh, don't talk about graves.'

Kathleen looked at her with concern. 'You look pale, Francine. It's just an expression. You're tired, we've exhausted you with all our questions. Bridget said not to keep you too late. I'll walk you home.'

'No,' Rory said, 'I'll take Francine. We haven't had a proper chance for a talk yet. I'll leave her at Bridget's then go on to Spinners End. The boss wants me to develop some prints later. A regular slave driver he is.'

After Francine said her goodbyes and promised to come again soon Rory said as they walked along the street, 'What's troubling you, Francine? Apart from worrying about me, that is?' Although his tone was light she sensed his underlying seriousness. After hesitating for a moment she told him about the meeting with her father.

He was shocked at Edwin Chayter's treatment of her. 'He can't just marry you off to some old man.' In the next breath he added, 'But of course he can, he's your father. Look, Francine, go back to school. After all, it will only

181

be for a year, or two at the most. What is that out of a lifetime?'

'Two years at school would seem a lifetime,' she retorted. 'I want a home life, want to learn photography and I *will* learn photography – even if I'm not allowed to live with my father like any other normal girl.'

'Now Francine, be reasonable. Who is going to teach you? I'm not - for one thing I wouldn't have the time and for another, I don't believe in women doing men's jobs.'

Francine stopped. 'You had better leave me because I'm getting more and more mad. There's the tram, goodnight.' She ran to the stop but Rory came after her. He got on to the tram with her and after he had paid their fares they sat in silence for a while, then Rory turned to her.

'Will you promise me one thing, Francine. If your father still insists on you going back to Oakleigh Manor, don't do anything rash like running away. I'll try and think of something to help you. I don't know what, but I just know you can't go roaming the streets of London hoping to find a job.'

He explained carefully all the terrible fates that could await her if she was tempted to run away; from being beaten up by some mob for her money to being forced into prostitution. To which Francine replied that prostitution might be a lot better than marrying some old man she hated.

At this Rory got really annoyed with her. She was talking like a spoilt child. She didn't know when she was well off, she had not only had a good education but had enjoyed a holiday abroad with all the attendant luxuries.

'I had to leave school at twelve years old,' he said, 'and take a job to help out the family.'

Francine turned to him and said quietly, 'But the difference is that you've had love from your family. I wouldn't have minded leaving school and working to help if I had your kind of life.'

'Oh, Francine.' Rory gave a sigh of despair. 'What am

I going to do with you? I would marry you, if I had something to offer. Not mind you,' he added quickly, 'that I want to get married and settle down. I have always wanted to travel – and you whetted my appetite more than ever today.'

There was a dreaminess then in Rory's voice and Francine too felt despair. How many people got what they really wanted out of life? She forced herself to say lightly, 'And who told you I would want to marry *you*? I had plenty of offers when I was away.'

'Then you'd better write to tell them all you've changed your mind and then choose the one with most money.'

'Oh, you, you -' The tram came to a stop and although she was a distance away from Bridget's she jumped up and got off. Rory jumped off too, and grabbing her by the arm he swung her to face him.

'Now listen to me. I care what happens to you, I missed you a lot when you were away. I wouldn't have admitted it had you not behaved the way you're doing now because you only care about yourself, but -'

'That's not true!' She shook herself from his hand and marched ahead, calling over her shoulder, 'You haven't even an inkling about me.'

Rory caught up with her. 'Yes, I have. I know you're warm-hearted, a girl who needs love. But I also know you'll have to climb down a bit and try and understand other people. At the moment you're only concerned with what suits *you*.'

Francine was silent for a while then she said quietly, 'No matter what my faults are I'm not going back to school. Nor am I willing to marry a man my father happens to choose for me, so I think it's best if we just drop the subject. I wish you luck with your career. Perhaps someday we might meet in the same profession and be rivals.'

They had reached Bridget's house and Rory said, with a kind of wonder, 'You really believe it, don't you? Well,

183

all I can say is that with determination like yours you might just get what you're after: but I won't figure in it. Never would I want anything to do with a woman photographer. Good night, Francine.' He kissed her gently on the lips.

If Sophie had not come running along the passage to greet her Francine knew she would have burst into tears. As it was she had to keep swallowing hard to control her emotions.

'I've been waiting ages for you,' Sophie exclaimed. 'I'm dying to know what your father had to say.'

Bridget had gone to look in on a neighbour who was ill and Francine, feeling the need to unburden herself, decided to tell Sophie everything that had transpired. When she described her father's reaction to her refusal to go back to school, Sophie said firmly that if Francine was not going then neither was she!

But when Francine went on to state her father's ultimatum Sophie had an idea.

'I'm sure Lord Holcombe would marry you if he knew. *He* would let you learn photography – and I could come and stay with you. Oh, it could be wonderful!'

'Sophie! I'm not marrying anyone, and especially not Lord Holcombe. He's old – he must be sixty if he's a day, or even older.'

'But you said he was so kind to you in Paris, and he *is* rich. Far better to marry him than some awful fat old ugly thing who would treat you badly. Do think about it, Francine.'

Francine said, yes, she would, but privately resolved to run to the ends of the earth rather than marry a man she didn't love.

CHAPTER FIFTEEN

When Francine learned two days later from Bridget that there was no hope of her father relenting about her return to school, she began to make plans for leaving, and was surprised at how calm she felt.

She did have money left over from her holiday, and her father would give her some more when she was supposedly returning to school. She had already made up her mind to go to a town, rather than a village, for she might be able to get domestic work and with any luck, find a photographer in need of an apprentice. Surely not all men were against females working. Serviceable clothes suitable for a girl seeking domestic work were no problem, as she had her navy blue costume and white blouses which she wore for walking out at school. She also had stout shoes. Her underclothes for school wear were plain and simple, too.

Sophie seemed surprised at Francine's calm acceptance of returning to school. She began to feel suspicious of her friend's complacency as the time drew near for them to leave for the autumn term. One evening she said, 'I think you have some plan in mind, Francine, and that you'll end up running away. If you have, for heaven's sake tell me, because I will definitely not go back to school if you don't.'

'Sophie, if I do go, I go alone. There'll be trouble enough if I run away. I can't let you be involved. I love you too much for that.'

Sophie argued that they were best friends, had shared all escapades, but Francine was adamant and in the end Sophie said with a grin, 'Don't think you'll get away without me, not if I have to keep awake every night.'

Francine, knowing that Sophie was a sleepyhead just smiled.

Reading was a place she had picked out on a map, simply stabbing a pin in that area. She would at least try there first. Francine wrote notes that same evening to Sophie, Bridget, to her father and Kathleen. In them she said they were not to worry over her, she had plans and would not come to any harm. She asked them all to forgive her for what she was doing, adding that no one could have made her change her mind about going back to school.

Francine packed her bag, put it in a cupboard under the stairs that was seldom used, and went to bed that night as normal. When she was sure that Bridget and Sophie were fast asleep she took her clothes downstairs and dressed there. Then, collecting her bag, she crept out of the house.

The only signs of life as she went along the next street were the sounds of some drunken men singing and the caterwauling of a cat. It was not until she opened the broken door of the warehouse and went in that she knew a pang of fear. Tramps could be sleeping there. But once she was accustomed to the darkness she was sure she was alone. She knew there were some wooden boxes she could sit on, and there was some straw if she felt she had to lie down. This last item had no attraction for her, there could be mice scuttling about. She put her bag on the floor and sat on one of the boxes and it was not until then that she realised the enormity of what she was doing. She was putting a load of worry on to other people's shoulders because of her own self-will.

Twice when Francine heard a faint scuffling among the straw she got up to leave, to return to Bridget's, then she sat down again. It was now or never for the break.

In spite of the dampness seeping into her body she catnapped and was eventually aroused by factory hooters. It was just breaking daylight. She felt stiff and chilled but her blood was circulating again by the time she had walked to a tram stop, and as she boarded a tram, fairly full of workers, she felt again the sense of adventure.

A middle-aged man got up to give her his seat, and she accepted it and thanked him, not wanting to draw attention to herself by refusing. The majority of the passengers kept nodding off to sleep. As some alighted at the various stops, others took their places.

Francine had to change trams and the sun was out and the morning seeming to warm up by the time she arrived at Paddington station. She had half an hour to wait for a train and so went into the refreshment room and bought herself a cup of tea and a bun. The tea was nectar to her after her uneasy night.

The train to Reading stoppd at every station, making the one and a half hour's journey seem like five. She felt jaded when she arrived.

Reading was a busy place, with the sound of machines pounding and farmers taking cattle and produce to market. To Francine, the roads here seemed as busy as those near the docks at home. Walking away from the station, she saw a notice in a tobacconist's shop that said, *Skivvy needed for lodging house. Temporary. Good wages.*

The words 'lodging house' put Francine off at first, but then she decided to make enquiries. She needed a roof over her head and to earn money; even though this was a temporary job it would give her a start. On enquiry she found that the house was just a short distance away. The man who told her added, 'Mrs Lomax has a tongue as sharp as a knife and she'll work you hard, Miss, but you will get good food. Her staff gets the same as her lodgers. The girl who's been skivvying is her niece but she's ill. You'll be out of a job when her niece comes back. Loyal to her own kith and kin, is Mrs Lomax, when it comes to it.'

Francine thanked him and was about to leave when he

187

called to her. 'If you come back when you're due to leave I might be able to find you another place. Just ask for Mr Naylor. I'm not promising anything, mind you, but customers do ask now and again if I know of a servant for this place or that.'

'Oh, thanks, it's good of you. By the way, do you happen to know of a photographer who might be willing to give me lessons?'

'Give you lessons?' He scratched his head. 'I don't rightly know. Never heard of a girl wanting to learn photography.'

Francine smiled. 'It's simply that I plan to be a photographer some day.'

'You do? Well, I wish you luck. I've never heard of a lady photographer but as my old aunt used to say, it takes all kinds to make a world. Pop in sometime and I'll have a word with Dan Beckett. He's retired, has ill-health, but he still uses his camera.'

Francine thanked the tobacconist again and left, feeling jubilant. It was Fate that she had picked Reading to come to. She felt sure now that she would get the job she was going for.

The house she was seeking was a three-storeyed building, and although it needed painting on the outside there was an air of cleanliness in the curtains and the scrubbed front step.

In answer to her knock a small boy opened the door and when Francine told him she wanted to see Mrs Lomax he shouted, 'Aunt Sybil, there's a girl here wants to see you.'

Aunt Sybil turned out to be tall, angular, her hair screwed back in a bun, her expression forbidding. 'What d'ye want?' she demanded. 'If it's lodgings you're after I don't take women, only men, don't believe in mixing the breeds.'

When Francine explained she was after the job Mrs

188

Lomax eyed her up and down. 'It's a skivvy I want, not a lady's maid.'

Francine nodded. 'Yes, so I've been told. I'm not afraid of hard work.'

'You look as if you've never done work of *any* kind,' snapped Mrs Lomax.

'Perhaps not, but I've suffered some hardships and I'm willing to try anything. I won't let you down. That's a promise.'

'You seem to have plenty to say for yourself.'

'Well, it's no use being tongue-tied if you're after a job that someone's not willing to give you, is it? But if you're not satisfied with the looks of me I'll try somewhere else. I have six addresses to try. Perhaps one of the other people won't be so unwilling to take a chance.'

Francine wondered where she had acquired so much cheek and although loath to leave, made to turn away. Mrs Lomax called, 'Wait, I'll take a chance! I'll know at the end of the day whether you're any good or not. Come on in.'

'Thanks, but first, what is the wage? It said on the advertisement that you pay well.'

'Five bob a week and that's good – I only pay my niece eight pounds a year. I'm giving extra money because the job isn't permanent.'

Francine stepped inside. 'I accept.'

Mrs Lomax asked her name and when told snapped, 'I can't stand fancy names, I'll call you Mary.' Francine accepted this, too.

She had expected the house to have a stale smell of cooking but there was air coming in from the open door at the end of the passage. Mrs Lomax said, 'Follow me,' and they went into the kitchen. It was big, with a shining black-leaded kitchen range and there was a gas stove to the left of it. 'I have ten boarders,' she said, 'and all with good appetites. I don't skimp them in food like some landladies do. I have a good name around here. Put your

189

bag down and I'll make you a cup of tea, but don't think you'll be drinking tea all day, this is special while we have a talk. You're a stranger around here, what brought you to Reading?'

Francine found herself happily lying. She said she had been orphaned and wanted to get away from London and all the unhappiness. 'I could have stayed with relatives,' she said, 'but I wanted to make my own way in life.'

Mrs Lomax gave a quick nod. 'And that's not a bad attitude to take. I've made my own way since I was twelve. I was put in the workhouse with me mam when me dad died. Then Mam died and I ran away. I've done all right, but I've worked for what I've got. And if you're prepared to work all hours God sends we'll get along like a house afire.'

Hardly giving Francine time to drink her tea, Mrs Lomax had her on her feet and was showing her the house. There were four bedrooms on the first floor, three of them with two double beds in them, and the fourth, a very small room, belonged to Mrs Lomax. The room Francine was to sleep in was on the floor above. An attic room. It was small like Mrs Lomax's, but it was adequate and it was clean, as all the rooms were. And Francine found the rooms the men slept in very tidy. When she remarked on this she was told if any of the men didn't put their stuff away they were out.

'I won't have untidiness,' the landlady said. 'It rubs me up the wrong way, makes me bad-tempered. And if you ever hear me in a temper you won't want to hear it again. Come on and I'll show you the dining room.'

There was one long table in it, laid with a red and white checked cloth and each place setting had a knife and fork and a spoon. None of the cutlery matched. There was a serving hatch in one wall that connected the room to the kitchen. Her husband's making, Mrs Lomax told Francine. 'He's been dead for four years, God rest his soul.'

All the floors apart from the kitchen were laid with

brown linoleum. In the kitchen it was bare boards, well scrubbed too, by the looks of them. There wasn't a single armchair in the house; they were all wooden straight-backed chairs and there wasn't one cushion to be seen anywhere. This was not exactly great comfort, but Francine felt pleased that she had found herself a home and job so soon. She was determined to have lessons in photography if this was at all possible, but she decided this would have to wait until she had proved herself capable of being a skivvy.

She was given a dark grey print dress and a big white apron to go over it while she was serving the meals and a coarse sacking apron to use when she was doing the scrubbing and cleaning. Mrs Lomax also insisted that all her hair be tucked under a mob cap, except during her off-duty hours.

Later, when Mrs Lomax explained all her duties Francine began to wonder grimly if she would ever have the strength left to enjoy any off-duty hours. The woman was a 'cleanliness is next to Godliness' fanatic. Everything in the house had to be dusted twice a day. She couldn't stand dust! A damp cloth was to be taken over every inch of linoleum in a morning; the kitchen floor was to be scrubbed after breakfast, which would be served at six-thirty, and again after supper in the evening, which would be served at seven. Sandwiches were packed for the men to take with them to have at midday. They went back to the factory after supper until nine or ten o'clock.

And there would be no making eyes at the men, Mrs Lomax declared. Some of them were married and she didn't want any of their wives to know the worry of their husbands getting mixed up with servant girls. And those that were not married had to be kept out of trouble, too. Her own lad who worked away had got some chit of a girl in service into trouble and he had had to marry her. She blamed the girl, who, of course, had worked her wiles with him.

During this recital Francine remained silent, nor did she pass any remark when she was told she had better start scrubbing the already spotlessly-clean floor in the kitchen. She had burned her boats so now she must put up with the consequences.

The nephew who had opened the door to Francine, had disappeared and she was told by Mrs Lomax that young Harry had come in a morning to help with the washing up while Florrie, her niece, was ill. Francine was shown how to get hot water from the boiler at the side of the fireplace with a scoop, and after Mrs Lomax had thrown a piece of old matting on to the floor to kneel on, Francine started scrubbing the bare boards of the kitchen.

The stretch of floor seemed as big as an ocean and thinking of the sea brought Monte Carlo back to Francine's mind. She thought she must be mad to be doing this kind of work when she could be sitting comfortably in a classroom. She wrung out the floorcloth, mopped up the suds and sat back on her heels. No, she had had all the schooling she needed. This type of job would at least teach her a little more about life and characters, which was necessary if she wanted to be a professional photographer.

After the kitchen floor was finished she was told to take a damp cloth over every inch of linoleum in the house. Then everything had to be dusted. At midday she was given beef sandwiches, with a piece of apple pie to follow. When she told Mrs Lomax how much she had enjoyed the meal the landlady said she was glad, and pointed out that she would not get anything else to eat until after eight o'clock that evening.

Francine stared at her in dismay. 'That's another eight hours to wait! I'll be on my knees by then because my legs will be too weak to hold me.'

Mrs Lomax nodded in agreement but explained it would only be for the first day – after that she would get used to it and come to no harm. Her niece Florrie never had.

When Francine asked what illness her niece was

suffering from Mrs Lomax replied promptly, 'A broken heart, that's what. The lad she was engaged to suddenly upped and went off with someone else and got married. Collapsed did Florrie, it was the shock, you see. Went into a coma. Never had anyone in *our* family have one of those!' Mrs Lomax sounded quite proud of the fact.

After the snack Francine was told to start on three basketfuls of clothes, sheets and pillow-cases. The clothes belonged mainly to the men, shirts and underwear. Francine had watched Kathleen and Evie taking turns with the ironing at Spinners End, and had laughed at the way they had spat on the sole of the iron to find out if it was hot enough to use. She had teased them about sweat running off the ends of their noses, but Francine was not in the mood to laugh when she felt sweat running off the end of *her* nose.

Her back began to ache and she kept pausing to press her palms against it, hoping to relieve the ache but it made no difference. Then Mrs Lomx, who had been busy cooking most of the afternoon, took pity on her and told her she could have a mug of milk and a slice of bread. The bread was spread with strawberry jam. Francine found it difficult not to wolf it down.

She hardly had time to finish it before Mrs Lomax had her on her feet again. She had to hurry up and finish the ironing and get it out of the way before the men came in for their meal. Mrs Lomax added that Francine was not to think she would get milk and a piece of bread every day, that was special because it was her first day.

The smell of rabbit pies cooking had saliva dripping down the side of Francine's mouth. However was she going to last out until after eight o'clock?

At ten minutes to seven the back door burst open and the men came in *en masse*. There was shouting and bursts of laughter as they washed their hands and their faces under the pump in the yard. Then came the strong smell of the midden privy as the door kept opening and closing.

193

Although Francine had been vaguely aware of the smell from the privy she now felt nauseous as the door was opened so many times.

A middle-aged man looked into the kitchen and called, 'We're all here, Missus,' and Mrs Lomax replied if they all sat down they would have the meal in a jiffy.

She had set up a trestle table in the kitchen and laid out ten warmed plates. Then Francine was ordered to put so many potatoes on each plate served from a big bowl and also a scoop of cabbage. And as Francine coped Mrs Lomax put a piece of crust on each plate followed by meat and gravy. Francine was then to carry the plates to the hatch for the men who were lined up to collect them. Some of the lodgers made remarks. 'Ho, a new lass . . .' 'What's your name, love?' At this Mrs Lomax called, 'It's Mary. And don't get fresh!'

Some passed comments about her pretty face and others her lovely eyes, to which Mrs Lomax shouted, 'Enough of that! Get your suppers and shut up.'

The talk and laughter went on. While the men were eating their first course, jam roly-polys were taken out of the cloths they had been cooked in and cut into portions. The portions were generous. Francine's stomach was rumbling with hunger. When Mrs Lomax's back was turned she nipped a piece of crust from the pie dish and also managed to stab a piece of meat and get it into her mouth without her slave-driver mistress noticing. She felt she had made a step in the right direction.

When the empty plates had been passed back after the main course Francine had been too flustered to notice any of the men but when the pudding plates were returned she felt more relaxed and noticed there were several attractive younger men among the lodgers. Some were shy, but the bolder ones whispered and asked if she was walking out with anyone.

Guessing that Mrs Lomax would not have her holding conversations with the men she smiled, nodded quickly and said, 'Yes, it looked an excellent meal. I'm glad you enjoyed it.'

One man said, 'Where do you come from, love? You talk like a toff.'

Mrs Lomax called, 'Mary! There's not time for gossiping, there's washing up to be done. Here, take this pot of tea, they help themselves.'

The pot was enormous, so was the enamel jug of boiling water that followed. The man who took them whispered, 'You're real bonny. We must get to know one another. I'll arrange it.' Francine turned away thinking that no one could arrange anything with Mrs Lomax there, nor did she want any assignations. What she wanted was food and a bed to rest her weary body.

After half an hour the men prepared to leave for work again, and as they trooped out Mrs Lomax called to them to come in quietly later and not wake up the entire household when they returned or they would be out on their ear! They all promised, and some laughingly crossed their hearts.

Mrs Lomax pronounced them to be a good lot of lodgers but you had to keep them in their place or they would take the very house from you.

When Francine sat down to her supper at eight o'clock she felt almost too tired to eat it. The pastry was dried up but the meat was tasty. She ate the pastry too, knowing that without food in her stomach she would not be able to cope the following day. She ate some of the jam roll but then her lids began to droop. It was Mrs Lomax who roused her and told her to get upstairs to bed. There was a note of kindness in her voice. She gave her a mug of warm milk to take up with her, but Francine flopped on the bed, the milk untouched.

When she roused it was dark, the house was silent and she found she was still dressed, even to her coarse sacking apron. She undressed and got under the covers but seemed only to have closed her eyes before Mrs Lomax was knocking on the door and telling her it was time to get up. Francine washed in cold water, her eyes closed, and they were still closed when she was dressed. It was impossible, she couldn't go on like this, she would have to look for something else.

But she perked up a bit when she smelt bacon cooking as she went downstairs. She would take it from day to day, see how she got on.

The men were quiet as they came down for their breakfasts, but all of them greeted her. 'Hello Mary, had a good sleep?' were the general comments.

There was bacon and egg, a piece of fried bread and plates stacked with thick slices of brown bread. Marmalade was on the table, but no butter. Francine's mouth was watering as she took the plates to the hatch. She hoped she would not have all the washing up to do before she sat down to something to eat herself.

While the men had their breakfasts she helped Mrs Lomax to make ham sandwiches for them to take to work. The slices of bread had been cut earlier. The sandwiches seemed neverending. To each tin lunchbox she added a piece of fruit cake. The smell of the ham had Francine's mouth watering again. She did manage to sneak some small pieces, but that was all.

When the men had gone Mrs Lomax told her to get on with clearing the table and doing the washing up. Francine decided to rebel.

'Mrs Lomax, I'm sure you realise that I'm a willing worker, but I know this much, I can't work on an empty stomach. The stomach is like an engine, it needs fuel to work. So, either I have my breakfast now, or I shall have to look for another place.'

Mrs Lomax opened her mouth as though to protest then she gave a nod. 'All right, you shall have your breakfast. You are a good worker, I'll grant you that, and I don't want to lose you, but I must admit I don't like my routine upset, but I suppose needs must when the devil drives. And more often than not he does the driving!' she added grimly. 'I'll cook your breakfast. But clear the table next door first, I can't stand the mess.'

Francine sat down to bacon, egg and fried bread and had two slices of brown bread and marmalade and three cups of tea. Afterwards she felt prepared to tackle anything. When she mentioned this Mrs Lomax's face relaxed for the first time into a brief smile. 'Right,' she said, 'then let's get started.'

Every day there was something extra to be done – windows to be cleaned, a big bread-making session; washday, which to Francine was a nightmare, with sheets to be possed, boiled in the copper in the washhouse, blued, and dried on five stretches of lines in the lane and yard. There were the men's shirts and heavy underwear besides Mrs Lomax's garments and Francine's. The womanly wear was dried in the house in front of the kitchen fire. The following day after all the ironing was done, Francine gave her employer another ultimatum; she had to have some time off, she needed fresh air in order to survive. Mrs Lomax grudgingly allowed her two hours off the following afternoon.

Francine felt as if she were off on a big adventure. She went straight back to the tobacconist's shop and was greeted with a warm smile by Mr Naylor.

'Well, and there you are, Miss. I've been hearing good things about you. Mrs Lomax has been telling folk that you're the best worker she's ever known. How d'ye get on with her?'

Francine smiled. 'I nearly gave up after the first day, but it was the thought that Mr Beckett might teach me about photography that kept me going. Have you asked him?'

'Yes, I have and he's willing. He'd charge you sixpence an hour if that would be all right. Perhaps you could get time off one afternoon. He'll fit in to suit you.'

'Oh, that is good of you, Mr Naylor. I'll have to arrange

something with Mrs Lomax. Of course I'll only be there until her niece is well again.'

Mr Naylor gave a knowing wink. 'And that'll be when her store of sweet stuff is finished.' To Francine's puzzled look he went on, 'Florrie is a compulsive eater, especially anything sweet. She saves up the money her aunt gives her and sets up a store, like a squirrel, then takes to her bed and stays there until it's done.'

'But I thought she was in a coma?'

Mr Naylor guffawed. 'It's another one of her ruses. Florrie is an actress, she ought to be on the stage. She does work, mind you, when she's at her aunt's, but not the way you do.'

'But don't her mother and Mrs Lomax know what she gets up to?'

'I think they do but they turn a blind eye to it. She's the only girl in the family and they both dote on her. And Florrie is a likeable lass. You can't help but like her. When her store is finished she'll sneak in my back door, she lives opposite in the lane, and ask for a pennorth of sweets. And when I threaten to tell her mother what she's doing and say I won't give in to her coaxing, she gets well again and goes back to work.'

'Well!' Francine said. 'I've never heard of anyone doing such a thing as that. I think I would like to meet her.'

'You will, and when she does come back, let me know and I'll try and get you fixed up in a decent place, one where you don't have to work so hard. In the meantime I'll let Dan Beckett know you'll be coming for lessons. He's a nice chap, a very gentle soul.'

Mrs Lomax would only agree to Francine having two hours off on a Wednesday afternoon and Francine accepted it, knowing the job was only temporary. Once she was in the routine of the work she skipped the second dusting of the rooms and simply made a damp patch here and there on the floors of the bedrooms, using the time saved to write letters home.

All the letters were brief, simply stating that she had found a job and was in good health. Her problem was to get them posted from some place other than Reading. She decided to confide in Mr Naylor and ask his advice, explaining that although she wanted relatives and friends to know she was all right, she did not want any of them to try and persuade her to return to London. She just had to prove she could earn her own living.

'No difficulty,' he said. 'My son is going to London in the morning and will post them from there.'

Francine smiled. 'You've been very kind to me, Mr Naylor, I do appreciate it.' He returned her smile, saying it was his pleasure to help her. Then he suddenly cocked his head in a listening attitude and his smile widened.

'If I'm not mistaken that's Florrie sneaking in the back way. If it is she'll pop her head around the door any moment.' As he spoke a door leading from the shop to the living quarters opened and a head came round. 'Come in, Florrie,' he said, 'you're among friends. There's someone I want you to meet.'

For some reason Francine had imagined Mrs Lomax's niece to be tall and thin like her aunt and to be in her mid-twenties, instead of which she appeared to be little older than Francine herself. She was small and as round as a barrel, had a moon-shaped face and a double chin. Her hair was dark and looked as if it had been cut with a pudding basin on her head. Francine thought her very plain with her snub nose and pursed-up mouth, until Mr Naylor explained who Francine was, then deep dimples appeared in Florrie's cheeks and her eyes held a world of mischief. She looked then most attractive.

'Caught out, aren't I, I'm supposed to be in a coma. Don't you dare tell Aunt Sybil you've seen me.' Francine promised and Florrie went on, 'I heard me mam tell a neighbour that Auntie thinks you're a real find. Mind you, I want me job back because I like meeting the fellers. How d'ye get on with them?'

'I only get a glimpse of them at mealtimes.' Francine smiled. 'Your aunt sees to that.'

'Oh, you have to play clever. I manage to meet one of them in the evening, later on, that is. Life would be dull otherwise, wouldn't it?'

Mr Naylor chided her gently. 'Now don't you be leading this young lady into trouble.'

'Taking chances makes for fun.' Florrie's dimples were very evident. 'I think I'll have to come out of me coma, perhaps tomorrow. In the meantime I'll have a penny-worth of aniseed balls, Mr Naylor. They last a long time. Then I must go before I'm missed. Nice to meet you, Mary. Don't start looking for another job yet. When I do come back I'll plead weakness and have to take it easy, so she'll still need some help.' She handed over the penny for the sweets. 'What I do miss is Aunt Sybil's cooking. She's good, isn't she? It's also awkward to sneak food out of the pantry at home. Me little brother Harry is getting the blame for it, had his ear boxed last night for a chunk of cake missing. Poor kid. I'm away then, ta-ra.'

In spite of her bulk she seemed to slide out of the door and was gone.

Mr Naylor smiled. 'What a character, you just can't help but like her. But I'm sure she'll land herself in trouble one of these days.'

'I must go too, Mr Naylor. I'll let you know how I get on with my photography lesson with Mr Beckett.'

'Please do, my dear, I'll look forward to that.'

A few minutes after Francine left the shop she had renewed her decision, made in Monte Carlo, to concentrate on photographing people rather than landscapes. In all the photographs she had seen of people they were all serious, but how different they might be if they were smiling. Take Florrie. Her whole character had undergone a change when she smiled. She would have to have a word with Mr Beckett about this. Francine felt a sudden thrill go through her. To think that after all these years she was at last going to get to know about the art of photography! At that moment three days seemed an age to wait.

CHAPTER SIXTEEN

When Mr Beckett showed Francine into a room cluttered with negatives, photograph frames and photographs and other items to do with the work, she felt the thrill of pleasure of entering into yet one more new world.

'You like them?' he enquired.

'Oh, yes.' He was a big, broad-shouldered man with a shock of white hair, a strong-looking man yet his voice was soft and his movements slow.

'I get customers in to buy various things, but I don't do much photography as such nowadays. I leave that to a younger man, I've had my days of toil. The doctor told me I must rest. So tell me, young lady, what made you become interested in the work?'

Not wanting to explain about her father being a professional photographer and perhaps give her identity away, she said smiling, 'I fell in love with a camera.' Then she added quickly, 'Unfortunately, the people who could have helped me to understand the technology of photography do not believe in a woman taking up a profession.'

The old man nodded. 'I think I'm with them on that score and yet,' he rubbed his chin, 'I do have a great admiration for the work of Julia Margaret Cameron. She was married, had six children and it was her daughter actually who aroused her interest in photography. Mrs Cameron did take it up only as a hobby, of course.'

Francine said earnestly, 'I'm not interested in making a lot of money out of the work, but I'll have to earn enough to indulge my yearning to have my own camera and all the equipment.'

Mr Beckett gave her a benign smile. 'I like your dedication, my dear, and I shall teach you all I can. I can talk forever on the subject and as I'm sure there must be many questions you wish to ask, we shall need some sustenance. I shall ask my housekeeper to bring some tea and cake. Have a look around, I won't be long.'

Francine was in a state of delight. How lucky to have met Mr Beckett, who though not entirely in agreement with her needs was prepared to indulge her. She went to look at the photograph frames and novelties. There were lockets and tiny albums containing photographs, and then there were the framed miniatures. Larger frames were made of bamboo, plaited straw, carved wood, chased silver, bronze − the varieties were endless. She was about to have a look at the photographs on the walls when Mr Beckett returned.

'These miniature albums,' she said. 'Aren't they wonderful. How do you make the pictures so tiny?'

He motioned her to a chair. 'We shall come to that later. First, we shall go through the fundamentals, the study of lighting, which is so important. Are you interested in portraiture or landscapes?'

Francine told him that after observing the changing expressions with the change of the person's mood, she thought she would prefer portraiture.

He nodded in approval. 'I like the reason for your choice of subject. You have a feeling for people. Now first, I should like to quote you a small piece from Vincent Van Gogh who, among other wise things said, "*One may make mistakes, one may exaggerate here and there, but the things one makes will be original*".' Mr Beckett paused then went on, 'The originality is in the thought and technique of each individual. Photography today has reached a high standard, in architecture, scientific work, industry, fashion and high-class portraiture. But the emphasis, after technical points have been mastered in this last subject, must be centred on communication with other human beings. This is something that I feel sure you have.'

He talked at great length and Francine became so absorbed that the tea was lukewarm by the time they remembered to drink it. Mr Beckett apologised for his negligence but Francine dismissed it, saying 'I could listen to you for a day without food. You make it all so fascinating. Oh, Mr Beckett, you have no idea what this means to me. I've wanted to know about photography since I saw my first camera when I was eight years old and . . . fell in love with it.'

He laughed softly. 'I take back all I said about not agreeing with women going into the profession. Why should such love, such dedication, be wasted? Now, where was I?'

The two hours flew by and it was hearing a grandfather clock striking that made Francine jump to her feet. 'Four o'clock. Oh, I shall have to go. Mrs Lomax was most insistent that I had only two hours off.'

The old man held out her coat for his new pupil, then taking two books from a table offered her the loan of them. 'Study these and next week we shall discuss the contents. It's been a pleasure teaching you, Miss Chayter, you are so enthusiastic, so willing to learn. I shall look forward to seeing you next Wednesday. And, if you can persuade Mrs Lomax to let you have an extra hour's tuition I shall not charge you for it.'

'Thank you, Mr Beckett, it's been wonderful. I shall just live for next Wednesday. Bye!'

Francine ran all the way back to Mrs Lomax's and was greeted with a sharp reminder that she was ten minutes late. Francine simply smiled and said, 'What is ten minutes out of a lifetime?' which had the landlady gawping at her open-mouthed for a moment, before telling her to get on with peeling the potatoes, and to hurry up about it.

Francine was in a dream for the rest of that evening and was teased by some of the men. One dark-haired young man said, 'Only a feller could have put that look in your eyes,' and Francine said softly, 'Yes, it was a man.'

'Lucky feller,' came the reply. 'I'd like to have a try to repeat it.'

Francine smiled and shook her head. 'That would be impossible, you haven't the qualifications.'

To this Mrs Lomax shouted, 'And it doesn't need qualifications to get these plates of pudding to the hatch! Now come on, my girl, move – or they'll all be here till ten o'clock.'

During the next few days, Francine sneaked minutes out of her work-load to have a read of the books Mr Beckett had lent her and soon she became familiar with the names of the early pioneers, like the French physician and inventor Nicéphore Niepce, who had one of the strangest names she had ever heard. Then there was Henry Fox Talbot, Nadir, Daguerre – who was responsible for the Daguerreotype photographs, Tom Wedgewood and Sir Humphrey Davies. So many . . .

She lit a candle and read in bed by its flickering light and was sure she would dream photography; but instead had dreams in which Tyson and Rory both featured. Another night, the whole O'Reilly family were in her dreams and she awoke the next morning suffering from awful waves of homesickness. She had put everyone firmly to the back of her mind, knowing if she started thinking about them she would want to return to London. Her dreams were responsible for bringing them to the surface. She felt really unhappy when she went downstairs and might have remained in this mood had not Florrie turned up.

Mrs Lomax greeted her with, 'Well! Look who's here! You've soon come out of your coma, Florrie Gibson. I hope you're back here to work and not to moon around.' Although the voice was sharp there was affection in the woman's eyes.

'Course I'm back to work, Aunt Sybil.' Florrie's expression was all innocence. 'I wouldn't have come back else, you know that.' She turned to Francine and gave her a huge wink. 'So you'll be Mary, glad to know you. We'll have to share the work for a bit, won't we? I'm feeling better, but not on top, as it were.'

Mrs Lomax gave a 'humph' and told her she had better get her pinny on and get started, then added, 'And don't think I'm going to go on paying out two wages, because I'm not: money doesn't come in by the bucketful.'

Florrie just grinned at Francine and put on the coarse sacking apron. They went upstairs to do the bedrooms. Florrie was a great talker, she was also a shirker. She said she didn't agree with floors being washed so much and did as Francine had done, put a few damp patches on the floor, then she stretched out on the bed. Francine began to laugh then and Florrie laughed with her and said she could see they would get on like a house afire.

Francine was surprised that Florrie not only knew the christian names and surnames of each of the lodgers, but knew which ones were married, how many children they had and which of the younger men were courting. Florrie said she didn't mind who she spent a few minutes with in an evening, they were all men and working away from home. They needed a bit of young company, just as she needed men in her life.

Florrie's words reminded Francine of Sophie, and she wondered how her friend was getting on at school . . . She realised just how hurt Sophie must have been by her actions, as previously they had shared every little secret, all the fun and sadness in their lives. She must write to her again, a proper letter this time, reiterating her regret at having to leave her friend behind.

Florrie moved back into her old room which Francine was using, but although they shared the double bed and chatted at bedtime and had laughs together, Francine knew that with Florrie she would never have the close, sisterly relationship she had enjoyed with Sophie.

What did bother Francine was the way Florrie would wait until her aunt had settled in bed and then sneak out, saying she would only be a few minutes. Once, Francine got up and saw with foreboding the girl and a man go into the wood-shed in the back yard. They were not there long then Florrie was back saying, a note of satisfaction in her voice, 'That was a nice little chat to brighten the week. Brightened it for both of us.' Then she put something into her drawer and clambered back into bed, her feet cold, her body a dead weight as she snuggled into Francine's back for warmth.

One evening Florrie was away such a long time that Francine dropped off to sleep, and was aroused by hearing raised voices. She drew herself up in bed and realised it was Mrs Lomax and Florrie quarrelling. Mrs Lomax had once mentioned her temper, and she was certainly in a rage as she called Florrie 'a whore' and began slapping her around the face. Florrie was yelling back that she had only brought a bit of happiness into a man's life and Mrs Lomax shrieked, 'Happiness, that's not happiness, that's sin! And may the fires of hell consume you. *And* him that you tempted!'

Francine slid out of bed and creeping across the room opened the door and peeped out. Some of the men were on the landing below. When Mrs Lomax began slapping Florrie again one of the older men said, 'Take it easy, Missus, she's been ill.'

'Ill my foot, she's a Jezebel! Only I was too daft to see it. Your mate's gone and if there's any more carryings on like there's been this night, the lot of you will go. Is that clear? Now get back to bed and you, Miss, come with me where I can keep an eye on you. Tomorrow I'll let your mother know what you've been up to and if I'm any judge she'll have you put into a home for wicked girls.' She began to push Florrie in front of her and they went into Mrs Lomax's room with Florrie in tears, begging that her mother shouldn't be told.

Five minutes later the house was so quiet Francine could hear the creaking of wood as it seemed to settle down for the night. She lay in bed shivering. Mrs Lomax had called Florrie a whore but she had been in the shed only minutes.

Francine had a sudden feeling of utter exhaustion and soon she fell into an uneasy sleep.

The next morning Florrie was not in the house, nor was the dark-haired young man who had teased Francine about having a dreamy look in her eyes. The breakfast was served in almost total silence. And her homesickness was back. By the end of the day she knew it was only the thought of the coming Wednesday that made her stay in the job.

Mrs Lomax mentioned Florrie only briefly. She was sick again, sick in her mind this time and would not be coming back.

The atmosphere was terrible and at supper-time one of the men pushed a note into Francine's hand. He said he wanted to talk about what had happened to Florrie. Would Mary meet him in the back lane outside the door about eleven o'clock? When Francine went back to serve the pudding she shook her head at him. His eyes pleaded but she remained adamant. What had happened to Florrie could happen to her, and she was not going to end up having 'chats' and being pushed into any home for wicked girls. Her future was with photography.

The next Wednesday morning Francine asked for an extra hour to visit Mr Beckett, as the two hours off in a week was not enough. At first Mrs Lomax began to protest but when Francine told her she would leave to get a job where she could have a whole afternoon off the woman gave in, but warned her she had to be back prompt at five or she could leave. Francine was not to think she was indispensable – there were plenty of other girls who would be glad to do the job at five shillings a week. It would be a small fortune to some. Many a woman had practically to keep a family on that amount. Mrs Lomax was still calling after her when Francine left.

She had sufficiently recovered from her homesickness at that moment to be able to smile at the tirade.

Mr Beckett greeted her with a warm smile and without wasting any time they sat down for the lesson. After questioning Francine about the books he had lent her he pronounced himself delighted at the result, telling her she had a most retentive memory. He then answered her earlier question about miniature photography, explaining that a professional would reduce the photograph himself, but that there were men constantly experimenting. There was microphotography and photomicrography, the latter having been used by a man called John Dancer who reduced a whole page of *The Times* to an eighteenth of an inch across.

'An eighteenth of an inch?' Francine exclaimed. 'My goodness. I suppose you can use this technique to put photographs inside jewellery, like a ring or a locket.'

Mr Beckett nodded. 'But more importantly, it was used during the Franco-Prussian war to transport documents by pigeon post, tiny films being put into quills.' He added, laughingly, that the earliest micrographic was of a flea, taken by a man called Reade.

Francine arrived back at Mrs Lomax's, cockahoop with this new knowledge, only to be faced with her tight-lipped employer who told her she had a visitor. Francine stared at her, frozen. A visitor? Her father?

A voice behind her said quietly, 'Francine, we've all been terribly worried about you.'

She turned slowly to find Tyson de Auberleigh eyeing her with compassion. 'I'm sorry to be the one to find you, because I shall have to let the family know where you are.'

'How did you find me? I thought -'

Mrs Lomax interrupted, 'I'll give you five minutes to clear out.' She left, slamming the door.

Tyson said, 'I think you had better pack your bag now,

209

Francine. I'll get a cab to take us to the station then we can talk on the train.'

Francine drew back. 'No, I'm not leaving. I can't just walk out and leave Mrs Lomax to do all the work. She has lodgers.'

'I think Mrs Lomax will cope all right. She's evidently had to cope on her own a few times in the past. We have had quite a long talk. Go and pack, Francine.'

Her head went up. 'I'm not going with you, Tyson. For the first time in my life I'm doing what I want. I'm having lessons in photography and I won't give them up.'

'I'm afraid you'll have to. I don't think you realise what repercussions there have been because you chose to do what *you* wanted.' Tyson's manner had changed, there was now an anger in him.

'Sophie ran away from school, saying she was not going to stay without you; my aunt Helena was distressed when she found out that my uncle had given Sophie a sound thrashing; the O'Reilly family have been in a terrible state, feeling they had failed you in some way; the sons have been out scouring London for you and not getting any work done. Your father, at great expense, even hired private detectives to look for you, without success I might add.'

Francine, who had lowered her head with a feeling of shame at her thoughtlessness, now looked up. 'And how did *you* find me?'

'By one of those chance moments in life. I had come to visit one of my college friends and, to my astonishment saw *you* going into a house. I was about to knock on the door when a woman came out, carrying a shopping basket. I asked about you and she told me you were having a photography lesson and had strict instructions from Mr Beckett they were not to be disturbed until three-thirty, when she would take in tea. She added that if I wanted to get in touch with you later I would find you at Mrs Lomax's. She gave me the address.'

Francine stood a moment then said, 'I'll go and pack. I can drop a note into Mr Beckett on our way.'

Tyson managed to hail a cab, but although he chatted about his college friend and tried to make small talk, Francine remained silent until they were at the station and waiting for the train. Then she said, 'If you return me to my father, Tyson, that will be the end of my hopes, my dreams. He threatened that if I did not return to school he would find a husband for me, not a young man, but someone older who would be strict with me.'

Tyson glanced at her quickly. 'He probably only said it to make you take notice and go back to school.'

'My father would never say anything he didn't mean,' she answered grimly. 'He hates me and I think it would give him pleasure to see me suffer. He wants his revenge for what my mother did to him.'

'Oh, Francine, I'm sure you're wrong.' Tyson now seemed full of concern. 'He wouldn't have bothered about you running away if he hadn't cared for you. He had every chance to say good riddance. Don't you agree?' His voice was coaxing.

Francine met his gaze steadily. 'No, I don't and neither would you if you knew him as I do. He's cold, implacable. He would be determined to get me back just to punish me, teach me who is boss in his house.'

Tyson was silent so long after this that Francine wondered if he was toying with the idea of letting her go. But his next words showed her that he too could be determined about something.

'I have to take you back to your father, Francine. If I didn't and something awful happened to you I would regret my weakness for the rest of my life. I'm doing what I think is for the best. You must believe me.'

'And would you not repent if I were married against my will to an old man whom I hated and who made me submit to his orders?'

Tyson dismissed such a possibility with a laugh. 'Oh,

211

come on, Francine, now you really are exaggerating. Your father is not an ogre. I'm sure you'll get a scolding, quite a severe one, but I'm sure too that the worst that will happen to you is to be sent back to school.'

Francine thrust out her jaw. 'I won't go, nor will I submit to a forced marriage. I'll talk to everyone, try and explain how I had to get away, out of my father's clutches. I'm sure they will understand, even if you don't.'

'Now you are being melodramatic.' Anger was back in Tyson's voice. 'I think you behaved selfishly to run away as you did and cause so much distress to so many people. It's time you grew up and listened to reason. You were lucky in finding a job with Mrs Lomax who kept you out of harm's way. There were ten men in that house. Men who were away from home. Heaven knows what could have happened to you.'

'Well, it didn't, did it?' Francine was angry now. 'I do have a code of behaviour myself without having to rely on someone else taking care of me. I *can* take care of myself and I'll prove it when I run away the next time.'

Tyson declared he had lost all patience with her and when the train arrived and they took their seats in a first-class carriage they remained silent for a long time, Tyson's face closed against her. Francine felt she hated him for what he was doing to her, and found it difficult to believe he had ever told her he had fallen in love with her. Was it only weeks ago that she had been by the sea in a languorous climate, experiencing so much luxury? Tyson had been so tender towards her at times, now she found a coolness in him that reminded her of Edwin Chayter. So much for her romantic interludes with Tyson!

Before they reached Paddington, however, Tyson approached her again, this time his manner was more gentle. 'Francine, I don't want to do anything to hurt you, I don't want to be responsible for making you unhappy. Where would you like to go when we arrive? To see Bridget, my aunt and Sophie or the O'Reillys, or do you feel you must see your father to put his mind at rest? Believe me when I say he was upset that you had run away and I know there was no suggestion of any revenge in his mind when I spoke to him.'

Francine, on the verge of tears at the change in Tyson's attitude, answered in a low voice that she would like to go straight to Bridget's house. Bridget would perhaps have suffered the most because she had been in her care.

'Bridget's it shall be then,' Tyson said, with a sudden forced cheerfulness. 'Perhaps the whole thing will blow over once you're returned to the fold.'

'Perhaps,' she said, but knew deep down she would have a load of trouble to face. Even facing Bridget would not be easy.

Tyson left her when they arrived, saying he would keep in touch. There was warmth in the smile he gave her and in the squeeze of his hand.

Bridget burst into tears when she saw Francine standing there, and held her close, but by the time she was putting the kettle on for a cup of tea the scolding began and she did not spare Francine the brickbats. How could she have done such a thing – didn't she know all the trouble she could cause? Had she no feelings for anyone else? Think of all the people who had become involved, people who had worried themselves sick. Yes, she knew Francine had sent letters but anything could have happened since. Gran O'Reilly was sure she could have been taken by gypsies or was lying at the bottom of a river.

How did Francine think *she* would feel, Bridget wanted to know, realising she would be held responsible? Her father had called her incompetent. Heaven knew what would be the outcome. One thing was certain; her father would no longer allow Francine to live with her.

The full implications of her actions really hit Francine then. She had never thought of Bridget being so involved that her father might stop her from living here. Bridget had become like a dear aunt to her. Big tears welled up and ran slowly down her cheeks and she ached to be once more cocooned against misery.

Bridget poured them each a cup of tea then drawing up a chair reached out a hand to Francine. 'Don't cry, my love. I've been hard on you, but I've felt ill with worry, not knowing what had happened.' She held out a handkerchief. 'Dry your eyes, love. You'll feel better when you've told me the whole story.'

Later, she sighed, 'Oh, dear, working as a skivvy in a lodging house. We must never let your father hear about this, Francine. I don't rightly know what we can tell him ... I don't think I ought to lie, but scrubbing floors, looking after lodgers, men – it's terrible!'

When Francine was calmer they agreed they would simply say that Francine had found lodgings and had paid to take photography lessons, and would have gone on living in this way as long as her money lasted.

'Surely, with his love of photography your father must understand the need in his own daughter,' Bridget said. 'But of course, as you well know, he is a difficult man. You look worn out, Francine dear, I suggest you go and lie down for a while. I shall go with you later to see your father.' Bridget gave a shaky laugh. 'Beard the lion in his den, as it were.'

Francine said wearily she would rather go right away and get it over and done with. And so they caught a tram to Spinners End.

As they arrived at the house Rory, who was coming down the steps, stopped dead and stared. 'Francine! Well, I'll go to the divil. Where've you been? Do you know that everyone's out of their minds at -'

Bridget held up a hand. 'Francine's gone through enough, Rory, without any more scolding. She does have her father to face.'

'Yes, of course, sorry. Does Gran know you're back?' Francine shook her head and Rory looked gleeful. 'Just wait until she knows, she'll get the flags out. I have an

214

errand to do, I'll call and tell her. See you later, in the meantime don't run away again. We missed you, missed you like hell – sorry, like anything.' He left, laughing, glanced over his shoulder and gave her a wave.

Kathleen, who opened the door to them, exclaimed, 'Glory be to God, you're not dead and in your grave as Gran was convinced you were.' She drew Francine fiercely to her and they cried together. Then Kathleen drew away, wanting to know if Bridget and Francine would come to the kitchen first and have a cup of tea, or whether Francine wanted to get the interview over with her Da first. Francine said they would go straight upstairs if that would be all right. Kathleen went upstairs and moments later was waving them up from the landing. She whispered, 'He's been very quiet these past two days, but be prepared for anything. And don't answer him back whatever you do.'

Francine found herself wondering when they went into her father's study how many times they had met under similar circumstances, with her father sitting writing at his desk and not bothering to look up until he had finished what he was writing.

When he laid down his pen and she saw the anger in his eyes she knew that she was not going to be let off lightly.

'So, the prodigal returns. Well, my girl, there will be no fatted calf for you. Who do you think you are, just leaving everyone and going off to seek your fortune, or whatever it was that you were after?'

'To learn photography,' she said quietly.

'Don't you dare answer me back! And I have very few more words I want to say to you. A suitable husband will be found for you and then I shall wash my hands of you. You've been nothing but trouble since we met, defying me in everything I asked you to do. You can stay with Mrs Brogan until you are married, and if you don't, if you try running away again, I shall see Mrs Brogan made homeless. And don't think I cannot do it.'

215

'But that isn't fair,' Francine protested. 'Bridget had nothing to do with me running away.'

'Was it fair that you left so many people in ignorance as to your whereabouts? People who had shown you every kindness. You, my girl, are beneath contempt and if you want Mrs Brogan to keep you at her home you know what you have to do. That is all.' He picked up his pen.

Francine opened her mouth to protest again but Bridget nudged her and shook her head. She got up and pulled Francine to her feet.

They were at the door when Francine turned and said, 'I'll do as you command but I don't think I deserve such cruelty. You are more than cruel, Papa, you're sadistic. Perhaps once you've taken revenge on me you might at last find peace of mind. I hope so.'

Bridget pulled her outside then closing the door shook her head at her. 'Oh, dear, when will you learn to keep quiet, Francine? You do your cause no good. Your father might have relented.'

'No. He never would. He might have suffered in the past for the way my mother behaved, but his punishment to me is almost too much to bear. It's my life in ruins.'

On their way downstairs to the kitchen Bridget said, 'I know your father sounds cruel, Francine, but he's a proud man and his kind suffer slights deeply. Given time I still think he might relent.' Bridget paused outside the kitchen door. 'We can tell Kathleen later what has happened, but I don't think it's wise to let Cook and Evie know what has transpired. Leave it to me, I'll simply say you were soundly scolded and that will be that.'

Cook accepted it and told Francine she was very lucky that she had had no more than a scolding. Evie nodded to this. Kathleen raised her eyebrows and Bridget whispered, 'Later.'

They sat down to a cup of tea and piece of seedcake, with Cook trying unsuccessfully to wheedle from Francine where she had been. Afterwards, they left to visit the O'Reillys.

On the way in the tram Francine expected to be roundly scolded by every member of the O'Reilly family, but her welcome was warm and loving and when Francine told them she was sorry for all the trouble she had caused, Mrs O'Reilly said, 'Ah, now, don't be apologising, it might all have been to the good. I think that most people feel like running away at some time in their life and if they do they usually learn something from it. Either they learn that their family aren't so bad after all, or that they've found just what they've been seeking. I hope with you it's the latter. Come and sit down and tell us all that happened. That is, if you want to, of course.' Francine said she did and told them everything, apart from Mrs Lomax calling Florrie a whore.

There were plenty of interruptions during the telling. Fancy their little Francine getting down on her hands and knees and scrubbing floors, especially when they didn't need scrubbing. What a foolish woman . . . Ten men lodgers did Francine say? . . . It was good that she was well fed . . . Took lessons in photography? Well, it was what she had wanted, wasn't it? This from Mrs O'Reilly, who went on about it. Just like their Rory she was, photography mad.

Then the old lady said suddenly, 'Francine, child, what did your father say when you came back?'

Francine hesitated for a moment then she sat up straight. 'He told me he's going to find a husband for me.'

'A husband?' they all echoed. There were murmurs of consternation. Therese said, 'But you're only sixteen!'

Mrs O'Reilly crossed herself and with eyes closed whispered, 'Then please God he'll be a man you could love.'

Francine, knowing that this would be the last thing her father would consider, felt full of despair.

CHAPTER SEVENTEEN

Although Francine was longing to see Sophie she was also dreading meeting Mrs Denton, who had always been so kind, so gentle with her. But like the O'Reillys, she too was warm and loving towards her.

'Oh, my dear,' she greeted her, 'I can't tell you how pleased I am to see you safe and well. I should have realised how unhappy you were to want to run away. If only you had told me I might have been able to help.'

When Francine said how sorry she was for all the trouble she had caused Mrs Denton answered, 'I'm sorry you felt it necessary to run away, Francine dear, but now, we are going to forget all about it. Sophie will be so glad to see you. She ran away from school, as you know. Her father insisted she went back but she made herself so ill that I arranged for her to leave.'

Mrs Denton smiled and there was an imp of mischief in her lovely eyes. 'I might say it's the first time in my life that I've had my own way.'

Francine knew then that if there had been any ice to break it would certainly have been broken at that moment. They were fellow conspirators.

Sophie, who had been upstairs reading a story to Roderick who was in bed with a chill, came running into the drawing room.

'Francine! I thought it was your voice I could hear as I came downstairs. When did you come back, where have you been? It was rotten of you not to tell me you were running away. If only you knew what I have been through -'

Mrs Denton said quietly, 'Sophie, take Francine upstairs

and don't start scolding her. I'm afraid she must have had a very trying time. Off you go!'

Francine had to go through the whole story again and this time she included the part about Florrie being called a whore. She ended the tale by telling Sophie about her father's latest threat.

Sophie stared at her, dismayed. 'Oh, Francine, he really meant it, then.'

'Yes, with Papa it's simply revenge. *How* he must hate my mother.'

'I think he's a pig taking it out on you. I used to like him once but now I hate him. I wonder who he has in mind for you to marry? It could be someone personable.'

'Definitely not young,' Francine said firmly. 'He made that very clear. He told me earlier it would be an older man who would be strict with me.' Francine looked at Sophie with appeal. 'What am I to do? I can't even run away again because Bridget would suffer.'

'Marry Lord Holcombe – he might not live long,' Sophie offered hopefully.

Francine gave a sigh of despair. 'Forget Lord Holcombe, Sophie, *please*. He could live ten, twenty years, but living one year with him would be more than enough. I'm young. I want to marry eventually but I had hoped it would be to someone I loved. If only I had a lot of money I could go away – take Bridget away with me. We could live in France or – or somewhere.'

Sophie suggested that Francine write to her mother, pointing out that if she knew what Francine's father was planning she might step in and lend her the money to leave England.

Francine shook her head. 'I don't think my mother would be interested even if she knew Papa was about to marry me off to the devil!'

Sophie grinned. 'Now that could be interesting. Oh, let's stop fretting. You know what Bridget is always saying

– it's no use worrying about what could happen because it might never take place.'

Francine made an effort to forget her worries for the moment and asked Sophie what she had been doing recently. She said, very little, as she had been more or less confined to the house on her father's orders after running away from school. She had seen Tyson when he came to tell them that Francine was safe, but only for a few moments.

'He has his worries too,' she said. 'He's been seeing a lot of Octavia Manning, but she blows hot and cold and he never knows where he stands. Apparently, my uncle is becoming more insistent that he goes into banking and Tyson is dead against it. If Octavia won't have him, I wouldn't be surprised if he doesn't try to marry some girl with a large dowry, so that he can do what he likes in the way of any business he chooses or just laze his way through life, travelling and socialising.'

Francine refused to believe this, and said so. 'I don't think that any man of his calibre would marry without love. He could lead a terrible life if he found he had married a difficult woman.'

Sophie laughed grimly. 'Don't you believe it, he would simply go and find a mistress. That's what men do, after all. And most of the wives accept this way of life. Women are just chattels, Francine.'

Francine felt a sudden terrible ache. 'Sophie, supposing this man my father chooses for me refuses to allow me to mix with all the people I know and love. What could I do? I don't think I could stand it. It's all of you – you, your mother, Bridget, Kathleen, the O'Reillys, that have made my life so wonderful. Without you all I might just as well be dead.'

Sophie gave a shiver. 'Stop saying things like that. You make ice go down my spine. I'll think of something – I'll ask Mama. She could talk to my uncle, as he knows your father and puts a lot of business in his way, I've heard

Mama say this. Perhaps Mr de Auberleigh could make your father see sense. Uncle likes you, I remember how kind he was to you the first time we had dinner with the family in Monte Carlo. He's never once talked to me like that. Oh, Francine, I couldn't bear it if I couldn't see you. We would have to meet in secret. Do you remember when we first went to school and we both cut a little nick in our wrists and put our wrists together, swearing we would be blood sisters for life? Well, we are not going to allow any miserable husband to part us, are we?'

'No,' Francine said, her lips trembling, and the next moment they were both in tears.

When Bridget came for Francine later both girls felt happier, hopeful that they would get help from some source.

Later that week, a note was delivered summoning Francine to see her father.

Kathleen opened the door to them. She was pale but gave Francine a quick hug. 'He's waiting, my love. He's been quiet all morning. You'd better go straight up.'

Francine, who was trying to be reconciled to her fate could not, nevertheless, stop the trembling of her limbs. She clasped her hands tightly together when her father called, 'Come in,' to Bridget's knock. For once he was not sitting at his desk writing, but was standing, his back to the fire.

Two chairs had been placed facing him. He motioned them to sit down.

When they were seated he began without preamble. 'Several men have offered for your hand, Miss, but I have considered a proposition from Lord Holcombe. And I might add I'm being kind to you in considering it, after your appalling behaviour.'

Francine's heart began a dull pounding. 'You mean that Lord Holcombe wants to marry me?'

'I said he has a proposition to offer,' he retorted. 'He'll be here in a few minutes, having recently returned to his country seat in England. When he arrives I and Mrs Brogan will leave you together, so he can explain his plan fully. I would advise you to accept it.' Edwin Chayter walked to the window and stood there, his back to them. 'If not you will accept the man I choose for you.'

Francine and Bridget exchanged glances. Francine mouthed, 'Proposition?' and Bridget raised her shoulders in a helpless shrug.

At that moment Lord Holcombe arrived and after greetings had been exchanged Edwin and Bridget withdrew. Lord Holcombe gave Francine a sad little smile. 'My dear, I'm sorry we meet under these rather difficult circumstances. I only hope we can reach an amicable conclusion.' He sat on a chair facing her then added, 'If I had been a younger man I would very quickly have asked for your hand. As it is . . .'

Francine waited, puzzled. If he did not want to marry her, then was it his intention to ask her to be his mistress? The thought chilled her. Surely not.

'I will try to explain the situation as simply as possible, Francine. Mr de Auberleigh informed me that his son Tyson would be willing to marry you, under certain conditions. I do understand that you have a liking for one another?'

Francine's heart was now a wild thing. Tyson? She nodded. 'Yes, I like him very much and he did tell me when we were abroad that he thought he could – love me, but since then -'

'Then that is splendid. We are halfway there. Now then, as you know, I have no children of my own and I would like to take you both under my wing, as it were. Tyson will be my right hand, accompany me when I have to go abroad on business – he enjoys travel. When we are at home, he will help to run the estate. He is an outdoor man. You will make your home at Holcombe Manor, which is in Windsor but will of course have your own suite of rooms.'

222

Francine was becoming more and more bewildered. 'I don't quite understand Tyson accepting these terms. I was told he was seeing a great deal of Octavia Manning and was deeply in love with her.'

'Octavia has recently become betrothed to an American millionaire. She wanted a wealthy husband.' His tone was dry. 'I believe they are to live in the United States.'

'Tyson must have been very upset,' Francine said.

'His father was more upset. The poor boy made rather a fool of himself over her in public. I'm being honest with you, Francine. You have to know the position. Mr de Auberleigh has been annoyed that Tyson would not go into banking and he's told him if he does not accept my proposition and marry you, he will cut him completely out of his life.'

Francine stared at Lord Holcombe in astonishment. 'His father wants him to marry *me*? After the way I behaved?'

'He thinks you were driven to it and puts no blame on you whatsoever. He apparently has quite a fondness for you, thinks you are a very sensible young lady and will be good for his son. Oh, yes, he realises of course, as I do, that it will not be roses all the way, at first that is. It's an odd situation. But the fact that you and Tyson do like one another gives us hope for the future.'

Francine thought wryly she wished she could share his sentiments. She could see nothing but trouble ahead. And yet there was an underlying excitement about the idea. She would not be pushed into marriage with some hateful older man.

Lord Holcombe leaned forward, a look of pleading in his eyes. 'Do please accept the situation, Francine. Tyson is young and handsome and I must tell you that the next man on your father's list is an odious person, wealthy, yet very mean.'

'I accept,' she said with a smile. Then soberly she added, 'I'll do my best to be a good wife and I thank you from

223

the bottom of my heart for giving me this chance, Lord Holcombe. You've always been so kind to me.'

'You brightened my life in Monte Carlo, my dear. Even in a crowd a person can be very lonely. You always listened, in an interested way, to what I had to say. You were kind to *me*.' He got up. 'Now we must let your father know the glad news.' He went to the door.

When Edwin Chayter knew he showed no reaction, but simply said, 'Well, that is settled. We shall arrange a date for the wedding later.' To Francine he added, 'Mrs Brogan is waiting for you. She will be informed in time of the arrangements.'

Just like that! Francine thought. Then she turned to Lord Holcombe and thanked him for all he had done. He bade her goodbye and gave her a huge wink, like a fellow conspirator. She left without bidding her father goodbye.

Both Kathleen and Bridget were waiting for her at the end of the landing. She hurried towards them and gasped out her news. Kathleen gave a glad cry and hugged her, Bridget's face widened into a broad smile. 'Thank goodness for that. Protégés of Lord Holcombe, eh? My goodness, Francine, you *are* lucky.'

Kathleen, bright-eyed, said, 'Tyson de Auberleigh! You really are marrying into the aristocracy. When are you seeing Tyson? Come along, tell us everything, we'll go to the kitchen.'

In the kitchen the talk never stopped. Evie oohed and aahed, while Cook was impressed by the de Auberleigh family. Why, they went back to the flood! She had worked once for a cousin of Mr de Auberleigh. They had more money than they knew what to do with. Would it be a white wedding? Where would it be? Perhaps Westminster Abbey.

Francine, caught up in it all said, 'I don't know and I don't care. I only know that I'm not having to marry some hideous old man. Just wait till Sophie knows.'

224

Sophie squealed her delight. 'Tyson? Great heavens, wonders will never cease!'

Mrs Denton was quietly pleased; it seemed to be no surprise to her. She told Francine to count on her for any help she needed with the wedding. Francine asked what Mrs de Auberleigh thought about the arrangements, and Mrs Denton replied calmly that she was sure her sister was pleased but they had not as yet been together to have a talk.

A great sadness suddenly descended on Francine. She had no choice but to marry Tyson: would she have wanted to marry him if she had been free? He could be moody. And what would his reactions be towards her, after this coercion? How could they even establish a friendly relationship if he was still deeply in love with Octavia Manning? Would time help him to get over his obsession with the fair-haired beauty? Francine, remembering the times that Tyson had been really nice to her, had hope. After all, Octavia was definitely out of reach now and if Tyson was pleased to be able to travel and do more or less as he wished without his father plaguing him to learn banking, he might turn out to be quite amiable.

But any hope of accord between them was dispelled the next day, when she met him at the Dentons. He stood up when she came into the room, acknowledged her, said 'I'm glad we've met,' and glared at her, his expression stormy.

Mrs Denton motioned to Sophie who was lapping it all up, and looking as if she were enjoying herself and she left at her mother's command, seeming quite disgruntled. 'I'll leave you together for a while,' Mrs Denton said tactfully. 'There will be several things you will both want to discuss.'

When they had gone there was a silence. Tyson stared towards the window, with his chin out-thrust in a stubborn line. Francine waited and when he made no effort to speak she said, 'Well, there must be something you want to say.'

225

He turned his head and Francine felt a chill go through her as she saw the coldness in his eyes. 'There's quite a lot I want to say, but I'm afraid if I start I shall overstep the mark and say something I shall regret.'

Francine forced herself to reply calmly, 'Say what you wish, Tyson, I won't take offence. After what has been said to me I think I've developed a skin as thick as a rhinocerous.'

He sat up. 'If you had not been so foolish as to run away, you idiot girl, I would not find myself being forced into marriage!'

Francine sat up. 'May I point out that you *do* have a choice, and I suggest you use that choice because I have no wish to go through a ceremony to have my husband blaming me for his indiscretions.'

'What do you mean by indiscretions? I've done nothing to be ashamed of. I fell in love, the girl prefers someone else. I am not to blame for that.'

'No, of course not, but as I understand it you have no wish to go into banking and in order to be free of your father's dominance you accepted Lord Holcombe's offer to have a life more to your liking.'

'And in return I have to tie myself to someone I -' He paused and looked embarrassed.

'You don't love? You did tell me once you had fallen in love with me, but anyway, the important thing is that you have no need to tie yourself to me. Simply tell Lord Holcombe that you have no wish to accept the arrangements he suggested. I will marry someone else, someone my father will choose for me, and you will go into banking. It's so simple – I don't know why you are sitting glowering at me.'

'Because *I do not* want to go into banking.'

'Nor do you want to be married. I suggest you give the matter a great deal of thought. But if your choice is marriage, then I shall not accept recriminations for what will be your own choice.'

He sat for a time looking as if he were made of wood, then he stood up and paced around the room. 'You can't possibly understand my dilemma. You haven't lived.'

'Oh, yes, Tyson, I've lived. I'm surprised at how much I've learned about life since my father brought me to live with him. Have you ever mixed with people who have to work for a pittance, and perhaps have one meal a day and that a crust of bread each; have you seen children going barefooted to school *and* in winter, their clothes thread-bare? These people live in a harsh, real world. Those you mix with live in luxury, have three good meals a day, a dinner perhaps consisting of five, six or seven courses. You drive about in carriages or motor cars.'

Although a flush rose to Tyson's cheeks he said, 'If you are trying to make me feel shame because I've been brought up with a certain amount of luxury, you've failed. I didn't choose to be born into my family. If I had been born into a poorer class then *I* might have been going barefooted as a child. And like you, condemning those who have wealth.'

'It's easy to say these things when you're not suffering,' Francine retorted.

'Look, let me explain something.' He spoke in the patient way an adult might reason with a child. 'I have been bound by parental discipline, like so many other offspring. My father is in the banking world so I am expected to follow in his footsteps. I don't *want* to be in banking. I would prefer to work on the land.'

'Well, now you have your chance; you would be involved in land-management if you came under the guidance of Lord Holcombe. But I would like to point out that you would also have an opportunity to indulge your desire for travel. Not exactly the prerogative of a farm-hand, is it?'

'Do you know something, Francine Chayter, you can be really infuriating. I would have welcomed the chance to travel and have been willing to work my passage on a tramp steamer, if I had been allowed. But no, a de Auber-leigh could not do anything so demeaning.' Tyson ran slender fingers through his thick dark hair. 'And now, in order to break the ties that bind me I have to make a sacrifice.'

'The sacrifice being me, of course,' Francine snapped.

'Yes. It would be wrong to lie about it. I had no inten-tion of marrying for some time.'

'But you would have married Octavia Manning like a shot, if you had had the chance.'

Anger flared in his eyes. 'I have no wish to discuss Octavia. And now, if you will excuse me.' He gave her the slightest of bows and left. The next moment she heard him ask a maid to give his apologies to her mistress, he had to leave.

Mrs Denton came into the drawing room alone. 'I take it that all did not run smoothly, Francine?'

'Far from it.' She explained what had passed between them and Mrs Denton said it was really no more than could be expected, two young people being forced into a situation that neither really wanted. 'But,' she added, 'given time, it might work out very well. Many a young girl has had an arranged marriage and love grows between husband and wife.' At that moment Francine had very little faith that this would be so in the case of Tyson and herself.

Two days later when she went with Bridget to the O'Reillys she faced an aggressive Rory. Why had she agreed to marry Tyson de Auberleigh? To her reply that she had had no choice he replied in scathing tones: 'You could have got out of the arrangements had you wanted to.'

'How, tell me that? I'm sixteen, I have no money, I'm answerable to my father. I ran away once and here I am back and without having achieved anything. Except that is, that I did find someone who was willing to give me lessons in photography, which, I might add, was more than you were willing to do.'

'Because there would have been no end to it, that's why!' he shouted.

Soon they were both yelling at one another in the passage, which brought Mrs O'Reilly bustling out of the kitchen demanding to know what was going on. They were both trying to explain, with Francine near to tears when the old lady said, 'That's enough. Rory, you get back to your job. Francine, come with me.' She took her arm and urged her towards the kitchen. Rory went out, slamming the door behind him.

Mrs O'Reilly said quietly, 'He's full of hurt, Francine. He's fond of you, I know he doesn't show it, but I think deep down he saw you as his girl and that one day you would be married.'

'Well, he didn't try very hard to show it,' Francine said, her lips trembling. 'He's always been on at me, always trying to upset me.'

'Not when you went for bicycle rides together,' the old lady reminded her gently. 'But since then you've been abroad, mixed with the upper class and now you are to be married to the son of a wealthy man. Rory's to blame for taking you for granted. He'll get over it. Now, just you sit there, love, and I'll make you a cup of tea.' Francine was aware then that there was pain in Mrs O'Reilly's voice. Rory was very much her favourite although she would never have admitted it.

The following day Bridget told Francine that the wedding had been set for the end of May, and that her father had asked for it to be a quiet affair. This pleased Francine but not apparently Mrs de Auberleigh, who expected a fashionable wedding for people of their status. But according to Sophie her uncle had agreed with Edwin Chayter, pointing out that Tyson, who had gone against his wishes in relation to a profession, did not deserve the kudos or publicity of a big affair.

229

Sophie, who had appointed herself chief bridesmaid with a retinue of bridesmaids and page boys, was furious, pointing out that her uncle should not have had any say in it. It was a woman's affair and the arrangements should have been left to her aunt.

To this Bridget asked wryly, 'And would you agree that Mr Chayter should be faced with a massive bill for a lavish affair? After all, the marriage was arranged as a punishment for Francine.'

Sophie subsided, but grumbled a great deal more when they learned some weeks later that the time of the wedding would not be known until the evening before the ceremony.

'It's diabolical,' she declared, 'and I know why it's being kept secret. So the O'Reilly family won't turn up at the church. Oh, yes, your father is certainly having his pound of flesh. He knows that you regard them as close family. He's a pig. I've said it before and I'm saying it again. I hate him.'

It hurt Francine that the O'Reillys would not be at the church but she was powerless to change anything.

She was to be married in white, in a simply-styled dress and hat, and instead of carrying a bouquet of flowers she would hold a prayer book. Sophie, her only attendant, would be wearing pale blue.

Mrs Denton had tried to talk to Francine once about the duties of a wife to her husband, but was so embarrassed she ended up by telling her that she was to accept any unusual behaviour on the part of her husband.

'Unusual in what way?' she asked Sophie. Sophie suggested she ask Bridget . . . and was offered more or less the same advice given by Mrs Denton. In the end it was Kathleen who explained what being married really meant. Francine was horrified. 'But that's dreadful, it's well, it's unhealthy. I won't do it.'

'You must,' Kathleen said quietly, 'otherwise you'll be

a wife in name only. And Francine, I understand it can be quite pleasurable once you become used to the idea.'

Francine said, 'Never,' but was secretly curious about such a rite and confided her news in Sophie.

Sophie looked at her goggle-eyed at first then she began to laugh. 'So, that's what the mystery is all about. Well, it must give *some* pleasure or we would have hundreds of women killing themselves. You will let me know how you get on, won't you?'

Francine, knowing it would be impossible to discuss such an intimate subject, even with Sophie, turned the talk to the wedding breakfast, which was to be held at the Dentons' house.

Late one evening, Francine learned the wedding would take place at the local church at nine o'clock the following morning. She was also told that her father would meet her at the church. Francine felt wooden.

How could he do this to her? He was not only denying her the courtesy of travelling in the same carriage, as any other daughter would do, but was denying her the warmth and love of the O'Reillys to help her along. There was not even to be a honeymoon as such, for after the wedding breakfast she would leave with Tyson to drive to Holcombe Manor.

The future at that moment certainly looked bleak.

CHAPTER EIGHTEEN

At twelve o'clock the following morning when Francine was driving with her bridegroom to Holcombe Manor she wondered if any bride had ever set off on her honeymoon with a more grim-looking husband. To be fair, Tyson had made an effort to be pleasant at the wedding breakfast, not so her father. When she had walked down the aisle on her father's arm and saw Tyson waiting, she wondered which of the two men was the most ferocious-looking. Tyson had simply inclined his head in greeting and she felt she had hated him then for not making an attempt at a smile.

The chill of the church had crept into her bones and although a coat had been provided for the drive she felt herself trembling at times.

There had been no sightseers inside or outside the church. The Denton family, the de Auberleighs, Lord Holcombe and Bridget were the only people there who were not involved in the ceremony. Her father left right after the service without even saying goodbye to her. Lord Holcombe set off before the end of the wedding breakfast, saying he wanted to be at Holcombe Manor to welcome the newlyweds.

To be fair also to Tyson's family, they had been pleasant to her and Mr Denton had put himself out to wish her well. It was Tyson and her father who had made the whole ceremony seem a sham.

The chauffeur-driven limousine had been Lord Holcombe's gift to them and when Tyson had seen it his whole face lit up.

Francine, feeling she must make an effort to lift the

gloom said, 'Lord Holcombe has been most generous with his gift.'

Tyson looked at her and studied her as though seeing her for the first time. 'Yes, indeed. Quite a surprise. It almost compensates for–' He stopped and a flush rose to his cheeks.

Francine said drily, 'Compensates for having to be saddled with me.'

'I didn't mean that, not in that particular context. I was thinking of being answerable to someone for my daily bread. In other words, Lord Holcombe. I wish that I had had sufficient money to do exactly as I pleased.'

'So do I,' Francine said on a grim note. 'Being married to you is not something that I had bargained for.'

'Bargained for? I say, that is a bit strong. Most young ladies of your age would be delighted to – well to have found a presentable husband. And I say that with all modesty.'

'Presentable? You are boorish, petty, childish and have been utterly spoiled by your mother. Don't expect me to go down on my bended knees and thank you for marrying me. Nor shall I promise to try and be a good, obedient wife.'

'I hope you will be obedient,' he retorted. 'I shall have enough to contend with, a work schedule and–'

'And trips abroad. What troubles are you anticipating? I shall keep out of your way as much as possible.'

'Thank you, that will certainly help.'

Francine thought if there had been anything at hand to throw at him she would have done so. The arrogance of the man.

The car slowed then turned left between big iron gates and travelled along a gravelled drive towards a three-storeyed stone built house with mullioned windows.

The garden was formal with a small pool in the centre where a cupid poised on one leg was preparing to shoot an arrow. A small fountain spilled into the basin. They drove up to wide stone steps where at the top a big oaken door was set in a balustraded terrace.

The door opened and Lord Holcombe came out and waved to them, an upright, elegant figure in his morning suit that he had worn for the wedding. Francine felt her first real warmth of the morning at his welcoming smile.

As they went up the steps he held out a hand to each. 'Welcome, welcome to Holcombe Manor Mr and Mrs de Auberleigh and may you spend many happy days here.' Tyson actually smiled and his smile this time was sincere.

They were ushered into the hall where several servants were lined up to greet them. Although on first appearance the hall had seemed gloomy, Francine felt a warmth stealing into her. This *could* be home to her.

Lord Holcombe led the way upstairs to make sure they approved of their accommodation. The boot boy and a sturdy-looking maid followed with Tyson's trunk and Francine's hamper. There was a sitting room made cosy with red velvet upholstery and curtains; a double bedroom with a tester bed in which all the furnishings were of chintz, and a dressing room led from this. There were two smaller bedrooms and a bathroom with the largest bath Francine had ever seen. Lord Holcombe joked about it, saying his predecessor had been blessed with ten children – four sets of twins with a year between each pair, and two singles to follow.

'Blessed did you say?' Tyson queried. 'I hope to have children but not in such a quantity.'

Francine, oddly enough, had not thought of children until then and as she remembered Kathleen describing how she must submit to her husband she felt blood pounding in her temples. How was she going to cope with such a dreadful thing?

Lord Holcombe smiled from one to the other. 'Well, I shall leave you to sort yourselves out. Francine, the maid will unpack for you. Tyson, you can borrow my valet if you wish, he's on an errand for me at the moment.' Tyson said it would not be necessary and Lord Holcombe told them drinks would be ready when they came down.

The maid had unstrapped the hamper when Francine, needing to be alone with Tyson, told her to leave it for the moment. When the girl had gone she said, 'I think we must remember, Tyson, that we *are* in someone else's house and make an attempt at amiability.'

Tyson walked to the window and thrust his hands into his pockets. 'Which is not going to be easy. All the land you can see from here and beyond belongs to the estate. I shall have my work cut out and I feel sure I shall be resented by the steward. It's not something I'm looking forward to.'

'But I was told you wanted an outdoor life!'

'I do and shall have to make the best of it, but I'm not exactly the happiest man around.'

'Nor I the happiest bride,' Francine retorted. She lifted the top from the hamper and, pulling out a dress threw it on to the bed. Tyson turned to watch her.

'Flying into a temper is not going to help the situation.'

'Oh, yes, it does. I'm getting rid of all the resentment that has built up since I met my father at the church. I was not allowed to travel with him.' She pulled out a second dress and tossed it beside the other. 'And when I walked down the aisle and saw your miserable face I could have turned and fled.'

'Why didn't you?' There was bitterness in his voice. 'I would have been free.'

'Is anyone ever free? No, Tyson, don't blame me for the position you are in. You chose the easy way. Yes, easy, you have the whole countryside before you, you can go riding, mix with the gentry, go abroad with Lord Holcombe when he goes on business. Stop behaving like a spoilt child and act like a man.'

This last sentence got him on the raw. 'You'll know this evening whether you've married a man or a spoilt child!

And believe me you'll know not to speak to me again in such a fashion.'

To Francine's surprise she felt a small surge of excitement go through her body, with a strange throbbing in sensitive places.

Was this because of her husband's threat to manhandle her?

She turned her back on him. 'If you'll excuse me I want to get changed out of my – wedding finery.'

'No, excuse *me*,' he snapped. He dragged the trunk into the dressing room then seemed to go out of that door. A few minutes later she heard him opening and slamming shut drawers in one of the spare bedrooms. Did he intend to sleep there? And if so, would he not share her bed at any time that evening?

That morning she would have been relieved at such a thought. Now, she was not so sure. Kathleen could be right, there could be pleasure in having a husband invading one's body.

Twenty minutes later Tyson came to see if she was ready to go downstairs. His eyes looked mutinous. Francine, who had changed into a pale grey skirt and blouse put on a jacket. 'I'm ready.'

The logs on the fire in the hall were being stirred as they went downstairs and Lord Holcombe looked up, poker in hand. 'It's started to rain. I had thought we might have had a walk as it might only be a shower. A drink, Tyson? Francine, perhaps you would prefer tea, I have ordered some.'

Francine thanked him, then sat in an armchair that Lord Holcombe had pulled forward. The men began talking about racing and as the logs sparked and Francine listened to the rise and fall of the men's voices, she found it difficult to believe there had been such anger between Tyson and herself earlier. Perhaps it only needed time for him to settle down to marriage. It must have been a dreadful shock to him when his father had delivered the ultimatum – marry this girl or be disowned.

A maid came in with the tea and after it was poured Francine sipped some then replaced the cup in the saucer. This manor house could be home to them with a little understanding between Tyson and herself. And if she had a child he might be a totally different person.

The rain stopped and when later Lord Holcombe asked if she cared to join Tyson and himself for a walk she asked to be excused. She felt drowsy. They left, saying they would not be long.

Francine closed her eyes, and after a few moments images drifted under her lids; Sophie, making up to one of Tyson's brothers at the wedding reception . . . Mrs Denton looking sad . . . Mr Denton stern; Mr de Auberleigh smiling at her, welcoming her as their daughter-in-law. His wife echoing it, but without conviction.

Then the images changed and she was in Monte Carlo, with Tyson telling her he felt he had fallen in love with her. How different he had been then, so gentle, so tender towards her. There were many facets of character to each individual. She must make allowances for that. Rory had been such fun in the past. Recently he had been angry, sullen, because she was marrying Tyson. She slept.

She roused to hear whispering voices. 'She's sleeping . . . poor thing, she's so young, he must have got her into trouble. It's good of the master to give them a home . . .' The voices drifted away.

Francine opened her eyes. 'Got her into trouble?' Was that what most people thought because they had not had a big wedding? Well, time would prove them wrong, wouldn't it. She fumed, seeing the quiet wedding now as something to be endured by her father and the de Auberleighs. She was simply a photographer's daughter, not worthy of anything better than a hole and corner affair. Not even a proper honeymoon.

Well, she would see that Tyson de Auberleigh did not

violate his wife's body, just to get his revenge on her for calling him a spoilt child. She would lock her door when she went to bed.

Which she did. And then had to unlock it because he threatened to break the door down. She had lain shivering in bed when she heard him coming upstairs, had waited for his reaction all the time he was preparing for bed in the bedroom he had allocated to himself. There was a silence for a while and she was beginning to relax when she heard the door handle turn. The next moment he was calling, in a low but passionate voice, 'Open this door at once Francine, if you don't want me to wake the household by kicking it down.'

Francine leapt out of bed and dragged on a dressing gown, her heart thudding madly. She ran across the room, turned the key in the lock then ran back to the opposite side of the bed and watched him come in, a terrible fear in her. He looked thunderous.

'What do you think you are doing, locking me out. I do have rights. Did you hear what I said?' She was surprised at how much venom there could be in such a low-pitched voice. 'Answer me.'

'I was afraid of you. You more or less told me I would suffer for the way I had spoken to you.'

'And you are right, you will. Take off that nightdress and get into bed.'

'Take it off—' She clutched the nightdress at the neck. 'No, I – I can't.'

'Then let me help you.' He came round the bed, knocked her hand away and catching hold of the nightdress at the neck he pulled it and the tiny buttons flew in all directions. He then caught hold of the hem and whipped the fine lawn garment up and over her head. She crossed her hands over her breasts and stared at him horrified. Her lips began to tremble and she whispered, 'Tyson please, please don't hurt me.'

Tears welled up and rolled slowly down her cheeks. He

put his hands to his face and said, 'Oh, God, what am I doing?' He picked up her dressing gown and thrust it at her. 'Put that on.'

He turned his back on her, stood a moment, then went out, closing the door quietly behind him. Francine dropped to her knees and wept.

This was only the start of her marriage. How could they ever make a life together with Tyson so bitter, so full of hate?

She climbed into bed where she lay shivering, in spite of the bed having been heated with the warming pan. The cold was deep inside her.

She would have said she had not slept at all but she must have cat-napped because she was roused by Tyson shaking her and saying he must talk to her. It was just breaking daylight and she saw he looked haggard. Francine drew herself up in the bed. 'What is it?'

'I apologise for my behaviour last night. I must have been mad. It was your attitude. You admitted you knew what to expect so you had no right to lock your door.'

'I know,' she replied in a small voice. 'It was just that I was afraid, it seemed such an awful thing for a man to do to a woman.'

He paused then went on, 'I won't be easy to live with. I'm full of resentment at the way my father has treated me. It was cruel of him to have forced me into marriage with you, knowing that I'm still in love with Octavia. Cruel of you, too. I will make an effort not to make your life too unhappy, so try and bear with me, will you?'

'Yes, I'll try. Do you – I mean if you want – well,' she half-raised the bedcovers and he gave a wry smile and shook his head.

'I'm sorry, but I'm not in the mood. Thanks for offering.' He turned and walked away, a slight droop to his shoulders.

Francine sank down into the bed. They had both had a raw deal, and all because of her father's uncaring attitude and, it seemed, of Tyson's father too. This last fact grieved her. Mr de Auberleigh had seemed caring, he had shown her kindness, a gentleness. But then that might be just part of a studied charm. There were plenty of charming rogues in the world.

When Lord Holcombe was there Tyson would be outwardly pleasant to her, draw her into the conversation, but when they were alone he would sit silent, either reading *The Times* or studying papers to do with the running of the estate. When he went out it was in the company of Lord Holcombe, and John Binks the steward would accompany them. Then Francine would feel at a loose end and yearn to be with Sophie, Bridget or the O'Reillys. She would go out on her own, and walk across the fields or along by the river. Other times she read, for there was a big and varied selection of books in the library. But even books could not take away the feeling of aloneness.

One morning she awoke when it was still dark and heard voices beneath her bedroom window. She got up and looking out saw John Binks, a grizzled-haired man, and Tyson talking together. They were both wearing tweeds and each man had a gun under his arm. They walked away and Francine heard her husband laughing. At least there was no obvious strain between the two men at that moment.

Feeling full of despair at the way her life had turned Francine went into the library, took a book from the shelves at random and sinking into an armchair stared into the heart of the glowing fire. Was this to be the daily routine to the end of her days – walking, reading, staring into space, sitting in the dining room with Lord Holcombe and Tyson, either discussing the affairs of the estate or the unrest in South Africa? Several times Lord Holcombe had stated emphatically that there would be war, it had to come. Last night Tyson had sounded excited about it. If war did come he would join up, go out to South Africa, it would be an adventure.

Lord Holcombe told him grimly there was no adventure in war, only bloodshed and hatred. He then changed the subject, but Francine, thinking of it now, decided she would welcome Tyson leaving, being abroad. Then she would have no contact with him. At the moment it was a torment to her, waiting every night, not because of any sexual feelings but because if they were to live together a rapport would have to be established between them. If he did know he was to go abroad he might be willing to consummate the marriage. She could even have a baby.

Francine was sitting daydreaming of having a child of her very own to love and thinking how wonderful it would be when a voice said quietly behind her, 'Francine, my dear, I think we must have a talk.' Lord Holcombe came round the chair. 'That is, if I'm not intruding.'

'No, no, of course not, you could never intrude.'

He brought up a chair and when he was seated he steepled his fingers under his chin and sat studying her. 'You are unhappy, Francine. Is there anything I can do to help? Would you like me to take you for a drive? Tyson is very busy getting involved with affairs of the estate.'

'It isn't that.' Francine clasped her hands tightly. 'It's our marriage, it hasn't – he, well, no, I was to blame, I locked him out of the bedroom on our wedding night.' The last words came out with a rush.

'I see.' A look of compassion came into the old man's eyes. 'Well, Francine dear, it isn't the first time a newly-wed bride has done such a thing and you certainly will not be the last. The trouble is, a husband's pride has suffered. A man expects to be master.'

'I know, I – well, I did offer later to . . . but he refused.'

Lord Holcombe smiled then. 'Naturally, he could not give in right away, it would then seem like a weakness. Give him time, Francine. You see, apart from anything else Tyson was not planning to marry yet. You were both plunged into marriage. Why don't you ask Sophie to come and stay for a few days? Mrs Denton would probably accompany her. You've been cut off from all your friends.'

'Tyson may not like it. I'll wait. Perhaps, as you say, he will be – friends with me again.'

Lord Holcombe got up and held out a hand to her. 'Come with me for a walk, we can go to the Home Farm. Mrs Binks will be pleased to meet you, she's a kindly woman.'

Francine did not particularly want to meet anyone new, she wanted to be with those she loved and could be at ease with, but she accepted the offer. Lord Holcombe was doing his best to be kind and helpful.

Although they were into the end of May there was a sharp nip in the air and Francine gave a little shiver. The day before when she had been out for her walk the May blossom had been in bud, but now the buds were in full blossom and the scent from the lovely clouds of white drifted on the air. 'How beautiful,' she said.

'Indeed it is. Do you ride, Francine?' When she told him no he said, 'Why not try it? I have friends who have stables. They live over there.' He indicated a house which could be glimpsed beyond a spinney. 'The Forsters have no children, but they do have nephews and nieces who come over to ride. Tyson has ridden with some of them.'

This had Francine shrinking from the idea. She had no wish to be looked over by strangers and found wanting as the wife of Tyson de Auberleigh. So many times she had heard women being discussed by gossipers in Monte Carlo and had despised them for their catty remarks. She said, 'I would rather not, Lord Holcombe, not yet anyway. Perhaps later.'

He turned to her. 'When are you going to stop addressing me as Lord Holcombe? My name is Hammond. If you find it difficult, how about using my mother's nickname for me, Andy. My second name is Andrew.'

Francine looked up at him and smiled. 'I think that

Andy might come more readily to my tongue. But I think I could only use it in private. Otherwise I shall try to use Hammond.'

'So be it, that makes me happy.'

They met Mrs Binks coming out of the byres. She set down the pail she was carrying and curtsied first to Lord Holcombe then, when introduced, to Francine. She was a rosy-faced, plump woman with bright eyes.

Lord Holcombe said, 'Well, Mrs Binks, I've brought Mrs de Auberleigh to meet you and I'm hoping you are going to offer us a cup of tea and a slice of your excellent plum cake.'

'It will be an honour, my lord. Binks and Mr de Auberleigh should be back soon, they've gone a-rabbitin'.'

She was a lively woman, who although treating Lord Holcombe as a master, seemed nevertheless quite at home with him, talking about the farm as she pushed the kettle from the bar on to the fire and brought out cups, saucers, cream and sugar and the plum cake. She turned to Francine.

'And be you settling in, ma'am? Things seem strange at first, don't they?'

'Yes, they do, Mrs Binks. I'm just beginning to get to know my way around the fields, the spinneys and the river.'

'Well now, ma'am, there's a fine view from the top of Beacon Hill over yonder,' She pointed towards the window. 'And as pretty a waterfall and dene as you'll see anywhere up left along river.' Her eyes twinkled. 'Fairies be there. I've never seen them, but I'm assured you'll see them if they take a fancy to you.'

Francine laughed. 'Oh, how delightful. I must go and see if they like me.'

'Oh, they will, ma'am, they will. You be a dreamer, I can tell by your eyes.'

'I think I believe in them. I have Irish friends and they have all but convinced me about fairies and the leprechauns. I want to go to Ireland sometime, God willing.'

'You'll go, ma'am, you'll go. The fairies'll see to that.'

Francine was utterly captivated by Mrs Binks and knew she was someone she would want to be friends with. The woman knew all the lore of the countryside, knew about herbs and the cures they effected. She talked about the animals as if they were humans and could talk to her. Old Bessie the cow was telling her this morning that she wasn't feeling too well, she'd get Mr Binks to have a look at her when he came back.

When they left it was with Francine's promise to call in at any time she liked. She would be more than welcome.

Francine felt surprisingly happy as she set off with Lord Holcombe to see the waterfall. 'What a delightful woman,' she said. 'She seemed to have a wealth of knowledge about animals and the countryside.'

Lord Holcombe smiled. 'She's a character, a wonderful character. Her family originated in Dorset, but she's been in service in a number of places over the country, that is, until she married John. And now she says she wants to settle here. They have two daughters, both who married farmers and live away, one in Scotland and one in Surrey. She misses the girls and I'm sure she would be very pleased indeed if you would drop in and see her from time to time.'

'Oh, I will, I won't need any persuasion to call. What is her husband like?'

'John? Outwardly a very taciturn man, but with animals he's a gentle, caring person. He and Tyson get on splendidly.'

When they came to the waterfall Francine declared herself entranced and swore laughingly that she could see fairies. The water did not fall from a great height but it tumbled down in a rush, the spray rising from the pool, rainbowed by a shaft of sunlight. A weeping willow on the bank dipped its branches to the water and the foliage all around was a rich tapestry of greens.

'How rewarding,' Francine said softly. 'How peaceful.' She talked, calling Lord Holcombe Andy, explaining how unhappy she had been until meeting Mrs Binks and how she had come to realise that it was an attitude of mind that could make or mar one's life.

They sat on a dry rock a way from the waterfall and were silent for a while. Apart from the rushing and splashing of the water there was no other sound until a bird began to sing and the sweet notes had Francine feeling near to tears. There was so much beauty in the world, as well as poverty and strife. She felt privileged to be in this place and she found herself thinking, I hope the fairies *do* like me.

They strolled back to the house and when Francine thanked Lord Holcombe for being so kind to her he said softly, 'Having you and Tyson here has changed my life. You make me feel that I have at last a family.' And when they stopped before going up the drive Francine stood on tiptoe and kissed him on the cheek. He whispered a thank you and seemed deeply moved.

Francine was in a lovely mellow mood when Tyson came storming in. 'Did you have to tell your life story to Mrs Binks?'

Francine stared at him. 'What are you talking about? I never mentioned my family.'

'No, but you talked about the O'Reillys, giving the impression that they are your family. Mrs Binks thinks they are, said you had some Irish in you and that you believe in fairies. I would just like to remind you that you are *now* a de Auberleigh. Or have you forgotten?'

'I've had every chance to forget, haven't I?' she retorted. 'I'm a de Auberleigh in name only! And the fault is not mine, but yours. I enjoyed meeting Mrs Binks, she's a caring person. I was happy this morning, now you've taken all my pleasure away. How could you? You thought your father was cruel for delivering an ultimatum, but you are more cruel, because I think you really enjoy making me unhappy. It's a revenge to you, just as my father made me marry you to get his revenge for what my mother had done. I hate you both.'

She got up and was at the door when Tyson shouted, 'Come back here. Don't you run out on me when I'm talking to you.'

Francine stopped and turned to face him. 'Yes, *sir*, what is it? Do you want to cast me into a dungeon for the rest of my days?'

'Stop making a jest of what I say.'

'A jest? Oh, Tyson, this is no jest, it's just the ruination of a marriage that has not even had a chance to take off.'

'And whose fault is that? Yours. You locked the door.'

'It's been open ever since,' she said quietly.

'Why should I satisfy *your* lust?' he demanded.

'Satisfy my – lust?' She gave a bitter laugh. 'I dreaded you coming to me and demanding your nuptial rights, but I was willing for you to have those rights, I thought it would help to perhaps make us closer. How wrong I was. You're mad.'

'Yes, I'm mad, mad for you. Your very look every time I see you torments me.'

'Then you know how to get rid of your torment,' she taunted him.

He suddenly caught her by the hand, ran her out of the library and up the stairs, and she thought he *is* mad, completely mad.

Yet she made no attempt to resist. There was this strange excitement in her, a throbbing in her limbs. Was it a throwback to an age when men dragged women to caves, a mastery? But then surely she should make a stand, she had rights too . . . didn't she?

Her heart was pounding by the time he dragged her into the bedroom and made to undress her. When he fumbled with the fastenings on her dress she said, 'I'll do it,' and her voice trembled. Tyson began to undress feverishly, and Francine tried to match his haste. It had to happen now, it was her only hope of them making a life together.

Before she removed her last petticoat she went to the window and drew the curtains. They were velvet and cut out most of the light. It made it easier to strip to her white cotton drawers with the fancy lace and beribboned edging. Francine found she was breathing heavily and there was a tormenting teasing in parts of her body. She knew that she would find it unbearable if Tyson was suddenly to leave.

Even then she hesitated before stepping out of her drawers and was left just wearing her shift.

Tyson, stark naked, came over to her and with one swift uplift of her shift had her naked, too. Francine gasped. The next moment he picked her up and practically threw her on the bed, then he clambered up beside her. His breathing was ragged.

'Oh, God, I can't wait, Francine.' One hand was holding her breast, the other was under her buttocks. Kathleen had told her that before the consummation of the marriage there would be kisses, a tender caressing of the body, but there were no kisses, no tenderness now. Tyson was rough, penetrating her with an urgency that made her cry out. She was also totally unprepared for the movement. She had thought that once the penetration had taken place that was it. But Tyson was moving with an almost frantic rhythm. At first she felt only pain but after a moment she became aware of a pleasurable feeling of not wanting him to stop. Kathleen had said a woman could get pleasure out of it, too. The pleasure was building up when suddenly Tyson gave a groan, then was still, and the throbbing in her body died away. He lay heavy on her for a moment then rolled away. Francine now had a feeling of being thwarted.

He was silent for quite a while then he said, in shamed

tones, 'Francine, I'm sorry. I behaved badly. It ought not to have been like that. It was the waiting, the wanting you these past few days then being unable to wait.'

When she did not reply he leaned up on one elbow. 'Please forgive me, I behaved like an undisciplined oaf.'

'That's a husband's privilege, isn't it?' She could not keep the sarcasm from her voice. 'A woman, in the eyes of most men, is a chattel.'

'No, you're wrong. Although, to be fair, I must have given you that impression when I dragged you upstairs.' He touched her cheek. 'It will be better the next time, I promise. I want you again now.'

She tensed and because he had just cupped her breast he was aware of it. 'Francine, relax, I won't hurt you this time.' He moved closer and she felt him hard against her side. A tiny throbbing began inside her once more and when this time his mouth covered hers she responded.

But again he was too eager and just when she was beginning to feel what amounted almost to an ecstasy it was over, with Tyson rolling away from her.

'Sorry, sorry, I really am Francine, it's you, you're so desirable. When I saw you stripped I knew I had to take you there and then. But this is only the beginning. We have all the time in the world.'

All the time in the world, what a lovely sound it had. Could they make a successful marriage?

The lunch-gong suddenly boomed and Tyson gave a mock groan. 'Now wouldn't that just spoil our lovely interlude?' He dropped a kiss on her brow. 'We mustn't keep them waiting, we do have the evening to look forward to.' He threw back the bedclothes and dressed almost as quickly as he had undressed. When Francine made no effort to move he said, 'Come along, we don't want old Holcombe to guess what we've been doing, do we? See you downstairs. I want a drink.'

Francine lay for a few moments more, knowing now that they were still very far from making a successful marriage. All that had been in Tyson's mind was the evening of love-making to come. There had been no real tenderness in him towards her, no holding her close and telling her he loved her. For Tyson, love-making was just an act; any other woman could have satisfied him. She got up.

CHAPTER NINETEEN

To Francine's disappointment Tyson's love-making that evening was no different to that of the morning. He was an impatient lover. He kept apologising, saying lightly it was Francine's fault, she had such a beautiful body. Once he saw her stripped his body demanded he take her right away. But he didn't have to see her naked to be roused to a frenzy. Three times during the night he took her with the same urgency.

She remonstrated with him. She was getting little pleasure because of this. This was after their fourth coupling and Tyson seemed a little annoyed. Although he did not say so in so many words he hinted that a wife should not expect pleasure. This, of course, infuriated Francine, but with an effort she managed to control her anger.

'I understand that some women do derive a great deal of pleasure from the act, but then I suppose it depends on the man. Some will be more skilled at it than others.'

'Some men are more passionate than others,' he retorted. 'You should count yourself lucky that I fit into this category. I've been celibate since I knew we were to marry and some men would not give a wife that consideration.'

'And do you expect me to say thank you very much for this?'

Tyson sat up. 'Francine, you can be so infuriating I could slap you. Perhaps the ladies who informed you of the proceedings of nuptial rights forbore to tell you that a man on his honeymoon is a different animal to one who has settled down to married life. I cannot help that my passions run high when I see you naked, or when I feel your warm, desirable body next to mine. Believe me, you *are* desirable.'

Francine might have melted then had not Tyson added in a low voice, 'Almost more so than Octavia.' He had reached for her but she pulled away.

'Octavia, Octavia! Isn't it time you forgot her? You are married to *me*.'

'Yes and God help me, aren't I starting to think it was the biggest mistake I ever made. Not only am I married to a shrew but to a wife who thinks that *she* should be pleasured by her husband.' He threw back the bedclothes and got out of bed. 'You can sleep alone from now on. I shall find my pleasure with a woman whose only aim is to see that I am satisfied. Good night.' He stormed out of the bedroom and she could hear him later moving about in the spare room.

Francine swallowed hard to try and prevent a sudden rise of tears. What a mess she had made of everything. If only she had been patient Tyson might in time have been more leisurely in his love-making, have caressed her, wanting to rouse her before taking her. Now she had ruined everything. Should she go to him, apologise? No, it would be like getting down on her knees and this she felt was all wrong between a married couple. There must be a closeness, a oneness, so that the husband understood his wife's needs. She would not settle for less. Not even if it meant that Tyson took a mistress.

He had left the house when she came down for breakfast the following morning but Lord Holcombe was there, and although he gave Francine a cheerful good morning she sensed he knew that all was not well between Tyson and herself. It was the glances he kept giving her. And when she fell silent, not wanting to make conversation, he asked her gently if there was anything he could do to help, explaining that Tyson had hinted at a rift between them.

Francine looked down at her plate. 'I think I need to talk to someone, a woman.'

'I see. Would Mrs Denton be able to help, or perhaps Mrs Brogan?'

'No, I think the one I really want to see is Kathleen O'Reilly, she's my father's housemaid.'

Lord Holcombe made a pellet of a piece of bread then dropped it on his plate. 'Well now, I think perhaps we can arrange something. I shall write to your father making an appointment to have a photograph taken – I can say a relative wants one of me taken in evening dress. You write to Miss O'Reilly and while I am with your father the two of you can have a talk.'

'Oh, Andy,' Francine exclaimed, 'you are just so kind to me, so understanding. I only wish that Tyson–'

'Tyson needs time,' he said gently. 'An arranged marriage is a very different affair from that of a couple who are crazily in love.'

Francine nodded. 'Yes, I suppose so. It's just that I feel I've failed so dismally and right at the beginning of my marriage.'

'Not at all. I'm sure that wherever you feel you've failed can be put right after a talk with your friend.' To this Francine gave a wan smile and said she hoped so.

Tyson did not come in until the evening and to give him his due he did make an effort to be pleasant, but he slept alone again and did so on the following evening.

On the third morning Francine was watching from the window for the third postal delivery of the day when she saw Lord Holcombe's limousine coming up the drive. And a minute later she gaped in astonishment as Kathleen stepped out of the car.

She knocked on the window and Kathleen, glancing up and seeing her, waved. Francine raced down the stairs and all but fell into Kathleen's arms. 'I can't believe it, oh, Kathleen, I just can't believe it. How did you, I mean to say, what happened, I – Oh, come upstairs. I don't know where Lord Holcombe is.'

'He's up in London with your father. He talked Cook

into letting me have time off to see you. He told her you were homesick. I'll go back in a couple of hours and then his lordship will come back in the car.'

They went upstairs with Francine talking all the way. How was the family, and how was Bridget, Cook and Evie? Had she seen anything of Sophie?

Kathleen answered that everyone was fine. Sophie had called to see Bridget and was dying to be invited to Holcombe Manor. Francine said she really must get down to some letters. Once in the sitting room she rang for tea and cake to be brought, and after the maid had left Kathleen began admiring the furnishings. Then she said, 'But there, I'm talking about furnishings and I understand you have a problem.'

Francine in a low voice told her about her marriage. A look of understanding came into Kathleen's lovely blue eyes.

'I know how you feel, Francine, but you do realise that a marriage has to be worked at? I think you've been a little hasty in condemning Tyson for his lack of thought. No, no, don't protest yet, let me finish. Which do you prefer, a weak man or a masterful one? A masterful one, of course. A man must be boss in his own house. And although a woman should not behave like a slave, you should make an effort to understand Tyson, to go along patiently with him until you've both settled down to married life. This is no time to regret that you *are* married to Tyson.'

'But I do regret it. I'd rather be married to anyone but him.'

'Listen, Francine. I think that Gran hoped that you and Rory would be together, but you would have had a divil of a life with our Rory. He flares up, just as Tyson did. The trouble is, Francine, that you flare up, too. If you have a couple constantly at one another's throats then life will be hell.'

253

Francine looked resentful. 'So you think the wife should give in?'

'You're not listening to a word I say. You *pretend* to give in. You tell your husband you enjoy his love-making, not tell him that other men are more skilled. This is a terrible blow to a man's pride. Every man thinks he is the world's best lover.'

Francine began to laugh. 'Oh, Kathleen, you're so good at sorting things out. I can't tell you how marvellous it is to have you here to talk to. Not that I think I can flatter Tyson into thinking that *he* is the world's best. How can I? I've never been with any other man.'

'I should hope not! But you still haven't taken the point. You want heaven without having tasted a little of hell. He's hot-blooded, madly passionate. Lucky you. He has to get rid of all that wildness in him before he'll be able to control his feelings.'

Francine teased her, wanting to know how she came to know so much about men and Kathleen, a twinkle in her eyes, replied, 'I would like to say it was through experience, but I'm simply quoting the experience of friends and of women I've overheard talking about the subject when I was in service. I've been party to some very daring conversations, my dear, which was quite an experience in itself. Women in high society seem to think that servants are deaf and dumb.'

The two of them covered a lot in the two hours that Kathleen was with Francine. Francine learned that Rory had done some superb outdoor photography and that her father had been pleased with the results. Rory, of course, was overjoyed and in his eyes was already established as a well-known photographer in his own right. Mary was finally pregnant after years of waiting, and was gradually getting over her morning sickness. Milo was going round like a dog with two tails, telling everyone he was going to have a son, he just knew it. Business was good at the moment and Himself had not been in any dire trouble lately. Evie was going to be married in two months' time, but would stay on at Spinners End working in the kitchen. She and Jackie Pennystone would need the money.

Francine then said softly, 'And what about you, Kathleen? When are you going to settle down with a man and get married?'

'Oh, one of these days. I'm not in a hurry. I quite like my work. Your father seems to be a lot quieter these days. I suppose he's pleased that you are married and have a husband to take over the responsibility.'

'No doubt,' Francine snapped. 'I have no wish ever to see him again.'

After Francine had shown Kathleen around the house they went for a walk by the river and when Kathleen said, 'You don't realise how lucky you are,' Francine began to wonder if she had not behaved a little pettishly. After all, she was a married woman now with responsibilities. She must try and behave that way.

The two hours went by and Kathleen left with Francine's promise that husband or no husband she would be coming to see them all, which brought the rather sad request from Kathleen not to defy Tyson, but to make sure to win his permission.

For a while Francine had a bereft feeling then, thinking over her talk with Kathleen she decided to follow her advice to win Tyson over. And at five o'clock when she saw him coming towards the house alone, she went out to meet him, greeting him with a smile.

'Hello, have you had a good day? I've had a visitor. Guess who? Kathleen. She was only here two hours but it was lovely to see her.'

'Yes, I'm sure it must have been.' Tyson seemed to be surprised at her light-hearted mood. 'Mrs Binks was asking after you.' He smiled. 'She thinks you're beautiful.' Then he laid an arm across Francine's shoulder. 'Which of course you are.'

Francine felt happier than she had been for days and

when Tyson told her they had been invited to dinner by the Forsters for the following week, she said, lovely, it would make a nice change, even though she did not particularly relish the thought.

Lord Holcombe was back in time for dinner that evening and though he and Tyson talked livestock and farming, she tried to show an interest. And was rewarded later by Tyson saying in an indulgent way, 'I think we might make a countrywoman of our Francine yet.' To which Holcombe agreed and he was smiling, as though accepting that the couple's marital problems were settled.

But Francine was to spend another night alone. Two friends of Lord Holcombe arrived later and the four men settled down to a game of bézique. It was in the early hours when Tyson came to bed and, perhaps not wanting to disturb her, he went to the spare room.

When she went down to breakfast Lord Holcombe told her that Tyson had already left for London on a business matter for him, adding that he should be back the following day.

But it was three days before Tyson returned and then he came only to pack, saying he would be away for a few weeks this time. He gave his wife a hasty peck on the cheek, saying he mustn't dawdle, the car was waiting. When Francine, feeling somewhat bewildered by this sudden decision, asked Lord Holcombe where Tyson was going he seemed evasive. Tyson would be settling up some business in London first then going on to Geneva.

'Geneva?' she echoed. 'What type of business, or am I not allowed to ask?'

'Man's business,' he answered, half-smiling, but Francine still felt he was being evasive about it.

'Well,' she said, 'if Tyson is going to be away for several weeks then I must have something to do. I was being tutored in photography while I was in Reading by a Mr Beckett. He was excellent. Would it be possible for me to go to Reading, perhaps once a week, to resume my lessons?'

Lord Holcombe looked doubtful. Tyson might not approve. He suggested instead that Francine invite Sophie to come and stay for a while, and perhaps Mrs Denton would come too, and bring her little boy for a change of air. Or would she like Mrs Brogan or perhaps Kathleen to come, if she could get time off?

Francine pleaded to be allowed to go to Reading; photography was close to her heart. 'It would fill in such an empty gap,' she went on. 'I would like to see Sophie too and all my other friends, but they could also be fitted in for a visit. Please, Andy, I would be eternally grateful if a visit to Reading could be arranged.'

He was reluctant to give in, saying it could perhaps cause another rift in their marriage, but when Francine went on begging him for this one chance, he agreed, saying with a wry smile, 'On my head be it for giving my consent.' Francine was overjoyed and gave him a hug.

A letter was despatched to Mr Beckett and a reply came promptly, offering his congratulations on her marriage and saying he would be delighted to see her. Would she perhaps care to come for the whole day? His housekeeper would arrange meals. He suggested the following Wednesday.

Francine wrote back accepting and she also wrote to Sophie asking if she and her mother would care to come for a visit. She explained about going to Reading on the following Wednesday.

By return came a letter saying that Mrs Denton and her offspring would be arriving the following day, with a postscript from Sophie adding, '*I have so much to tell you, I can hardly wait to see you* . . . '

It was a joyous meeting with Sophie and while Mrs Denton strolled around the garden with Roderick and Lord Holcombe, Francine took Sophie upstairs to their apartment. Before she had even a chance to look around

Sophie said in a dramatic way, 'Octavia is back in town and Tyson has been seen in London, although he has not been to his home. What is going on?'

Francine's limbs went weak. She sank into a chair. 'Octavia back? I thought she went out to America with her fiancé.'

'She did, but apparently they fell out two days after they had arrived and she came straight back home. It's just the sort of thing Octavia *would* do. But if Tyson was in London why did he not go and see the family? Do you think he knew that Octavia was home? Surely he wouldn't take up with her again. And yet–' She eyed Francine in concern. 'Has something gone wrong? With your marriage, I mean.'

Pride made Francine pull herself together. 'No, everything is all right. Tyson and I are not terribly demonstrative people but are getting along on an even keel, as they say. Tyson went to London to do some business for Lord Holcombe then he was going on to Geneva. I should think it was just coincidence that Octavia happened to be back in London at the same time. And I should imagine the reason he had not been to see his family would be the time factor. No doubt he'll call on his way back from Geneva. Now, tell me all your news.'

Tyson and Octavia were forgotten as Sophie described a young man who had come into her life. 'He's madly attractive, very distinguished-looking and is in the Diplomatic Corps, which naturally pleases both Papa and Mama. Papa especially. We met at a party and he's been paying attention ever since. We've been for drives, accompanied by Mama of course, and we once met clandestinely. Oh, Francine, it's so exciting. His name is Randolph Merefall-Powy. He wants to ask for my hand in marriage, but although I like him a lot I'm not in love with him. And I don't want to be married, not yet, I want some fun. What do you think?'

Francine forced a smile. 'Have some fun, you have plenty of time.'

Sophie was suddenly serious. 'Are you happy with Tyson? What was it like on your wedding night? You did say you would tell me.'

Francine had not said any such thing but decided to treat it lightly. 'Before you are due to get married I shall tell you, but not before, because you might be tempted to sample the pleasure beforehand.'

'Oh, so the woman *does* get pleasure. What happens? Oh, Francine, do please tell me.' Francine just smiled and shook her head, promising to tell her when the right time came, and no constant coaxing on Sophie's part would make her change her mind.

Sophie's visit came at the right time for Francine, preventing her from dwelling too much on Tyson and the thought that he might have gone to see Octavia. In fact, she began to take a philosophical view that she must accept whatever Fate had in store. Nothing she could say or do would alter anything. Mrs Denton, when alone with Francine once, asked gently if she was happy and Francine said yes, she was. It was strange being married, but she was sure they would both adapt to their new life together.

The five of them visited Mrs Binks, who was not the slightest bit put out that gentry should walk into her kitchen. 'Come away in,' she invited, and she made tea and brought out cake and chatted away happily with them, making a great pet of Roderick. Francine promised that they would call again when they were out for a walk.

The visitors left on the following Tuesday, and Mrs Denton begged Francine to come and stay with them soon. It was so good to keep in touch. She looked a little tearful when she left and Francine wondered if she knew about Octavia's return and about Tyson. Sophie said that only she and the friend who told her knew about it.

The next morning Francine set out full of excitement for her visit to Reading which was within easy reach of

Windsor, and when she arrived she marvelled that such a short time ago she had been scrubbing floors and serving meals to ten men in a lodging house. Had Mrs Lomax taken Florrie back to work in the house, she wondered.

Mr Beckett gave her a warm welcome and said how surprised and delighted he was to hear that she had been married since their last meeting. She asked about Florrie and was told she was still 'ill' at home, Mrs Lomax had employed another girl, who was buxom and according to Mrs Lomax as strong as an ox.

Mr Beckett had a gentle voice but he spoke quickly, and as the lesson progressed Francine found it difficult to take in all the details. Obviously aware of her bewilderment, he said, 'I'm giving you a lot of information, Francine. You'll only remember some of it but later you'll find certain things emerging. It was the method my father used and it was effective.'

He went on to talk about developing, the method and the chemicals used, about light and shade, discussing the latter at great length because of the importance of both.

At the end of the lesson it was names for various reasons that sprang to Francine's mind. She had remembered the name Joseph Nicéphore Niepce from a previous time, because she had thought it so strange. Now she remembered John Dancer and could see him dancing around as he pioneered Microphotography and Stereophotography. With John Joly she conjured up a jolly, plump man, one of the later photographers who was responsible for using a process introducing colour into photographs by putting the negative through a screen, microscopically checkered in red, green and blue.

Paul Martin was vivid to her because he loved gadgets and took excellent unposed photographs of street scenes with his camera concealed in a suitcase, and was known as the 'Candid Cameraman'. But more vivid still to Francine was Viscountess Hawarden, a distinguished amateur who produced hundreds of photographs of her five children, as well as fancy dress and genre scenes.

The viscountess was the only woman's name Mr Beckett had mentioned, apart from that of Julia Margaret Cameron, whom he had spoken of earlier. Francine suspected it was to promote her interest. She thought it must be lovely to be able to photograph one's children.

She had arranged to meet Lord Holcombe at Windsor station and he was there, waiting in the chauffeur-driven limousine when she arrived. He held out a hand to her. 'Come along, my dear, tell me all about your day. I missed you. I think we must try to persuade Mr Beckett to come and stay with us for a couple of days a week. I can send the car for him and return him home. I shall speak to him on your next visit.'

Francine said she thought it a wonderful idea, but of course they lacked the cameras and all the equipment, so she could not become familiar with the various processes. In that case, said Lord Holcombe he would buy everything Francine needed and use one of the rooms as a studio.

'Oh, no,' she protested. 'Tyson would be furious.'

'Not if I say I want them for a hobby.' Lord Holcombe nodded. 'Yes, I think it would be a good idea if I had lessons, too. I didn't realise until yesterday, Francine, how lonely I was until you were away. The house seemed so quiet, so empty. We really must have more people to come and visit. I realise too how necessary it is for you to have something to occupy you. Tyson could be away for quite a long time.'

He seemed uneasy again and Francine, after studying him for a moment said, 'Andy, I want to ask you something. If you are bound to secrecy and are unable to answer I'll accept it, but if not I'll be pleased if you'll answer my question. Did Tyson go to London to see Octavia Manning? I was told she was back from America and Tyson was seen in London at the same time.'

Lord Holcombe was a long time in answering. 'Yes, he

261

did, Francine, and I regret that I gave him the opportunity of seeing her. He was desperately unhappy, said he had to see her to finish with her for good. Then he begged that I give him the opportunity also of getting right away from this environment for a time so he could work out his life. Then he said he felt he could come back and settle down with you. He assured me he was very fond of you and that he could love you, given time.' Lord Holcombe paused and a look of sadness came into his eyes. 'Unhappily, I had a letter from him this morning. He and Octavia have gone to Switzerland together.'

Francine's heart constricted. 'Then that is the end of our marriage.'

'I don't think so, Francine dear. I do sincerely believe that after he has been away for a time, alone with Octavia, he will realise what a shallow person she is.'

Francine got up and walked over to the window and stood, her body tense. 'And would he really expect me to take him back?'

'You are his wife, Francine.' Lord Holcombe sounded surprised, as if that was the answer to everything.

She turned to face him. 'It might be a way of life in this kind of society for a man to take a mistress or to have an affair with any woman he fancies, but it's not my way. We had an arranged marriage it is true, but in my opinion an agreement was entered into too, and Tyson should honour it. He did have a choice. It was greed that made him choose marriage with me.' Her lips trembled.

'Francine dear, let me explain something. I sowed my wild oats when I was young. I had an affair after I was married. Ours was an arranged marriage but I only had that one affair because I grew to love my wife and she to love me. We had a very happy marriage. The same could happen to you and Tyson.'

Francine's chin set in a stubborn line. 'I don't want it to happen. I would have no respect for Tyson.'

'You could learn to respect him,' he said gently, 'just as

262

he will learn your ways, even though it might be against his will. Give him this chance when he comes back.'

'If he does come back,' she said, a bitterness in her voice.

'Well, while we are waiting, let us enter into the world of photography together. Please.'

She nodded then asked to be excused. Upstairs in the bedroom the tears came. Tears of utter misery. She seemed destined for unhappiness. Her father not wanting her, nor her mother, and now her husband. There was only one thing she could do to make life seem worthwhile and that was to study photography with Lord Holcombe.

And with that decision reached she began to feel better.

Mr Beckett agreed to come to Holcombe Manor for two days a week, and took a great deal of pleasure in advising Lord Holcombe on what to purchase in the way of photographic equipment. So yet another kind of life opened up for Francine — a life of complete freedom and she enjoyed every minute of it. Sophie came to stay again, Bridget and Kathleen made visits, and once, Kathleen even brought Rory with her. Francine's heart leapt. She had not seen him recently and he looked different somehow, taller, more attractive, more mature. His roguish grin was evident when he greeted her, but underlying the lightness was a look of . . . longing?

'The boss is away so I thought I'd come and take a look at the set-up.'

Francine replied in equally light vein, 'I don't know that I feel flattered at being called a set-up.'

'Stupid.' He came up and dropped a kiss on her cheek. 'The camera set-up. Spoiled rotten, that's what you are, I'd give my right arm to have a camera and all the equipment. And it's not right you know, no woman should be in this line.'

That set her off, and they argued good-naturedly. When Lord Holcombe met Rory in the house the two of them began talking photography as if they had known one another for years. 'Come up to the studio,' Lord Holcombe said. 'You might be able to offer some good advice. I am just a novice, Francine is the expert. You should see the photographs of objects and flowers she's taken. Mr Beckett, who gives us lessons, is full of praise for Francine's work. He says she's a born photographer. The study of light and shade, he said, is an instinct with her.'

Rory held up a hand laughing. 'Stop, or I'll be so envious I'll never want to speak to her again.'

He was impressed with the studio and equipment, and when he started talking about the work and Francine realised that Kathleen was waiting patiently in the background she said they would leave the two men to talk photography.

They went out into the garden and Kathleen said, 'I hope you don't mind Rory coming with me. I don't think it was only the camera and stuff he wanted to see, but you, Francine. He's kept talking about you so much lately, wanting to know how you're settling down to marriage. Is everything all right? I know you said that Tyson was away on business, but I feel there's something that's worrying you.'

Francine had not told even Sophie about Tyson and Octavia going to Switzerland and although she felt she wanted to confide in Kathleen, she decided against it. She said, 'I wish that Tyson was back home, of course, but really I'm delighted to have this opportunity of learning all about photography. It's such a fascinating subject, Kathleen, do you know—' she stopped and laughed. 'I'm as bad as the men, talk, talk, talk. How are Cook and Evie? It shouldn't be long before Evie's wedding day.'

'No, it isn't. Bridget picked up a piece of white silk in the market and between us we've made her a wedding dress. Francine, that girl is positively glowing. You would hardly recognise her. She wants to leave, wants to make a proper home, but Jackie doesn't earn much. She says she'll leave if she falls with a baby.'

A baby? Francine had hoped that at least Tyson would have made her pregnant, but her monthly cycle had come around as usual and put an end to her dreams.

Lord Holcombe and Rory came out and the four of them went for a walk by the river. Once Rory stopped and nodded to the hills ahead. 'It reminds me of Ireland, and it's a long time since we lived there. I was just a lad.' There was a dreaminess in his voice. 'There are times when the hills and mountains don't look real. They have a texture of velvet. When the snow melts, the water cascades into the river below and the rising spray, with the sun on it, is like hundreds of rainbows. Ah, but it's a lovely thing to see.'

The next moment, looking a little self-conscious, he went on, 'But there, I like the bustle of the city too, the people and the noise.' He turned to Francine. 'His lordship tells me you like photographing people. I'm glad of that. If you have to be a photographer, it's a good thing to do. But I still don't approve of women taking up a profession.'

'Well, whether you approve or not, Rory O'Reilly, that is what I am going to do!'

'And what does your husband say about it? I understand he doesn't know about the camera yet.'

Francine's head went up. 'He'll be told when he returns from his business trip. Then I shall let things take their course. Come along, let me show you and Kathleen my waterfall and the lovely little dene. It's a secret place.'

Rory admitted he was impressed by Francine's secret place. Then asked if she had photographed it. She told him no, not yet, but she would when she was more proficient.

Talk was general after that and over tea the possibility of war with South Africa was discussed by the men. Lord Holcombe said it was looming nearer every day. Rory said if it did come he would enlist and go out to South Africa.

War had seemed so remote to Francine that it had not

occurred to her that Rory might want to enlist. And what about Tyson? He wanted to go, too. Francine felt a sudden pang realising that both men had a place in her heart, yes even in spite of Tyson being obsessed with another woman.

After tea Lord Holcombe took Rory off to show him his collection of guns and then Kathleen said suddenly, 'Francine, I have something to tell you. I've kept putting it off because I thought you might be upset, but you'll have to know sooner or later. It's - well, I am–' she paused then, looking distressed said, 'I'm going to be married.'

'Married?' Francine gave a joyful shout. 'Why should you think I would be upset about that? I'm delighted.' She gave her a quick hug. 'Who is the man? You've never mentioned anyone special.'

'It's your — father I'm marrying, Francine.'

'My father?' She stared at her aghast. 'I can't believe it. How could you, Kathleen? How could you *do* this to me?'

'We both wanted it. I think I must always have loved him and that was why I never wanted any other man. Also I'm . . . carrying his child.'

Francine repeated, 'His child,' but no sound came. She felt utterly betrayed. Kathleen, whom she had always thought of as an elder sister, loved, and now she would be her . . . *stepmother!*

Francine turned and ran from the room and out into the garden, her fist pressed to her lips, the word step-mother beating in her brain. How could Kathleen do such a thing, marry the man who hated her, who had been so horribly cruel to her? Oh, God, when would these terrible things stop happening to her? She ran on blindly, tears running down her cheeks.

CHAPTER TWENTY

Francine sat on a rock near the waterfall, her knees drawn up to her chin, her arms wrapped around her legs, trying to fight the dreadful hatred for her father that consumed her. She was convinced now that he had done this thing to Kathleen as a further revenge on herself, knowing how fond she was of Kathleen.

But how could Kathleen, who was so level-headed in other ways, be duped by him? It was not that he was a man who would soft-talk a woman, he was hard, steel hard. Francine tensed as she heard the snap of a twig.

This was followed by a rustle of undergrowth then Rory was saying quietly, 'It's no use shutting yourself away from people, Francie. Lord Holcombe is upset, so is Kathleen.'

Francine looked up sharply. 'And do you think that I am not upset? Kathleen knew how I felt about my father, how he felt about me. She's a woman and knows the way of men, not an innocent young girl. She must have known what the consequences of such an affair could be, knew how I would feel.'

'And have you ever given a thought to what *she* would feel, how Gran feels?' Rory hunkered down beside her on the rock. 'Gran is aching with hurt, with guilt, feeling that she is responsible in some way for what has happened. Kathleen has a special place in the family. She's much loved. She must be crying inside for the situation she's in, crying inside for you, knowing what your reaction would be. I want you to come to her, tell her that you understand.'

Francine looked up at him with tear-filled eyes. 'I can't, Rory, I can't, not yet. I'm too hurt, I looked up to her.'

'But you are also angry because you feel she had no

right to allow such a thing to happen. There are hundreds of people in this world who think as you do, think only of themselves and not of the people involved. Few have seen the quiet side of your father. I have and so has Kathleen, we both know he's been tormented by what happened in the past.'

Francine jumped up. 'Don't make excuses for him to me! You've never suffered from his cruelty, never been savagely beaten by him. Yes, beaten, and by a grown man. I was a little child, who had been sheltered since birth. I knew nothing of cruelty. A child's flesh is delicate and so is her soul, at eight years of age.'

Rory stood up. 'I didn't know, Francie, I'm sorry. But please come to Kathleen. I can't bear to see her so hurt. She knows she's sinned, knows she has the wrath of the Lord to contend with. Help her.'

'The wrath of the Lord?' Francine stared at him. 'The Lord is just. He won't condemn her. He understands our weaknesses.'

'Then pray to Him to help you with yours,' Rory said quietly.

Francine lowered her gaze against the steady look that he gave her. After a long silence she said, 'I'll come with you.'

Kathleen was waiting in the sitting-room. She looked drained. Without a word being spoken she and Francine went into one another's arms. They shed a few tears together then Kathleen drew away. 'Will you come home for a while soon, Francine? Gran wants to see you, she's missed you.' Francine nodded and said she would see them all the following week.

They prepared to leave. Rory kissed her and held her close for a moment and she drew comfort from his strength. When the limousine left Lord Holcombe took her by the hand and they went into the house. Francine said, 'I never expected such an ending to our day. Perhaps it's just as well we don't know what is in store for us, otherwise we mightn't have the strength to face up to all the troubles.'

'I must agree with that.' Lord Holcombe spoke gently. 'Shall we have a game of two-handed whist?' Francine agreed, not wanting to think any more about recent events.

On the Saturday morning Bridget arrived to travel with Francine to the O'Reillys. She was as sombre as though they were going to a funeral. It was a terrible thing Kathleen had done to the family, they would never live it down. She could only pray that people would accept the child as being premature.

But when they arrived at the O'Reillys Francine had a joyful reception from them. And wasn't it wonderful to see her. How did the wedding go? Just fancy being married and living in the house of a real live lord.

Her hat and coat were taken from her and the family all followed Mrs O'Reilly and Francine into the kitchen to hear all the news.

Tea was poured for her and a piece of cake cut but Francine had no opportunity to partake of either for answering questions. And she knew a happiness then that took away all the upset of the news of Kathleen marrying her father.

These people were excited that she had married so well, bore no grudge that they hadn't been invited to the wedding, but treated her as though she were one of them. The true salt of the earth, as Cook would say. Francine talked and they hung on to her every word as she described Holcombe Manor and told them about Tyson who had had to go abroad on urgent business. Then they aahed in sympathy and said wasn't it a shame then, a young bride being separated from her husband almost on their honeymoon.

Mary asked Francine softly when her husband would be coming back.

Francine smiled, 'Soon, I hope,' and felt strangely confident that he would return.

Mr O'Reilly, who was standing next to Mary, laid an arm across her shoulder. 'Soon we'll be having a wee great-granddaughter or a great-grandson. And we'll be having another great-grandchild when Kathleen's little one is born.' He beamed at Francine. 'And if you were to have a wee one too, then we would be a lovely big family, wouldn't we?'

The family had gone silent when the old man had mentioned Kathleen. His wife said sharply, 'Your mouth's too big, Mr O'Reilly, embarrassing poor Francine who's hardly over her honeymoon. Drink your tea, child, and eat your cake.' She shooed the family out. 'Get on with your work, you'll have plenty of time for talking. Francine's staying overnight.'

'Am I?' she said. 'Oh, that's lovely, I didn't know.'

'Neither did I until this minute,' declared Mrs O'Reilly. 'But I think it'll take all day and the morning to catch up on the news.'

Francine stitched dolls' clothes while she sat with the family in the workroom and they all talked. Kathleen came for an hour and Rory soon after. It was a quick call, he said. He turned to Francine . . . 'Back to slumming again then, are you?'

There was a gasp from the others then his grandmother smacked him across the face. 'Don't you dare say such a thing to a member of this family. You'll apologise to Francine.' She pushed Rory out of the room then called Francine to follow. Gran then went back into the workshop leaving the two of them standing. Rory looked at Francine, shame-faced.

'I'm sorry, I don't know what made me say such a thing. I think it is that I'm jealous. I hate the thought of you marrying into the de Auberleigh family. They're snobs.'

Francine was trembling at Rory's barb. 'They've been kind enough to me,' she said in a low voice. After a pause she added, 'And you were kind to me when we were by the waterfall. Why are you so horrible now? I'll stay away

270

if it offends you, my being here. I don't think I can stand any more upsets.'

Rory drew her hastily to him. 'Francine, I'm sorry, I'm sorry, I don't want to hurt you, I don't know what got into me. The trouble is I care too much about you, I don't want you to be married to anyone else.' He drew back suddenly. 'And I'm sorry about that. I have no right to hold you. Forgive me.'

Francine, near to tears, whispered, 'There's nothing to forgive. These things happen, we all say things at times we don't mean. I said I would stay away if you didn't want me here, but I want to come, it's the only real home I know.' Her voice broke.

'Francine, don't,' Rory said in an anguished voice. 'I can't bear to see you cry. I want you to come here, I wish you lived here and then I could see you every day.'

'Oh, Rory, you mustn't say such things. I'm married.'

'I know only too well you are,' he replied with bitterness. 'And you shouldn't have been. No one can tell me that you're happy. No husband worth his salt would leave his wife to go on business while you're still honeymooning. I don't know what's happened between you, I don't want to know, I only wish you weren't married.'

Mrs O' Reilly looked out. 'Has that lad not apologised yet?'

Francine said, 'Yes, he has. We're – friends again.' She gave Rory a brief smile then went back into the workroom.

Rory, who said he had to be leaving, turned on his heel and left. His grandmother said, 'He blows hot and cold does our Rory, but then don't we all at times.'

When Kathleen was ready to leave she motioned to Francine to come to the door with her. There Kathleen said, 'Try not to let our Rory upset you, Francine. He's in love with you, that's his trouble.' She paused and touched Francine's cheek. 'Do you still hate me because I'm going to marry your father?'

'No, I love you, Kathleen, and always will. I shall love

271

the baby too, but I'll never have any love for my father. Come and see me at Holcombe Manor when you can.' Kathleen promised then they kissed and she left. Although Francine no longer felt upset by Rory's snide remark, most of the joy had gone out of the visit. She told herself that she didn't want Rory to be in love with her, yet knew she was clinging to the fact that he was. More than anything in the world she needed to be loved. And she could be married to Tyson for the rest of her life, he who might never love her.

For the first time Francine began to understand why a man took a mistress: why a woman had an affair with another man. Many marriages were arranged. It was said that a lot turned out well but there were others in which the partners had no love to give to the other.

Life went on, with Francine looking forward more and more to the photography lessons and visits from Sophie, Mrs Denton and Bridget. Her father was quietly married to Kathleen early one morning at the Register Office, with only Mr and Mrs O'Reilly attending. The old man had given his granddaughter away and apparently had been deeply touched by this, but Gran had sworn she would never forgive Edwin Chayter for not inviting Francine, his only child. The couple had gone straight back to the house and there had not even been a wedding breakfast.

'Terrible,' Bridget said. 'With an attitude like that the marriage is doomed from the start and Kathleen is the fool for having let herself get pregnant.'

Evie was quietly married, but in church. Apparently, Mrs Pennystone had given a wedding breakfast and, according to what Cook had been told, it had been quite a happy affair. She, of course, had been unable to go and Evie was back at work the following morning.

Lord Holcombe had been in London a number of times on business and Francine had taken to calling on Mrs Binks, who always seemed so pleased to see her. Francine thought that when she was proficient with a camera she would dearly like to take a photograph of Mrs Binks, who had so many changing expressions. When she spoke of her husband it was with a fondness. Binks didn't have much to say, but he was a kind and thoughtful man. And then her eyes would twinkle when she talked about her own childhood and the fun the children would have running about the countryside, climbing trees, riding on the haywagon and singing hymns in the evenings, even when it wasn't Sunday.

Lord Holcombe started to go to London regularly for several days at a time. He said it was on business, but Francine suspected he was attending gaming parties because when he returned he would sleep for two whole days and a night. When he was away Sophie and Bridget would come to stay. Francine enjoyed these breaks, although she longed for Tyson to write to her from Switzerland, to let her know where she stood. When Lord Holcombe had missed a lesson with Mr Beckett Francine would explain all she had learned. One lesson had been about placing the sitter's hands, so important. There were numerous positions that could be used. It all depended of course on the type of sitter. Another lesson was about taking photographs in the right light outside. Dan Beckett showed Francine beautiful outdoor scenes, pointing out cloud formation, the reflection of buildings, of trees in still water. She began to understand why her father had won an award for his landscapes.

She had learned about developing and then came the day when Mr Beckett suggested she could take her first portrait photograph. Sophie was to be the sitter. Both girls were excited. Francine's hands were shaking so much she was sure she would have a failure. But once she was behind the camera with the black velvet square over her head and was seeing Sophie upside down through the lens, she became quite calm. Mr Beckett let her arrange everything, the position she wanted Sophie to adopt. Sophie was in a modest gown, with a high neck, but she was sparkling. Her hands were restless. Francine told her to calm down and placed Sophie's hands, lightly clasped, on her lap. She sat her sideways then told her to look in the lens, and asked her to try and look pensive. Sophie giggled and said it was quite impossible, but when Francine pleaded that this photograph was very important to her Sophie settled down.

Francine's most exciting moment was in the dark room when the image of Sophie appeared on the paper. Mr Beckett and Sophie were with her. When Francine picked up the photograph with tweezers and held it up, Mr Beckett said, 'Very good! It has faults, which I shall point out later, but it is an excellent first effort, and Sophie's smile is very natural.'

This to Francine was praise indeed and she was quietly jubilant. It was a start; how soon would she be proficient enough to have a business of her own?

But she soon realised that there was a great deal more to learn before she could treat photography as a means of starting a business. She was, however, a willing pupil and might have gone far had it not been for two things. Word came from Mr Beckett's housekeeper that he had suffered a heart attack and would not be able to come to Holcombe Manor for a number of weeks, if ever again. This grieved Francine, poor dear Mr Beckett.

And right on top of that tragic news came word from Lord Holcombe, who was in London, that England was at war with the Boers.

'*We were expecting it,*' he wrote, '*yet it still comes as a shock. People are going wild with excitement, and are waving Union Jacks, as if the war was already over and England had won. There will be a lot of bloodshed from now on.*' He ended the letter saying he had some urgent business to deal with but would be home in two days' time.

Sophie thought the news of the war terribly exciting, even though it would be taking place so far away. Bridget said in a voice of doom, 'There is no excitement in war, there will be boys and men maimed and killed. For them it is all glory and our very own men will be joining up, I'm sure.'

The O'Reillys? Francine's heart began to pound. Would the boys volunteer, Milo, Declan, Michael . . . Rory? Oh, no, pray God, no.

When Lord Holcombe did arrive back four men were with him. After greetings had been exchanged they went into the study and when they emerged an hour later they looked grim. Sophie, who had done some eavesdropping, as usual, said she formed the impression that a great deal of money had been lost on the stock market because of the situation.

Three of the men left but one stayed and during lunch the war was discussed, with the two men at times seeming to forget they were not alone.

When Sophie ventured to ask how Britain had come to be at war with South Africa, Lord Holcombe spoke of a man called Jan Smuts, who as leader of the Boers, had called on the British Government to remove their troops from the frontiers and send away all British reinforcements. The Government had refused and Chamberlain had been shocked when Smuts had taken on the onus of aggression. 'But,' Lord Holcombe added, 'you have no need to worry, Sophie, we will soon end this war, one that should never have been started.'

Later, Sophie talked about how exciting it must be in London with all the troops leaving and although she was not due to return with Bridget until after the weekend she made up her mind to leave the next day. And Francine, who was worried about the O'Reillys' grandsons joining up, asked Lord Holcombe's permission to accompany them.

'Of course, my dear,' he said. 'But you have no need to ask my permission, you are a married woman in your own right.'

Francine eyed him in an anxious way. 'And Tyson? Do you think he will return to England to enlist? If only I knew where he was, how he is.'

Lord Holcombe shrugged. 'Who can tell? Most young men think of war as a great adventure and Tyson is more adventurous than most.'

Francine said no more, but went upstairs to pack a bag for a few days' stay in London.

The few days developed into weeks. Sophie had been right. It was exciting being in London, with soldiers marching to the docks to the rousing music of the brass bands. For the first time the troops were in khaki and wore their sun helmets. The streets were lined with a cheering crowd. Some of the older men grumbled about the dreary colour of the khaki, nothing like the glorious scarlet uniforms that put fire into your blood and made you proud to march. To this a woman said wryly, 'In red they were targets for the enemy and we all know why the men were blood-coloured, so the enemy wouldn't know if they were wounded until they fell. Give me this khaki colour every time.'

There was a sea of Union Jacks being waved and Francine, Sophie and Bridget waved theirs as vigorously as anyone else. There had been a frenzy of fund-raising so that the men could have clothing, tobacco and cigarettes and to help dependants left to keep the home going on a pittance. Women also handed the men lavender sachets and bibles to go into their kitbags.

The Princess of Wales, who was head of the Red Cross, helped to organise hospitals to receive the wounded and also hospital ships. Americans in London, led by the widow of the late Randolph Churchill, financed the hospital ship *Maine* as a gesture of Atlantic brotherhood.

When Francine went with Bridget to the O'Reillys they found the family in dissension over the war. Old Mr O'Reilly's sympathies were with the Boers, declaring that any man would fight to save his land, his home.

Mrs O'Reilly said, 'All I know is, I don't want my lads to go and get killed fighting someone else's troubles.'

Her husband flapped his hands at her. 'Calm down, woman, they might never have to go. The regulars'll go first, then the reserves and by then I've no doubt that the war'll be over. The Boers will wipe them all out. They *know* the land.'

This last statement brought the boys into the argument and it was obvious by their comments that it was the adventure of going abroad that had them eager to volunteer. When their grandmother upbraided Milo for wanting to go and fight, knowing his wife was going to have a baby, he was aghast that she should expect him to stay behind for such a reason. Would they have his child know that his or her dada had shirked his duty when he was needed? 'Don't put that shame on *me*, Gran,' he exclaimed.

Francine thought about Tyson then. And wasn't he shirking his duty, being with his mistress and enjoying the peace of Switzerland when he was also needed. Not now, perhaps, but later. No war ever stopped in a few months.

It was Mrs O'Reilly who brought the argument to an end. 'Here we all are fighting about a war and Francine and Bridget have come to visit. Sit you down and we'll have a cup of tea.'

A week later Francine had just arrived at the Dentons' to stay for a couple of days when Tyson was announced. Her heart began a slow, painful beating. He came breezing in, looking incredibly handsome and immaculate in silver grey. 'Aunt – Sophie.' He kissed each of them on the cheek then suddenly became aware of someone else in the room. His eyebrows raised in surprise.

'Francine! I thought you would be at Holcombe Manor.'

'No, I – I've been staying here in London for a few weeks, the war, there's so much going on. I -' She stopped, with a feeling of helplessness, unable to think of anything else to say.

Sophie said to Tyson, 'Well, give Francine a kiss — she is your wife.'

'Sophie!' her mother scolded.

Tyson walked over to Francine and leaning forward kissed her on the lips. When he drew away he said, 'Tact is not one of Cousin Sophie's strong points.' He was smiling and there was a warmth in his eyes that Francine had not seen since the Monte Carlo days.

Mrs Denton said she would order tea but Tyson held up his hand and told her not for him, he had simply called in for a few minutes before going home. He had some business to discuss with his father. He gave a quick glance at Francine then turned to Mrs Denton again. 'Actually, I did want some news of Francine, but now that she is here, perhaps I could have a few words alone with her?'

'Of course, Tyson. The morning room.'

With the door closed Tyson drew up two chairs and when Francine was seated he sat facing her. 'I came back because of the war. I want to volunteer. I know I will have to undergo some training but in the meantime I want to stay at Holcombe Manor. I'm hoping that you will be there, too.'

She stared at him, furious. 'I had better settle one thing right away. I do not want to live with you as your wife, ever again.'

'I wasn't going to suggest that you did,' he replied calmly. 'I know I have behaved badly, but it's all beyond my control. I'm still in love with Octavia. It's simply that I want you to know that you will be provided for while I'm away in South Africa.'

'Thank you very much,' she retorted. 'At least I'll know that I won't have to take a job scrubbing floors in order to live.'

Tyson, his palms pressed together between his knees, regarded her steadily. 'The trouble is, Francine, we are both rebels, both desperate for independence. My only regret is that you had to be sacrificed so that I could achieve my freedom. Unfortunately, neither my father nor yours anticipated that I would behave over our marriage the way I did.'

Francine sat, straight-backed. 'Are you surprised at that? You entered into an agreement and were paid for it. You cheated and I find cheating despicable.'

'I didn't cheat, I fulfilled my obligations when I married you.'

'Obligations? Ha! You couldn't get away quickly enough to be with your mistress.'

'Octavia is *not* my mistress.' Now Tyson was ruffled.

'Then what would you call her? Does she perhaps dispense her services to a number of other men?' The moment Francine had made the accusation she regretted it. Tyson jumped up.

'How dare you denigrate Octavia in this way. If you'll excuse me, I'm leaving. I may, or may not see you again before I leave to go to South Africa.'

He was away and the front door had slammed before Francine pulled herself together in order to apologise. She went to the window and watched him walking along the crescent with lengthening strides. Oh, God, she had said a dreadful thing. She had almost suggested that Octavia was a whore. It was unforgivable. Tyson had reached the corner when he stopped abruptly. He turned, stood a moment then came striding back.

Moments later he was being ushered back into the morning room. He swept off his hat. 'I couldn't leave without putting a few things straight. I went to Switzerland as a house guest of the Mannings. Octavia did invite me but apart from walks and skiing with her we were never alone. I wanted to make love to her, but for your information, Octavia is not free with her favours. She is chaste, yes, chaste. She wants to keep herself for the man she marries.'

A wryness touched Tyson's lips then. 'And she made it quite clear that I would not have been that man, not even when I was free. I was glad when the war was announced so that I had a good excuse for returning to England.'

They were both silent for a while then he said, his voice quiet, 'There were times after I left you that I longed to see you, Francine. I had always found you desirable. I did when we were at Monte Carlo. Do you remember when I told you I could fall in love with you?'

Francine almost succumbed to the sensuousness in his tone, then she realised why he had wanted to talk to her.

' "Desirable" you said. Are you sure you didn't mean "available"? Octavia rejects you so you come back to your wife to satisfy your – lusts.'

He took no offence. 'You have every right to think such a thing, Francine. But I'm not such a wretched creature that I would come back to you to satisfy my lusts, as you call it. I have to admit that I still think of Octavia at times, can't get her out of my mind, dammit, but I could so easily love you. And that is the truth.'

He really did seem sincere and as Francine thought of Tyson making love to her, pulses began to beat wildly in her body. It had been so long.

He began to plead. 'Come with me to Holcombe Manor, Francine. I need you, no not to make love to you, but just to walk with me, to stroll over fields, by the river, explore woods. *Please*.'

It was not his pleading that made Francine give in but the terrible bleakness in his eyes. She had experienced rejection, had suffered that awful feeling of aloneness. She held out a hand to him.

'Yes, Tyson, I'll come with you.'

CHAPTER TWENTY-ONE

Lord Holcombe greeted them, visibly emotional. 'How wonderful to see you together again. I'm so glad you arrived now. In a week's time I will be on my way to France. Come along and tell me what news there is in London of the war.'

Francine went upstairs to change, leaving the men to talk. It felt strange returning with Tyson. He had been quiet, thoughtful on the way to Windsor and she wondered if she had done the right thing. When he talked, it was about the wonderful scenery in Switzerland, the towering snow-clad alps, the lakes, the skiing and she was very much aware that Octavia was on his mind. Once, he started to talk about a walk that he and Octavia had taken together, then he quickly changed the subject.

Francine thought of Sophie, who had openly showed disappointment when she knew she was returning to Holcombe Manor with Tyson. 'I'll miss you terribly and it won't be the same coming to visit you with Tyson there.' Then she cheered up. 'But no doubt soon he'll be off to the war then we can have some fun again.'

Mrs Denton, Gran O'Reilly and Bridget were all despondent that Francine, who had been married such a short time, would be on her own again if Tyson went to war. Kathleen, like Sophie, treated it more cheerfully. 'Don't think of Tyson leaving, think of the reunion when the war is over.'

Francine was surprised at how happy Kathleen seemed to be, married to her father. Had marriage softened him? Had having someone special to care for him rid him of some of his bitterness? Or was it the thought of perhaps having a son? Francine hoped it would be a boy, a girl she felt might be too much of a reminder of herself.

When she came down to the drawing room the two men got up. 'It's all right,' she said, 'you go on talking, I'm just going to sit here quietly. I have a slight headache.' The headache was an excuse, she wanted to think over the past few weeks in London. She sat in a small alcove at the far side of the window.

The men went on talking and Francine studied them: Lord Holcombe, with his aristocratic bearing, tall and thin, a shaft of autumn sunshine lighting his silvery hair, his cheeks finely boned. Tyson's features were stronger. At times he had a slightly arrogant air. A lock of his dark hair fell over his forehead as he eagerly described an incident he had witnessed in London.

Then Rory came into her mind. She had tried desperately not to think about him. He had been cool when he knew she was returning to Holcombe Manor with Tyson.

She had a vivid image of him, strong-featured, blunt, a stubborn thrust to his chin. 'For your sake, Francie, I hope you'll be happy, but I doubt you ever will with de Auberleigh. You're not really his type.'

She had been angry. 'What exactly do you mean by that? Do you consider that Tyson is above the salt and that I'm below it?'

'No, of course I don't, and you know it. He goes for the daughters of the wealthy, hoping to get an easy living. Oh, yes, I know all about him. He has such a big opinion of himself.'

'So do *you*,' Francine retorted. 'You think you know everything. I suppose it didn't occur to you that he could fall in love with someone so ordinary as I am.'

'I don't think you are ordinary,' Rory said quietly. 'You're special, very special to me. I hate to see you tied to Tyson de Auberleigh who'll break your heart. I know it.'

'You know nothing.' Francine had turned and left him

then, and although Rory had called after her she had ignored him.

Now, looking back over the incident she realised that in different ways she was in love with both men. They had two things in common: they both had the same colouring and both were selfish. Tyson had no thought for her when he went off to Switzerland with Octavia Manning, and Rory was just as selfish by refusing to tutor her in photography. If his feelings for her had been really deep he would have been more than willing to help, wanting to please her. Surely that was what true love was all about.

Tyson was asking Lord Holcombe how long he thought it could be before he would be shipped abroad, and the answer was, 'It might never come.'

Tyson looked vastly disappointed. 'Never?'

'It's like this, my boy. The powers to be would feel incompetent if the regulars were not able to finish off this uprising in a few weeks. They will hate it if they have to call on the reserves, so you can imagine how they will feel if they have to send volunteers out. Thousands *are* volunteering, however.'

'And you think they might not be needed?'

'For Francine's sake I hope not.'

They both looked towards her and seeing she was watching them Holcombe got up. 'Come and join us, my dear, I feel we are neglecting you.' She came over, and although at first the talk was general the two men were back once more to the various angles of war.

A neighbour, Mr Milton, dropped in that evening after dinner, having just returned from London. At ten o'clock, he was still there and the talk of war had not ceased. Francine excused herself and went up to bed, where she lay, shivering a little not knowing whether Tyson would come to their room or sleep in the spare bedroom.

Although Francine tried to convince herself that she would prefer to sleep alone, she had only to start thinking

283

of Tyson making love to her for her body to start throbbing. She lay awake a long time listening for him to come upstairs, but eventually feeling drowsy she slipped down in the bed.

She roused with the feeling that someone was in the room and when she opened her eyes, Tyson was standing by the bed looking down at her. He was in his dressing gown. 'I want you, Francine,' he said softly. 'Please don't turn me away. I want to see you, touch you.' He reached out and began undoing the buttons of her nightdress. Francine tensed. Leisurely, this time, he drew back the bedcovers, reached for the hem of her nightdress, then raised it slowly, and as he drew it over her breasts he drew in a quick breath.

'Oh, God, Francine, you're so beautiful.' He raised her then drew the nightdress over her head. By then, small frissons of ecstasy were making her own breathing ragged. Tyson rid himself of his dressing gown and climbing on to the bed laid his nakedness to hers. She gave a little moan and he began kissing her breasts, her throat, her eyelids. 'Francine, Francine, I can't wait.'

He thrust into her and with a frenzied rhythm he was bringing her to a climax when it was suddenly all over and he was a weight on her. She could have cried with frustration. 'You're selfish,' she accused him. 'You think only of yourself.'

He laughed softly. 'You are the one to blame, you're so beautiful, so desirable.' He rolled away then slipped an arm around her shoulder. 'Be patient, just give me a few minutes and then -'

She said pettishly, 'I'm sure you wouldn't treat Octavia like that. You would see that she enjoyed it, too.'

He pulled away from her, got out of bed, pulled on his dressing gown and exclaimed, 'You're so stupid, Francine! You have no idea of how to pleasure a man.'

Francine had regretted mentioning Octavia the moment

she said her name. Now she was angry with herself for having spoilt everything.

'Whores and mistresses pleasure men,' she said, making matters worse.

'And wives if they have any sense,' he retorted. She wanted to say she was sorry, but the words refused to come. He knotted the cord of his dressing gown. 'It's wives like you who drive husbands to seek solace elsewhere.' He had his back to her. Now he swung round to face her. 'I'm trying to get over Octavia. I'm still crazy about her, but I was doing my best to make our marriage work.'

Francine drew herself up in the bed. 'You lied to me when we were in Monte Carlo and you told me you were head over heels in love with me!'

His face was thunderous. 'I was not lying! You were so refreshing, so lovely then, so – so innocent. But you're like every woman, as soon as you are married you become shrewish and want to own a man body and soul.'

He turned and stormed out and Francine put her hands to her face. What a mess she had made of everything. She had behaved like a shrew again and why? Because she wanted satisfaction from their love-making. She was unwilling to wait, so she picked on Tyson's obsession with Octavia and killed all his attempts to try and make a go of their marriage. Fool, fool . . .

Should she go to him, tell him she was sorry? But supposing he refused to accept her apology? Francine stayed where she was, unable to bear one more rejection. Perhaps when Tyson cooled down they might draw together again.

But she didn't see him for the next four days and Lord Holcombe postponed his trip to France, making the excuse that he wanted to know more about the South African situation before he left. Tyson had left a note on the hall table saying he was going to do some concentrated riding for a few days so he would be in trim for when he went to South Africa.

'Well,' Lord Holcombe said, 'I suppose it's sensible, but veldt riding is very different from cantering over English fields.'

Tyson came back weatherbeaten and looking extremely fit. He greeted Francine as though she was his much-loved wife.

'Darling, have you missed me? Sorry I ran off the way I did. I just felt I had to be prepared to face up to the Boers.' His smile only touched his lips. 'I'll be having another long ride the day after tomorrow. Perhaps you would like Sophie to come and stay with you.' He turned to Lord Holcombe. 'And you sir, I know are itching to get to the casinos. I shall be here every evening from now on until I'm called for training for the army.'

Sophie said in answer to Francine's letter that she would be with her in a week. There were a lot of parties going on. Everyone was celebrating before the war had been won.

Lord Holcombe left for France, with reluctance. He even asked Francine if she would like to go with him, but she said no – he was not to worry, she was fine.

Tyson was out every day, but he did come home every evening as promised, but although his manner was pleasant towards her and in fact at times almost affectionate, he made no attempt to come to their room again. And it was pride that kept Francine from making any advances towards him.

The days were long to her. She spent some time in the studio, which Tyson still knew nothing about. She went for walks, calling every day to see Mrs Binks. One time she met Mr Binks, who as his wife had said, had little to say.

Mrs Binks knew about Tyson riding most of the time. 'He's quick, he is, he can wheel Hannibal round in the space of a heartbeat and he's shooting too as he's riding and could knock a piece of twig from under a sparrow.

Mr Binks says he's good and if he says so, he is. Not one for much praising, is Binks.'

Francine went one day to the fields where Tyson was riding but there was a girl there, jumping fences with him, and she left feeling full of heartache, doubting now whether she and her husband would ever be close again.

Once when Francine was in the Binks' kitchen a huge spider walked over the stone-flagged floor close to her foot and she jumped up, knocking over the chair. 'Oh, it's horrible, I can't stand spiders.'

Mrs Binks looked at her in faint astonishment. 'Why, they'm lovely creatures, they'm spinners of silk. Have you ever watched one, ma'am?'

She went on to describe how the female lays hundreds of eggs then when they hatch some of them swing down on silken lines, others are lifted into the wind and the rest float away like petals. 'When they grow *they* make webs, gossamer threads so fine you can only see them with a magnifying glass. They come from tiny openings in the spider's body which are called spinnerets.'

Francine said, 'If the mother goes on laying eggs there must be thousands of spiders.'

'No, ma'am, she don't go on laying eggs. After the first hatch she dies, her life's work is done.'

'Oh, how sad.'

'You mustn't think that way, my dear. She leaves beauty behind. Think of the silken web and add a jewelled dewdrop and you'll see one of the loveliest miracles of nature.'

Francine said, 'Mrs Binks stop it, or you'll have me weeping. You're a poet.'

'Nay, ma'am. It's Binks who's the poet, he has a way with words. He writes some wonderful pieces that make me want to cry at times. People don't seem to see beauty these days. At the moment all they can think about is war. Me and Binks have ten nephews all anxious to go and fight. How many of them'll come back? But there, we're

287

getting on to unhappy things. Come, I'll show you a web just finished this morning.'

Francine left the cottage feeling chastened. She had secretly felt that Mrs Binks must have a dreary life with her taciturn husband and yet they shared such beauty together. 'Spinners of silk'. What a lovely expression. She repeated it, then Spinners End came into her mind. There was Gran O'Reilly, who had worked so hard to bring up her orphaned grandchildren, who shouted at her husband when he was drunk, but who would, Francine knew, love him no matter what he did. Gran had learned many philosophies through all the hardships. And what have I learned, Francine wondered? Very little, it seemed. She had a husband who had called her a shrew, and he was right. She had only herself to blame for being miserable, full of self-pity. She must try and think differently. Make excuses for Tyson's faults. See beauty in things, spin beautiful thoughts. She would try and patch up the differences between Tyson and herself.

Unfortunately this was denied her. Sophie arrived with Bridget unexpectedly that afternoon and when Tyson came home he said now that Francine had company he would go and stay with his parents for a few days, there were one or two things he wanted to discuss with them.

Sophie raised her eyebrows when he had gone and asked how the marriage was working out, remarking that it was strange Tyson should disappear the moment they arrived.

'He's restless, like most of the young men wanting to get away to the *adventures* of war.'

'Or to have a fling with some other woman,' Sophie remarked wryly.

'Possibly. Who knows what husbands get up to when they're away from home.'

'Don't you mind? You're very calm about it.'

Francine, not wanting to make a drama of it, told Sophie about her talk with Mrs Binks and about spiders being the spinners of silk and how it had made her want to think beautiful thoughts and Sophie found this all very amusing. She laughed and Francine laughed too, otherwise she felt she would have been crying, having learned it was very hard to get beauty into one's soul at short notice.

Sophie was always a tonic, and although Bridget was in a low state about the war as several of her relatives had gone to South Africa, she always had plenty to talk about.

Kathleen was really happy in her marriage, she said, and according to what she had heard, Mr Chayter was looking forward to the birth of a son. 'Oh, yes,' she added, 'he's made up his mind it's going to be a boy.'

When Francine asked after Evie and how Cook was managing in the kitchen without help, Bridget said that Evie seemed contented enough running her own little home and expecting her first and, as for Mrs Dodge having help, Kathleen was never far from the kitchen. She was always popping in and out, and was in there all the time when her husband was away...

The following day Sophie said she had decided to return home. She was missing Randolph. 'Yes, really and truly I am, Francine. Perhaps I am in love with him after all.'

Bridget said she would stay, unless Francine wanted to come back to London with her. Francine knew she would have done so had not a letter come from Mr Beckett by the next post to say he was over his indisposition and would be willing to resume the photography lessons if Francine was agreeable. She wrote back straight away to say she would be delighted to have him come to Holcombe Manor and would look forward to his visit.

Seeing that Mr Beckett would be staying in the house, Francine knew she would have to tell Tyson, who had returned from his visit to the de Auberleighs, about her lessons. She was prepared for him to raise some objections, but was totally unprepared for his anger.

How dare she go behind his back and arrange such a thing. She had behaved in a most deceitful manner. He

289

would not have his wife take up such a role. Before long she would be opening a business.

At first she matched his anger, asking him why not, seeing that he was never at home. She needed something to occupy her. He shouted that she should do as other wives did, take up embroidery or some other interest. There was a library of books that could keep her occupied for years. Then he added that she must get rid of the camera and all the other paraphernalia in the studio at once.

Francine was suddenly calm, pointing out that it did not belong to her – all the equipment had been bought by Lord Holcombe, who had shared her lessons and indeed, encouraged them.

This took Tyson aback for a moment then he said, tight-lipped, 'Lord Holcombe can resume them when he likes, but I will not have my wife learning the art of photography. And that is that.'

'No,' she said quietly, 'you are wrong. If you refuse your consent then I shall leave you. And this time when I run away it will be to a place where you won't find me so easily.'

'I would find you, you can rest assured on that.' His tone was grim. 'I will not be made a laughing stock because my wife has run away to be a photographer.'

'Far better to be a laughing stock for that reason than for me to tell my friends you are such a weakling you've only been able to make love to me several times since we were married.'

His face flamed. 'You are an insufferable liar!'

'Am I? Ask yourself how many times we have slept together. I had hoped for a child, but obviously you have no interest in children.'

'I do want children – I want a son, but I will not be blackmailed into it. As for being a weakling -'

'Either you are or you're taking your pleasures elsewhere.'

'I am not taking my pleasures elsewhere!'

'Then you are a weakling.' Francine was beginning to enjoy herself when he grabbed her by the hand and pulled her across the room, saying he would soon rectify that situation.

She tried to pull back but he was strong and in a dreadful temper, and she knew if she shouted she would not only bring Bridget running but some of the staff.

When they reached the foot of the stairs Tyson swept her up in his arms and she knew if they were seen it would be taken that he was a romantic, passionate husband unable to wait to make love to his wife. But there was nothing romantic about Tyson's love-making, it was rape; he was brutal to her and when it was over she lay, slow tears sliding down the sides of her cheeks. Tyson, still in a fury, was hastily dressing. He pulled on his jacket, turned suddenly then seeing her, an anguished look came over his face. 'Oh, God, Francine, what have I done?' He sank into a chair. Francine turned her face away and wiped her tears with a corner of the sheet. Tyson got up and came over to the bed.

'Francine, I don't know what came over me. Forgive me. I've behaved as though I were someone else.' He turned her face towards him. 'I hurt you, I'm sorry, so very sorry. I think a devil must have got into me.'

'I had a devil in me,' she whispered. 'I was tormenting you. It was wrong.'

'I'll leave you to rest,' he said gently. 'I'll say you have a headache and don't want to be disturbed.' He touched her cheek. 'We'll have a talk later, we must. I only pray you'll forgive me.'

He left then, closing the door quietly behind him, leaving Francine disturbed. She *had* taunted him, but why should it have made Tyson behave so brutally? Was his obsession with Octavia so strong that her rejection of him had made him feel inadequate, which was a terrible way for a man to feel?

There was no question of her not forgiving him. She had behaved badly, had actually enjoyed taunting him, but at the same time she was not going to give in about relinquishing the photography lessons. She made to draw herself up in the bed, but quickly lay back. Her whole body felt bruised at the way Tyson had handled her. Men forgot how strong they were.

She slept and on opening her eyes, found Bridget sitting by her bedside.

'How are you feeling, Francine?' she asked, her voice gentle. 'Tyson told me he had behaved badly towards you. I can only guess that you had a rather serious quarrel. He seemed very upset. He might not have told me but a letter came from the War Office asking him to go for an interview about enlisting. It's for early tomorrow morning. He said he would go home and stay there overnight. But he'll be back tomorrow, even though he might be late.'

'Enlisting?' Francine sat up, wincing as she did so, which she felt had not gone unnoticed by Bridget. 'He'll be leaving to go to war?'

'Not before he's had some training, Francine. I've brought you a cup of tea. Try not to worry, you'll make up your quarrel.'

Francine thought she must be grateful for that at least. It would be terrible if a husband were called up right away, with a quarrel hanging between him and his wife.

The following evening she sat up until midnight and had just decided that Tyson would not be home when she heard the car coming up the drive. She was composed when he came into the drawing room.

'I knew you were still up when I saw the light.' His eyes were bright with excitement. 'I've been accepted for training. I go to Aldershot. So do my brothers.'

Francine gave a shiver. 'Your poor parents, they must be terribly upset.'

'Mama is, Papa is terribly proud.' Tyson came towards her and said softly, 'And you, Francine? How do you feel?

Are you glad to be rid of me? I haven't been much of a husband to you, have I?'

'I think we both have our faults. I only know that I don't want you to go to war.'

'Have you forgiven me? Please say yes.'

'I love you, Tyson, no forgiveness is necessary.'

'You love me? After the way I behaved towards you? Oh, Francine, I don't deserve it. At this moment I feel sure I'm in love with you. I couldn't get your face out of my mind during the drive to town.' He drew her to him, and even though he was gentle she felt every bruise and was unable not to tense. 'Dear God,' he exclaimed. 'Will I ever forgive myself for what I did? I must have been temporarily deranged.' He released her. 'Francine, I'll be away for about a month then I'll have leave before I sail for Africa. Perhaps then we can . . . make up our quarrel.'

She managed a smile. 'I'm sure we will.'

Tyson left the next morning and Francine couldn't stop crying after he had gone. She was crying for a marriage that had never really been a true marriage right from the start, not with Tyson longing for Octavia. Although he had told Francine that he was sure he loved her, she was not convinced. Octavia was ever-present in his thoughts. All she could do now was to live life from day to day and hope that once the war was over Tyson might be through with his obsession.

It helped her when Mr Beckett came to stay for a few days: she felt she had come alive again. They went outdoors photographing, taking the camera with them in a large trap, arranged for them by Mr Binks. The steward showed a great interest and watched them from a short distance. Mr Beckett invited him to join them to have his photograph taken and he took off his cap, replaced it then gave a nod. And when the plate was developed Francine saw not a taciturn man but a gentle person with dreamy eyes. What had his thoughts been when he was being photographed? When she asked him he said, 'Well now,

I was thinking about the sow that dropped her piglets this morning, and the little runt that got his snout in before the others. A regular little pushy chap, he be.'

And his expression was that of a father who was apt to indulge the less strong one of the family.

Mr Beckett showed Francine how to superimpose one negative on another to give an effect of mist. When she wanted to photograph birds in flight he explained that their flight was too swift for the lens to capture. To give her an example, he showed her a photograph taken of a busy thoroughfare: when the plate was printed, only one stationary cart was shown.

Ever since Mrs Binks had talked about the spinners of silk, Francine had a more keen awareness of beauty in the countryside. She had always enjoyed her walks with her Aunt Amelia along the country lanes, loved the colour of poppies in a cornfield, the beauty of the bluebells in the woods. Now she appreciated the delicacy of ferns, the veins in a leaf, and the way the skin of the willow herbs curled back, the tiny seeds flying away as light as the dandelion balls.

Francine had letters from Tyson but they were all short. The training was concentrated, exhausting, he had little time for recreation. He hoped she was well and had plenty of company. He signed the letters, *Your loving husband* . . .

A week after Tyson's last note, Francine had letters from Sophie and Kathleen in the same post. Sophie asked when Tyson was expected to sail for South Africa as she and the family wanted to say goodbye to him. Then she went on, '*He was home last Sunday, but only stayed for an hour. I suppose he went on to see you* . . . '

Francine tensed. No, he had not come to see her, so where had he been? The fact that he had not mentioned having time off from training showed he had wanted to keep it secret. So much for hoping they might get close before he left to go to war!

In Kathleen's letter she said that Edwin was going abroad for two weeks and she wondered if she could come and spend a few days with Francine. Scribbled lines in Rory's handwriting followed this.

'I'm also free, how about me coming with Kathleen? I can sleep in the stables.'

Oh, yes, let Rory come too. He at least was honest even though he might sulk at times. And he loved her, really loved her, she was sure of that, and how desperately she needed to be loved . . .

CHAPTER TWENTY-TWO

When Bridget knew that Francine would be sending the car for Kathleen and Rory she said she would travel to town with the chauffeur and return when the visit ended. It would give her a chance to dust her house. Francine suspected that she missed her chats with Mrs Forbes, for the two women had become firm friends since returning from Monte Carlo.

When Kathleen and Rory did arrive Francine was astonished at the change in them. Kathleen looked elegant in a costume of forget-me-not blue, which matched her eyes, and a long fur stole, disguising her pregnancy. Rory was immaculate in a fawn suit, with an overcoat in a matching colour draped around his shoulders. She ran out to them and Rory swept off his hat and bowed low. Then he grinned.

'To the manner born. How do I look?'

Francine laughingly dropped a curtsey. 'Handsome and elegant, your lordship.' She turned to Kathleen who was waiting, arms outstretched. 'Kathleen, you look beautiful. Oh, it's so good to have you both here.' She linked arms with them. 'I've been waiting at the window, watching for you this past hour. Come along out of this wind, lunch will soon be ready.'

Kathleen had gone with the maid to her room and Rory was suddenly still, looking at Francine.

'It's grand to be here again. How are you, Francie?' His voice was low.

'Fine, fine. I enjoy the country air, but if I'm truly honest I miss Spinners End, all the hustle and bustle at the docks and market. On the other hand, I'm making headway with my photography.'

Rory inclined his head, his eyes teasing. 'Now, is that so, and what have you been photographing?'

'Oh, birds, animals, hedgerows, trees, lakes, the river and people. And what about you?'

'A lot of miserable wealthy folk who have never learned how to smile. I used to think the joy of my life would be owning a studio, but now I know I want to be a journalist photographer. Winston Churchill has gone out to Africa. They say he's a bit of an upstart but also that he is a fine writer like his father. I would like to photograph out there, but you have to be among the higher-ups to stand a chance of that kind of job. I wish the powers to be would send for me. This war'll be over before we even get out to Africa.'

'And I hope it will be,' Francine retorted. 'I can't understand men rushing to enlist in order to kill people.'

'We don't enlist to kill people – it's just part of the job of protecting our rights.'

Francine had just said heatedly that the Boers had rights too, when Kathleen came in, scolding them. 'Enough of that you two, we haven't come here to quarrel about the war.'

When Francine asked after Gran and Grandad O'Reilly Kathleen said, 'Himself went on the rampage last week. Herself hit him over the head with a dish, then she was all over him, had she hurt the dear man? She could have killed him. Then Himself started calling her names and she hit him again. After that all was peace. Same old story.'

They all laughed and Rory told Francine how his grandmother had insisted he got dressed up to come for this visit; she was not going to have the name of the O'Reillys sullied by any member of the nobility. He added that she had bought the clothes from some secondhand shop.

Kathleen then asked how Tyson was getting on with his training and Francine said, 'Fine, I think. He'll be home for leave before he has to sail. I think I'll be coming to town more often when he's gone. Apart from having my photography lessons there's nothing really to keep me here.'

'Good,' Kathleen said, 'then we'll be seeing you more often. The family are forever talking about you.'

Kathleen looked in sparkling health but she did say after lunch that she would like to lie down for an hour, and suggested to Rory that he take Francine for a walk.

The wind was still sharp but the sun had come out, giving light and shade to the scene. Rory, after taking several deep breaths, said, 'You don't know how lucky you are to be living here. What sort of social life do you have?'

'None, and I don't want any. We were invited out once when Tyson was here, but we never got to the house, as he had to leave on business. No one called to see me. I suppose there are callers when Lord Holcombe is here. I have made friends with the steward's wife, though. She's a lovely person, reminds me of Gran with her philosophies.'

Francine told Rory about the spiders being called the spinners of silk and Rory glanced at her. 'Spinners of silk? They're cannibals, they trap and eat flies and other insects.'

'Don't, Rory,' she said quietly. 'I know what spiders do but Mrs Binks made me more aware of the beauty in nature. I see weeds and plants and hedgerows through different eyes now. And they don't cannibalise anything. I've also known there was plenty of poverty around but I didn't think deeply about it because it didn't affect me.'

Rory stopped and put his hands on Francine's shoulders. 'Tell me, Francie, what is wrong. Your marriage isn't happy, is it?'

'It's not as happy as it might be, but the fault is mine. I wasn't ready for marriage. I think Tyson and I might get on a little better when he comes home. I've had time to think things out. My photography has helped.'

'I wish,' Rory began, but Francine, not wanting him to say any more, drew away and walked on.

298

'At one time, Rory, I wanted to photograph people, then I wanted to capture landscapes on plates. Now I know it will be mainly people I want to take, not studio photographs but general ones. Last week during one of my walks I came across two children standing outside a cottage. It looked derelict and the children were bare-footed and ragged.' Francine paused. 'The little girl would be about six years old, the boy three. He was crying silently, tears rolling slowly down his cheeks. The girl was holding in her arms a small bundle of straw, which had been tied in places to represent a doll.' There was a catch in Francine's voice then and it was a moment before she could continue.

'I had some pennies in my pocket. I spoke to the children and handed them some money but before they could take it a woman came out of the cottage. She knocked my hand away then hustled the children inside and shut the door. I felt terrible.'

'She was poor,' Rory said gently, 'but she had her pride. She didn't want charity.'

'It wasn't charity. I thought of the pleasure it would give the children to perhaps buy some sweets.'

'And give pleasure to you, Francine. We are all inclined to indulge ourselves when we feel charitable.'

Francine looked up at him, her eyes brimming with tears. 'No, you're wrong. It wasn't to indulge myself. I was well-clad when I was young, well-fed, but I never knew the pleasure of having a penny to spend on sweets. My aunt was not built in that mould. My own father certainly never indulged me, but your grandfather did. He gave me a penny once to spend on sweets and I'll love him forever for that. I'm sure that he was not indulging himself in giving it to me.'

'Poor Francie,' Rory said quietly.

Francine's head went up. 'No, don't say that. I've been very fortunate that I've met so many wonderful people. Very fortunate indeed, and it's time I stopped feeling any self-pity for myself.' She gave a wan smile. 'It was one of my resolutions after I knew about the spinners of silk. Mrs Binks did me a good turn.'

Unconsciously Francine had been leading the way to her dell. She said, brighter now, 'The last time we were here I was in despair because Kathleen was marrying my father. Tell me honestly, is theirs a happy marriage? Kathleen always seems happy.'

'Yes, it is. Your father has definitely changed. Not that he acts exactly like the Archangel Gabriel, but he can, believe it or not, be pleasant to *me* at times. And I have seen the two of them laughing together.'

'My father laughing? Well, now I've heard everything.'

They were close enough now to hear the cascading of the waterfall and when they walked through the short avenue of trees Rory cupped Francine's elbow, warning her to be careful and not to trip over the exposed roots. At his touch she felt a tremor go through her and felt ashamed at her thoughts. Once they were in the clearing she drew away from Rory.

They sat on a rock and were silent for quite a time. Francine broke the silence by asking Rory what he was thinking about and when he answered softly, 'You,' she regretted having asked. To detract his attention from herself she pointed out a small plant growing from a crevice in the rocks.

'How does it manage to exist? It's being drenched all day long by the waterfall.'

'Because it's a survivor, like you. You have all sorts of set-backs, but you recover and set out to reach your goal. I have never encouraged you in your photography, firstly because I'm against women taking up a profession, but also because I never thought you would get anywhere with it. Now I'm sure you will. You have talent, Francine.'

She bobbed a curtsey. 'Thank you for those kind words, sir.'

'I mean it, Francie. You not only have a grasp of the

300

technique, but you've learned about people. You've learned about their little quirks, their good points and their failings. You're learning too from nature. I think you should concentrate on taking photographs of children.'

'Why only children?'

'Because you understand them, because you are finding so much beauty in nature. Children are not yet in a mould, they have no secrets to hide, they are vulnerable, innocent. Oh, if only we could see that innocence in an adult.'

Francine looked at him in surprise. 'And where has all your knowledge come from? Not from my father?'

'Yes indeed from your father – where else? You've never seen that side of him, which is a pity. He's a tormented man because he knows his own failings, but if you could hear him talking about life, about people and yes, about the beauty of nature, you would realise why he won awards for his work.'

'Then why oh why, should he have treated me in such a way when I -'

'Because he loves you. Yes, Francie, he does, but he can't admit it, he has that quirk in his nature and he hates himself for it. He may never show you any affection but you can be assured it's there.'

She shook her head. 'No, I can't accept that.'

'Just accept it and you may at some future time understand his nature and forgive him for what he did.'

'Never. No, never.'

Rory's eyebrows went up. 'So, in spite of all your big talk you haven't learned a thing from your Mrs Binks and her "spinners of silk".'

Francine was silent. How long did it take to learn lessons? A year, five, ten, twenty?

Rory said, as though reading her thoughts, 'Some people are never big enough to learn lessons, they only talk big.'

'Like you,' she retorted. 'You haven't learned much from your grandmother's wonderful philosophies, have you? You fly off the handle, you sulk when you can't have your own way, you –'

'Who is sulking? And anyway, if I was perfect I'd be impossible to live with.'

'Perfect, you?'

He got up. 'Oh, stop nagging, come on, let's walk. This place gives me the creeps.'

She looked around her then stared at him. 'The creeps? It's a beautiful place, secret –'

'That's the fault of it. It makes *you* moody.'

'Who is moody? I'm not. You are always the one to start a quarrel.' Francine got up and brushing past him made for the path between the trees. 'You can be really nasty when you like.'

He followed her. 'Just calm down, will you. There's evil here. Find somewhere else to come and meditate.'

She stopped and turned to face him 'Evil, here? No, Rory. If there is any evil, then it's in me. It's in my thoughts of my father, hating him, being unable to forgive him. I can't.'

She suddenly burst into tears then she was in Rory's arms and he was saying softly, 'Don't, Francie, don't cry. I'm sorry for the way I behaved.' He smoothed back her hair. 'I didn't mean it when I said you were nagging. I'm wanting to hit out at you for having married Tyson de Auberleigh. He's wrong for you. I know it because I love you so much.' When she made to pull away he held her tightly. 'It's all right, I won't say any more, just let me hold you for a few minutes.'

Francine knew a sudden longing to respond, but she resisted, whispering, 'It's wrong.'

'Is it?' Rory took her chin between thumb and forefinger and tilted her face to his. 'I need to be loved and so do you.' His face came closer then his mouth covered hers, his lips gentle at first but then they moved sensuously, which set her blood on fire. She responded and for seconds there was a wildness between them. Then, into the silence

302

came the sweet, clear notes of a blackbird. The sheer purity of the song made Francine realise the enormity of her intentions. She drew away.

'No, Rory,' her voice trembled. 'We would hate ourselves afterwards. I'm married to Tyson and I love him.'

'You don't, you can't!' Francine knew a weariness then, but when he went on, 'He's not your type, I've told you before,' she was suddenly angry.

'Why do you keep telling me that Tyson is not my type? He is and I love him, he's a wonderful lover, I enjoy his love-making. I don't want him to go to war. I shall miss him, do you understand?'

Rory stood staring at her and his eyes held a sorrow. 'Yes, I understand. I'm sorry I tried to take advantage of you. I won't ever again. Shall we go?'

The bird had stopped singing; the sky had become overcast, they walked in silence. Francine's thoughts were in a turmoil. She had responded to Rory's passion. She was at fault for having given him the wrong impression. On the other hand Rory knew she was a married woman and had no right to tempt her.

She found herself thinking of the night that Tyson had raped her and was surprised to find it set her pulses racing. He had been so brutal that it was only now that some of her bruises had faded altogether. Was it an inborn primitiveness that had stirred her emotions? And yet it was tenderness, a loving tenderness she longed for. She needed to be gently caressed, coaxed into love then brought to an ecstasy . . . an ecstasy that Tyson had found it impossible to sustain for her.

She tried to dismiss such thoughts, but Rory's nearness, his obvious unhappiness made her want to put her arms around him and tell him it was all right, she bore him no malice. And yet, if she did he might take it as surrender.

On the other hand they had Kathleen to consider. She stopped. 'Look, Rory, we must be sensible about what has

303

happened. The three of us have a few days to spend together. If both of us go about with long faces Kathleen's going to ask what's wrong, and we certainly don't want her to know what happened between us.'

'Heaven forbid! My life wouldn't be worth living.' A trace of a smile touched Rory's lips. 'She'd have me paying penance for years. I'm sorry, Francine, I really am. I had no right to do what I did. Am I forgiven?'

'I'll forgive you if you'll forgive me. Yes, I was just as bad for letting my feelings run away with me. But from now on -' she held out a hand and Rory slapped it and said it was a deal. After that he linked arms with her and to all intents and purposes it was as if nothing had happened between them, but Francine was very much aware how strong her feelings were towards Rory. Did this happen to many women, women with arranged marriages who knew a yearning to be loved by someone other than their husbands? But if Tyson had behaved differently they could, perhaps, have had a good and loving marriage. Confused, Francine began to talk about the beautiful late autumn colours, all the lovely russet shades, and saying what a pity it was that a camera could not capture these.

To this Rory remarked that it would happen sometime in the future. During the rest of the way their talk was of photography.

During the next three days Francine, Kathleen and Rory did a lot of walking, talking and laughing, but every now and again Francine noticed that Rory would talk about Ireland with nostalgia, as though he would never see it again. He had come to England when he was two years old, but an aunt and uncle who had come across for his parents' funeral when he was nine years old, had taken him back with them.

'I was there a year,' he said, 'and I didn't realise until I came back to London what a wonderful experience it had been. The peace, the easy way people took life, no one ever hurried. If they told a story it could take over an hour in the telling, but you never thought of it as rambling on, there were so many characters in the story, so many incidents. And then of course there were the mountains, the sea, the lakes.' He had paused then and added in a low voice, 'I hope to live so I can die there.'

And Kathleen had given a shaky laugh and said, 'And isn't that a typical Irishism now?'

They were, overall, three very happy days. Kathleen talked to Francine alone one evening while Rory was out with Mr Binks (he had taken to both the Binks) and said how much she was looking forward to having the baby. She hoped it would be a boy for Edwin's sake. She was sure, she said, that it would make a big change in him.

After a pause she added, 'And I hope in his attitude towards you, Francine my love. He has asked about you once or twice, which gives me hope that he will finally accept you into his life. He should too, it's so wrong to have treated you the way he's done over the years.' Kathleen smiled suddenly. 'Have you accepted me as your stepmother?'

'No, I shall always think of you as my sister, Kathleen, and love you.' Francine changed the subject then, not wanting any more talk about her father.

Before they were due to go back to London Rory said, 'When we've all done our training for the army and have a sailing date for Africa we're going to have a party at home, so you must come for that, Francine. You will, won't you?'

She promised but thought it would be a sad time having to say goodbye to Rory and all his brothers. And then there would be the goodbye to Tyson. Until then the war had seemed so unreal, with Africa an unknown territory. But now, with the realisation that all the young men would be going out of her life and she would be living more or less in a woman's world, it hit Francine hard. She said, distressed, 'Let's hope the war will be over before you even have your training to do.'

'What!' Rory exclaimed, 'and would you have us miss the big adventure?'

Kathleen scolded him for calling war an adventure, but it fell on barren ground. It was change, excitement. Rory was waving and smiling when he and Kathleen left to return to London, and calling 'See you soon.'

A few days later Tyson arrived home, looking tanned and cheerful. The training had been quite an experience; he talked about it, but after a while Francine realised he was on edge. Did he think she might know he had been on leave for a day and gone to his parents' home? She decided to tell him she knew. He had a ready answer – it was to conduct some business, something to do with finance. By the time he had finished the business it was too late to come over to Holcombe Manor to see her.

She accepted this explanation and thought he seemed relieved. After that he seemed different, behaved quite tenderly towards her, but although he asked her how she had been while he was away, she hardly had a chance to tell him before he was back to his army experiences.

That night he came to their room and they made love, but there was no change in his technique. Francine was left, as usual, unsatisfied. He did, however, put an arm around her afterwards and talked softly of their coming separation. He had been selfish, he said, but thought he had learned a lesson.

'I think I was expecting too much out of life, Francine, and marriage had not come into my mind. But we are married and I do love you in my own way, and I feel sure when this war is over we shall make a good go of it.'

He ran his fingers gently over her cheek. 'Perhaps we shall make a baby before I leave. Would you like that?'

'Yes, I would,' she whispered. 'I would like that very much.' She pressed her cheek against his fingers. 'I love you too.'

After a pause she went on, 'Tyson, would you make love to me as you would to a mistress?' She felt him tense.

'Are you implying that Octavia was my mistress, because if you are -'

'No, no, I didn't mean that at all. I mean, well, I'm sure you must have made love to other women. I just felt that making love to one's wife might be different from -'

'Other women pleasure *me*,' he said, a coldness in his voice. 'You don't even attempt it.'

'But I don't know how,' she exclaimed. 'I didn't know until I was married what really does happen.'

'Then now is the time to learn. Touch me.'

When she hesitated he became impatient. 'Oh, come, Francine, you surely must know what I mean.'

'Yes, I, it's just that -' She touched him. He was flaccid for a second and she felt revulsion. Then there was a rigidity that astonished her with the quickness of the response. But because she felt no emotion whatsoever at this action she instinctively moved her hand to his body, her fingers moving lightly over his skin. This brought him across her and it was the quickest act of fulfilment yet for Tyson. Francine felt insane frustration.

'You're learning, darling,' he said, his voice ragged. 'There's an art in making love, one you'll learn fully in time. And then it will be perfect.'

Yes, for you, she thought, but not for me. Tyson was one of the takers that Grandad O'Reilly had talked about.

Francine learned a lot more about the technique of making love during the following week, but she still had no pleasure out of it. Never once did she experience the feeling of ecstasy that she had once known, even though at that time she had not reached complete fulfilment. But because she sensed what a perfect mating could be, she simply kept on hoping that once she and Tyson might achieve it.

He spent most of his days riding and when she mentioned Mr Beckett's visits, he offered no more objections; in fact, he treated it in an indulgent way. It would keep her occupied while he was in Africa.

The following week Tyson had his calling up papers and he was so excited he went around letting everyone know. Even Lord Holcombe arrived home after a telephone call to Monte Carlo.

'My dear boy, I had to see you,' he said in answer to Tyson's protest that he need not have come home. 'Also, I wanted to see Francine – I have missed her.' He held Francine close. 'My dear, this is a worrying time for you. But I'm sure we shall have Tyson back safe and sound. In fact, I wouldn't be a bit surprised if the war won't be over by the time he gets out there.'

Tyson made it very plain, like Rory, that the war being over before they had taken part in the adventure, would be a disaster.

Tyson planned a visit to relatives and friends to say goodbye and Francine felt hurt that he did not ask her to go with him. Tyson explained it would not be a happy occasion, as people would be upset, weeping, but she still felt she had a right to go.

He said he would be back in three days, but returned on the day before he was due to sail, looking haggard. 'Too much drink,' he complained, 'too much celebrating. It was just as well you didn't come with me. You would have hated it. I must get packed and go back to London, we're sailing at half past nine in the morning.'

Francine said she would get ready and come with him but he told her no, he didn't want her to. 'Why?' she snapped. 'Is it because darling Octavia will be seeing you off at the docks?'

She expected a sharp retort but Tyson spoke quietly. 'No, Octavia will not be there, nor will I allow any of my family to be there. I've insisted on it. It might sound wonderful, the bands playing, people waving Union Jacks, but Francine, it's harrowing, women weeping, families not knowing if their men will return. I don't want you to suffer that. And it's the truth.'

She knew he was sincere and she put her arms around

him and wept. He held her close and talked soothingly to her.

'My father says that when I come back I'll have all the edges knocked off me, and will have learned some sense. I think he's right. I'll be a settled-down husband. I might even be a daddy.' He tilted her chin. 'When will you know?'

She told him two weeks and then with a tremulous smile added, 'I'll write and let you know.'

'You had better,' he said. 'Come along, darling, help me pack.'

An hour later he had gone and Lord Holcombe who had stood in the drive with Francine waving, took her by the hand.

'Let us go in, my dear, that wind is chilly. Pray heaven the sun will be shining warmly when you come out to welcome Tyson home.'

CHAPTER TWENTY-THREE

The following day, Francine had a letter from Kathleen to say that all the boys had their calling-up papers and were to report in three days' time. According to what they had been told, their training would only be two weeks. They thought they would like to have a party before they left for training, because they might have to sail almost right away at the end of it. Could Francine come for the party? They hoped so. She need not reply, just turn up.

When Francine told Lord Holcombe this he said of course she must go, he would send her in the car. She must go that very day and be with them as long as possible. She kissed him on the cheek, touched by his thought for her.

The car arriving was enough to bring half of the street out. The house too seemed to be swarming with people, who had come to wish the boys well. But everyone had time to greet Francine and make her welcome. Rory took her aside.

'I'm so glad you could come, Francie. It would have been awful to have sailed without saying goodbye.' His eyes were shining with excitement. 'It's been like a madhouse here since we had word, everyone we know has called. No work has been done. Oh, they're leaving now. I think Gran's looking for you.'

The old lady came bustling over. 'Francine, come and have a drink of tea and a piece of cake then we can hear your news. Your husband has sailed, I hear. It's a dreadful time, but to see the boys you would think they were sailing to heaven. Even Milo is caught up in the fever, and poor Mary expecting. But she understands, men are just like children she says. Kathleen is coming along later.'

They went into the kitchen and when the tea was poured Gran O'Reilly prompted Francine to tell her what was happening in her life. Old and young commiserated with one another about husbands, fathers and sons having to go to war. The old lady's manner was aggressive as she called all those in higher places names for making a war, but underneath the aggression was a woman who was full of heartache. Would any of her boys come back?

Mr O'Reilly had little to say but he looked at his grandsons, his rheumy old eyes full of love. 'They've got to come back,' he said, 'we can't do without any one of them.' Then, as though a little ashamed of being thought sentimental he said in a complaining voice, 'Who's going to do all the work, tell me that? The government don't care, don't give a tinker's cuss how folks will live.'

'We'll live,' declared his wife. 'We lived when they were little and at school, so I reckon we'll jog along.'

The girls had a say, they would make up the time, they would work all night if necessary. But to this their grandmother said, a sudden sadness in her voice, 'I doubt whether there'll be the work. It won't be dolls that's wanted, but bullets for guns.'

Rory said, in a cheerful tone, 'You might be surprised, Gran-fathers will be wanting to buy their little girls a doll before they leave.'

'Those that have the money,' Gran retorted drily, 'and there won't be many of them.'

Francine had become familiar with various names – Jan Smuts, Kruger, Kitchener, Buller, Baden-Powell, but now it was names of places they were discussing. There had been a lot of changes since the battle at Elendslaagte: yes, there had been defeats, but there had been victories, too. No one needed to worry, all the places would soon be in British hands.

Mary said to Francine later, 'You have a husband on his way to war, and soon Milo will be away and he might never see our baby.' Her voice broke. 'It's not fair, he

311

ought not to have volunteered. No, no,' she corrected herself, 'he had to, especially with all the boys going, it would have made him feel a coward.'

'He'll come back,' Francine said, speaking firmly. 'In fact I'm sure they all will. And who knows but they might arrive in Africa to find the war is over. We must pray for that.'

In the afternoon Rory said to Francine, 'I want some fresh air. Come with me. We'll take a tram to the terminus then walk along the country lanes. It's a bit nippy but it'll be invigorating.'

Francine hesitated, feeling she could be asking for trouble. Rory's dark eyes were full of love. 'All right,' she said, 'I'll get my coat.' She was moving away when he caught her hand.

'There'll be just the two of us, I don't want anyone else.' She nodded, her heartbeats quickening.

When Gran O'Reilly was told about the outing she said, 'It'll do you both good. Are you well wrapped up? There's a touch of frost in the air. Francine, take this scarf.' She reached for one hanging on a peg and wrapped it around Francine's throat. 'There, that's better, now off you go.'

Outside Francine had a sudden feeling of exhilaration, of playing truant from school, which she and Sophie had done several times and had been severely punished for each time. The clattering sound of a tram approaching had Rory seize her hand and start running.

They clambered aboard and laughing, went upstairs. The wind was strong on the open deck but Francine lifted her face to it. 'This feels good.' She turned to Rory. 'Are *you* well wrapped up?'

'I'm wrapped up in you,' he said softly, moving closer to her.

'Now Rory O'Reilly, you behave yourself, do you hear?'

He grinned. 'You sound just like Gran.' There were only three other people on the top deck, a middle-aged couple and a boy on his own. Rory unfolded the rain apron from the seat in front and drew it over them, then under its cover he took hold of Francine's hand. When she made to draw it away his grip tightened.

'Let me have this small pleasure, I'll not be here after tomorrow.' She told him in a low voice it was blackmail, but she did not attempt to withdraw her hand again.

He began to talk of the times they had cycled out into the country and the races they had had and knowing he was trying to draw her into the nostalgia of these times she answered lightly 'Yes, and twice you nearly had me off my cycle, crowding me.'

'But you didn't come off, did you, clever clogs,' he was smiling.

By the time they reached the terminus there was only one other passenger to get off, a woman, who took a path to a farmhouse. Rory and Francine set off along the country lane, with Francine pointing out various species of plant life. She stopped, indicating a cluster of ferns. 'Aren't they beautiful?'

'And so are you,' he said softly. 'The Lord made a wonderful job when He fashioned you. If you could see your face, your rapt expression. Your changing expressions have always intrigued me. You can look so appealing one moment and the next so indignant.'

Francine released the fern. 'I'm no different from anyone else. Every person's expression changes with his or her mood.'

'Oh, but you *are* different, very different. There's just no one quite like you, as far as I am concerned.'

Francine walked on, trying to think of something to say that would stop Rory making such remarks, yet knew at the same time she wanted his admiration and felt ashamed. She said, holding out her hand palm upwards, 'I'm sure I felt a spot of rain.'

'If it rains,' he said, suddenly cheerful, 'I know just the place where we can shelter.'

313

'No, we'll get the next tram back. Perhaps we'd better go right away.'

'Don't be daft, we've only just arrived and I can't feel any rain. We came for a walk and a walk we're going to have. I'll show you where the boys and I used to play when we were kids. We used to come in the summer and visit our godmother and her family. She's dead now. See those cottages across the fields, they're derelict, but they were pretty at the time, every one with roses round the doors and clematis and jasmine on the walls. And all the gardens used to be full of colour. We'll walk that way. There's a stile further along.'

Rory climbed the stile first then reached out a hand to Francine. She stood on the top step ready to take the few steps down on the other side when she felt Rory's hands on her waist and he was lifting her down. Her heart fluttered then began a mad racing when he held her to him for a moment before releasing her.

'You're as light as a feather, with a waist my two hands could span.' He gave her a wicked grin. 'And without the artifice of whalebone and lacing up.'

'Rory!' Her face flamed with embarrassment. 'That's a dreadful thing to say. A man does not mention such things.'

'Sorry, but let me say this, when you live in a house with three sisters and a gran you can't help knowing what they wear, even though pieces of muslin cover corsets when they're hung on the line to dry, which I think is stupid.'

'It isn't stupid, it's, it's, well, I don't know how to describe it, but – '

Rory flung out his hands. 'You, of all people, amaze me. You want to be an enlightened woman and work for a living and yet you have this foolish mock modesty about corsets.'

'It's not mock modesty, it's just a question of decency.'

'All right, we shall be very decent and hide corsets under

the carpet.' There was laughter in his voice and she wanted to be annoyed with him and couldn't. A smile trembled on her lips at the thought of corsets being hidden under the carpet.

She hated the wretched things and wore them only for social occasions, which annoyed Bridget, but this was one thing that Francine stood out against, especially now she was a married woman and Bridget a friend, not a nurse looking after her.

Francine concentrated on the activity going on in the various fields. In one men were harrowing wheat; in another a woman and three children were loading mangolds on to a cart; further on a youth was driving a cartload of turnips. To the right of him the roof of a barn was being thatched. There was an elderly man dyking and another lopping branches off a hedge beside a fast-running brook.

Francine said, the corsets forgotten, 'There must always be jobs to do in the country. I know that Mrs Binks is forever busy.'

'All but the wealthy are busy,' Rory replied wryly. 'When I was a kid I used to think it would be wonderful to work on a farm. Now I can't imagine myself doing anything other than photography. This way.' He cupped a hand under her elbow and Francine responded immediately to his touch. They had been walking round the edge of a field. Now he stopped and opened a gate and, laughing, said, 'This way to the secret cave.'

She looked up at him. 'Cave? But there are no rocks.'

'It's an earth cave. It seemed very big to me when I was young, but it's quite small really.' They went through a spinney and its dimness gave a feeling of intimacy to Francine. Did Rory have any ulterior motive for wanting her to see this cave? Her mouth went suddenly dry. If he had, would she refuse him? Common-sense took over. Of course she would. She must be mad to think otherwise.

They came to the derelict cottages. Window-frames had

fallen in, giving them an eyeless look, and the most of the roofs were open to the elements. Francine gave a little shiver. Then Rory was saying, 'Nothing is ever quite dead, is it? Look at that clump of chrysanthemums.'

They were bronze and had been hidden from her momentarily by a pile of stones. She stopped to look at them. They were a thing of beauty in a garden of decay. 'This would make a wonderful photograph,' she said. To which Rory replied, a twinkle in his eyes, that it would indeed. She had the feeling for the camera all right.

After that she felt brighter. Where was this wondrous cave, she wanted to know.

Rory pointed ahead. 'See that hill at the end of the field? It's in there.' The wind suddenly began to gust bringing a fine rain, needle sharp on the cheeks. He began to hurry her. 'We'll be there in a few minutes. This will just be a shower. I'm a born weather prophet.' Francine told him wryly she hoped he was right, otherwise they would be in for a drenching in the open country. They ran the last hundred yards.

Francine could see no sign of a cave until Rory began to pull away branches and then with a flourish, he ushered her towards it, chanting, 'For all ye who enter here happiness will be yours.'

When Francine protested that it was dark Rory said he would soon alter that when the lamp was lit. She glanced at him with suspicion. 'A lamp? All very homely, isn't it? How many girls have you brought here?'

'None, you are my first guest.' He struck a match and the next moment the wick in the lamp was giving a feeble glow. 'I think it must be a meeting place for courting couples, or perhaps just one couple. I haven't been here for a while. Sit down,' he indicated a large flat-topped stone.

'All the comforts of home,' she quipped, 'and do I get a cup of tea too?'

'You will when I get a fire going.'

316

She laughed a little shakily. 'I don't believe you don't bring girls here.'

'Cross my heart and hope to die. I brought a pan and mugs yesterday, hoping I would get you to come with me. There's a spring a few yards away.' Francine made fists of her hands.

'Rory, I'm not staying, I know why you planned all this.'

'No, you don't,' he said quietly. 'All I want is for us to be completely alone, isolated, so that you can belong to me, not physically, just in mind. It came to me yesterday, then I planned it.' He paused then he turned up the lamp and going to a corner of the cave, lit twigs set between stones. They ignited at once. Rory turned to her. 'The memory will be something I can carry with me when I'm away. I joke about war being an adventure, yes, crossing the ocean will be, but I've talked to men who've been to Africa, who know the Boers, know the terrain and I know it's not going to be easy. After the war your husband will be with you for the rest of your lives. I sense this. All I ask is one half hour to be alone with you.'

Francine held out her hands with a helpless gesture. 'What can I say? I feel it's dangerous, you in this mood and I – '

'And you in what, Francine?' he said softly.

She had been going to say – and she needing to be loved. She said, 'No, I don't want to say any more. I'll enjoy this quiet interlude with you, but only for half an hour. Can I get the water?'

'No, I will. You put some of that wood on to the fire. I won't be long.'

The small logs were bone-dry and the spirals of smoke rising as they caught were tongues of flame by the time Rory came back with the water.

'Now isn't that a cosy sight,' he declared. 'I could live here.'

'Not with me, you wouldn't,' Francine replied.

'Who asked you?' Rory's smile was teasing. 'We'll soon have some tea brewed.' He chuckled. 'I wonder what Gran would say if she could see us? She would probably be pleased. I think she always had a feeling that you and I might get together.'

'Rory stop it, or I'm leaving. I really have no right to be here with you. I dread to think what Tyson would have to say if he could see us.'

'What the eye doesn't see,' he quoted, seeming determined to remain cheerful, which Francine thought was just as well and yet, deep down she wanted him to be serious. Wanted ... ? Well, what did she want? To be made love to, by Rory, that's what. Not that she would allow it, but it was right that she should admit it to herself. In that way she would not be taken unawares if Rory made an advance towards her. She concocted all sorts of arguments, and prepared a speech to say if he as much as touched her.

But when Rory did touch her, all her resolution faded into the background. They had drunk their mugs of tea, with the flames from the wood fire making all kinds of shapes on the walls of the cave, and Francine understood exactly what Rory had meant. It was an incident that would stay in her memory always, something for Rory to think over when he was all those thousands of miles away from home. There was a closeness between them now that she had never really and truly known with Tyson. At that monment she wanted nothing more than to sit in silence. But then Rory took the empty mug from her saying he would rinse it with his at the spring, and a finger touch on her skin sent shivers of sensuality through her body.

She looked up at him and he was still watching her. The gaze of each was steady then, without a word being spoken he laid the mugs down and knelt beside her. He touched her cheek, ran a finger-tip lightly around her mouth, then laid his lips gently to hers. She sat passive, although every nerve in her body was responding.

Rory undid the buttons on her coat, then the two top buttons of her dress and paused. 'I love you,' he whispered.

She wanted to say it was wrong, but found herself saying instead, 'I love you, Rory.' He went on unbuttoning the front of her dress and remembering how Tyson stressed that women should pleasure their men she undid Rory's shirt and slid her hand inside. He tensed and his breathing was ragged as he said, 'There must be no regrets, Francine.'

'No regrets,' she whispered, and after that there was a feverishness between them to divest themselves of all clothing. With body against body Francine felt tingling shocks running through her; she expected Rory to take her as quickly as Tyson always did, but Rory explored every part of her body, kissing, caressing, murmuring words of love. She touched him and he gave a moan of pleasure.

With both it was a questing of knowledge, both wanting to pleasure the other. When at last Rory entered her Francine raised her back moving with him, as Tyson had taught her. By then her body was one big throb and when Rory held back, wanting her to know fulfilment too, she was the impatient one. The ecstasy that had started up when he entered her was building up into a beautiful tormenting agony, and then sunbursts were exploding and she cried out with the joy of it. Rory buried his face against her neck.

'Francine, Francine, my darling.' He lay spent, the crescendo of throbs gradually easing. 'I tasted heaven. Could a man ask for more?'

Francine, knowing that she could not ask for anything more perfect, made to move, wanting to keep the memory of this wonderful experience for ever, but Rory held her tight. 'No, Francine, not yet, I want you again, at this moment,' His arms tightened and he moved his lips over her throat, her eyelids, then his mouth covered hers. At first she was unable to respond but a small tingling began which within seconds had love-nerves twitching. 'Oh, Rory,' she breathed, 'we shouldn't.'

He gave a chuckle that held a tremor. 'Shouldn't? With you the complete temptress? Oh, God, Francine, how can I leave you. We'll run away, hide.' His hands were at her thighs and moving and she dug her nails into his back.

Their love-making was even more fierce this time and the reward so deeply intense it had both of them crying out. Francine was as crazy as Rory then with his talk of running away and hiding, and she was thinking up places they could run to when the aftermath of the act and commonsense took over.

Rory too, had come to his senses, and there was an anguish in his voice as he said, 'Why, oh why did you have to marry Tyson de Auberleigh? If only you could have waited.'

The fire in the cave had died down and she shivered. Yes, she was married and had sinned: she deserved to be punished. She drew away from Rory's arm and got up quickly, and to his plea that there was no rush she reached for her clothes.

'There is a need to rush, Rory, to get away from this place. We've done wrong. I don't regret it, but I should!'

Rory groaned. 'We love one another. I want to come back from the war to your arms, Francie. It will be the only thing that will help me get through the fighting.'

Rory got up and began to dress, talking all the while. They could set up house miles away, they could go to Ireland, rent a cottage. They could get a living from the land.

Francine said no and she spoke firmly. She had obligations to fulfil. Tyson would expect to come home to her. There was Rory's family, whom she loved, Bridget, Sophie and Mrs Denton. Then after a pause she added, 'And then there is my photography.'

'Is your photography more important than I am?' he demanded.

'Let me say, equally important. No, Rory, I'm not willing to sacrifice so many things.'

'In other words you don't love me. Not in the way I love you.'

He was angry and she made no effort to try and soothe him. 'I want to leave, Your grandmother will be wondering where we are and would be horrifed if she knew what we had been doing.'

'Yes, we'll leave,'

There was desolation in Rory's eyes then that made Francine say softly, 'Don't be cross with me, Rory. It was a wonderful experience and nothing and no one can take that away. I'm sorry I'm the way I am, but perhaps it takes a greater love than mine to make sacrifices.'

He came to her then and took her hands in his. 'No, Francine, I don't want you to make sacrifices. I was selfish.' He gave her a wry smile. 'You know me, the big sulker when I can't get my own way.' He touched her cheek. 'I'll have this lovely memory for the rest of my life.'

'So will I, Rory,' she said in a low voice and he took her in his arms and held her tight for a few moments before releasing her.

'Well, there we are then, I'll hide the pan and the mugs. Perhaps someday, who knows ... ' He brightened. 'Don't forget we have the party this very evening.'

'This evening?' She eyed him in dismay. 'I thought you had one more day at home.'

'No, we're leaving in the morning. Cheer up now, we don't want to go home with long faces, we must keep up Gran and Grandad's spirits. And poor Mary's, too.'

Francine felt suddenly guilt-ridden. Here were two elderly people about to part with all their grandsons and Mary her husband and all she could think about was her love-making with Rory.

She talked a lot when they did get back, about the countryside, the weather and she noticed that Rory did too. Then Francine apologised, saying she really should have stayed in to help with the preparations for the party that evening, she had thought it was the following evening.

'Nonsense,' said the old lady. 'The walk has brought colour to your cheeks, you were looking a bit peaky. And anyway, the preparation is done. People will be dropping in for a bite to eat and drink, but they'll all bring a mite of something.'

People started 'dropping in ' about six o'clock and by eight o'clock one guest who had just arrived said the noise could be heard five streets away. Francine could believe it. It was impossible to hear what anyone said until he or she spoke close to her ear. It was not only the talk and the laughter, but one man played a concertina and many of the people there joined in with the singing.

Nearly everyone brought something to eat, plus a bottle of home-made wine or ale. By nine o'clock Francine was feeling heady and very loving towards Rory who never strayed far from her side. His touch had her longing for them to be alone. It was Kathleen who separated them, ordering Rory to go and have a talk with one of the aunts who was asking about him. To Francine she said, 'Are you all right, Francine? You look a little flushed. Would you like to go and have a lie-down?' This made Francine pull herself together.

'No, I'm all right. I had a little too much to drink. I won't have any more.' Kathleen, her expression full of understanding, patted her arm and told her she thought that wise.

It was nearly midnight before the last of the visitors left . . . most of them with a great deal of reluctance. Some of them had been prepared to stay until the next morning. It was Gran O'Reilly who sent them home, saying she was not going to have her lads looking bleary-eyed and half-witted when they arrived for their training.

Bridget, Francine and Kathleen were staying overnight, but when Bridget said they would get off to bed the old lady declared they would not be going to bed until they had all had their sing-song. It was something very special.

And it was. It was beautiful, with the boys and their sisters harmonising. The rest listened and there was not one dry eye.

They were all the lovely Irish songs. Francine remembered the first time Rory had sung a solo. Then his voice was sweet and pure. Now it was a man's voice, a rich tenor, and pulling at one's heart strings. He sang to Francine, his eyes full of love, and Francine knew if she lost control she would be sobbing. She felt no regret at having let Rory make love to her. He would always be her true love, but she vowed then if both men were spared she would stay with Tyson, for he was her husband.

The boys were leaving for their training camp at six o'clock the following morning and they insisted there would be no one getting up to see them off. When Rory kissed Francine goodbye he whispered, 'Don't forget our secret cave.'

'I won't,' she whispered back, and the grip of his hands on her arms was exquisitely masterful.

She lay awake for a long time thinking she must see Rory once more before he left, but when she did awake the boys had gone.

And now another phase in her life was beginning, one that would perhaps turn out to be the most painful.

CHAPTER TWENTY-FOUR

Francine went back to Holcombe Manor after Rory and his brothers left, wanting to be alone to think about the wonderful interlude in the cave. She lived in a semi-dream world, in which only she and Rory existed, then reality set in when she realised she was pregnant. From then on she suffered a turmoil of emotions. Whose baby would it be – Tyson's or Rory's? Would she ever know, for both men were dark-haired and dark-eyed. Who did she *want* to be the father? Sometimes she would think it right if Tyson were the father, other times she wanted it to be Rory's baby, a baby born out of true love.

There had been no other girl in Rory's life, at least none that she knew of, but with Tyson there had been not only Octavia, but those he had taken to his bed to satisfy his needs. She longed to hear from Rory but when she did it was secondhand. Kathleen dropped a line to say a letter had arrived from the boys: the training was hard, but they were enjoying the life. There was a chance they would be home for a couple of days before sailing; if so, the whole family was going to see them off – Francine must come, too . . .

The dockside was crowded with relatives gathered to see their loved ones away. There was a sea of small Union Jacks being waved, intermingling with bobbing, coloured balloons. There were also placards held up with messages written on them so that Francine began to wonder if any individual on the quayside could be seen by the men on the ship. There seemed to be thousands of khaki-clad figures on deck, all of them waving and shouting.

Red-coated bandsmen struck up with the tune *Goodbye Dolly Gray*, and the crowd and the men began to sing, but many of them, Francine felt sure would like herself be too choked to utter a word.

> Goodbye Dolly I must leave you,
> Though it breaks my heart to go,
> Something tells me I am needed,
> At the front to fight the foe.
> See, the soldier boys are marching,
> And I can no longer stay,
> Hark! I hear the bugle calling,
> Goodbye Dolly Gray.

When the song ended there was wild cheering and by the time it had died away the band was playing another favourite music hall song, *Jolly Good Luck to the Girl Who Loves a Soldier*.

There was a constant shifting of the people in front of her, but despite the movement Francine was unable to spot Rory or his brothers. Then suddenly the whole family was yelling, 'There's Milo ... Declan ... Michael ... Rory.'

'Where?' Francine asked, and they were pointed out to her standing next to a very tall man. When she saw Rory her heart contracted. The boys were frantically waving at everyone on the quay and laughing.

Then Rory stopped waving and appeared to be searching and Francine unpinned her hat and began waving it; immediately he raised his hand as though acknowledging it, and she felt choked, sure it was a special greeting for her alone. Then she felt an unbearable ache that she was unable to tell Rory that she might be carrying his baby. Nor could she tell him in a letter, knowing that other eyes might see it.

Francine became aware of all the other activity, the loading, the neighing of horses as some were hoisted by crane and others herded into the holds from the quayside.

Massive crates were being manhandled aboard, food, ammunition, guns ...

A man behind them said, 'Nobody realises the tons of stuff that have to be carried – cattle goes with them, tents, *baths* for the bloody colonels and what have you. Yes, baths! A disgrace when the men can stink with muck for all they care.'

The brass band was now playing *Ta-Ra-Ra-Boom-De-Ay!* and the people joined in.

Rory was lost from view for a while as someone else took his place, but then he was back again and just stood there, waving every now and again. Gran O'Reilly said, 'I don't want them to leave but I wish they would. It must be terrible standing there, when they can't reach us. Oh, my lovely lads.' Her voice broke.

The old man put an arm around her. 'Now then, Mother, you can't let the boys see you weeping.'

It must have been an hour later when there was a change in the atmosphere. 'They're leaving,' someone shouted. The derricks were still; gangplanks were being drawn up; bells were clanging; orders were being shouted. There was a sudden stillness in the crowd and in the men on the ship. A deep-throated sound came from the funnels. Then came the tugs like so many fussy beetles as they manoeuvred into position.

When the moment of departure came at last and the ship began to move the band began to play the National Anthem.

'God Save Our Gracious Queen,' sang the people and as voices quavered Francine felt a terrible coldness go up and down her spine and her throat ached as she made an effort to sing the words. How many of the men aboard the ship would return?

When the anthem ended cheers went up, Union Jacks were being frantically waved and released balloons went drifting away, the only brightness in a grey afternoon.

The soldiers had taken off their sun helmets and were

326

waving them. Only a few shouted to people on the dockside.

There was a mournful hooting of tugs as they pulled their 'charge' up the river. No one moved and it was not until the ship was out of sight that the crowd began to disperse and men were weeping as unashamedly as the women.

During the next two weeks, Francine relived the scene at the dockside many times, seeing Rory full of high spirits at first, laughing, shouting, then when the ship was leaving his sombre expression making her regret not having gone to London sooner, to have another talk with him. She had behaved stupidly. Or had she? What purpose would it have served? If she had told him she was pregnant he would have gone away with a load of worry on his mind, wondering if the baby was his.

She had not told anyone yet about being pregnant and knew when she did it would be Kathleen she told first, not that she would bring Rory into the picture. Sophie had been for a visit but she was unhappy, her young man having volunteered to go to South Africa.

'When he does come home,' she said, 'Randolph and I are going to be married. We wanted to before he went away but the parents wouldn't allow it, Papa saying I could be left a widow.' She burst into tears. 'I'm just so unhappy, Francine. I love him, I really do, I hadn't realised until now what real love meant. I dream about Randolph all the time. He doesn't want anyone else, not like my cousin Tyson who married you but who goes on mooning for Octavia.' In the next breath Sophie wailed, 'Oh, forget what I said, I'm being utterly stupid. Of course Tyson doesn't love Octavia, he was just besotted with her.'

From then on Francine's life revolved between news of the war, lessons in photography, visiting Mrs Binks, the Dentons, Bridget and the O'Reillys and having return visits. Lord Holcombe went off again to France, knowing that Francine was never without company. She thought he did not look too well but when she asked about his health he smiled and said it was only the gambling fever that was troubling him.

The newspapers at first were full of good news of the war, of British victories, but then word seeped through from other sources that there had been defeats with a heavy loss of life, and this had Francine in despair at times. How was Tyson faring? And Rory?

Many times she daydreamed about the interlude in the cave and she would run her hand gently over her stomach and wonder if it would be a boy or a girl. There had been no morning sickness and she prayed there would not be any because then other people would know she was pregnant and she felt she wanted to keep it to herself.

But one evening when she and Kathleen were alone and both had been busy with their own thoughts, Kathleen said suddenly, 'When are you expecting the little one, Francine?' Her voice was soft.

Francine looked up, startled. 'You knew?'

Kathleen smiled. 'I guessed by the way you keep touching your stomach. Also, I've seen Gran watching you. I think perhaps she has guessed. She'll be delighted. I know I am.'

Francine blurted out, 'Would you still be pleased if you knew it could be Rory's baby?'

There was a silence, then Kathleen said gently, 'Don't feel sorrow, Francine dear. Sometimes these things are inevitable. I think I've known that Rory has been in love with you from the first time you met. And I feel sure that you love him. But, if you are to save your marriage, and you must, for the sake of the baby, then he must never know.'

Francine knew it was sensible advice, but she wept slow, painful tears that brought an ache of guilt. 'We were so foolish. I only hope that the baby will not be punished in any way because of our sin.'

'Francine, you mustn't even think such a thing. I take

it that it *could* be Tyson's child?' When Francine nodded she went on, 'You must think positively; if you don't, you'll be carrying a burden of guilt for the rest of your life. I doubt whether you will ever know the truth, for both Tyson and Rory are dark-haired and dark-eyed, and there's nothing really to distinguish between them. They are both attractive men. Also, the baby could take after you and have chestnut hair.'

'Or be like my mother, fair,' Francine said a little tentatively. 'I'm glad I told you, Kathleen, and I don't think I need to tell you that it must remain a secret between us.'

Kathleen patted her hand. 'No need at all. Now let's have a cup of tea and we can talk babies, which is very close to both our hearts.' They covered a lot of ground and Kathleen persuaded Francine to let her grandparents and her sisters know. They would be so delighted.

After hesitating a moment Francine said, 'Kathleen, why did you marry Papa?'

'I think because he needed me, and because I have always loved him. I know he's fond of me and has come to depend on me quite a lot.'

'Why is he so bitter about me? Will he feel any differently towards me if I have a son? Somehow I don't think he will. How long can he go on hating me? And why, why? I haven't done him any harm.'

'But you are Gabrielle's daughter as well as his — it's a sad fact, and I don't know how long he can keep up this dislike of you. Some bitterness in families is carried on for generations. It's dreadful, but there it is. We can only pray that when the babies are born it will touch a softer core in your father. He can be tender, that might surprise you. It's this that gives me hope for the future.'

The talk with Kathleen had given Francine a different outlook on her pregnancy and she shared the joy of the O'Reillys when they knew. The old man had tears in his eyes when he hugged her. 'Our little Mavourneen with a wee one of her own. The Lord is good.'

Gran O'Reilly was the more practical one, offering advice on the way Francine should behave. She must have good food and plenty of good clean air when she had the chance. And she was to take things easy. She was in a position to do so. She busied herself, talking as she worked. 'Just wait until our Rory knows! He always had a soft spot for you, loves you like a sister he does.'

The way the old lady stressed the word 'sister' made Francine feel sure she knew about Rory and herself.

The first direct news Francine had of the war came in a letter from Tyson. It was short. He had enjoyed the voyage even though things were a bit rough at times. They had not yet been into battle but were expecting to any day. There had been heavy rain and they were glad to get under canvas at night. Everything was damp, of course. It was an astonishing undertaking, involving so much. Lord knew how they would get on in battle, oxen having to pull cannons in thick mud. The foot soldiers would be up to their mid-calf in it. He concluded, *'Must stop there, take care of yourself, Francine, your loving husband, Tyson.'*

There were no kisses. Francine read it over several times, but could glean no more from the contents. That evening she sat down to pen a letter and told him about the baby. *'I'm sure you'll be pleased,'* she wrote, *'it really is quite exciting. I'm keeping well.'*

She told him about going with the O'Reillys to see their grandsons off at the docks and said he was right, it *was* a very emotional time, but she did think it would be an interesting thing to tell their children in the future. Francine followed this with any other little item she felt would be interesting to him and concluded her letter by telling him he must take every care, she was longing for the war to be over so that they could be together again. She signed it, *with my love, Tyson, Francine*, and put two small kisses at the end.

The following morning she wrote to Rory. She talked about the family and her lessons in photography: Mr

Beckett, who was not overwhelming in his praises, had told her how some outdoor photographs she had taken were quite professional. This, of course, had pleased her very much.

Then she told him about the baby, saying that Tyson had known about it before he went away and was very pleased, but sad that he might be in Africa when it was born and—

Francine stopped there and tore that letter up and started again. And this time she made no mention of the baby. His grandmother or Kathleen would tell him and Rory would have to reach his own conclusions. It was wrong to lie to him, to let him think they had made love while she was carrying her husband's child. Francine gave the letter to the postman the next morning then she took a train to London and a tram to the place where she and Rory had visited the cave. The wind was sharp and she pulled up the collar of her coat. Perhaps it was wrong to come and keep a vigil with her lover, but she wanted to be close to him. It would be the last time she would come. The branches that Rory had put in front of the entrance looked as if they had remained undisturbed. Francine pulled them aside and went in.

There was a strange earthy warmth inside the cave and she sat on the slab of rock and stirred the ashes of the fire that Rory had made. Dead embers. That is what their love must be. But would their love ever be dead with this tiny living embryo inside her? If only she could have told Rory, been positive about it, how pleased he would have been. It would have been something to dream of in the alien South Africa, something to fight for. 'Oh, God, please send Rory and Tyson back to me,' she prayed. 'I know I don't deserve any happiness ever again for what I did but please spare them both.'

She stayed quite a long time reliving their time together in the cave and wondering if she would ever know such joy again. Eventually it was hearing voices that made her leave hastily and replace the branches. But the people she had heard were quite a distance away.

When Francine returned to Holcombe Manor she made up her mind to go to her dell. Rory had called the place evil but she was sure she would always see the beauty of it, feel the peace in it. But this time the peace was denied her, and all through seeing a hazel bush almost stripped of its leaves.

Every time she had seen the bush she had found beauty in its twisted branches. Today, bare, she found evil in the convoluted shapes: coiling snakes, witches' talons; she ran from the dell, stumbling over roots and stopping only when a stitch in her side made her gasp.

When the pain eased she walked on slowly and then felt she had been wrong to run from the dell. There was no evil in nature, it was her own guilt that had made it seem so. Tomorrow she would go again.

She did, but found no peace there. How could she achieve it? She had to, for the baby's sake. 'Think good thoughts,' Kathleen had said, 'then all the goodness will go into your baby.' Truth or an old wives' tale?

The day Francine received a letter from Rory she took it to the dell to read. It was a calm day with a shaft of sunlight shining on the hazel bush. The branches to Francine then were beautiful, the branches curling as though the smaller ones were exploring the rest of the branches, like children seeking knowledge. She sat on the fallen trunk of a tree and opened the letter.

'Francine dear,
This is the only letter I shall write, telling you of my love for you, then you must destroy it. I was so pleased to hear from Gran your news of the baby, and although I know I would have no claim to it I do hope the baby is ours. I dream of you so often, dream of the wonderful time we spent together. I am back with you in our cave. Do you ever go? I pray you have no regrets. I feel it would

be wrong. In the eyes of the law, in the eyes of people it would seem wrong, but somehow I know that God understands. Otherwise why did He plan it so that we should fall in love? There must be a purpose to it. Everything in life has a purpose. I had never realised that until we came out here. War does strange things to people. It straightens one out, possibly because we know we might never get back home. And Francine, I don't want you to grieve if I don't. I'm so grateful to you, my darling, for loving me that short time. No, it was not a short time, it was a whole lifetime. It sustains me. Possibly, if I do come back, I shall be the same cocky, selfish Rory, thinking only of what I want, teasing you, getting mad at you because you don't see things my way. Forgive me if I do.

We arrived to dust-storms but now we are in the rainy season. It's deluging rain, turning the ground to mud. But in places there is a lot of green, an incredible green in the valleys and hills. So much beauty. I long to have a camera.

The camp awakes at daybreak and mist surrounds the hills. At five o'clock, the horses are taken in the morning parade to water, a lovely sight with their muscles rippling. There are gentle meandering streams in some places, torrents in another. At times it's impossible to believe we are in the middle of a war. But we have been involved in the fighting. More of that in my next letter. This really is a love letter, my dearest Francine, the only one I must permit myself to write. But remember this, I will love you forever. God keep you safe. Think of me at times. In quiet moments, and they are not many, I feel so close to you I know I am in your thoughts. Write to me when you can, a few lines will be so welcome. All my love, Rory.'

There was a line of kisses underneath. Francine did not weep then, her tears came later when after reading the letter over and over again, she destroyed it. It had to be, but it was like tearing her heart out.

In the following weeks she followed all the war news,

read *The Times* and listened whenever war was being discussed. In the battle of Nicolsen's Nek over a thousand British were lost; there were more heavy losses at the battle of Modder River. Buller's forces were defeated at Colenso. Mafeking was beseiged . . .

Then came the unhappy news a week before Christmas that poor Mary had had a miscarriage. The O'Reillys and Francine were bereft. Christmas was something to be got over.

And the war news got no better. In January Ladysmith was under siege then Kimberley. This was followed by the battle of Spion Kop, with severe losses. Everyone was in despair. More and more women were wearing mourning and Francine lived in fear of hearing that Tyson and Rory had been wounded or killed.

Lord Holcombe, who had been abroad again came to see Francine and much to her surprise, Mrs de Auberleigh was with him. She said, 'Lord Holcombe suggested I came to see you, Francine. I've wanted to very much in the past, but Tyson said you would not welcome me.'

Francine stared at her mother-in-law in astonishment. 'Tyson said that? Surely you misunderstood him. I've been hurt that none of you have been in touch with me since we were married. I presumed that you were not willing to accept me into your home.'

'Oh dear.' Mrs de Auberleigh looked distressed. 'Indeed there *has* been a misunderstanding. I've longed to see you, Francine, especially since knowing about the baby. It will be our first grandchild, so wonderful and–' Her voice broke and Francine was full of concern.

'Please, Mrs de Auberleigh, don't get upset. You are here now and I'm delighted about that. Do sit down, I'll order some tea.' Francine rang the bell then turned to Lord Holcombe. 'It's lovely to see you home again, Andy.'

'It's good to be home, Francine dear.' He kissed her on both cheeks then hugged her briefly before drawing away. Francine noticed that he looked drawn.

After tea was brought in Mrs de Auberleigh talked about Tyson. He was not as good a correspondent as his brothers. Her three daughters were helping at a hospital for wounded officers – and how very few of the people knew just how many officers had been wounded and killed.

She then begged Francine to come and stay with them, if only for a few days, and she promised. While they were talking, it worried Francine that Lord Holcombe looked so poorly, but she made no mention of it until Mrs de Auberleigh left to return to London in a waiting limousine. When she had gone Francine turned to Lord Holcombe.

'And now, sir, I think you need some mothering. I also think you need to see a doctor.'

'A little mothering from you, Francine dear, would be welcome, but a doctor would be no help for what ails me.' His attempt at a smile was overshadowed by the bleakness in his eyes. After a pause he went on, 'I've lost the Manor to a fellow gambler, and this time there will be no chance of winning it back. My other debts are too heavy for that. It's you I worry about, Francine.' He broke down.

When Francine was over the first shock, she tried to console him. 'You have no need to worry about me, Andy. I can stay with Bridget or the O'Reillys – they would be pleased to have me. But what will you do?'

He dismissed this with a wave of the hand. 'I have plenty of friends who will accommodate me. It's the baby, your photography ... There are so many things. You enjoyed having the studio so much. The camera and all the other equipment is in your name, so no one can take that away from you. I have also created an annuity for you, my child, so you will have an income as long as you live.'

'Andy.' Tears filled Francine's eyes. 'You've always been so good to me. How can I thank you?'

'Having you here has been my thanks,' he said softly.

'I was so pleased to be able to offer you and Tyson a home. When he comes back perhaps you'll be able to set up house in the country again. He enjoys riding and shooting.'

Francine said yes, but wondered what sort of life they would have together. Tyson had lied about her not wanting to see any of his family, so what other untruths would he tell.

CHAPTER TWENTY-FIVE

When the O'Reillys and Bridget learned about Lord Holcombe losing the Manor they nearly fell out about who was to give Francine a home. Kathleen was the peace-maker, suggesting that Francine lived with Bridget but used the attic at the O'Reillys' for her studio. 'It's full of Grandad's rubbish,' she said, 'but we'll soon get it cleaned up and scrubbed out.'

Everyone was happy at this. Francine grieved at having to part from Lord Holcombe, but was relieved to know he had accepted the offer of friends in Surrey to stay with them for as long as he wished.

'So, Francine dear,' he said, 'we shall be able to meet when I come to town. Can't stay away from the big city too long.'

They had a tearful parting. Francine went to say goodbye to her favourite dell, and found it an emotional experience.

She talked to her baby in quiet moments, speaking about Tyson as its papa and how they would all be together when he came home from the war. It was impossible to put Rory out of her mind with the family talking constantly about the boys. What would they say when they knew Francine had a studio in their attic? The others were very proud of this fact – all the neighbours knew about it. When Francine was settled in she was going to take a photograph of them all to send to the boys. Even before Francine had the dark room set up Gran O'Reilly had settled in her mind how they would all be placed. 'Himself' would sit on the chair, she would stand beside him, her hand on his shoulder, and the girls would stand at either side. They would all wear their Sunday best.

But before this could take place, Francine had to spend a few days with Tyson's parents. Mrs de Auberleigh had all but demanded it, she had been most upset about Francine living with Bridget. No mention was made about the studio, Francine knowing it would have been looked on with strong disapproval.

Mrs de Auberleigh felt that Francine ought to live with them; after all she was Tyson's wife and expecting his baby. Francine explained as calmly as she could that Bridget had been a part of her life since she was eight years old. She *wanted* to live with her.

Mr de Auberleigh insisted they respected Francine's wishes. They wanted her to feel settled and happy for the baby's sake. To Francine's surprise Tyson's sisters were also on her side and Mrs de Auberleigh had to give in.

To be fair, all of them were kindness itself to her. The sisters, in fact, had never been kinder. All were greatly interested in the baby and Francine found out why on the second evening of her stay at the house. She was ready to get into bed when there was a gentle tap on her door. On opening it she found the three sisters there, all in dressing gowns. Verity, the eldest, asked in a whisper if they could come in. Francine said yes, of course, and the three girls crept in, all after a hasty glance over their shoulders. When Francine looked at them questioningly there were self-conscious giggles then Verity asked if Francine would tell them how the baby got into her stomach.

Francine was completely taken aback. She had thought that the girls with their busy social life would have known all about marriage and child-bearing. Should she explain? If she did she would have to extract a promise from them not to tell anyone where they had acquired their knowledge.

But even after the promise was given she found it difficult to start. In the end she began, 'You have brothers so you do know that boys differ bodily from girls.' They nodded, they had seen their brothers once in the bath

338

when they were all young. So, Francine took it from there and watched three pairs of eyes going rounder and rounder. Victoria, the youngest, was the first to speak. 'I can't believe it! It isn't nice, is it? Imagine a man putting—' She stopped and Francine explained quickly there was a certain amount of pleasure in it. At this their interest increased. In what way?

Francine found herself almost tied in knots, but the explanation brought gratitude from the girls, who had been dying to know. Francine warned them never, never to let any young man take advantage of them . . . and felt like an elderly aunt with the girls all being older than herself.

Marguerite said, 'We're so glad to have you for our sister-in-law, Francine. We've always been a little shy of you, you're so clever.'

When Francine protested that she was not in the least bit clever they insisted she was, and mentioned the evening on the Mannings' yacht when so many people had been impressed by her knowledge. She had spoken so sensibly and Marguerite said she thought it was on that particular evening that their papa had decided she would make a good wife for Tyson.

A good wife? Francine flushed. If only they knew.

They all looked up startled as Mrs de Auberleigh could be heard calling her daughters' names. The girls asked eagerly if they could come again for another talk and when Francine agreed each kissed her on the cheek then fled.

Francine sank on to a chair. Who would have thought she would have been asked for sexual instruction. She smiled as she thought what Sophie would have to say if she knew. But Sophie was away with her mother for a month visiting relatives. And anyway, it was not a subject she would want to discuss with anyone else.

When Mr Beckett learned of Lord Holcombe leaving the Manor, he assured Francine she was perfectly capable now of taking photographs on her own, but added she would need help with the camera and equipment if she wanted to do outdoor work. He suggested a man he knew who hired out his barrow and his services.

'He lives in the dock area. His name is Shaun McTinnock. His father used to be a photographer, but although Shaun did not follow in his father's footsteps he is knowledgeable on the subject. He's an eccentric, wears strange clothes sometimes, but he's clean, honest and hardworking. I'm sure you would get on with him, Francine. I'll give you his address.'

Francine thanked Mr Beckett for all his help and promised she would keep in touch.

Although she had been sure she would lack confidence without her tutor's presence, Francine was surprised at how much she had absorbed from his teachings and books, and there came a time when she told Mrs O'Reilly she would be ready to take the family group on the coming Saturday.

Francine was pleased with the studio. She had hired a man to paint a mural on one wall and at his suggestion had opted for a scene of a terrace in a garden, overlooking a lake.

The special chair had a rest on which the client could put his neck. Gran O'Reilly had declared that Himself would need a straitjacket to keep him still, but he was the one who sat motionless while the others fidgeted, smoothing hands over skirts, tidying hair, repinning a brooch or toying with a silver chain. Francine spoke to them firmly.

'Now listen and listen carefully. This photograph is to go to the boys at the front. We want it to be the very best we can do. So will you all stop moving about! I want to get you in focus.'

They fidgeted a bit more, cleared throats, then said they were ready. Therese giggled when Francine put the black cloth over her head and was sharply reprimanded by Gran.

Francine let them think it was to be a trial photograph, wanting them to be relaxed, but when she said, 'Well, that's it!' there were groans. They had not been smiling, they would be stiff.

Francine smiled. 'It looked good to me.'

And it was. As Kathleen said, 'Himself was sitting as upright and looking as important as the Lord Mayor, and Herself, well, didn't she look as elegant as a titled lady?'

The old man laughed. 'And the girls look like princesses. Never realised how beautiful they were.'

When they saw the finished photograph they were all over the moon. It was so good of them all! Old Mr O'Reilly told Francine that when she sent it to the boys she must enclose one of herself that Mr Beckett had taken, it was a lovely portrait.

Francine felt a pang, thinking of Rory seeing it but not being able to claim it for himself.

The following day she wrote to Shaun McTinnock explaining she needed transport to do some camera work at the docks, and mentioning that Mr Beckett had recommended him. By return came a letter written in a beautiful copperplate handwriting, saying he would arrive at ten o'clock the following morning, clear weather permitting. Gran O'Reilly, seeing the letter, declared he must be a gentleman for sure to be writing like that.

But when, the next morning, Francine saw Shaun McTinnock from the window waiting with his barrow at the kerb she drew a quick breath. She went to the front door. He was tall and beanpole thin and puffed on a short clay pipe. His ginger beard was long, he wore a hard-topped black hat with a big dent in it and his dark over-coat, tied at the waist with string, reached to his ankles.

On seeing her he raised his hat and greeted her cheerfully. 'The top of the morning to ye, ma'am. Would this be the contraption ye want taking to the docks?' He indicated the wooden box containing the camera and equipment at the foot of the steps.

'Yes, it is. Would you be very careful with it, Mr McTinnock please.'

'I will that, ma'am.' He lifted it effortlessly and placed it on the barrow.

Gran O'Reilly who had come up muttered, 'Glory be to God, did I say gentleman?' She called out, 'You take great care of Mrs de Auberleigh now.'

He waved his pipe at her. 'Indeed I will, ma'am.' Shaun was away with a loping stride and Francine, walking on the pavement, had a job to keep up with him.

The air was crisp with the sky a surprisingly clear blue for the January mornings which recently had been shrouded in mist.

There was a constant movement of people and the usual congestion on the roads, with drivers of carts and drays and barrow-boys yelling for others to make way. The dockside itself was even noisier; seamen competed with workmen shouting orders; the thump of timber being stacked vied with the clanking of anchor chains, and all this against the constant hooting of tugs and the deep-throated boom of steamers leaving and arriving.

Francine felt a rising excitement – what a wealth of scenes to photograph! A neighing horse close by brought her back to the present.

Shaun, who was waiting ahead called, 'Watch out, ma'am!' and Francine stepped quickly aside to avoid a dray drawn by two beautiful shire horses. Following the dray were two hefty men carrying a piece of long, squared timber on their shoulders. Several more drays passed stacked with crates and Francine was thinking she would like to photograph the animals when Shaun called again, wanting to know where to put the 'contraption'. She darted across.

She indicated a piece of ground out of the line of traffic and people then said, 'I would like to take a photograph of you first, Mr McTinnock.' They were beside a high

342

stack of large round baskets which looked like a tower and she asked if he would stand with his back to them.

He looked amused as he struck a pose which told Francine he was well used to having his photograph taken, but was serious when she took it. After Francine had chosen three more scenes to photograph and Shaun had set the camera at the correct angles, she eyed him with some curiosity. 'Mr Beckett told me your father was a photographer, Mr McTinnock.'

'He was that, and a good one, but although I learned from him I didn't follow in his footsteps. I wanted to travel the world and did so.' He moved the camera a fraction. 'There, and if you don't mind me telling you, ma'am, there's some fisher girls coming who'd make a good subject for you.'

There were five of them, girls who gutted the herrings brought in from the East coast. They knew Shaun and joked with him and it was he who got them to quieten down and stand still while Francine took the photograph.

All in all she felt it had been a good morning's work. She had photographed a vagrant woman, two Chinamen, several urchins, a decorated barge which had appeared unexpectedly, a drunken man asleep in a gutter with a bottle in his hand, and a baby in a wooden box on wheels, whose mother helped gut the fish.

Although Shaun accepted Gran O'Reilly's invitation to have a meal with them, he prepared to leave soon afterwards. He had another job to do. He was on his way out when Bridget arrived. She was introduced to him and greeted him tight-lipped. When he had gone she made her annoyance known. She had presumed that Francine was working in the studio. What was Mrs O'Reilly thinking about, allowing her to go to the docks among rough men, and to have such a ruffian as an assistant. This had Gran on her high horse.

'Shaun McTinnock might be shabbily dressed,' she said, 'but he's a gentleman at heart. He's sailed the seven seas and is well able to take care of Francine. No harm will come to her with Shaun there.'

Bridget was not appeased, declaring he looked like a tramp and what would the Dentons or the de Auberleighs say if they saw her with him?

Francine not only pointed out it was unlikely that either family would be anywhere near the dock area, but that she had already asked Shaun to call for her the following morning for another photographic session. Bridget gave in but only on condition that she accompanied them.

The following morning, to the surprise of all, Shaun arrived looking, if not a gentleman, certainly more respectably dressed. He was wearing a dark brown suit, a tweed cloth cap which looked fairly new, and also he had had his beard closely trimmed, which took fifteen years off his age. Even Bridget seemed impressed, but what won her over was the way Shaun swept off his cap when he knew she was coming with them and said it would be a pleasure to have her company.

'A charming man,' she declared when they returned. 'And so interesting. I would have no hesitation now if Francine was ever left alone with him.'

This time Shaun offered to help with the developing. Francine accepted and realised more than ever what an asset the Irishman would be in her work.

When Kathleen saw the photographs she was so impressed with them she asked if she could take them to show to Francine's father. Francine agreed to her taking the family photograph only, saying she did not want any snide remarks from her father about her outside work.

Kathleen said quietly, 'Your father has his faults, Francine, but he is an honest man and I know he would praise you for your work.'

Francine gave a grim laugh. 'Papa, praise my work? Never.'

'He's changed a great deal.' Kathleen spoke earnestly.

'He asks about you, Francine. I feel sure he will be inviting you soon to come and see him.'

Although Francine said she had reached the stage when she had no feelings at all for her father she knew that deep down there was still a strong urge to be accepted by him.

Every day that followed became a joy to Francine working under the guidance of Shaun. There were many grey and rainy days when it was impossible to work outdoors. Then they would work inside, with Francine photographing an ornament, a piece of fabric, lace, a fern. Once when she brought in a sheaf of chrysanthemums Shaun said, 'No, no, not a bunch of them, photograph a single one, concentrating on the light and shade. Place it on a dark background.'

They studied photographs she had taken and Shaun would point out what he thought were faults . . . a face at a wrong angle, or taken at a time when the expression was sombre. He laid out a photograph of Kathleen. 'You've concentrated too much on her hands and forgotten her expression. Now look at this one of you taken by Mr Beckett. What was he talking about when he took your photograph?'

Francine said at first she couldn't remember then added, 'Yes, yes, I do, he was talking about birds nesting in his garden and his pleasure in the fledglings.'

'Exactly. Now compare the two photographs.'

It was a while before Francine realised that Mr Beckett had captured a warmth, a gentleness, in the one of herself and that Kathleen looked wooden.

'Study the people you are going to take,' Shaun went on. 'See this one of the fisher girls? Their expressions are serious but their eyes are still full of mischief because we had been joking. If you open a business you would have a much better result from a woman if you admired her dress than if you talked about the awful weather we were having.'

Francine laughed. 'I see what you mean.'

Shaun drew attention to the one of the O'Reilly family. 'The old lady, bless her lovely heart, is very serious, but there's a sparkle in the eyes of her husband and the girls, why?'

'I should imagine because they were all laughing inside because of the way Gran O'Reilly had placed them all as *she* wanted them in the photograph.'

Shaun nodded. 'And that's a lovely thing to be sure. They were laughing because they love her and her ways.'

Francine looked up at him. 'You're a very discerning man, Mr McTinnock.'

'Ah, well now, I've been to a lot of places and met a lot of people to do some discerning.' His smile was wide.

Later he asked casually about the O'Reilly girls. They weren't married, were they courting? Francine said they had all been courted at times but she thought they hadn't married because it would mean leaving home and their grandparents depended on them for the work on the dolls.

'Not that Gran O'Reilly wants to stop them marrying, or her husband, in fact it's the other way around. Both, I know, would be delighted for the girls to be married and have children.'

Shaun rubbed his chin. 'Then something must be done to rectify it. I have a fancy for Therese. I did the first moment of seeing her. And that's a strange thing. I've known women but never wanted to marry one until now. I wouldn't mind her working, I'm out all day. I have a nice wee house and I make a fair living.'

'But is that enough?' Francine asked, doubt in her voice. 'Shouldn't love—?'

Shaun pulled himself up. 'I must be in love with her, otherwise why should I want to marry her this very minute. Yes, I do, I really do. I must go and speak to the old people right away.' He crossed the studio and was at the door when he turned and said with a broad grin, 'I'll be back with permission to court the lovely girl, I know it.'

346

And he was. There was a celebration and no one was happier for her than Cecilia and Graine. Just imagine, only a short while ago they had never met and here was Shaun talking about marriage. Such an impatient man, how romantic.

How romantic indeed, Francine thought with an ache, to have a man sweep you off your feet. Tyson had never done that, and in fact he had been thinking of another girl when they married. Rory loved her but she had to forget him. She *must*, if she was to make the marriage work when Tyson came back. She had not heard from him for some time, nor had the O'Reillys heard from Rory.

For days on end when Francine looked at *The Times* under the heading of *War News* there were the same words: '*Siege of Ladysmith.*' How long could the men hold out? Mafeking was still under siege, also Kimberley. Wounded men who had been sent back to England talked of the Boers as being cleverer than they thought and losing far fewer men in the field than the British.

A week after this Francine received a letter from Tyson and the following day the O'Reillys had a letter from Rory.

Tyson's was much more loving than the last one. He said how much he was missing her.

'*So very much, Francine,*' he wrote. '*I hadn't realised until I had been out here for a while how important relationships were. I dream of holding you, of loving you and I could cry because I treated you so offhandedly. I think of the baby often and feel proud that I will be a father, something I had never imagined at home. Take care of yourself, my darling. I've written all the war news in the letter to my parents. Go and see them, Francine, I want us to be a really close family when this wretched war is over. All my love, Tyson.*'

Francine was deeply moved by Tyson's letter. It took a lot for a man to admit his faults, and she felt that they could now, with Tyson declaring his love for her and feeling pride in being a father, make a success of their marriage.

She wrote to the de Auberleighs, asking if she could come for another visit and had a welcoming reply. But before she went there she had heard the contents of Rory's letter and could see the different attitudes of each man on the subject of the war.

Tyson called the Boers cowards; as soon as they felt they were losing they went galloping away. Rory praised the Boers for their skill and ingenuity. They would gallop away on their ponies, disappear and when the British advanced, would suddenly reappear. *'Away we would be clambering up a steep rise when lo and behold they would appear from nowhere right along the ridge . . . They can find a hiding place behind the flattest of rocks. One minute they're there then they melt away but before you know where you are you're surrounded by them. It's only the big numbers of the British that's kept us from being wiped out.'*

Tyson called the Boers cruel, they killed British women and children; Rory said that they cared for the women and children, also for the British wounded, removing jackets from their own dead to cover the sick men.

Tyson hated everything about the Boers, the way they attacked without notice – it was not gentlemanly; Rory acknowledged their cunning in using smokeless powder in their cartridges, making it impossible to spot their position.

Francine wrote back to both Tyson and Rory, telling Tyson that she and his parents were getting to be quite close. This was true, for Mrs de Auberleigh was always pleased to see Francine, wanting to know how her health was with regard to the baby. The girls, as soon as they could, got her away again so they could have another little session with her. What happened when the baby was born?

When Francine passed on the knowledge she had had from Kathleen they were once more wide-eyed. How was it possible? Francine wondered this herself and at times felt a little afraid, afraid that something would happen to the baby, that it would be born with a cleft palate; would have duck-billed toes; be cross-eyed; have a hideous birthmark, or horror of horrors, be born with withered legs! All these things had been told her by Mrs Binks. 'It's best to be prepared,' she had said sagely. 'Being prepared is half the battle.'

And if this were not all there was a chance of a breech birth which meant that the child was the wrong way round and if the midwife couldn't manage to turn it, then it would be stillborn.

When Francine tearfully told Kathleen what Mrs Binks had said she was furious. 'Don't think such things. You're healthy and strong, you've taken care of yourself. Of course your baby will be all right, and so will mine. Do assure Tyson on this score. He's bound to be constantly worrying about you.'

Francine had already done so, she had told Rory too she was keeping well. She told him about her meeting with Shaun McTinnock, about his help with the photography and about his falling in love with Therese.

A week later Francine had a letter from Sophie. She and her mother were back home and they wanted her to come for a visit. They had a surprise for her, she *must* come. Francine would have accepted anyway. She thought that perhaps Sophie was going to be married, but she found Lord Holcombe there on arrival.

'Francine dear, when I knew that Mrs Denton was going to invite you I asked if she would invite me too. How lovely to see you. Let me look at you, you are positively blooming.'

'It's wonderful to see you too.' Francine was near to tears. 'I've missed you.' Lord Holcombe said he had missed

349

her and Sophie scolded them, saying they would have them all weeping in a minute.

But Sophie and Mrs Denton's welcome was warm, too. 'Do sit down,' Mrs Denton said, 'I've ordered tea.'

There was so much news to catch up on. Francine thought that Lord Holcombe looked so much better and when she told him so he said, 'It's the Surrey air. And, of course, no gambling, no tension.'

He, Sophie and Mrs Denton all wanted to know what Francine had been doing and so the Shuan McTinnock story had to be retold. Francine had brought photographs and showed them one of Shaun. 'This was the first one I took of him.'

Sophie laughed in delight. 'Oh, what a character. But he looks old, too old for Therese.'

Francine handed her another one. 'This is Shaun, tidied up.'

'Well! What a change,' Sophie exclaimed. 'What a mischievous look he has, I do like him. You have a more exciting life than anyone I know, Francine. I wish I wanted to be a photographer.'

'You have to be dedicated,' Lord Holcombe said quietly. 'Francine is.' He had been looking through the photographs and held one up of a bird, sitting on a lawn, head cocked. 'This is exquisite.'

They studied the photographs and all were full of praise for Francine. She would go far, Mrs Denton said, if only Tyson would let her continue with her work when he returned from the war. Pray God all the boys would return.

It was all talk of war from then on for a time, with Lord Holcombe knowledgeable about what was happening in different sections of South Africa, knowledge gleaned from the sons of friends who had been shipped home with wounds.

'The incompetence of some of those in charge makes one see red! It's the lack of communication, according to those who have seen action, and generals who bumble their way along. I heard some very apt phrases the other day and I quote: "Boers go to great lengths to conceal their guns; the British expose them. They place men in a straight line with the exact measurement between them, then order them to advance, making a target of each one." They've learned nothing from the Crimean war. In many cases, the same types of guns are being used. The Boers are using long range, ninety-four pounders called Long Toms, terrifying things. One of the Boers' sayings is, "You English fight to die; we fight to live." How true that is. Signals are sent by heliograph in many cases, but if it is misty they have to use runners. And what happens? They are picked off by the Boers. They seem to smell them out. But then the Boers know every inch of the land.'

Mrs Denton said a little tentatively, 'But we must have some competent people in charge.'

'Yes, of course, I've painted a very black picture. We will win, we have thousands of men from the Empire, we have them from Canada, Australia – of course we will win! And now, no more talk of war. Francine, tell me, what are your plans with your photography, once your baby is here?'

Francine laughed. 'I shall put him in a wooden box on wheels, like the fisherwomen do, and take him with me.'

'Oh, so you've decided you are going to have a son?' His smile was teasing.

'I don't mind either way, but I know that Tyson would like a son.'

Mrs Denton nodded. 'Yes, he would, he told his parents so in his letter. He is greatly taken with the idea of being a father.'

The maid came to announce a visitor. Mrs Denton looked at the visiting card then around at them all, her expression puzzled.

'What on earth has brought Octavia Manning here?'

Francine felt an icy finger touch her spine, sure that this

was not just a courtesy call. And she was right. Octavia asked to see her alone and in the morning room it took only six words to shatter Francine's temporary safe world. 'I'm expecting your husband's child . . .'

CHAPTER TWENTY-SIX

When Francine stood facing the elegantly dressed Octavia Manning she felt that the six words had been burned into her brain and she could not stop her limbs trembling. But then she became aware of the sneer on the lips of her husband's mistress and she was calm.

'I only have your word that you are carrying Tyson's baby. It could be another man's child.'

'It isn't, and for your information Tyson married me before he married you.' Octavia eyed Francine up and down and there was a sneer on her lips as she said, 'So you see, you have a bigamous marriage and will have a bastard child.'

Francine felt as though she had been dealt a number of heavy body blows. It couldn't be true – Octavia was lying, she *had* to be. Tyson had his faults but he wouldn't do such a thing, he couldn't. He had even denied ever making love to Octavia. In a mechanical way she turned and walked to the door and when Octavia asked, her voice sharp, where she was going, Francine replied, 'To call Lord Holcombe and Mrs Denton. I need advice.'

'No! I don't want anyone else to be involved. This is between us.' For the first time there was a note almost of panic in Octavia's voice. 'I don't want my parents to know, my mother is ill, very ill.'

'You should have thought of that before you came here.' Francine went into the hall and called to Lord Holcombe and Mrs Denton, who came quickly. She went back in to Octavia and they followed. When Lord Holcombe asked what was wrong Francine asked Octavia to repeat what she had just told her. Octavia did so, but with some reluctance, reiterating that she did not want her parents to know.

Mrs Denton looked shocked. 'This is ridiculous, I don't believe a word of it. I know my nephew, know he would never do such a thing.'

Lord Holcombe held up a hand. 'Wait.' He asked Octavia where the marriage had taken place and when. She told him Gretna Green, two months before he married Francine. She had proof.

Octavia now had a defiant look about her. 'No matter what you say or do you can't alter anything. Tyson is my legal husband.'

Lord Holcombe shook his head. 'Tyson might have been foolish in his youth but he's an intelligent man and would not, I'm sure, be so stupid as to marry Francine while he was married to you.'

'He did! He asked me to keep it quiet. He needed money desperately. He had big debts. I suppose he thought he would get a substantial dowry from Mr Chayter if he married his daughter.'

'Why didn't you tell your parents when this marriage with Tyson supposedly took place?'

'I couldn't. My mother was ill, she didn't like Tyson, she thought he was weak.' Octavia was really agitated now.

Lord Holcombe said quietly. 'I suggest that this story is a figment of your imagination, fabricated to hurt Francine. You are jealous of her.'

'I'm not, I'm not, it's all true. Tyson loves me, he always has, I *am* carrying his baby. I *am* his wife. You'll find out in time and then you'll be sorry for accusing me of being a liar. If you dare to tell my parents I shall kill you, I swear I will.'

With that she rushed out, brushing past them. Mrs Denton started to go after her but Lord Holcombe detained her. 'No, let her go, it would serve no purpose at this time to bring her back. We shall have to go into the matter.'

Francine, who had sunk into a chair, sat white-faced, trembling, unable to believe that such a thing had happened. She looked mutely from one to the other and Lord Holcombe took her hands in his.

'It's all right, Francine, I'm quite sure that none of what Octavia told us is true.'

Mrs Denton said soothingly, 'I think Lord Holcombe is right. Try not to worry. When my husband comes in we shall discuss the matter. Come upstairs and lie down for a while. Sophie will sit with you.'

Sophie, who had obviously heard most of what had been going on, was furious. 'That bitch!' she exclaimed. 'I always did hate her. She's really stooping low to say such things.'

'But are they true, Sophie? There were times when I didn't know where Tyson was. Times when I felt sure he was with Octavia. You know how obsessed he was with her. He was very anxious to get away to South Africa.'

Although Sophie normally delighted in scandals she was gentle and caring with Francine. 'You must stop worrying or Octavia will have achieved her object, upsetting you and consequently your baby. She hates you, always has, knowing that Tyson does really love you.' Sophie gave a self-conscious smile. 'Do you know that I fancied cousin Tyson a little myself and was jealous because in Monte Carlo he was always watching you? Yes, he was, that's the truth.'

Sophie's words were consoling but Francine could not get out of her mind that there must be some truth in Octavia's statement. No woman in her right mind could have made up such a thing.

In her right mind? Suppose Octavia was not quite stable? She had always seemed such a unnaturally cold person, aloof, whose only interest was in men. Like my mother, Francine thought. Men, men. Her head began to throb. How could she bear it if Octavia's story was proved to be right?

She began to cry, slow painful tears and Sophie held her, rocked her in her arms. 'Don't, Francine, everything will be all right, I know it. Try and have a little sleep then the parents and Lord Holcombe will get it all sorted out.'

With the aid of a headache pill Francine slept.

Sophie aroused her, telling her dinner was ready and that the de Auberleighs were here and the adults had all had a long talk. She was to come downstairs if she felt like it. Francine, anxious for any word on the subject, washed and changed.

The de Auberleighs could not have been kinder. Mr de Auberleigh told Francine that Octavia's mother was in the best of health and pointed out that if Octavia would lie about such a serious thing she would lie about others.

Although it calmed Francine to a certain extent the underlying worry was with her for nearly a week, when after many enquiries, Lord Holcombe told her that Octavia's story had definitely been a figment of her imagination. She had enjoyed the power it gave her to have Tyson pining for her, following her all over the place. She enjoyed rejecting him, but once she realised his feelings for her were cooling, and then learned about the baby, her attitude changed completely. *She* wanted *him*. She panicked at the loss of her power, and it preyed on her mind that he had by now completely rejected her.

'I think we must feel sorry for her,' Lord Holcombe said. 'Her mind is slightly unbalanced. Her parents have sent her to a sanatorium for treatment and are praying that she will recover.'

Francine hoped so too, lest Octavia never fully recovered and continued to plague her and Tyson when the war was over. When she told Lord Holcombe of her fears he said gently, 'Live for the present, Francine dear. Put Octavia out of your mind. Concentrate on your baby, stay well.'

Francine tried, but she was full of unease until Lord Holcombe gave her a present, saying he hoped it would keep her mind from any worry. Francine undid the wrapping, discovered a leather-covered box about six inches by three in a carrying case with a shoulder strap and after studying it looked at him questioningly. 'A camera?'

He smiled. 'It is. It's called a Kodak. It has a paper roll film and takes a hundred small circular pictures, two and a half inches in diameter.'

'A film?' Francine felt a quiver of excitement, and could hardly contain it as he went on to explain how to use it.

'To take a picture you pull a string, which cocks the shutter. Then you point the camera at the subject and press a button. That releases the shutter and makes the exposure. Finally you wind the key, which moves the film on its way and readies the camera for your next picture.'

Francine jumped up and hugged him. 'Oh, Andy, you couldn't have bought me a more wonderful present. Thank you a thousand times over. What happens after you've used up the film?'

This, he said, was where she would have to be patient. The camera with the film in it would have to be sent to the Kodak company in America, with the money for processing the film, then the camera would be returned, ready loaded to take a further hundred pictures.

Lord Holcombe had had an interesting discussion with an American connected with the Kodak company and during the next half hour he was as excited as Francine as he explained the coming developments of the firm. There would soon be a larger version of the camera and they hoped to produce a celluloid film.

'But remember this, Francine,' he added. 'Your Kodak is just to play around with – you will never get professional pictures on this as you do on your George Hare camera.'

Francine said she realised this but could hardly wait to use the Kodak. However, she didn't take any photographs until she had talked to Shaun about it. He was as intrigued

357

by it as Francine. They studied the directions carefully and went out the following morning to take some open air scenes. In the afternoon they took each member of the O'Reilly family separately, then Bridget and Sophie who came for a visit and finally, photographed Kathleen with the Kodak.

Kathleen urged, 'You must tell Rory about this, he'll be so interested.' Francine said she had already started a letter to him and she must also write to Mr Beckett.

During the following week Octavia Manning barely crossed Francine's mind and when she did she was able to dismiss her. Octavia with her lies was unimportant. When she wrote to Tyson she made no mention of her. There was no point – he would only worry and he had enough to cope with fighting the Boers.

In February there was great jubilation when first Ladysmith was relieved then Kimberley, but when in May Mafeking was relieved, after a seven month siege, the people went wild. There was dancing in the streets, as they sang to brass bands, waved thousands of Union Jacks and marched through streets draped with bunting.

And Francine like everyone else was sure that soon the war would be over and the men coming home. The men thought so too, but it still dragged on.

In Rory's next letter home he spoke of the courage of the Boer women who fought beside their husbands. No man approved of this but these people were fighting for their homes, their land, their very existence. Who were they to stand in judgement? He said that food was in short supply at the moment but they were not starving, there were plenty of rats. Quite tasty, really!

Francine shuddered at this, yet was it any worse than killing and eating rabbits?

He talked about the heat and of how quickly the land had dried up after all the torrential rain. In places it was parched. Streams had disappeared completely. He spoke of General Buller and how they had heard he and his men were well-fed. They had also heard he was the biggest bumbler of all the Generals.

'*It's a funny old war*, he went on. '*Some of the Boers go home after a big battle to see how their families are faring. They don't wear uniform, just their ordinary clothes. One Boer General went into battle wearing a top hat and frock coat! We wanted to laugh but couldn't. He was killed and was apparently a very brave man.*

Don't worry about us folk. Me and the lads are all fine, fighting fit in fact. We all send our love . . . '

A postscript said, '*We had to laugh when we heard that armchairs had been sent out for the officers with strict instructions that the enemy were not to be allowed to sit in them. Laugh? We nearly died laughing. We're with a great bunch of men. When we're not fighting we really enjoy ourselves so you are not to worry. We all send our love. It's Michael's turn to write to you next. He's already started a letter . . .* '

The war dragged on, with small victories and heavy losses. Kathleen, after a short labour gave birth to a son. He was a lusty boy who apparently delighted his father.

'Like a dog with two tails,' Kathleen laughingly described Edwin. Then, more soberly, she added, 'I hope that your baby is a boy too, Francine – it might bring you and your father close.'

But Francine, after a long and painful labour, produced a girl and in her weakened state knew a swift disappointment. A girl? Her father would not want anything to do with it and Tyson would be upset too that she had not given him a son and heir.

But when the baby was placed into Francine's arms tears welled up inside her. Rory's eyes looked up at her from the tiny face, and Francine felt a deep peace and certainty fill her heart. Rory, her childhood friend, her own true love. She held the baby close and whispered, 'Oh, my darling, forgive me, I love you.' The next moment the nurse took the baby away, telling Francine she must sleep.

It was morning when Francine saw her baby again and every moment spent with her after that was a delight. Francine just loved the way she fed so hungrily, the touch of the dark, downy hair against her skin, hair that curled when damp; those familiar blue eyes that tried to focus when her mother spoke softly to her, the dimples that appeared at either side of her mouth.

Weeks before the baby was due Francine had been told that there could be complications with the actual birth and had agreed, with a great deal of reluctance, to go into a nursing home and be attended by the de Auberleighs' own physician. Now she realised she had done the right thing, but it meant that she was restricted with visitors. Mr and Mrs de Auberleigh had been in to see her and declared themselves thrilled with the baby, insisting that when Francine was well enough, she must come to them to recuperate.

Although Francine agreed she longed to be back with the O'Reillys.

Kathleen was the next visitor. She gave Francine a hug and a kiss. 'Oh, we're so glad it's all over, we were all so worried. And a little girl: a niece for Edwin Junior!'

Francine laughed. 'How strange that two babies should be uncle and niece. How is wee Edwin?'

'Beautiful, but a great cryer at the moment, I think it's just bad temper.' Kathleen, who had been laughing too, suddenly sobered. 'You father is here, Francine. He asked to see you. It's a good sign.'

Francine's heart was beating a great deal faster when her father came in. His expression gave nothing away as he greeted her. 'Francine, how are you?'

'Fine now. I – made you a grandfather.'

'Yes, you did. Quite an achievement to have been presented with a son and a granddaughter within the space of a few weeks.'

With these few words Francine knew that her father had accepted her as his daughter at last and experienced a quiet joy. He asked what the baby was to be named and after a small hesitation she said, 'Gabrielle, Papa, after Mama.'

Edwin nodded. 'I thought you might.'

When she and Edwin saw the baby, Kathleen drooled over her, for wasn't she the bonniest wee thing she had ever seen? Edwin pronounced her to be quite a healthy-looking child. He then excused himself, saying he would leave the two mothers to have a chat.

After he had gone Kathleen said, 'Honestly, did you ever meet such a man? At times you would think he was made of wood.'

'He's accepted me,' Francine said softly, 'and more important still, my baby. That means a great deal.'

'And to me, Francine. It's grieved me all these years that he would never show he had accepted you, yet I knew he did. Bridget and all the family are dying to see you, but although Bridget wants to come here, the family said they'll wait until you come home.'

'Home,' Francine whispered. 'I can't wait.'

It was some time before the de Auberleighs would part with Francine and their first grandchild, but it was worth the waiting for the welcome mother and baby received. The O'Reillys had even hung a Union Jack outside one of the windows and there were sprays of leaves and wild flowers in jam jars all over the house.

The two old people wept over the baby. Just like their own wee great-grandchild, she was. Gran O'Reilly, taking the baby in her arms exclaimed, 'You little beauty! Just look at those dimples, me sister Anne and me sister Moira had such ones – and those eyes! Oh, you'll be breaking a lot of hearts when you grow up, sweet child.'

Francine had tensed when dimples were mentioned, feeling sure that Gran O'Reilly could see the resemblance to Rory, but the others took no notice, they were all too busy baby-talking Gabrielle.

Mary asked shyly if she could hold the baby and when Gran handed her over with a look of compassion the old man said, 'And will you all now come and let wee Gabby see her presents.'

The presents were a knitted shawl, a gossamer fine head-shawl, bootees, a white embroidered cot blanket, a rattle and several knitted animals and dolls.

'They're lovely,' Francine said warmly. 'What a lot of work you've all been putting into them. I'm sure Gabrielle would thank you herself if she could.'

'Ah, now but wait,' said the old man, 'there's something else and everyone in the family has contributed to it. The lads asked for something to be taken out of their savings at home to buy it and Shaun has given, too. If you'll just wait I will get it.' He went out of the room and came back with an oblong box. When he handed it over, his smile was from ear to ear.

Francine, wondering, undid the pink ribbon and raised the lid. The next moment she gave a gasp. 'Oh, how absolutely exquisite. I've never seen such a doll. The eyes . . . ! The clothes!'

The old man nodded. 'It's a Jumeau doll, the eyes are its speciality.'

The eyes were a clear light blue, eyes that all but spoke to you, and there was a life-like expression on the face. The doll was dressed in an ice-blue velvet dress and cloak, trimmed with fur. The hat was trimmed with lace, pearls, petals and feathers. The shoes were ice-blue kid.

'The clothes, everything,' Francine said, a wonder in her voice. 'It's a beautiful present and I know it will be something Gabrielle will treasure when she's old enough to understand.'

It certainly was a day to remember. A high tea followed during which Gran O'Reilly told the news of how they had been approached by a firm to dress better class dolls.

'It will mean a lot of work,' she said, 'because we want to go on making our wooden Betties, but we'll do it. We want to put something by for the boys when they come home.'

After tea Shaun arrived, made a great fuss of the baby and took pictures of her and the rest of the family with the Kodak camera. No war news was discussed at all. Gran said that was for another day, not this one.

The baby had received a silver christening mug from the de Auberleighs, toys from the girls, clothes from Bridget and by post came money from Lord Holcombe and a tiny model of a pianoforte in silver, which was inscribed with the words, *May she dance to music every day of her life*.

He was away at present but said he would be home soon and was looking forward to making the acquaintance of Gabrielle.

Francine had written to her mother with the news, and she wrote back to say how delighted she was about the baby, but begging her daughter not to tell anyone who knew her. Just imagine! A grandmother and still playing ingénue parts. She sent a beautiful hand-embroidered christening gown, which, she said, Francine had worn at her own christening. She had kept it out of sentiment.

Francine thought she would never, ever, understand her mother, who could keep a christening robe out of sentiment yet would not allow herself to be acknowledged as the grandmother of her only daughter's child.

Francine had written to Tyson telling him of the birth of the baby and wrote again, enclosing a photograph. She also sent one to Rory and the boys and felt a pang that Rory would not know for sure that he was looking at his own child. Gabrielle had his sturdy build, as well as the dimples of his great-aunts.

Letters were spasmodic during the remaining months of 1900 and the news was seldom good. Tyson had declared his delight about the baby. No, he was not disappointed to have a daughter. He dreamed of seeing her, of holding her in his arms. '*And of holding you, my darling Francine,*' he wrote once . . . which made Francine weep. When would this wretched war be over and they could be together as a family? Tyson was missing all the loveliness of Gabrielle's growing up. She was gorgeous, a happy baby, and in danger of being thoroughly spoiled with so many people making a fuss of her.

Francine had gone out photographing with Shaun again and although there were times when she wanted the baby with her she would be talked out of it by Gran O'Reilly.

'The dockside's no place to take a baby. Leave her with us, we love to have her and poor Mary gets so much pleasure from looking after her.'

In the middle of December 1900 the de Auberleighs had a letter from an officer from Tyson's regiment who was in hospital in England, recovering from war wounds. Could they come to see him?

They went distressed, expecting bad news, and came back jubilant. Tyson could be due for a Victoria Cross — for bravery beyond the call of duty. Although wounded himself he had led his men and taken a vital position that had seemed impossible. Fortunately, his wound had not been serious.

The de Auberleighs were indeed proud of Tyson's bravery and the O'Reillys were full of praise for Francine's husband and told the baby, 'Your papa is a hero.' But Francine felt only guilt that Tyson was not Gabrielle's papa.

The de Auberleighs were still basking in the glory of their son's achievement when they had word from the War Office to say that both their other sons had been killed in action.

And three days before Christmas the O'Reillys were told that Milo had been killed.

So Gabrielle's first Christmas that had been going to be so special was spent in houses of grief and despair.

CHAPTER TWENTY-SEVEN

Mrs de Auberleigh became a broken woman after the death of her two younger sons and Francine visited as often as she could because her mother-in-law's only seeming interest was in her granddaughter.

Gran and Grandad O'Reilly hid their grief, there was the living to think about. There had to be money put aside for when the boys came home. Mary too, after this second tragedy, put on a brave face and she also seemed to find solace in having Gabrielle with her.

When Tyson wrote to Francine about his brothers he was in a depressed state. Why had he not been taken instead of his brothers, for he was the least liked by his father.

The O'Reilly boys also said they would rather it had been one of them, instead of Milo who had left a lovely wife.

But whereas Tyson's letter continued in a depressed state about the war going on so endlessly, Rory tried to cheer the family up a little by telling them funny little pieces about the men doing their own washing and asked them to imagine bread having to be baked for twenty thousand men. He described how line after line of trenches were dug, fires lit in them and the bread baked.

'*Nothing could ever taste like your wonderful bread, Gran, but after living on biscuits as hard as a rock we enjoyed it.*' He also described the meals, cooked in pans that were built up like a pyramid. It was horse meat, he said, but a welcome change from other things they had eaten.

He also told them about Queen Victoria having sent a tin of chocolates to every soldier, but they hadn't eaten theirs, they were sending them home. They thought they would be a treat, and the boxes could be kept as momentos.

The family protested at this; the boys should have had the treat, but Gran said the tins would be lovely for their great-grandchildren to have.

In June Shaun and Therese were married. The wedding was quiet but the celebrations went on until well after midnight, all relatives and friends having contributed food and drink.

When Shaun had first talked about Therese he had spoken of having a lovely wee house to offer her and, to the surprise of all it turned out to be just that. He had papered it, freshly painted it, and it was furnished comfortably from pieces that had been turned out from some of the big houses.

Therese was back home and working the day after the wedding and Shaun back out on his rounds. When he could spare the time, he and Francine would go out photographing. Sometimes they would photograph people living in dire poverty, at other times they would find a country lane and photograph nature. One day when Shaun asked Francine what she would do about her hobby when her man came back she was a long time in answering.

'I'm not sure. I think he may accept it. I feel he's changed since going out to fight, feel he's more tolerant.'

Shaun nodded slowly. 'War does change men. It changed me when I was out fighting earlier in South Africa. Death is so close it makes things that once seemed important, unimportant. Although you're with a lot of men there are times when you feel a terrible aloneness — I think it's knowing that no one can save you if your time has come . . .' Shaun jumped up suddenly. 'Heavens above, what a morbid subject, we came to capture beauty.' He waved a hand. 'Look at it all around us, let us enjoy it, then you can go back and enjoy that lovely wee child of yours.'

It was always a joy to get back to Gabrielle. She was a happy little soul, beautiful, with dark curly hair and a winsome smile that won all hearts. When Lord Holcombe came home on visits he would hardly let her out of his sight. She was toddling all over the place and with a young child's curiosity explored everything in sight. Although she had been given toys of all kinds her favourite was a rag doll that Kathleen had made her, reminding Francine of her first doll and the pleasure and warmth she had drawn from it. It seemed sometimes an era ago.

Little Edwin was a sturdy boy, an endearing child too, but although rough in his games he was surprisingly gentle with Gabrielle. What did hurt Francine was that her father had never once invited her to bring Gabrielle to Spinners End. In fact, he had shown no interest in her since the day he came to see her when Gabrielle was born. Yet Kathleen insisted he loved them both. 'He just can't show it, Francine. He asks after you, after Gabrielle. Someday I'm sure he'll change, and be able to show his feelings.'

Mrs de Auberleigh was always asking Francine to bring Gabrielle over, her daughters wanted her there, too. Gran and Grandad O'Reilly loved having her with them and the girls, especially Mary, made a fuss of her. Sometimes bedtime was the only occasion when Francine felt that Gabrielle was wholly hers.

She would hold her little daughter in her arms and sing her to sleep with a lullaby, and when the lovely eyes closed and the long dark lashes fanned the creamy cheeks, she would feel a wave of love sweep over her. There were times when she would let her mind drift back to the secret cave where the baby was conceived and wish it were possible that Rory could see his little daughter, if only once.

Sometimes she dreamed about Rory and always they were walking hand in hand through fields. But one evening she dreamt that Rory was running away from her and she was unable to catch up with him. She awoke, sweating. Was it a bad omen? Had something happened to him?

The next morning, however, there was a letter from him, and it was as cheerful as always. Supplies had got through and they had had some good meals. Then two days later, the mail had come and that was a joy! '*Letters from the family and from you, Francine. It was quite wonderful to hear all your news. I'm becoming envious of your photography sessions with Shaun. You'll be teaching me new techniques when I get home! Had a letter from your father. He seems greatly taken with his son and lovely granddaughter. Lucky man. Wish I could see them. Let us hope it will be soon. Although* nothing *seems to get settled.*'

Rory then said something that set Francine's heart racing. He was talking about the Boer guns, then added, '*They say that the Mauser guns make a clean hole that mends quickly, so let's hope if I have to have a bullet in me that it will be a Mauser . . .*'

Was he tempting fate? It was terrible to think that even while she was reading this letter he could be lying wounded or even . . . *No*, Francine refused to think about it.

When tragedy did strike again it was unexpected. Lord Holcombe died suddenly in France, and was buried there at his request. Francine could not stop crying. If only she had known he was not well.

'We mustn't grieve over him,' Mrs Denton said, a great sadness in her voice. 'He lived his life the way he wanted and he died in France, which he loved.'

But nothing could get Francine over his death until Sophie said, 'You're serving no purpose crying your eyes out, Francine. Do something to help the living, the men who are fighting. Knit some scarves or some gloves. The African winter is on them. Come to the knitting session with me. There are twenty of us.'

It was the idea of the rebel Sophie actually knitting, that

helped Francine over her grief and so she started knitting for the army.

In a later letter to Kathleen from the boys Rory said he had been reading a book, lent to him by one of the men. It was all about Egypt and he thought it would be a wonderful place to visit and photograph. When Gran O'Reilly read it she was up in arms.

'He'll not be rushing off abroad again if I have any say in it. He could be lost in the jungle or eaten up by a lion. Me cousin Michael went out there and was bitten by a rattlesnake, or was he kicked by a rhinoceros, or perhaps it was India he went to. Well, wherever it was Rory isn't going there and that's that.' She had then burst into tears, an unheard-of thing for the old lady, and when they all cried with her she got more mad than ever. What was the matter with them? Couldn't she indulge herself now and then? If Rory or any of the lads wanted to go to the end of the world they could go, it was their lives, wasn't it?

This made Francine realise more than ever the close family ties of the O'Reillys and of how lucky she was to be a part of it.

The war dragged on and on, with small victories and defeats. There were plenty of attempts to reach a peace settlement, but the Boers refused to accept the terms offered by the British.

Towards the end of November Kathleen called to see Francine one morning and asked her if she would come and see her father. She seemed agitated. 'Edwin isn't well. He's been overworking, as his last assistant has gone out to South Africa. He's asked to see you, Francine. I think he wants to ask your help.'

'My help? With the photography? I don't know how he dare after the way he's treated me, *and* Gabrielle.'

'I know and I can't say I blame you if you refuse.' She looked at Francine with appeal. 'But I love him and I can't bear to see him so worried.'

'No, I'm sorry, Kathleen, I couldn't go to him under

those conditions. If only he had asked me once to come home, but he's just ignored us. He's hurt me ever since the day I went to live with him. And it's no use saying he's built that way, that he loves me but can't show it. Let him be hurt for a change, but in his case it will be only his pocket that will suffer.'

Kathleen got up. 'It's all right, Francine, I know how you feel. I'll see you again.' Francine let her go, despite knowing that Kathleen was suffering because she loved her husband.

Shaun, who arrived ten minutes later, asked Francine what was wrong. When she told him he said, 'It's a small thing to ask, be charitable.'

She flared. 'Be charitable? To my father? He doesn't want to see me to tell me he loves me, he only wants help with his photography.'

'Then he must think very highly of your work to ask your help. It's his way of asking forgiveness.'

'Then he won't get it. I'm not going to absolve him of his sins.'

'You'll leave it to the Lord to do it, when he dies, is that it?'

'All my father is suffering from is overwork,' she retorted, 'and that is because he's greedy and wants more and more money.'

'You father *is* dying, Francine.' Shaun spoke gently. 'He sent for me, he knew my father, knew that you and I were working together.'

'Dying?' Francine stared at him, disbelieving. 'Kathleen didn't say anything, never even hinted that it was anything more than – '

'She doesn't know. Your father wants to keep it from her.'

Francine sank into a chair, realising how right Shaun had been when he said earlier that when death is close the important things seem unimportant. She had never tried to understand her father. Perhaps if she had called before, taken Gabrielle with her? She got up. 'I'll go now, Shaun.'

Kathleen was so pleased to see her it made Francine ache.

'Oh, Francine, your father will be delighted, he's just been talking about Gabrielle. I'm sure that seeing you will be a tonic.'

Francine was shocked at the change in her father. He was gaunt, looked years older, there were streaks of white in his hair. Why had Kathleen not realised he was so ill? Was it a determination not to accept this fact?

Edwin held out a hand to Francine, and there was a brightness in his eyes. 'I'm so glad you came.' His voice was little above a whisper. 'Sit down.'

Francine felt choked, yet knew she must control her emotion if only for Kathleen's sake. She put her hand over Edwin's. 'Papa, don't try to talk. I'm sorry for the rift that's been between us. It was as much my fault as yours.'

His head moved restlessly on the pillow. 'No, Francine, I am wholly to blame. There was a . . . blackness inside of me. I . . . could never dispel it. So . . . wrong . . . so very wrong.' His breathing was ragged and she begged him not to say any more, but after a short rest he seemed to rally again.

'Francine, I've denied you access to my studio all these years. Would you consider taking over the business? Shaun would help you.'

Francine felt a momentary panic. The house was alien to her, held so many unhappy memories.

Before she could think up a reply Edwin whispered, 'Think about it, there's no hurry.' He closed his eyes.

Francine leaned over and kissed him on the brow. He opened his eyes and smiled. It was a smile that hurt. She went out of the room and Kathleen followed.

'You've made your peace at last,' she said, her eyes filling with tears. Francine, realising that Kathleen had known all along about Edwin was unable to answer. She put her arms around her and held her close.

The following day Edwin's condition worsened, but he told Kathleen that Rory must be given a chance to work in the studio too, when he came back from the war. He was most knowledgeable. He would go far and be a big asset to the business.

The last ones Edwin embraced were his son and grand-daughter. Then there was a look of torment in his eyes, as though he wanted to cling to life. But in death there was such a look of peace on his face that Francine shed no more tears.

A telegram was sent to Francine's mother and a reply came to say she was deeply grieved to hear the news. In the letter she wrote how she had never stopped loving Edwin and wished she had been able to attend the funeral, but she was in the middle of rehearsals for a new play.

Francine tore the letter in little pieces and watched them being consumed in the heart of the fire. It was the end of any contact with her mother.

Two days after the funeral Kathleen said to Francine, 'I know that Edwin would have liked you to take over the business, but of course he wouldn't realise all the problems it might entail. The war could soon be over and Tyson come home. Then he would naturally want you with him all the time and, who could blame him?'

'Could you perhaps get an experienced photographer to take over?'

'I might, but actually I don't need the money, Francine, as your father left me comfortably off. Shaun did say he would come and help out but it would be only temporary. He likes his barrow work.'

As it turned out Kathleen did find a suitable man and Francine was pleased, knowing it would be an interest for Kathleen.

Francine continued her own work in the studio she had

set up in the attic at the O'Reillys but she saw Kathleen regularly.

CHAPTER TWENTY-EIGHT

It was not until May 1902 that the Boers surrendered, and the peace treaty was signed in June. In that time Queen Victoria had died and later, in August, Edward was crowned king.

Francine neither attended the funeral nor the coronation, for her life was completely wrapped up in her work. She experimented again with ghost pictures and found a ready sale for them. She also photographed children whenever she could and received high praise from Shaun for these. He made disparaging remarks about the ghost pictures. 'Leave that to others, Francine. You are prostituting your talents.'

To this Francine replied she just had to experiment and pointed out that everything new she tried added to her knowledge.

All three de Auberleigh daughters were married by now and Graine and Cecilia were courting and making plans to be married. All that everyone was waiting for now was for the men to come home from South Africa.

Tyson's letters were full of love and longing to be with his wife and daughter; he spoke of how he dreamed of holding Gabrielle in his arms. To think she would not even know who he was!

Rory had not accepted Edwin's offer to come back and help run the business. '*Sorry, Francine,*' he had written, '*when I go into business it will be one that I run. No woman bosses me.*' He had teased her, reminding her of how bossy she had been when she was younger. Several times she had sensed an underlying longing to see her. He would mention certain parts of the countryside they had visited. Had there been any changes? Was the old cave still used by people wanting to shelter? Then Francine would experience feelings she had only known that day with Rory in the cave.

Sophie's fiancé Randolph was the first of the men to arrive home and they planned their wedding right away. Then word came from Tyson and Francine was in a fluster, feeling that a stranger would be coming home.

Mrs de Auberleigh just looked vague when told her eldest son would be home soon and simply said, 'Oh, yes,' which was heartbreaking. What Francine really dreaded was having to live with the de Auberleighs when Tyson came back, that is, until they found a house of their own. But what was going to happen to her business? Shaun had agreed to take it over, but stressed it would be only a temporary measure.

The day Tyson was due Francine felt a bundle of nerves, but when he did arrive there was so much excitement, so many people there to greet him that it was easier than she had imagined. He swept Gabrielle up in his arms and hugged her, wept over her and Gabrielle looked at him in a babyish, puzzled way. Francine said, 'Give her time, she has to get used to you.' Then Tyson put his other arm around Francine and drew her close.

'Oh, my darling, how I've waited for this moment, longed for it, you are more beautiful than ever.' Putting his lips to her hair he whispered, 'I can't wait to have you alone.'

Although Francine had experienced strong emotions while he was away, she felt no response, but thought it would be different this evening, when there were just the two of them.

But she knew a swift disappointment when Tyson, over-excited, left her unsatisfied as always. 'Don't worry, my darling,' he said, 'the night is still young.' He kissed the tip of her nose. 'Don't you dare go to sleep on me.'

It was Tyson, however, who fell asleep first and Francine was up the next morning before he awoke. He teased her, saying she had run out on him, but just wait until later! He wanted to make love to her at all times of the day, and although she was embarrassed that the family would know what was happening she made excuses in her mind for him – after all, he had been celibate for so long.

She did her best to please, making a pretence of enjoying the love-making, and he was happy with her and Gabrielle for two weeks, but then he began to be restless. He wanted to ride. They would go into the country, visit the Binks, borrow a horse. He had friends who would put them up. Francine, who was longing to get back to her work, suggested he went on his own. He was reluctant, he wanted his wife and daughter with him. She persuaded him he would enjoy his riding better alone. She would be here when he returned.

After he had gone Francine went to Spinners End, saying she wanted to work.

Kathleen told her gently she thought she had made a big mistake in not going with Tyson. 'He needs you, Francine, and Gabrielle. Don't forget he's been away over two years fighting a war.'

'Yes, I know, but I've worked hard to get where I have with the photography, it's become a part of my life. I can't give it up.'

'Then treat it as a hobby, do it occasionally but don't be obsessed by it, which you are at the moment. Francine, *please* take my advice, you have so much to lose.'

Because Kathleen kept on about it Francine said she was probably right and left soon afterwards. But instead of going back to the de Auberleighs' she went to the O'Reillys', saying she wanted to do a little bit of camera work. Within minutes she was getting the same scolding from Gran O'Reilly as she had had from Kathleen.

'You're mad, girl, neglecting your husband and child. And where is Gabrielle today? Being looked after by one of your in-laws, I presume? Get yourself back home and at least be there when your husband does return.'

Francine, huffed, said she would leave at once, she didn't want to stay where she was not wanted. She was at the door when the old lady called, 'Come back here, my girl! I have a lot more to say to you, and don't you dare give me that sullen look.' More gently she added, 'Sit down, Francine, and listen carefully, because this is important. I know your father didn't want you. Supposedly it was because of what your mother had done. But I think he didn't want you in his life because he was obsessed with photography and he didn't want anyone to interrupt him.'

'No, that's wrong, he – '

'And your mother didn't want you because she was obsessed with the stage, she wanted the applause. She couldn't have you with her because she wanted to appear eternally young. Obsessed, both of them, and you were rejected.'

Francine was still.

'Don't, I beg of you, reject your child and your husband just because you want to take pictures.'

'I don't.' Francine's head came up. 'I've never neglected Gabrielle.'

'Oh, yes you have! You scold her when she's a little fretful because she interrupts you in your work . . .'

'No, no,' Francine protested, but the protest was weak because she knew that Gran was right.

After Francine had shed a few tears and been soothed by the old lady she left to return to the de Auberleighs', and was glad she had, for Tyson returned sooner than expected. He was brimming over with good humour and news.

'Francine, guess what! The new owners of Holcombe Manor have offered us accommodation, the same as we had when Lord Holcombe was alive. They only use the manor during the hunting season. They're a middle-aged couple, quite charming, you'll like them.'

At that moment all Francine could think of was having

her studio again at the manor. She could not work professionally but she could take pictures when she wanted to. 'Oh, Tyson, that's marvellous!'

He swung her off her feet. 'I think so too. It will be a splendid place for Gabrielle to grow up in, with all the animals and fresh air. Mrs Binks is delighted, you know how she loves children.'

This was one more thing in favour of the move, Francine thought. She would be free to do as she pleased and Tyson would be out most of the day.

Francine was full of nostalgia when they moved back into the the manor. It not only brought memories of dear Lord Holcombe to mind, but Rory, too and their walks to her secret dell . . .

'We have all sorts of invitations,' Tyson enthused, 'and of course we must start entertaining.'

Although Francine did not feel too enthusiastic about entertaining she gave in and pretended pleasure at having a social life. Some sacrifice must be accepted to have her freedom with her photography.

Tyson was always loving towards her but being loving meant making love, and Francine was seldom in the mood. She would find herself thinking of some work she had done, work that had a flaw, which must be rectified. She began making excuses when Tyson was amorous – she was tired, had a headache, felt she had a cold starting. Or Gabrielle was fretful, she seemed feverish, perhaps she ought to sleep in her room. Tyson suffered it for a time then flared up.

'You make excuses every night. I am your husband and have *some* rights.' Francine retorted she had rights too and it ended with a violent quarrel which had Tyson sleeping in the spare room and staying there.

Although Francine realised she had gone too far, she did at least not have to put up with Tyson groping for her during the night. She needed her sleep, to be fresh for her work.

She did however go out with him socially and accepted having people for dinner at the manor. But there came a time when she noticed that Tyson made up to other women, and although she knew she was partly responsible for this she was angry and jealous. To her accusations he replied quite calmly that if she didn't want him, there were plenty of other women who did. Although Francine seethed at this she said no more.

One thing that did remain stable was Tyson's love for Gabrielle, and she adored him. As soon as he arrived she would toddle to him saying joyously, 'Papa!' and when he picked her up she would wrap her plump little arms around his neck and put her cheek to his. This affection between them never failed to move Francine and one day she asked Tyson if they could have a talk.

'I've been a fool,' she said. 'It's taken me a long time to realise it. I had my values all wrong. I want to be a part of the life you share with Gabrielle. I'm sorry, Tyson, so sorry. Can you forgive me?' Her voice broke.

'There's nothing to forgive, Francine,' he said softly. 'I was arrogant, thought that I should be pleasured, never giving a thought to your feelings.' He took her in his arms. 'Tonight will be different, my darling, I promise.'

It was different. Tyson was patient, tender, wanting them to share the ecstasy of fulfilment. He slowed his rhythm when she begged him to wait, and quickened it when she gripped him in a frenzy. 'Now, Tyson, now.' A sob of joy escaped her as they rose on the crest of passion and later, when they lay spent, Tyson cradled her head against his shoulder and gave a deep sigh.

'Oh, my sweet, what I have been denying myself all this time. And denying you.'

It was the first of many such nights and she moved through the days in a haze of happiness, longing for evening to come.

Whenever they socialised they were like young lovers and there would be indulgent smiles. After all, when husband and wife have been separated for over two years . . .

One morning Francine awoke, her nose streaming, her throat raw. 'Oh, look at me,' she wailed, 'and we're due at the Craigs tonight for dinner. I couldn't possibly go, Tyson, you must go alone.'

He refused, he would stay with her. 'And catch my cold?' she exclaimed. 'Don't be foolish. You *must* go.' He gave in and Francine, at Tyson's insistence, stayed in bed.

Tyson was going with friends and he dressed and left early with the promise he would not be late. He was very loving and seemed really concerned that she was so poorly. 'Now, you have nothing to worry about. Mrs Binks will keep Gabrielle until you are well again, so do *not* get up.' Francine willingly promised, knowing she was really in the throes of a heavy cold.

She did not see Tyson until the next day when he told her that all had gone well at the dinner and everyone had been asking about her. He said he had arranged to go shooting with Mr Binks, but would stay if she wished. Francine shooed him out. 'You go, get out of this germ-laden atmosphere,' she joked, her voice thick.

It was three days later, when she was up and about again that she heard the news about Octavia Manning. A daughter of one of their friends gave the information.

'Quite a stunner, isn't she? You'd better beware, Francine, she couldn't keep her eyes off Tyson at the Craigs' dinner party the other evening.' She laughed. 'And not only her eyes, her hands, too.'

'And Tyson?' Francine forced herself to speak lightly.

'He lapped it up, of course, what man wouldn't? The other men were all envious.'

Francine felt wooden, but she still managed to treat it lightly. 'Don't worry, we both know Octavia. Tyson has her measure, he will know how to deal with her.'

'I hope so. They were riding together this morning.' The girl then changed the subject and began talking about a cousin's coming wedding, but Francine did not take much of it in for the fury consuming her.

If Tyson had not been interested in Octavia he would have mentioned it. How long had he been seeing her? Possibly for days. She spent the day in a torment waiting for him to come home. When he did she tackled him at once.

'Why didn't you tell me that Octavia Manning was at the Craigs' the other night?'

Tyson met her furious gaze squarely. 'Because I knew what your reaction would be, and I was obviously right.'

'Did you think to keep it secret, in this community? Everyone must know how besotted you are with her.'

'*Was*, Francine. It is all over – and that's the truth.'

'The truth! You don't know the meaning of the word! You went riding with her this morning, didn't you?'

Tyson sighed. 'To repeat to her that it is all over between us.'

'And you expect me to believe that? You didn't *have* to go riding with her, you could have told her when you met and then just walked away.'

'There were people standing around. I didn't want to air my affairs in public.'

'Your affairs is right. I wonder how many other women you've been having affairs with when you went out every day. You never told me where you had been.'

'You didn't ask.' Tyson was angry now. 'If you don't want to believe what I've told you, then that is your fault.' He went out, slamming the door behind him.

When he didn't return that day Francine went upstairs to pack. The marriage was over. She was not going to stand the humiliation of everyone knowing her husband had been seeing Octavia Manning. She would collect Gabrielle in the morning and go to the O'Reillys, or to Bridget's – anywhere to get away from here.

Although Francine could have sworn she had not slept that night, she must have catnapped because Tyson had been home and gone out again early. The maid said he had left word he had gone riding. He would see her later.

'Oh, no, Tyson,' she said aloud. 'You won't be seeing me, I'll be gone.'

But she had not even had the bags brought down when she heard the galloping hooves of a horse. On going to the window she saw Mr Binks dismount and throw the reins to a groom, and come hurrying to the house. Francine stood tense for a moment then went running downstairs knowing that the steward was bringing bad news.

Binks was in the hall, cap in hand, a curious greyness to his weatherbeaten face. 'There's been an accident, ma'am. Mr Tyson, he's had a fall. They're bringing him home, the doctor's with him.'

'How – bad is it?' She could hardly get the words out.

'He struck his head on a stone. I can hear the men now.' He went out and Francine followed. There were several men carrying a wooden hurdle. All Francine could see of Tyson was a paper-white face. She ran back into the house, calling to the servants, asking them to turn back the sheets of their bed upstairs.

For the next few minutes Francine was unable to still the trembling of her limbs and she found herself saying over and over again, 'Oh, God, please don't let him die.'

The men took Tyson upstairs and the doctor drew Francine aside. He shook his head, his expression grave. 'It's bad, Mrs de Auberleigh, a head wound.'

'What happened?'

'He was thrown. Someone – well, someone threw a branch of a tree at the horse.'

Francine stared at him. 'The branch of a tree? Was it a child?'

'No.' He looked uncomfortable. 'It was one of the guests of the Craigs. I must go up now and see to your husband.'

She caught at his arm. 'Octavia Manning?'

He nodded. She'd been ill, she was a little unhinged. He started up the stairs and when she made to follow he asked her to wait. 'Please, Mrs de Auberleigh, just give me a few minutes.'

When Francine was allowed to see Tyson she felt she was crying inside. His face was ashen, this man she loved, but whom she had lashed with her tongue the night before. He must have told Octavia he was finished with her and this was her revenge. She touched his hand. 'Oh, Tyson, Tyson, why didn't I believe you?'

The district nurse arrived and Francine was asked gently to leave.

Mr Binks was waiting in the hall. To Francine's questioning he said he was with Tyson when it happened. They were galloping across a field when Miss Manning suddenly appeared. She shouted, 'You'll suffer for what you've done to me!' and then she threw the branch. 'The master didn't have a chance, ma'am. Like a wild creature she was, eyes staring and sort of, well, foaming at the mouth like an animal. She must be mad. Is there anything I can do, ma'am? Would you like the missus to come and be with you and bring Gabrielle?'

'Yes, please, my husband might ask to see Gabrielle.' Francine put a hand to her brow. 'I don't seem to be thinking clearly. Telegrams will have to be sent, to his family, to several people. If I write them out will you see they are sent?'

'Yes, of course, ma'am, and just let me know of anything else you need.'

With the telegrams written and Binks away the nurse came to tell Francine she could go up now and see her husband. He was still unconscious, but he could come round.

However there was no change whatsoever in Tyson during the next two hours. Mrs Binks had arrived with Gabrielle then word having raced around about the accident, a constant stream of callers came enquiring.

At midday, Mr de Auberleigh senior arrived with the girls and his own physician. Soon afterwards Kathleen arrived with Bridget. Francine, who until then had been numbed with shock, shed her first tears, and they all wept with her.

Mr de Auberleigh went up with the physician and they were away a long time. Tyson's eldest sister said, as she tugged at the lace edge on her handkerchief, 'The awful thing is that Mama doesn't understand it. She keeps asking why Tyson should fall off his horse, he had always been such a good rider. What exactly did happen?'

After Francine had explained about Octavia Manning she felt all her tension go. 'I hated her so much, now I can't help feeling sorry for her, that her obsession with Tyson should have driven her to such action.'

It was strange, Francine thought, how familiar the word obsession had become in her life recently. Gran had accused her of becoming obsessed with photography, just as her father had been obsessed with his business and her mother her stage acting.

When the physician came down he said there was nothing more that could be done for Tyson. Only time would tell if he would recover.

It was the longest day Francine had ever known. At six o'clock Mrs Denton and Sophie arrived. They had been away when the telegram came. 'How awful, what a shock.'

Francine sat most of the time with Tyson but once when she was alone with Kathleen she learned that Rory and the boys had arrived home the day before.

Rory? Tyson's accident had made Francine emotional, vulnerable. 'How are they?' she asked, and was aware of a tremor in her voice.

'Looking surprisingly well,' Kathleen said. 'The sea voyage helped them to recuperate – they lazed and had good food.'

Later Kathleen told Francine that Rory had wanted to come with them. 'I told him no, not at the moment. Perhaps when Tyson is well again.'

Francine, tearful, wondered if he would get well, for

surely there should have been a change in him by now. Mrs Denton consoled her – her brother had had a fall and after being unconscious for three days, had recovered and was well today.

At nine o'clock that evening Tyson became conscious and asked for Francine. It was one time when she had gone downstairs. She raced up to the room, full of hope, a hope that died when she saw him. Icy fingers seemed to clutch at her heart. There was the pallor of death on Tyson's face. He whispered, 'Francine darling, I love you. I've never . . . loved, *really* loved, anyone else.'

'I know, I know.' She took his hand in hers. 'I love you too, Tyson. You'll soon be well and – '

He moved his head slowly from side to side. 'Gabrielle . . . give her a hug and a kiss. Tell her I – adored her.'

This was a terrible moment for Francine, Tyson declaring on his deathbed a great love for a child that was not his. Gabrielle was sent for but before she could be brought upstairs Tyson was gone, his last words being to his father, apologising for not having been the son he wanted.

Mr de Auberleigh, broken-hearted, protested that this was not true, that Tyson had always been his favourite.

Francine liked to think that Tyson had smiled faintly then. She certainly persuaded his father that this was so.

Francine wondered afterwards how she had managed to get through the next few days and the funeral, and knew that Sophie had helped a lot. They talked at night as they had done in their schooldays, giving voice to their inmost thoughts. In a way Francine had purged her soul.

The funeral had been harrowing.

Tyson had not lived to be presented at the Palace with the Victoria Cross but the award had been announced in the honours list in *The Times*. He was buried in London with full military honours.

Officers and men of his regiment marched to the

mournful tune of *The Dead March* from *Saul*. Hundreds of people attended the funeral; Tyson was a hero and deserved recognition.

It was not until the following day that Francine learned from Kathleen that Rory and his brothers had been to the funeral. Francine was distressed. 'Why didn't you tell me, Kathleen? Why didn't they come to speak to me?'

'Because you had enough to contend with. They'll come and see you in a few days' time. Here's Mrs Binks with Gabrielle.'

Gabrielle came toddling to Francine, arms outstretched. 'Papa?'

Francine picked her up and held her close, fighting a rise of tears. 'Papa has gone away, darling, but he asked me to give you a hug and a kiss.'

This satisfied the child and she began talking happily about the ducks and the chickens on the farm and Francine was grateful for this small mercy, that Gabrielle was not yet old enough to know the grief of losing a loved one.

It was ten days later when Rory arrived at Holcombe Manor. He was alone. Kathleen had said he looked well after the sea voyage, but Francine saw new maturity, of a man who has seen death daily, suffered hardships and been separated for over two years from his family.

It seemed natural for Rory and Francine to go into one another's arms.

386

CHAPTER TWENTY-NINE

After Rory had offered condolences Francine, wanting to get away from the morbid atmosphere that still seemed to cling to the house, suggested a walk. Rory agreed.

There was an autumnal chill in the air, with sudden rushes of wind that made beautiful moving patterns of the leaves that were already turning to russets and reds and golds. The two of them were silent for a while then Rory said, 'I still can't believe I'm home. At times I'm still over there. A chap was telling me once about being in hospital for six months and when he came home he felt he wanted to be back. Everything was strange.'

Francine glanced at him. 'I can understand that. It will take time to settle.'

'If ever I do.' There was a grim note in his voice.

'In one of your letters you said you thought you would go out to Egypt, do you still want to go?'

'No, I thought I would go to Ireland. I have an uncle who has a farm there. He could do with some help. I could try it for a few months and if I settle, I'll stay.'

Francine eyed him with dismay. 'To stay for good? What about your plans to be a photographer?'

'I did have such plans, but not any more. I thought at one time it would be wonderful to go out to South Africa and photograph war action.' He paused, was silent for a while then went on, 'After witnessing hundreds of men lying terribly maimed, dying and dead, I changed my mind.'

Francine reminded him of the beauty he had seen in the country in Africa. 'You told me about that, describing it so vividly I was moved.'

'The beauty was lost in the carnage. What about you, Francine, what are your plans?'

'I don't want to take any more photographs either, but for a different reason. It had become an obsession with me, and that is a dangerous thing. It made me blind. Oh, if only I hadn't been ill, hadn't shouted at Tyson. He might be alive today . . .' Her voice broke.

'Ah, no, Francine. You're wrong. It was his time to go and nothing could have stopped it. If you had been in a war you would know I'm right. Our lives are mapped out for us. You have a life to live, a child to love.'

Francine knew an unbearable longing to tell him that Gabrielle was his child, but she couldn't because of Tyson, he had loved her so dearly. She said, 'We're near the dell, do you remember it?'

'Yes, I do.'

When they reached it Francine found an air of melancholy about the place, but then the grass was suddenly leaf-dappled by a shaft of sunlight breaking through the clouds and the water cascading into the pool had a busy, happy sound. Rory had stopped and was looking up into the branches of a tree, where the bright eyes of a squirrel watched them.

Francine watched Rory. So often his dark eyes had twinkled in merriment, or teasing. Would that come back in time?

He caught her studying him and embarrassed, she said, 'You told me once that this place was evil.'

'I did?' His eyebrows were raised in surprise. 'I wonder why? Perhaps the evil was in me. Do you remember how I used to get so mad with you at times. And, if I recall the last time we were here we quarrelled.' He paused and looked up once more into the tree branches. 'Have you been back to the cave?' The casual tone he had attempted did not quite come off.

'Once.' Francine walked on, not wanting to discuss the cave, there were too many poignant memories. 'I think perhaps we ought to go to Mrs Binks and you can meet Gabrielle.'

'Mrs Binks? Wasn't she the one who talked about spiders being the spinners of silk?' Rory spoke softly.

Francine turned to face him. 'Fancy you remembering that.'

'I remember a lot more things, Francine, things it's perhaps best not to remember. They torment me. Shall we go?'

Mrs Binks was hanging washing on a line and Gabrielle was very busy, in her childish way, handing up the pegs. When Francine called her name Gabrielle looked around and came running to them. To Francine's consternation she held out her arms to Rory and cried, 'Papa!'

Rory picked her up and held her on high. 'Well, you little sweetheart, aren't you just beautiful.'

To Francine's further consternation she saw tears in Rory's eyes. Then he held Gabrielle close and she wrapped her plump little arms around his neck and laid her cheek against his, as she had done with Tyson. For Francine it was a heart-tugging moment to think that, unknowingly, father and daughter were embracing one another. She said gently, 'Gabrielle darling, this gentleman is your uncle Rory.'

For answer Gabrielle patted Rory's cheeks and said happily, 'Papa.'

Francine wondered why Gabrielle should mistake Rory for Tyson. Tyson had had the same colouring, dark hair and dark eyes, but he had been tall, slender, whereas Rory was sturdily built, his features rugged.

Mrs Binks, who had come up while Gabrielle had made the remarks, gave Francine a sad little smile and whispered, 'I would leave things be, ma'am.'

Mrs Binks said hello to Rory then Gabrielle wriggled to be let down. She went to fetch a rubber ball which she threw to Rory with a delightful squeal. He played with her, talking and teasing her, and Mrs Binks said, 'She needed her papa, I wouldn't disillusion her, not yet.'

Rory, Francine and Gabrielle spent the rest of the day together and Francine became worried, knowing that Rory had promised to return home that evening. 'How am I going to cope with Gabrielle, she won't let you go. I think I've laid myself open to a lot of trouble by letting her accept you as – her father.'

'Come home with me,' he said. 'Gran and the family are longing to see you. They wanted to come and visit when Tyson - but well, they felt it was a family time and they didn't want to intrude.'

'Intrude? Oh, Rory, they *are* my family, always have been from the first time they took me to their hearts.' She was unable to say any more for the restriction in her throat.

Rory gripped her hand and said softly, 'Gran will be able to sort out everything, she always has and always will. You must come.' Francine gave in.

It was an emotional reunion, but Francine knew she had done the right thing. Gabrielle was completely at home, as she had always been and was made so much fuss of by them all that she seemed to have temporarily forgotten about Rory being her 'Papa', especially when Grandad O'Reilly gave in to her every whim.

Kathleen had gone on a long-promised visit to a friend, taking little Edwin with her and Bridget was indisposed with a heavy cold, but Gran assured Francine she would be seeing them all soon.

A lot of ground was covered during the next few days and a lot of work, with Francine stitching dolls' clothes as they all talked. They discussed the future. Since peace had been declared the orders for dolls had increased, but Michael and Declan, like Rory were restless. They wanted a change. Why didn't the whole family go to Ireland? Grandad was willing and Gran had been saying for years she would like to go back home.

'So I have,' snapped Gran, 'but what work do you think we could all be doing over there? There would be no orders for dolls waiting for us, or a house and a workroom. No, I say far better stick with the divil we know than the one we don't.'

She ended up by saying she had been putting a little aside every week for years and that one day they would all have a little holiday in Ireland.

A month later, on a day that Francine had a sudden urge to take up photography again, Rory came to Holcombe Manor to say goodbye. He was going to Ireland on his own.

She felt a dreadful ache. 'To stay?'

'I want to see my uncle. I think I told you that I stayed with my aunt and uncle on their farm when I was young. My aunt died three years ago and Uncle Patrick never seemed to get over it. Then a few months ago two of his farm workers who went to war were killed.'

'How sad.'

'In the letters I've had from my uncle he sounded so terribly lonely.'

Francine had a sudden helpless feeling. She said, 'What did Gran say?'

'She said it would be good for Uncle Patrick to have some company and the change would do me good.'

'It will.' Francine could hardly get the words out. 'When are you leaving?'

He shrugged. 'Tomorrow or the next day. How are you getting on with your life, Francine?'

'I haven't been doing any photography lately, but oddly enough I had the urge this morning to start again.'

She saw a look of interest come into his eyes. 'It would seem strange to me using a camera again.' After a pause he asked, 'Francine, would you let me take a photograph of you?'

She felt an upsurge of spirits and spoke lightly. 'Yes, but only if you let me take one of you.'

'On condition that you make me look the handsomest man in the world.' The familiar roguish look was back in his eyes.

'Nature has already done that! The camera can't improve on it.' She was laughing. 'Come on, let's start photographing.'

The way Rory studied the light, placed her head, her hands, told her he had lost none of his skill. He took three poses, with her looking straight into the camera, sitting sideways, her arm resting along the studio garden seat and holding a book, glancing up as though she was aware that someone had come into the room.

'Splendid, splendid!' Rory exclaimed.

When Francine had taken three different poses of Rory they developed the plates.

And both complained about their individual work – they should have done this, and should have done that . . .

Then Francine said, 'Why are we complaining? We know they're all right, why won't we accept it?'

'Because we are both perfectionists.' Rory's mood had changed and he was now regarding Francine, his expression serious. 'I would like a photograph of the dell to take with me.'

'No, Rory.' She met his gaze squarely. 'We both have an image of it in our minds, both seeing it differently. To take a photograph might spoil those images.'

'You're probably right. It was just that . . . Francine, I –'

She put a finger to his lips. 'Let us take some more photographs, of objects this time. Yes?'

He nodded, but his eyes were velvet black with emotion. Then he looked around him. 'What do you suggest?'

It was a day charged with such deep emotions it was difficult to control them. Then when it was time to go Rory said, 'Give Gabrielle a hug and a kiss from me,' and Francine gave a small shiver. They were the words Tyson had spoken, a voice from the grave.

The next moment Rory kissed her gently on the lips and said softly, 'I'll be thinking of you always,' and she knew a sudden peace. He would come back and then perhaps the truth would be told.

A week after Rory had gone Francine began to look for the post and when no letter came she felt more and more restless. She would spend a day with Mrs Binks, take Gabrielle for walks, go to the dell and help to bake, but nothing could take away that yearning to see Rory again. She went to visit his family. No, they had not had a letter yet, but then he had hardly had time to settle in. It would come.

While Francine was at the O'Reillys she had a sudden urge to go to Spinners End. Which surprised her because in spite of her father's last words to her she had felt uneasy, the house alien to her on the two previous visits. Kathleen greeted her with her usual warmth.

'Francine, how lovely to see you. I was going to call home this afternoon. Shaun and I were talking about you only last night. Come on in, we'll have a cup of tea.'

Mrs Dodge had retired and a strange girl brought in the tea. When the maid had gone Kathleen said, with a small sigh, 'Yes, everything has changed, hasn't it? Do you remember when you first came here?'

They reminisced for a while and Francine suddenly realised that the house was no longer alien to her. When she told Kathleen this, Kathleen said softly, 'I'm so pleased, Francine. I was going to ask you if you would like to come and share the house with me, use the studio again. The man I employed was only temporary, and he's left now. To be honest, it's part selfishness as I'm lonely, but also it's because I want the studio to be used by someone like yourself, who loves the work so much.'

Francine felt a rush of tears. 'I'm lonely too, Kathleen. I can fill in the days because people are kind and I can visit, but the evenings when Gabrielle is in bed are endless. I would like very much to share, but I'm not sure about the studio. I would like to work in it, but not professionally. I couldn't do it on my own and – '

'Shaun would help,' Kathleen said eagerly. 'That was what we were talking about last night. He told me how much he missed working with you. This was after I had been telling him about a photographer friend of Edwin's praising your photographs of the children. He said they were exquisite and that you should continue photographing.'

The result of a long talk was that Francine accepted the challenge. She would move in to Spinners End and set up business, specialising in photographing children.

A week later the first letter came from Rory. It was to all the family, but included Francine. He wrote about the farm, their relatives, the people he had known as a child and the changes there had been. First Gran and then Grandad would make a remark. 'Well, now, fancy that, old Mr Clancy marrying again, and him nearly ninety . . . the ould divil . . . Did you read that, little Annie O'Hara, seems no time since she was starting school and her with six little uns . . . And Paddy Brennan as broad as he's tall . . . A skinny little runt he was . . .'

It was a month after this that Francine received a letter. The change Rory wrote about this time was within himself.

'At first I missed the hustle and bustle of the roads, the constant feeling of work having to be done with hardly time to stop and eat. Here everything is leisurely, no one hurries. My uncle can work for an hour without saying anything. At first I found myself talking, I felt I had to. Now I realise it's not necessary to talk to communicate. The people and the countryside have brought a new peace to me. When the work is done I can sit on the hillside and just watch the cattle grazing, and not want any more out of life.

'That, of course, is now, Francine. Perhaps I need this healing time. I enjoyed having your letter and hearing

394

about the move and you taking over your father's business. Shaun wrote to me too to tell me. He's excited, said he never would have thought he could have given up his barrow work. I myself still have no wish to work with a camera. Perhaps in time. I think of you and Gabrielle often, I think of your dell, and I ask myself if I could have found peace there in the countryside. Perhaps, I don't know. I send my love to both of you, please write again, Francine . . . '

Francine, who had waited so long for the letter felt disturbed. Would Rory want to settle in Ireland? He could change completely, find a girl, get married. If so, she must accept it. After all, she was finding fulfilment in her work. Every day was a joy. The number of clients was increasing. She was no longer lonely, for Kathleen was always there to talk to, to advise and little Edwin and Gabrielle played happily together, most of the time. If they did disagree and it was inevitable they would, they were soon sunny again.

The next time Rory wrote it was no more than a few lines, just to let her know he was still 'in the land of the living' and still enjoying the peace. Then he added, *'Although I must admit that I did enjoy the visit of Uncle's two nieces, my Irish cousins. Lively girls, who helped on the farm while they were here.'*

Although Francine had told herself she must accept it if Rory did find a girl and get married she knew now how upset she would be. Rory was the father of her child. Wasn't it time for him to be told? But what purpose would that serve? If he wanted to marry someone else Gabrielle could be a thorn in his flesh. She talked this over with Kathleen and Kathleen said to wait, she was sure that Rory would come back.

'He has to get the war out of his system, Francine, and when he does he'll want the life he knew — being busy and going back to his photography.'

Francine tried to believe it but was not so convinced as Kathleen.

As the weeks and the months went by she was persuaded to join the Photographical Society. Some of the members ignored her but there were others who praised her work and who talked her into entering for the yearly award. She worked to that end.

Rory's letters became less and less frequent and then in September his uncle wrote to say that Rory was not at all well. '*Gone right into himself,*' he said, '*spends hours staring at the mountains, at the lake. Someone should come and fetch him home. I don't want to lose the lad, he's a good worker, but neither do I want him going into a decline.*'

There was consternation. A decline? Francine, who was there when the letter came, felt her heart beating in slow, painful thuds.

Then Gran said, 'The only thing wrong with our Rory is that he's in love, and pining away because of it.'

'In love? Who with?' they wanted to know.

'Never mind who with,' Gran said shortly. 'The important thing is to get him back home. Someone will have to go and fetch him. No use me going, he'd feel he was being bossed around. The boys could go but sure as anything they'd want to stay. The girls haven't travelled anywhere. Bridget? No, she's never got over that heavy cold. Our Kathleen would go and Francine might go with her. Would you, Francine love? Would you go? You're well-travelled.'

Francine looked at her startled. 'Well, yes, but – '

'You and Rory understand one another.' There was a pleading in Gran's eyes.

'Yes, I'm willing.'

'There then now, that's all settled, we'll have to find out about the train and the boat times. I'll send the boys. You go and see Kathleen right away, tell her we'll take care of wee Edwin and Gabbie.'

Kathleen grasped the situation at once and she and Francine had their clothes and the children's packed and were back at the O'Reillys' when the boys returned from the station. They had all the details. The girls were to get the train to Liverpool, then travel on the overnight steam packet to Dublin. 'We've booked you seats on the train and a cabin on the boat,' said Declan.

'The money?' Francine queried. 'How much?'

'Gran has paid for it, it's her treat.'

When Francine protested strongly at this the old lady said, 'As you know, I've been saving a mite of something since the day I was married for us to go back home for a holiday sometime, but the sky could fall before that happens.' Her lips trembled. 'I want my boy back.'

Francine put her arms around her. 'We'll bring him back, Gran, never fear.'

Michael went on with further details of the journey. 'When you arrive at Dublin, you have to get from the docks to the station to get the Wexford train to Arklow. Now Declan and I thought if we sent a telegram to Gran's cousin Dermot he would meet you at the docks and see you on to the train.'

When Kathleen said this would not be necessary Gran said she thought it wise. That way, they would get news of the rest of the family, it would take but a short while.

Shaun was out while Francine was at Spinners End and she had left him a note. He arrived minutes later looking worried. There were the photographs to enter for the award, Francine could miss it. She said, 'Leave it, Shaun, Rory's more important.'

Declan said it was about time for the girls to leave and Shaun went to find a cab. Goodbyes were said, then the old man waved his pipe at them. 'All that lad needs is a bit of love, so see you give it to him, do you hear?' There was a tremor in his voice and it took Francine all her time not to weep.

The family waved from the doorstep with Gran wiping

her eyes, then they were out of sight. Kathleen said on a shaky note, 'Well, Ireland, here we come.' Then she added, 'For better or for worse.' Francine gave a little shiver.

It started to rain when they boarded the train to Liverpool, and it rained the whole way to Ireland, making the long journey more dreary being able to see only blurred images from the windows. A middle-aged couple who had done the crossing several times took them under their wing and saw them safely on to the boat and to their cabin, which had one bunk on top of the other. The crossing, they explained, took only about three and a half hours but they might snatch a little sleep. The girls were glad just to be able to lie down, but it was impossible to sleep, firstly because of the noise of people boarding and later because of the music and singing that went on above decks.

They both said they had slept fitfully and were bleary-eyed when the boat docked. It was still dark. They had been given a description of cousin Dermot O'Hara but he came to them at Northwall Dock, having recognised Kathleen, saying she was the dead spit of her ma when she was a girl.

He hailed a cab and although he pointed out the various buildings as they rode through the streets Francine was too tired to take anything in. Mrs O'Hara met them at the door and no two people could have been kinder. They were given hot drinks then Dermot's wife insisted they get into bed for a few hours, they could talk later. The deep feather bed had been warmed and Kathleen murmured, 'Heaven,' and if she said any more Francine was not aware of it. They were awakened by Dermot's wife with cups of tea and hot water to wash and told it was a nice bright morning, they were to come down when they were ready.

Later the girls sat down to a massive breakfast of bacon and eggs, sausages, fried tomatoes and fried bread and after the meal the talking began and it was non-stop because other relatives dropped in to see the girls, especially to see Kathleen, who was related.

By midday both girls were getting worried, wanting to be away, but then they had to have another meal, yes, of course, they must, they were not to go back home and say they had been half-starved. Kathleen laughed. 'Half-starved? I'm sure we won't be able to eat another thing for a week!'

It was eventually late afternoon before cousin Dermot took them to Western Row station to catch the train to Arklow. When they boarded the train he was talking and when it drew out of the station he was shouting to them to be sure to call on the way back with Rory.

Although the day was cold it was sunny and with the girls setting out fresh on the last stages of the journey they delighted in the variety of scenery. The train travelled along the coast for part of the way and they saw tiny coves where cream-edged waves rolled in leisurely among the rocks; saw bays where the sea surged in and climbed the rock face, fanning out into an iridescent spray. To the right of a lighthouse was an islet made white by the hundreds of screaming birds. Foliage and grass were an unbelievable emerald green, the hills purple with heather.

When the train left the coast they passed small villages, saw the chimneys of tin mines and ruined castles. There were derelict cottages as well as the ones with thatched roofs, white-painted walls and well-kept gardens.

Francine, entranced, said, 'I can understand Rory wanting to come to Ireland.'

Kathleen nodded. 'He was always talking about the time he lived with his uncle and aunt on their farm when he was a boy. The question is, will he want to come home?'

Francine glanced at her quickly and was about to say, 'But surely he would want to come home to die,' and stopped herself in time. She felt sick, knowing she would have been echoing what the whole family had been thinking.

No, no, not Rory, they would get him home, make him see a doctor.

It was nearly dusk when they arrived at Arklow. When they asked the porter the way to Patrick Brady's farm the man said to follow him, he would get someone to take them. He took their bags. Outside the station groups of men were standing talking, some of them fishermen in their navy gansies. Hailing an elderly man standing beside a donkey cart he asked if he could take the ladies to Patrick's farm.

'Sure, I will, indeed I will,' said the man, with a toothless grin. 'Be happy to.'

He, like the rest of the groups standing around, eyed the girls with some curiosity and before long was chatting away. 'So you'll be going to spend a holiday with Patrick then? He's had a bad time, losing his wife and both his regular workers killed in the war. But he had a grand young fellow helping him lately, a relative by the name of Rory O'Reilly.'

Kathleen said, 'Rory is my brother. My uncle wrote to say that Rory wasn't well.'

The driver scratched his head. 'Now there's a strange thing. He seemed all right to me at choir practice on Monday. In fine voice he was. They'll be singing in the cove tonight, it's Mary Donovan's birthday. She's a pretty lass.'

They had driven inland along several narrow lanes, crossed a main road then turned right along a high-hedged lane that brought them to a field gate. The old man got down to open it and before he climbed back to his seat he pointed in the direction of a greystone farmhouse across the field.

'That be Patrick's place.' There were outbuildings and quite a number of sheep grazing. 'Sold a lot of his animals lately, has Patrick. I think he lost his heart for farming when his missus died.'

A lamp had been lit in a downstairs room and as they neared the farm the front door opened and a big man was outlined against the light. He came to them as the cart drew up.

Patrick Brady's welcome was warm enough but it soon became clear that he was a man of few words. He said he had had a telegram saying they would be coming and there was a cold meal ready for them.

'Couldn't quite tell when you would be coming,' he said. 'The housekeeper's gone home for the night. Sit you down and I'll make you a cup of tea.'

There was a cosiness in the stone-flagged kitchen; brasses shining, a dresser full of blue and white crockery, the fire a red glow, two cats asleep on a home-made rag rug.

The uncle had fallen silent and Kathleen talked about the family, to which Patrick said no more than, 'Is that so,' or, 'Aye, they've had a struggle.'

The tea had been poured when Francine asked about Rory, and was told as the driver had told them, he was in the cove, for birthday celebrations. Kathleen asked, a sharp note in her voice, if he knew they were coming. And was told, 'Oh, aye, but he's singing with the others, you see.'

Francine, as annoyed as Kathleen, said, 'How is he? We've come because we thought he was really ill.'

'Oh, he's ill, well, let's say he's not himself. Far away all the time. After you've had a bite to eat you can go down to the cove and see him.'

Kathleen's lips suddenly tightened and Francine saw that her hands were clenched. 'Yes, we'll do that.' Under her breath she added to Francine, '*And* I'll certainly have something to say to him.'

CHAPTER THIRTY

As Francine and Kathleen set out across the fields to the cove they could hear the singing. The tune was the *Isle of Innesfree* and for Francine it was a heart-wrenching moment, the haunting air reminding her of the Sunday evenings when the boys always sang after supper. She would have stopped to listen, but Kathleen, still angry, was stepping out, reminding Francine of the brisk manner of Gran O'Reilly.

Before they reached the cove the glow of a bonfire lifted the blackness of the night. Now there were the sounds of voices and bursts of laughter. Francine and Kathleen stopped, looking down into the cove. The bonfire was big, lighting the faces of all those around it. There were people of all ages but the majority were young. There was another heart-wrenching moment for Francine when she saw Rory, his arm around a dark-haired girl. He was smiling into her face. Kathleen said quietly, 'The girl mightn't mean anything to him, Francine. One can get caught up in the party spirit.'

They set off down the path, with shingle and sand slipping away from their feet. When they were halfway down someone shouted, 'Some more visitors.' People turned, all looked towards them. Francine, her gaze on Rory's face, saw curiosity at first, then as he recognised them his expression turned to one of disbelief. His hand slid away from the girl's shoulder. He came forward slowly, paused, then came running.

'Kathleen, Francine! What's wrong, what brought you here? Is someone ill at home?'

'We understood *you* were ill,' Kathleen said, her tone clipped. 'But according to what I've just seen, you seem quite happy, healthy, and enjoying the company of an attractive girl.'

'It's a birthday celebration.' He looked from one to the other. 'Who told you I was ill? Uncle?'

Kathleen nodded. 'He did, said he thought you were going into a decline.'

'A decline?' Rory laughed but there was a shakiness in it. 'I don't understand. You mean you came all this way just to see if it was true? You could have written.'

'Then been told you were dead? It was Gran who bundled us off, Rory. She was worried sick, we all were, but it seems we are quite unimportant to you. You knew we were coming yet you weren't even at the house to greet us.'

Rory looked bewildered. 'I didn't know you were coming. If Uncle knew he never mentioned it.'

Someone from the group called to tell Rory to bring his friends to meet them. He called back to say they were family and had business to discuss. They would perhaps meet them tomorrow. He linked arms with Kathleen and Francine and walked them to the top of the slope. There he stopped.

'Forgive me, I haven't even greeted you properly yet.' He kissed them both then touched Francine's cheek gently. 'Coming all this way and I wasn't there when you arrived.'

'No, you weren't,' Kathleen snapped. Immediately she apologised. 'I'm sorry, I feel just about at the end of my tether and I'm sure Francine does too. It's been a long journey. But I do want to know what plans you have in mind.'

'Can we discuss that later? I want to know how everyone is.'

They walked on, with Kathleen talking about the family. Francine hardly spoke a word. When they arrived at the farm the old man had gone to bed. By this time Francine could hardly keep her eyes open and when Kathleen suggested that they go up to bed she agreed. Rory showed them up to the bedroom, stood hesitant for a moment then left, after saying they would talk in the morning.

Francine and Kathleen undressed in silence and when they were in bed and Kathleen said, 'I can't see our Rory coming back home,' Francine was unable to answer. The next moment she was asleep.

She awoke to the lowing of cattle and the smell of bacon cooking. For a moment she was unable to think where she was, then remembering, she saw that Kathleen was up. Francine slid out of bed and went over to the window. Fog blotted out the sea. Rory was in the yard below. He had rolled up his shirtsleeves and was wielding a broom. His arms were tanned and his muscles rippled as he worked. Sensuous emotions stirred in Francine and she felt ashamed. She turned away from the window and began to dress.

When she went into the kitchen, Kathleen, who was cutting bread said, 'I thought I would let you sleep. Rory's outside, so go out and have a word with him. I can't get any sense out of him about his plans. Don't stay too long, I'm going to fry the eggs.'

When Francine went out Rory looked up. 'Hello, Francine, did you sleep well?'

'Yes, thanks. Kathleen's sent me out. She seemingly wants to know your plans for the future.'

'I can't tell her, Francine. I just don't know at the moment. Uncle Patrick's not well.'

Francine said quietly, 'Is it perhaps that you don't want to come home, or is there another girl?'

Rory looked at her squarely and she saw a tormented look in his eyes. 'There has only ever been one girl for me. It's true that my uncle isn't well. I love him and I loved my aunt, I feel I have an obligation to him.'

Kathleen called then to say that breakfast was ready and they went in.

The housekeeper arrived, a small, wiry woman with bright inquisitive eyes. She apologised for not being there to see to the breakfast. It was Himself who told her not to come early, he had business to discuss with his relatives. She beamed at Kathleen and Francine. And wasn't it lovely then to meet Rory's sisters? He was a lovely man, so hard-working, but always dreaming and sometimes looking sad. Perhaps it was the sadness of the war that was still in him. She then suggested that Kathleen and Francine had a walk while she tidied up, and they agreed.

The fog had lifted and the sea lay calm under a cloudless sky. Francine took a deep breath of the seaweed-laden air. 'It's good.'

'About the only thing that is good,' Kathleen said in a defeated voice that Francine had never heard before. 'I'm sure our Rory has no plans for coming home and I'm also sure it's not the thought of the farm that is keeping him here.'

Francine's heart began beating in slow, painful thuds. 'You think he's in love with someone he's met?'

'No.' She looked at Francine. 'It's you. I've seen him watching you and there's a hunger in his eyes. But he can't very well tell you he's been in love with you for years, not with Tyson having just -'

'Oh, Kathleen, I love Rory too, but I can't very well tell him — it would seem as though I was desecrating Tyson's memory because I did grow to love him, but in a different way. I'm longing to tell Rory about Gabrielle, that he is her father. But again, there's this feeling of -'

'Tell him, I think he has a right to know. Put him out of his misery. I'm sure he's not going to rush back home, but given time . . .'

'But supposing he really does prefer farming?' Francine hesitated. 'I don't think I'm cut out for a farming life. My photography, I don't think I could ever give it up.'

The look Kathleen gave Francine this time held a great sadness. 'Then you don't love him, Francine. If you did, photography would be the last thing on your mind.'

Francine's thoughts at this were in turmoil. Was

Kathleen right? Was she willing to sacrifice something she had wanted for so many years and had progressed so far in that other professionals thought she was worthy of an award? But then, when she had thought that Rory was going into a decline the award had been unimportant.

They were making for the cove, but never got that far because of all the people who had come to call on 'Rory's family'. They went back to the farmhouse and the kitchen before long was full of people, all interested in England and all saying what a lovely man Rory was.

Francine liked them. There was a warmth, a close community feeling here, with everyone helping everyone else. But in spite of this she was not sure whether she could adjust to the life, that is, should Rory want her to share a farming living.

It was not until early evening that she found herself alone with Rory. Then he asked her if she would walk with him. There was a bay he would like her to see. Although they started out in the direction of the cove Rory took a path that led them across the headland. He talked about the people who had called and spoke of them as though they were old friends.

'A simple people,' he said, 'with a deeply religious faith and a love of the land. They'll talk of the terrible days of the famine when people were starving, but they also speak of legends and their belief in the mystical side. I've grown to love them.'

'Won't you *ever* want to come back home?' she asked quietly.

'I do get homesick, and I think often that I'm now ready to take up photography again. I see so many things I would like to photograph, the sky in all its moods, the sea, the mountains, and people, children especially. I meet a shepherd and I see a world of knowledge in his eyes. He talks of faraway places, wonderful places, yet he's never been away from here.'

There was something in Rory's voice that stirred

emotions in Francine, emotions she was afraid of, and when he said the bay he was taking her to had interesting rock formations she gave a shaky laugh. Rory glanced at her. 'What is it?'

Unable to tell him she spoke with a forced lightness. 'Well, here I am, walking in a deserted place with an attractive man and he talks of rock formations.'

'Ah, but in them are the stories of our childhood – dragons, witches, turreted castles, coaches drawn by six white horses with flying manes; the prince on a charger and . . .'

'And the princess?'

'Waiting to be rescued by the prince, of course.' A smile played about Rory's lips. 'In a few moments you'll see them.'

When they reached the bay Francine had a feeling of unreality. It was like being in a different world with the strange shapes of the various rock formations, the uncanny silence, the only sound being the gentle swish of tiny waves at the water's edge. In the distance were mountains that looked as if they had been painted on velvet.

'It's beautiful,' she said softly.

'Come and see the minnows in the rock pool.'

There appeared to be hundreds of them and they both picked up a piece of seaweed and trailed it in the water. When they turned away Francine said, 'Oh, is that a cave over there?' The moment she had said it she regretted it, thinking of their secret cave at home, but Rory showed no reaction.

'It leads to a warren of passages which must have been used by smugglers at one time. The main one goes straight through to the next bay. We can go through if you like, there are holes in the roof to let in the light.'

When Francine agreed Rory led the way. The passage was surprisingly warm. Each time they came to an opening leading off he would stop to show her then walk on. They were nearing the patch of light at the end of the passage when Rory said, 'There is a cave further along with movable slabs of rock, I suppose to store the spoils of the smugglers. Would you like to see it?'

Although he had asked the question casually enough Francine was aware of a tension in him. 'Why not?' she answered lightly, her heart beating a little faster.

Rory moved a slab, which seemed to swing out on an oiled pivot. When they both leaned over to look in the cavity Francine's cheek touched Rory's. They both straightened quickly and Francine was now aware of pulses beating all over her body. Rory replaced the slab.

'The others are all the same. I think we had better go, it'll soon be dark.' There was no mistaking the raggedness in Rory's voice and Francine knew she wanted to stay.

'At one time it would have been an adventure, wouldn't it, to be lost in a warren of passages?'

'Do you want to be lost?' he asked softly, moving closer.

'I wouldn't mind,' she whispered.

The next moment he had pulled her to him and his lips were on her eyelids, her throat, and then they sought her mouth.

'Oh, God, Francine, how I've dreamed of this. I've wanted you, longed for you. There were times when I would wake through the night when the longing was unbearable.' He began to undo the buttons on her blouse. 'I would get up and get dressed, determined to go back to England and then -' He slipped a hand inside her dress and caressed her breast, drawing a quick breath. 'Oh, Francine, it was awful because I knew I couldn't have you, you belonged to someone else.'

The thought of Tyson made Francine draw away. 'Rory, we mustn't, it would be wrong. Tyson -'

'You should never have been forced to marry him, *that* was wrong.' There was an anger now in Rory's voice. 'We belong to each other, we always have. I need you, love you to distraction.' His mouth came down on hers and she clung to him. He slipped the coat from her shoulders then taking off his jacket spread both on the ground.

'I'll keep you warm, my darling.'

Francine, almost sobbing now with a longing for Rory to love her, allowed herself to be drawn to the ground. But although the urgency was also in Rory he caressed her, teased her with the tip of his tongue, and she in turn teased him using the wiles that Tyson had taught her, moving her lips caressingly over his skin, stopping only when she reached the vulnerable part. 'Francine, Francine,' he moaned.

Then there came the wildness in their loving that they had known in their secret cave at home, but even then Rory had sufficient control to see that they climaxed together. He groaned, she shouted when they reached the agonising ecstasy of their fulfilment. Then they were still, exhausted, Francine's head cradled against Rory's shoulder.

After a while he ran the back of his fingertips down her cheek. 'I dreamed of this happening, but never thought it would. I can't tell you what it's meant to me, Francine. It will help me over the difficult days ahead.'

Francine, who had been warm until then, felt a sudden chill. 'Difficult days? You don't mean you're not coming back to England with us? You can't mean it, not after this.' She sat up.

'I can't go yet, Francine. There's Uncle, the farm.'

'You don't intend to leave here, ever, do you? You want to farm.' She got to her feet and started to dress. 'How *could* you? You've treated me like a – like a whore.'

Rory shot up. 'You mustn't say such a thing, Francine, mustn't even think it.'

'Why shouldn't I?' Francine, who had begun to button her blouse paused to say. 'Tell me Rory, why did your uncle write and say you were going into a decline? And don't please say that *this* is difficult to explain.'

'It is.' Rory was silent so long Francine prompted him. 'Well, are you going to tell me or not?'

'Uncle Patrick is dying.'

'Oh, Rory, I'm sorry. You should have told me.'

'He didn't want anyone to know. The reason he wrote home saying I was going into a decline was because he blames the loss of my aunt for his ill-health.'

To Francine's puzzled look he explained, 'He said he used to sit for hours when his work was done just staring into space and when he saw me doing the same he thought I was grieving over you. Yes, Francine I told him about you.'

'And so he wrote home wanting someone to come and fetch you. When I arrived with Kathleen did you tell him that you were going to ask me to marry you?'

Rory looked uncomfortable. 'No, I didn't and Francine, I have to stay. You do understand.'

'Yes,' she said, a hopelessness in her voice.

They both finished dressing.

When they left the cave they went back to the bay. It was nearly dark and all the romance had gone out of the strange rock shapes, to be replaced by monsters. Tears welled up in Francine's eyes. It was all over. Rory would never come home. He had found a different world and although she enjoyed the country she had no wish to take up a farming life.

'Francine,' Rory spoke gently. 'One must put priorities in order. I feel that Uncle needs me'.

She was about to retort that she needed him too when she stopped to think. She had made photography the most important thing in her life; made a camera her god. She loved Rory, loved Gabrielle, loved so many people but she was regarding them in a detached way.

She thought of the saying, 'Only a warm heart can melt the ice cold lens of a camera' and knew she had lost the warmth, lost the true caring she had once had for people. She was denying Gabrielle her rightful father; denying

410

Rory his own daughter. She turned to Rory and looked at him with appeal.

'Rory, I've made a lot of mistakes. I love you. If you want me to come to Ireland I will.' She gave a brief smile. 'Perhaps in time I'll learn to be a farmer's wife.'

'But Francie, I don't want to be a farmer. I want for us all to be close — you, Gabrielle and the family.' Rory paused then added with a slow smile, 'I have to get to know my lovely wee daughter.'

Francine's eyes widened. 'You knew?'

He nodded, 'Gran saw to that. She talked to me once about the family, making a special mention of her two sisters who had dimples at the corners of their mouths, and when, of course I saw the photograph of Gabrielle —' Rory drew Francine close. 'Oh, my darling, I've wanted you both so much. I want to hear Gabrielle call me Papa again. Do you remember the day she did, mistaking me for Tyson? I managed not to weep then but I did later. I would never have claimed the relationship had not Tyson . . . I have really nothing to offer.'

'You have love,' Francine said softly, 'and surely that is the most important thing in the world.'

'I agree.' He laid his lips gently to hers then, slipping an arm about her waist they walked away from the dragon, the prince and princess and left the bay to build their own castle of dreams.